GOLAN

This is the Future of War

FX Holden

Contact me:
fxholden@yandex.com
https://www.facebook.com/hardcorethrillers

KOBANI and GOLAN are prequels to the other Future War novels, Bering Strait (set in 2032), Okinawa (2033) and Orbital (2034). However all Future War novels are self-contained stories and can be read in any order.

Cover art by Diana Buidoso: dienel96@yahoo.com

With huge thanks to my fantastic beta reading team for their encouragement and constructive critique:

Bror Appelsin
Sim Alam
Nick Baker
Ken 'BBQ' Callan
Christopher Eadon
Johnny 'Gryphon' Bunch
Dave 'Throttle' Hedrick
Martin 'Spikey' Hirst
Greg 'Hawkeye' Hollingsworth
Joe Lanfrankie
Peter 'Gonzo' Reed
Yoav 'Joe' Saar
Therese 'T' Blakemore Saffery
Lee 'Streaky' Steventon

And to editor, Brigitte Lee Messenger, for putting the cheese around the holes.

"There's always some son of a bitch who doesn't get the word."

US President John F. Kennedy on learning that a US spy plane had blundered into Soviet airspace at the height of the Cuban Missile Crisis in October 1962.

Maps

Maps

Cast of Players

EXCOMM
US President Oliver Henderson
Vice President Benjamin Sianni
Secretary of Defense, Harold McDonald
Chairman of the Joint Chiefs of Staff, Admiral Austin Clarke
Director of National Intelligence, Lt. General (Retired) Carmine Lewis
State Secretary Kevin Shrier
White House Chief of Staff, Karl Allen
Director of National Cyber Security, Tonya Dupré

LCS-30 USS CANBERRA
Sonarman Elvis 'Ears' Bell
Lieutenant Daniel 'Dopey' Drysdale
Watch Supervisor, Chief Petty Officer Hiram Goldmann

USAF, 432nd Air Expeditionary Wing, Akrotiri Cyprus
DARPA Project Director, Unmanned Systems, F-47 *Fantom*, Shelly Kovacs
Flying Officer Karen 'Bunny' O'Hare, pilot, Royal Australian Air Force (RAAF), attached

RUSSIA, LATAKIA AIR BASE
Lieutenant Yevgeny Bondarev, pilot, 7th Air Group, 7000th Air Base
Second Lieutenant Sergei 'Rap' Tchakov, pilot, 7th Air Group, 7000th Air Base

IRAN QUDS FORCE BASE, DAMASCUS, SYRIA
Captain Abdolrasoul Delavari, Islamic Revolutionary Guards Corps (IRGC), Quds Force

BUQ'ATA, US 3rd Marines, 1st Battalion, 'Lava Dogs'
Gunnery Sergeant, James Jensen
Hospital Corpsman Third Class, Calvin Bell
Corporals Ravi Patel, Rae-Lynn Buckland
Privates Marta Lopez, Dominic Stevens, Brendon 'Rooster' Johnson, Belinda Wallace

BUQ'ATA, IDF and CIVILIAN
Amal Azaria, Engineer, Defense Research Directorate (Corporal, IDF Reserve, Unit 351, *Palhik* Signals Company)
Mansur Azaria, brother
Raza Azaria, Amal's son

BUQ'ATA, DRUZE SWORD BATTALION
Lieutenant Colonel Zeidan Amar (formerly Reconnaissance Battalion Commander, Golani Brigade), now Interim Commander, Druze Sword Battalion

ISRAEL, SUBMARINE FLOTILLA
Captain Binyamin Ben-Zvi, INS *Gal*
First Officer Ehud Mofaz, INS *Gal*

SAFINEH-CLASS FRIGATE, IRIN SINJAN
Captain Hossein Rostami, Islamic Republic of Iran Navy
Rear Admiral Karim Daei, Islamic Republic of Iran Navy

Praeludium

Return of Golan Heights is precondition
to Israel-Syria peace

Syrian President Assad said during an interview with Russian state media Thursday that any future agreement with Israel must entail a return of the Golan Heights to Syrian sovereignty.

Assad made the remarks during an interview with Russia's Rossiya Segodnya news agency, which was also mentioned by Syria's official SANA news agency.

"Our stance has been very clear since the beginning of peace talks in the 1990s ... when we said peace for Syria is related to rights – and our right is our land," Assad said.

Assad stressed during the interview that Syria can establish normal relations with Israel "only when we regain our land."
Jerusalem Post, October 2020

Iran's strategic objectives

Iran's objectives are to maintain the recently established land bridge that runs between Iran through Iraq and Syria into Lebanon, limit the influence of Sunni states and Israel, and expel US and Western influence from the region. • Iran's strategic geographic location enables it to threaten vital US interests in the Strait of Hormuz and the greater Gulf region and influence the Bab al-Mandab and Eastern Mediterranean. • Iran's military doctrine focuses on Hybrid Warfare operations and asymmetric response options aimed at reducing the will of the United States and its partners to fight in the region. • Iran's large military enterprise is split into two separate forces: the Iranian Army and the Iranian Revolutionary Guard Corps (IRGC). • Iran maintains the largest ballistic missile program in the region.
US Army Asymmetric Warfare Group, June 2020

Rouhani says most Iranians want peace

An overwhelming majority of Iranians want peace with the rest of the world, Iran's President Hassan Rouhani said Tuesday, defending the nuclear negotiations under way with major powers.

"We are determined to solve our problems with the world through logic, reasoning and negotiation," Rouhani said.

AFP, Tuesday May 26, 2015

All Domain Attack: Engagement

Buq'ata township, the Golan Heights, April 15, 2030

Her nickname was 'The Toymaker'. Her official title was Principal Engineer Amal Azaria, Directorate for Defense Research and Development (DRD), Israeli Ministry of Defense. But she didn't mind 'Toymaker'; it was accurate enough, if your idea of a toy was a wide-bodied unmanned aerial vehicle with a six-foot wingspan that could be 3D printed-to-order and configured for reconnaissance, swarming ground target attacks or – as for the drone she'd just been asked to deliver – assassination.

As she unlocked the padlock on the wide sliding door of her shed, the harsh sun was already radiating off the metal. Her new shed, her workshop and, behind her, her old family home in this Druze town in the north of the Golan Heights.

It had been her brother's lifelong dream to return to their birthplace so he could start a business with the money he'd earned in Tel Aviv, and he'd suggested she relocate with him. She hadn't been happy in Tel Aviv. Rather than say goodbye to one of their most creative robotics engineers, DRD had kept her on the payroll and let her take her workshop and a small team with her.

It had taken six months to prep the 100- by 50-yard building in Buq'ata for storing all her equipment, but less than a day for their tri-mode printer and supplies to be offloaded from the container in which they traveled and set up inside. Usually there would be at least four of them working in the shed, but because of the current security situation, her three junior engineering staff had been pulled back to Tel Aviv. So today, she was alone.

But to be honest, she liked it that way.

She booted up the printer. Given the right feedstock, it could print in metal, carbon or nylon, or combinations of all three. Her basic drone design was simple. Tail, propeller and wings were printed separately and then fastened with screws that would hold them together at forces up to 5G. The internal steering mechanism and propeller shaft were assembled from printed rods. The payload module in the center of the aircraft was customizable, and she had the different components with her, arrayed across row after row of folding aluminum shelves: electric engines with built-in power cells, GPS navigation units, high-powered digital zoom cameras, detachable mounts for anti-personnel or anti-armor grenades … the list was as varied as her client base, which included every branch of the Israeli Defense Forces.

But her favorite payload, because it was the newest capability she had added to the *Skyprint* Unmanned Aerial Vehicle or UAV, was the ability for the larger drone to deploy smaller microdrones. Circling high, out of sight of an enemy below, her *Skyprint* mothership could drop up to two of the quadrotor microdrones, each no bigger than a human hand, and then an operator could use the radio, camera and optical sight on the *Skyprint* to pilot the microdrones to their target. Just like their mother ship, the microdrones could be fitted with various payloads, most commonly microphones or other electronic eavesdropping devices, but also … other payloads.

Such as a box-shaped pistol.

The man watching Azaria painstakingly assemble the *Skyprint* and mount the assassination module had sounded skeptical on the telephone. He was a Captain in the Israel Defense Forces (IDF) *Sayaret*, or special forces. And he was Druze, like her: a separate ethnic and religious group that had coexisted with Muslims and Christians and Zoroastrians and Jews in Israel for thousands of years.

"I have to tell you, Azaria, I am a fan of old-fashioned methods. Proven methods," he'd said. "Men on the ground, looking at their targets through scopes. Or *Eitan* drones, armed with Hellfire missiles…"

Azaria had sighed. The army was still full of many such hold-outs. "You just explained, Captain Kasem, that the target

13

is always heavily guarded. You said, and I quote, 'The swine is never alone, never exposed for more than a moment,' did you not?"

"Yes. So I don't see how some build-a-bear hobby drone is going to..."

"Come over to my workshop," Azaria told him. "I will show you."

Now it was Kasem's turn to sigh. "Alright. I am at Camp Biranit, I will see you around mid-morning."

"Very good. And can you send me your ID photo before you leave? I will give you an email address..."

"Why?"

"You will need a photo ID pass. This is a secure facility."

"Alright, what's the address?"

Azaria had been smiling to herself as he read out his email address. The old shed in which she worked was the very opposite of secure. A stiff wind would probably carry the entire structure away. But it was large, and empty, and adaptable, which were her three main criteria.

Azaria didn't need Kasem's photo to make up a pass for him. She needed it to program into the facial recognition software for upload into the microdrone she had sitting on her desk. She hummed to herself as the software scanned the photograph, mapped Kasem's facial features and then fed the data into the memory of the microdrone. Then she loaded the microdrone into the payload module of a readymade *Skyprint* UAV – she always had a few preassembled, with assorted payload modules for clients who were in a hurry. Then she waited.

Kasem appeared at the shed about an hour later, just as he'd promised. He pulled the rusted metal door open and peered into the dark cavernous space, lit only by lamps over Azaria's workbench. "Amal Azaria?" he asked, dubiously.

In grubby overalls, long dark hair shoved untidily into a bun

14

behind her head, with freckles across an aquiline nose, Azaria looked up and waved. "Ah, Captain Kasem! Come in, come in. Leave the door open."

The Commando officer was lean, prematurely bald, with a hook nose and jutting jaw, and a stride that matched his countenance. The door was on rollers and he slid it open, then covered the fifty feet to Azaria's workbench in a few economical strides and frowned as he stopped up in front of the engineer. "I thought you said this was a secure facility?"

"I lied," Azaria replied simply. She looked behind him. "You are alone?"

"This is a sensitive operation. You may speak of it to no one, is that clear?"

She smiled. "Everything I do is sensitive. Now, would you like a demonstration of the system?"

Kasem looked at the UAV sitting on the bench. "This is it? I've seen UAVs before, Azaria."

"Of course you have, but indulge me. Stand wherever you like, as long as you aren't between myself and that door," Azaria said, picking up the UAV. It was light enough to hand-launch, it didn't need a slingshot. With the flick of a switch she turned it on, which booted up its electronics and started the propeller whirring. The noise reverberated inside the metal shed, making Kasem wince, but after checking two system indicator lights on the side of the small plane, Azaria planted her feet and hurled the plane toward the door. It dipped, righted itself and flew out into the daylight.

"Now, let's see..." Azaria said, reaching for a control pad with two small joysticks and a few other buttons on it. "If you'll come over here." She moved to another workbench where there was a small LED computer monitor and turned it on. It showed a view of the area around the workshop from about a hundred feet up. The shed was in a large yard behind her house, which backed up onto a quarry in the east of the town. "I'll just move the drone higher, give us a better view," Azaria said, as much to herself as to the officer behind her. When she had the drone circling where she wanted, the picture of the workshop below it centered and stable, she turned to look over her shoulder at a rather unimpressed Captain Kasem.

"It can fly up to 20,000 feet and has an endurance of 12 hours," Azaria said.

Kasem folded his arms, clearly not impressed. "Amazing."

"The camera has a Zeiss 40x optical and 200x digital zoom … see." Azaria zoomed the view in and centered on the wide-open door.

"Azaria, I have seen UAV video before."

"Of course, of course." Azaria reached for her control pad. "Now, keep watching the screen. I will deploy the microdrone."

"The what?"

"The payload. Watch, watch," Azaria said excitedly, pressing a button. The video jerked and then a second smaller window opened up on the screen, showing a new image of the workshop from above. Then the image moved as whatever was filming it moved away from the first drone. "See, they are separating, but the camera in the microdrone synchs to the target area you set for the *Skyprint* UAV so you don't lose situational awareness." The Lieutenant's face remained impassive. "I … I can switch from one feed to the other very easily, like this." She flipped the left joystick with a thumb, zooming one feed out and the other in, and then back again. "It has low light and infrared capability. The … the microdrone is a quadrotor, about the size of a hummingbird, based on a racing drone design."

"Azaria…"

"It can … well, it goes from zero to a hundred miles an hour in three seconds."

"I have a teenage son," Kasem said. "I am sure he would be impressed, but I…"

Azaria pointed at the screen. "Wait, wait. See the door, on the screen here. Watch."

As Kasem leaned forward, Azaria brought up a target

crosshair on the microdrone video feed and placed it in the middle of the doorway. Without saying any more, she tapped a trigger on the controller.

The video zoomed toward the door as the microdrone dropped toward it with lightning speed. Kasem was still watching the TV screen, but as the microdrone entered the workshop, its buzzing rotors just audible, he spun around, just as Azaria knew he would. The microdrone didn't even hesitate as it swooped through the door, crossed the distance from the door to Kasem inside a second, and smacked into the middle of his face before his flailing arms could even get above his shoulders.

With a loud report, the drone fired a noisemaker round and then dropped to the floor.

Kasem staggered backwards against the bench behind him, a shocked look on his face.

Azaria toggled her controller and restarted the microdrone, lifting it in the air to hover over Kasem's head.

"You might have noticed it went straight for *you*, not for me," Azaria said loudly, the sharp noise inside the workshop having set both their ears ringing. "That's because I used your ID photo to program you as the target. Of course, I cheated. I fed it a plan of the workshop and told it before it launched where you would be standing, but..." She tapped another button and the drone began moving carefully and almost silently around the workshop at head height. "... If you don't have the target's exact location you can set it into search mode and it will move around the inside of a structure, scanning. You can direct it via video as long as the target isn't jamming to stop drones. If they are, the *Skyprint* will detect that and stand-off outside jamming range; then you can launch the microdrone in autonomous mode. Requires no radio control, so jamming won't stop it. Of course, if you launch it in autonomous mode, you can't call it back."

Kasem no longer looked indifferent. He was wiping his forehead where the drone had smacked into it, and watching it move around the workshop with dread fascination on his face.

"It will avoid humans who are not the target, though: won't attack them. You know, sentries, guards, children, that kind of thing. Ideally you send it in through an open window at night, but an unguarded door is fine. It can go up and down stairs, can't open locks of course, but it's small enough to slide through prison bars and such. It can search a two-story, eight-room house inside about ten minutes."

"What did it fire?" Kasem asked.

"Well, that was just a noisemaker. You can use them for distractions. But for the mission you described, I'd go with .45 hollow point." Azaria pointed between his eyes. "Make a proper mess."

Kasem was still rubbing his forehead. Azaria turned, switched the video feed to the *Skyprint* still circling overhead, and instructed it to land on the dirt outside. She turned back to the *Sayaret* Captain. "This is my only prototype. I would need to print you a copy. So – when do you need it?"

The Red Sea, May 14, 2030, aboard
LCS-30 USS *Canberra*

"Contact! Bearing zero three zero, depth 150, range ten."

Sonar Technician (Submarine) 'Ears' Bell had been hunting the Islamic Republic of Iran Navy (IRIN) submarine *Fateh* for three days. He watched his screens for minute changes in the data that might give him a heading. It was possible the Iranian was maneuvering for a simulated torpedo shot.

Possible, but not likely, unfortunately for Ears. The *Fateh* was shy. Since the *Independence*-class warship USS *Canberra* had sailed from Oman and started its patrol in the northern reaches of the Red Sea three days earlier, Ears had picked up the acoustic signature of the first submarine in the Iranian *Fateh* class just three times, including this one, and never closer than 10 nautical miles away.

But the first contact had been a good one, long enough for Bell's AI to record and analyze the signature, confirming he'd hooked the *Fateh*. One of Iran's newest and most modern submarines, the *Fateh*-class boats were no easy target. They were small, only 600 tons submerged, and less than 150 feet long. Near silent twin-diesel electric engines could push them through the water at a modest 11 knots submerged, which made them unsuited for chasing their prey, but ideal for sneaking through the outer pickets of carrier strike groups and lying in wait to strike with their four wire-guided *Hoot* rocket torpedoes, or *Jask* anti-ship missiles.

Tensions between the superpowers and their allies were high in the Middle East. A simmering conflict between Syria and Turkey had turned into a full-scale shooting war six months earlier, and with Syrian tanks rolling across Syria's northern border into NATO partner Turkey with Russian air support, the US and its allies had been forced to step in to stem the Syrian advance. A ceasefire had returned Turkey and Syria to pre-conflict lines, with each back behind their borders and licking their wounds, but Russia's ambitions in the region had only intensified. From its new naval base at Tartus in Syria it had begun to challenge US freedom of navigation in the eastern Mediterranean and Red Sea. Russian destroyers had stopped and boarded a small US flagged freighter bound for Lebanon from Cyprus, claiming it had entered Syrian waters. And sheltering among the skirts of Mother Russia, Iran had also begun to lift its profile, sending submarines far into the Red Sea and through the Suez Canal on exercises with the Russian fleet. Two weeks after the boarding of the US freighter, the Iranian Republican Guard Corps spy ship *Saviz* hit a mine in the Red Sea and was towed to the Russian naval facility at Port Sudan. Iran accused an Israeli submarine of laying the mine, Russia accused the US.

Sabers were also rattling ashore, with Russian-backed Syrian ground forces, released from combat against Turkey, now being moved in strength to Syria's southwest military district: on the borders of Lebanon and Israel. Stock markets were jittery, and 24-hour news channel pundits were predicting trouble between Israel and Syria any day.

When Bell had first picked up the faint sounds of the *Fateh*'s screw cavitating, he'd hoped it was the Israeli submarine *Dakar*, playing hide and seek with them. Firstly, because there was a political element to any engagement with an Iranian sub that got in the way of prosecuting the contact the way he'd like. But also because if it was Israeli, he'd have a chance to compare notes with a sonarman off the Israeli boat one day and see how close it had really gotten before he picked it up. Unfortunately, the acoustic AI had tagged it as the Iranian. The *Fateh* often played tag with US and Israeli warships in the Red Sea or Persian Gulf, its crew testing their potential enemies to see how close they could approach before being detected. It usually kept its distance though, closing only to within standoff missile range. Occasionally it crept closer and tried for a simulated torpedo shot.

Israeli boat drivers weren't so timid. They loved getting their German-made diesel electric boats with their whisper-quiet Siemens 2.85 MW electric engines right in under the keels of American ships and then sending a compressed air shot out their torpedo tubes, to scare the *bejeezus* out of the poor sonarman who had let them do it. Which was nothing compared to the pain and suffering awaiting him when his Captain found out about it.

However, on one famous and highly classified occasion, the IRIN *Fateh* had broken the surface two miles from the Ford-class carrier USS *Enterprise*, deep inside that carrier's ring of protective frigates and destroyers. Of course it could have surfaced unintentionally, the Captain or helmsman misjudging his depth, but it had been interpreted by everyone who saw or heard about it as a definite 'screw you America' gesture. Bell heard the commander of anti-submarine operations in the *Enterprise* carrier strike group that day had last been seen sailing a desk. In Guam.

Whoever was driving the *Fateh* on this particular patrol wasn't interested in showing off. But he'd gotten sloppy. Bell refined the contact on his passive sonar and pushed it to the new 360-degree view wall of the *Canberra*'s refurbished Combat Information Center, or CIC. "Sonar to TAO, contact on passive sonar classified as Iranian submarine *Fateh*, designating target as Charlie one zero, bearing zero three one, heading zero niner eight, depth one fifty, speed six knots."

The *Canberra*'s circular CIC was lined with wall to ceiling screens showing a simulated view all around the ship. Around the bottom of the screens were compass markings and every civilian or military sea, air or subsea contact being tracked by the warship was visible as an icon on the screen, with data beside it showing its type, ID or ship name if known, and data on its bearing, course and speed. The icon for the *Fateh* appeared on the view wall as a flashing red symbol. The data was automatically pushed to screens for the attention of the various CIC supervisory officers, but Ears was old school and didn't like to assume his superiors were awake and alert.

Especially when the Tactical Action Officer, or TAO, on this watch was Lieutenant Daniel 'Dopey' Drysdale. Bell wouldn't have put Drysdale in charge of anything more complicated than an alarm clock, let alone the newest CIC on one of the newest ships in the Navy. Luckily, a lot of his job was automated and AI assisted on the *Canberra*, leaving less for him to screw up.

"Roger, Ears, contact confirmed. Subsurface Search Coordinator, spin up a quadrotor and get a *Hunter* over that sub pronto."

"Aye, sir, deploying quadrotor and *Hunter* for subsurface contact Charlie one zero," the Subsurface Contact Supervisor or SSC replied, repeating the order. The quadrotor was a drone that could drop a dipping sonar on top of the Iranian sub to get a more precise lock on it in case the ship's anti-submarine weapons systems were needed. The *Fleet*-class *Hunter* was an autonomous surface vessel that supplemented the *Canberra* as the warship's 'wingman', either following along behind it, or sweeping the sea ahead of it, trying to pick up mines, surface or subsurface vessels before they got within range of the *Canberra*'s sensors. It was fitted with the same towed sonar and phased array radar that the *Canberra* carried, which gave it a potent ability to detect hostile ships and submarines.

Bell watched the submarine's track as it started to develop. It looked like the *Fateh* was creeping south-southeast, trying to sneak past the *Canberra* in the flukey warmer waters of the Red Sea's northern inclines. They were shallower, but sound waves were more likely to be scattered by the different temperature layers between the *Fateh* and the *Canberra*, which was sailing in the deeper central waters of the sea. He checked their position. This part of the sea, right between Medina in Saudi Arabia in the east and the Sudan/Egyptian border in the west, was just about the widest part of the upper Red Sea, stretching about a hundred and fifty miles across. Further down, at the entrance to the sea near Djibouti, the navigable part of the channel narrowed to under twenty miles. Where they were right now was a favorite place for submarines to test their ability to pass surface warships undetected.

But why was the Iranian sub headed *south-east*? The Iranian government had just announced that the IRIN *Fateh* would be visiting Egypt's Berenice Military Base in two days' time to make a friendship visit before beginning exercises with Egyptian warships in the Red Sea. That was how *Canberra* had been alerted that it might be in their sector, and their brief was to try to locate it and then monitor the Egyptian-Iranian exercises. But Berenice was *north-west*, not south-east. The *Fateh* would have a hard time making Berenice inside two days if it was headed south-east here and now. Bell frowned. Could it have run into mechanical problems?

He checked the acoustic signature for any signs of mechanical irregularities, but he couldn't see or hear any. Its blade noise was faint, barely registering, but it was constant. He wasn't close enough yet to pick up engine noise, but he might be able to get a read on that once a dipping buoy was dropped. Still, it was…

A chime sounded in his headphones. "New contact!" he called out. "Bearing two seven four degrees, depth 200, range twenty-two klicks…" His towed array sonar had picked up a *second* submarine. He assigned his AI to continue tracking and refining the contact on the *Fateh*, and began working the new contact.

Though it was further out than the *Fateh*, he had a better read on it. The blade noise from its screw was coming through clearer, and there was even some engine noise. His AI got a close match, but not confirmed. It was registering as a seven-bladed screw, and the AI was calling it a possible Russian *Lada*-class submarine. But the acoustic signature didn't match any of the *Lada*-class boats in the database and there was no intel on a new boat in the class being launched. It could be an Israeli *Dolphin* class, shadowing the same Iranian *Fateh* that they were shadowing, but only Russian designs used a seven-bladed screw, and a quick check showed Ears that all the Israeli boats were either berthed or accounted for. It made sense for a Russian boat to be in the area, given everything that was going on, but the US Navy had built a solid acoustic signature database of every Russian submarine afloat, and this signature was not in it.

It made sense for the Iranians to have their submarines working in pairs, but the only other possible Iranian candidate was the IRIN *Besat*, and the last Bell had heard, it hadn't even completed sea trials yet. US ships hadn't gotten close enough to the newest Iranian submarine in the fleet, the *Besat*, to build a precise acoustic signature of it. He thought fast. The *Canberra*'s quadrotor and *Hunter* drones were already prosecuting the target that was the *Fateh*. He still had options, though. "Sonar, TAO, designating new contact Charlie one one, requesting MAD search on target position."

There was no reply. Walking and chewing gum were not Dopey Drysdale's strengths. Anything more than one active unidentified contact tended to send him into decision paralysis. Two Iranian subs at once? Luckily his second in command, the Watch Supervisor, Chief Petty Officer Hiram Goldmann, stepped into the gap. "Goldmann to weapons, you are clear to fire MAD on contact Charlie one one, commit."

"Aye, launching MAD shell at contact Charlie one one, Weapons out."

Unlike the quadrotor drone which took off from the helo-deck, the Magnetic Anomaly Detection or MAD drone on the *Canberra* was fired from the ship's 2-inch cannon like a homing artillery shell. It launched from the barrel of the gun inside a casing with fins that deployed as it was fired, before the casing dropped away and the UAV guided itself to the target using data provided by the CIC. When it reached the target area it plunged into the waves and began circling, looking for disturbances in the earth's magnetic field.

Almost as soon as it splashed into the water, the MAD drone started sending data on a large anomaly, two hundred feet below it. And looking at the numbers, Bell took a deep breath and started concentrating harder. After a couple of quick passes, the MAD had sent enough data for Ears to estimate the mass of the contact. One thousand, two hundred tons. He made a quick scan of likely candidates and found only one.

The *Besat*. It had to be! Announced in 2008, it had only been confirmed as a reality in 2020 and commissioned in 2026. It was Iran's largest indigenously built submarine, double the size of the *Fateh* and capable of deploying mines as well as firing torpedoes and cruise missiles. But it had done little more than a few sea trials in Iranian waters. It had never been sighted this far outside Iranian waters and no US or allied ship had been able to get close enough to build an acoustic signature for it.

And it was headed *north-west*, in the opposite direction to the *Fateh*.

Ears reached for his throat mike. "Chief Goldmann, I think the Iranians are playing us."

"You got something on MAD? Send it through, Bell,"

Drysdale ordered.

"It's a new class of boat, sir," Ears replied. He was circling the MAD drone manually, trying to paint a picture of the seemingly huge metal object beneath it. "I think it's the *Besat*. While we were trailing the *Fateh*, they tried to sneak the *Besat* past us."

"And I thought the *Fateh* was just being careless," Goldmann replied. "We nearly fell for it."

Bell ran his finger across the screen, mumbling to himself. "Chief, I've got propeller cavitation and increased engine noise at position Charlie one one. I expect the contact is moving to ahead full. We need to make a call soon – stay on the *Fateh*, or follow the new contact."

Drysdale broke in again, clearly annoyed his personnel were talking around him instead of to him. "Our mission is the *Fateh*," he reminded them. "We are supposed to follow it all the way to Berenice and then monitor the Egyptian navy exercises."

"The *Fateh* is heading south-east, sir," Bell pointed out. "It's turned around and it's headed toward Djibouti. Away from Berenice."

"So we stay on it," Drysdale said. "Toward Berenice, away … I don't care if it's going in damn circles."

Goldmann broke in again, ignoring him. "You're thinking the Iranians are trying a bait and switch, Ears?"

"Yes, Chief. It's the only explanation."

"I'm coming over." The CIC was arranged in a ring of concentric circles with the TAO and his assistant in the center and the specialist watchkeepers arrayed around them. Bell saw Goldmann rise from his station and make his way through the other stations toward him.

Chief Goldmann was a small man with black curly hair and a face that was all knuckles. He'd started his navy career as a submariner, which made him especially good at hunting them. "Let me see what you've got … seven-bladed screw? Twelve hundred tons submerged … Russians have nothing in that category. Swedish *Challenger* class?"

"Not made for warm water operations, sir," Ears reminded him. "No aircon."

"German Type 209? Egyptians had a few."

"All retired."

"Then it's got to be the *Besat*. Damn, that's sassy."

Bell watched the data pouring into their acoustic database. "Building the signature data now. That's my first new signature capture." It was rare to be the first to lock horns with a new submarine: like identifying a new species of whale. It would give him bragging rights when they finished their patrol.

"Stop preening. Does it have the same plant as the *Fateh*?"

Bell ran the numbers. "Seems so. Air-independent diesel."

Goldmann was drumming his fingers along the top of Bell's screen as he thought about what he saw, which was very annoying. But Bell knew better than to interrupt him. "Logic says they were trying to draw us off, sneak the *Besat* past us, but why? There has to be something about the *Besat* they're trying to hide, or they wouldn't go to all this trouble."

"Maybe they just didn't want us to know it's operational…"

"Could be that simple." Goldmann stopped drumming and keyed his throat mike. "Lieutenant Drysdale, I think the Iranians are playing a shell game. They've got us chasing the *Fateh* south, and they're trying to sneak their new boat the *Besat* past us headed north."

"Well, that's just impolite. You have confirmation it's the *Besat*, Chief?" They'd been briefed on the likely threat environment before starting their patrol, and the chance of bumping into Iran's newest submarine was one they'd all relished, though not expected.

Goldmann raised his eyebrows, looking a question at Bell. Bell nodded emphatically and said in a low voice, "I'd bet my next liberty on it."

"I do, sir," Goldmann said into his headset, sounding a lot more confident than Bell was feeling.

"Alright, that's a bigger prize. SSC, turn that quadrotor

around. Put it over contact Charlie one two and start prosecuting. I'll call it up to the bridge and see what they want us to do." Drysdale wasn't the sharpest tool in the shed, but he knew better than to ignore the instincts of Chief Goldmann.

Goldmann smiled and clapped Bell on the shoulder. "You're wrong, this is going to cost you more than your liberty, Ears."

RAF Service Custody Facility ('The Jug'), Episkopi Garrison, Cyprus, May 14

Flying Officer Karen 'Bunny' O'Hare had just set a record for the longest time served by a woman in 'the jug' at RAF airbase Akrotiri.

Forty days. That was the penalty for smacking a Squadron Leader in the jaw with your flight helmet. That and, of course, an administrative discharge without privileges – suspended. Bunny would have been shipped back home on the first available flight if the situation in Syria had been any different, but Coalition forces didn't have the luxury of saying goodbye to a combat-tested pilot like O'Hare. Not with all hell about to break loose two hundred miles south-west in Syria.

Forty days and then she'd be moved to a new unit for the duration of her tour. Which was fine by O'Hare. If she never saw her former CO, 'Red' Burgundy, again, it would be too soon. She'd just landed after a six-hour combat sortie in which she'd damaged a Russian Su-57 *Felon* stealth fighter and destroyed three Syrian ground units, and Burgundy had stalked across the apron to her machine and accosted her as she climbed down from her cockpit, barely able to stand, let alone take in what he was saying. She registered that he was angry at her though (again), which she decided was a bit rich considering she'd just flown her third combat sortie in 48 hours, so she had, in the words she'd used to the Defense Force Magistrate, 'gently prodded him in the face' with her 5lb. flight helmet and stalked off. Burgundy had been knocked out and lost a tooth, so probably it *had* been a little more than a gentle prod.

She had only two more days left to serve, however, and then she'd walk out to learn her fate. She had no idea what had been happening in the big wide world for the last five weeks. When she'd been put away, Coalition forces inside Turkey had just beaten back a Syrian armor attack on the NATO base at Incirlik in southern Turkey. In a serious escalation, Russian air force units supporting Syria had taken their gloves off and gone toe to toe with Coalition fighters in the skies over Turkey. It was the first time western and Russian stealth fighters had faced off against each other in combat, and she was pretty interested to find out what the final kill count was. When she'd touched down at RAF Akrotiri after her last mission, she'd have called it a Coalition win, but only just. The western Coalition fighters of the UK, Turkey and Australia had claimed a handful of Russian *Felon* stealth fighters and four *Okhotnik* stealth drones. The *Felons* had destroyed two Coalition F-35 *Panthers* and more than a half dozen of their 'BATS' drone wingmen. But the Coalition stealth fighters had proven highly effective in ground attack with standoff weapons, blunting the Syrian armored push right on the perimeter of Incirlik before US B-21 strategic bombers laid waste to the remaining Syrian tanks and troops with a blizzard of cruise missiles.

She'd heard Syria and Turkey had signed a ceasefire, but what did that mean? Was the conflict done? Would she be shipped back home in disgrace and demobbed now? She'd been bugging the British guards who delivered her food and led her out to the showers or for exercise to give her a radio at least, but they were annoyingly uncommunicative. She'd had a few phone calls from her mates at 3 Squadron and they had shared a rumor that the Turkish action was just a warm-up for something bigger, maybe a faceoff between Syria and Israel. But that couldn't have kicked off yet, or she would have heard a *lot* more activity in the skies over the garrison holding cells. She'd passed the time in her windowless cell trying to identify the aircraft flying overhead by the growl and whine of their engines. She'd picked up F-35s and F-15s, *Tempests* and *Typhoons*, some heavier transport and rotary-winged aircraft. The arrival of the F-15s was interesting. The RAF and RAAF didn't field F-15s, only the USA or its Middle East allies. If there were F-15s at Akrotiri now, maybe some of the F-35s she was hearing were American too. In which case, it was a clear sign the US had decided to have a little more skin in the game. Which told her maybe it wasn't all peace and harmony outside her cell.

She looked at her watch and then at the cell door. Eleven a.m. You could say what you liked about the Brits, but they were civilized. Eleven a.m. was morning tea time. The nice Corporal Georgiou of the Sovereign Base Areas Police Service would be along any minute with a mug of hot sweet tea and a biscuit. She stood and stretched, doing a few wall push-ups as she waited so that her muscles wouldn't completely atrophy. She looked at her watch again. Eleven oh seven. He was late.

Bunny heard the scuffle of feet outside and the beep of the lock. How many pairs of feet? Georgiou usually came alone. Something was up.

As the cell door swung open, she saw what. Georgiou was standing there with two mugs alongside a woman in her fifties, her hair tied back in a bun, with a curious look on her face as she peered around the door into the cell. She was wearing a white cotton blouse, blue jeans and sneakers.

"Flying Officer, 'ow you doin' this mornin'?" Georgiou asked in his best Greek Cypriot imitation of a British accent.

"Fine, Corporal, you?"

"Dandy, thank you. 'Ere you are, ma'am," the Corporal said, handing the civilian the two tea mugs. He walked in and placed a plastic plate with two cookies on it on the only other furniture in the cell apart from her bed, a fold-down plastic stool fixed to the wall. "'Ere you go, enjoy." He walked back to the door of the cell, where the woman was still standing with the mugs of tea, as though deciding whether this was a good idea after all.

"You can go on in, she don' bite." Georgiou winked at O'Hare as he stepped out of the way, closing the door behind the woman as she stepped into the cell.

"Hi, I'm Shelly Kovacs."

American. She pronounced it Ko-vach. O'Hare wasn't an expert at American accents, so all she could tell was the woman wasn't from Texas or the Deep South. O'Hare lifted the plate of cookies from the stool and indicated Kovacs should sit. "Hello Shelly Kovacs, I'm Flying Officer Karen O'Hare." The woman stepped awkwardly forward, offering her one of the mugs of tea, and O'Hare took it. As she sat on the stool, O'Hare looked at her again. She didn't look military. So not anyone's air force. US Defense Intelligence maybe? No. CIA? Definitely not. If anything, she looked like a poorly paid lawyer, a public defender perhaps. That thought did not cheer O'Hare up. "I haven't been allowed any visitors, Shelly Kovacs," O'Hare told her. "So how did you get through?"

Kovacs sipped the tea, then wrinkled her nose and set the mug down on the floor. "Well, actually, I'm a bit of a fan, Flying Officer."

"Uh huh."

"I mean … not the whole whacking your CO on the noggin thing. But I've been going through the data from all the air-to-air engagements of the Turkish conflict…"

"War. When countries are trying to solve their differences by shooting missiles and tank shells at each other, it's war."

"The Turkish war, yes. And I was particularly intrigued by a combat patrol you flew on April 2, defending the airspace over Incirlik. Maybe you remember it?"

O'Hare frowned. She'd flown a lot of missions in a short space of time, but of course she remembered April 2. The reason she was frowning was because she was wondering why Shelly Kovacs was interested in a mission Karen O'Hare had flown on April 2.

"You didn't really introduce yourself, Shelly."

"Oh, right, sorry!" The woman stuck out her hand

awkwardly. "I'm a project lead on the DARPA UMS program…" She paused, noticing that O'Hare was still frowning at her. "Uhm, Defense Advanced Research…"

"… Projects Agency, yes, I know," O'Hare told her. "The guys who develop the secret weapons."

"Well, not so secret. You can look up UMS on the internet. Unmanned systems. I'm on the unmanned combat aerial systems team. You've heard of the F-47?"

"The Navy drone?" Bunny nodded. "I heard of it. Haven't seen one. It's like the Russian *Okhotnik*, right?"

Kovacs leaned forward, a gleam in her eyes. "You engaged an *Okhotnik* flight, didn't you? I read your combat report and pulled the data logs. You…"

"I know what I did. I nearly got killed by one of those bat-winged mothers."

"You destroyed one. Your CO destroyed two. But in your final dogfight you used an unorthodox evasive maneuver that went directly against the algorithm your AI was telling you to follow, and it…"

"Would have got me killed, if that *Okhotnik* had been carrying missiles. But it wasn't."

"How could you *know*?"

"The flight profile of that *Okhotnik* flight suggested they were recon birds."

"Suggested?"

"Yeah. It was a gut thing. We bet on them not carrying missiles."

Kovacs looked disappointed.

"You DARPA types don't like pilots telling you it's a gut thing, am I right?" O'Hare guessed. "You can't program that."

"Oh, we can. Except it isn't gut. It's probability theory, not gut or instinct. Or you can call it what it is, a wild ass guess."

O'Hare laughed. "Fair enough. But you aren't here to talk about those *Okhotniks*. That mission was on April 3. Not April 2."

Kovacs looked suddenly serious. "You're right. I'm here to

talk about how on April 2 you overrode the command and control protocols for six Boeing Airpower Teaming System Loyal Wingman drones, took command of them and then used them to engage a wave of Russian *OVOD* cruise missiles."

"I was out of missiles myself. They were the only platforms airborne and available."

"You commandeered six drones by hacking my software mid-flight!"

"That was your software? Sorry. If you didn't want me to, you shouldn't have built it so I could."

"You shouldn't have known how! You used a diagnostic routine to open a command channel. How did you..."

O'Hare drew her legs up under her. "Shelly, do you own a car?"

"What? Yes."

"What is it?"

"A GM Zap."

"Don't know it. But I'd bet you if you gave me a beer, the manufacturer's handbook and a half an hour, I could get you an extra fifty miles per charge on the battery." O'Hare had finished her biscuit and took the other woman's without asking. "If you put me in the driver's seat of something, I want to know how it works so if it breaks, I can try to fix it. I read all the maintenance manuals, I go deep into the diagnostic menus, I get up in the weapons bay and learn how to mount the ordnance. I borrow testing tools from the Quality Engineers and I dig into the code..."

"You can read computer code?"

"Read and write. I know Java, C, C++ and Ada." Bunny gave her a tight smile. "But enough about me, you still haven't told me why you're here."

"Well, like I said, I was going through the combat logs of all the F-35 pilots who fought over Turkey. Yours caught my eye because most pilots follow the AI cues in combat, and you didn't, most pilots don't hack their own comms system mid dogfight, and you did." Kovacs looked around the cell. "And then when I approached RAAF liaison for permission to talk to you, I found out you were in here…"

"Two more days."

"Then what?"

"Haven't been told. I'm not going back to 3 Squadron, that bridge has been burned. I'm guessing a transfer to 75 Squadron until my tour is done. They're due to rotate in from Qatar last I heard."

Kovacs shook her head. "No. They're putting you on a desk. Operational Liaison, Coalition Air Ops, Nicosia."

Bunny crossed her arms. "Liaison? Seriously?"

"What they told me."

Bunny leaned her head back against the cell wall and closed her eyes. "Oh, God. A firing squad would have been better."

"What if I could keep you flying, in a sense?"

Bunny narrowed her eyes. "What does that even mean, in a sense?"

Kovacs got a gleam in her eyes again. "We have a development hub at Al Azraq Air Base in Jordan. Field testing a new F-47B for the US Marines…"

"Drones."

"Armed drones, able to carry 2,000lb. of ordnance. You've flown against the *Okhotnik*? The F-47 packs more punch per lb., flies faster, has a smaller radar cross-section, can see further…"

"It has shorter legs," Bunny said, arms still crossed. "And … did I mention? Drone."

Kovacs tried coming at Bunny from a different direction. "You like flying the F-35 *Panther*?"

"Sure."

"But when you fly a *Panther*, you're only flying one fighter."

"With a BATS wingman, two."

"How would you like to fly six at a time?"

"Six?"

"I've written experimental code that would allow a single pilot in a trailer on the ground to command up to six F-47s in combat. Just like you did when you commandeered those BATS over Incirlik, but with command and control routines designed to enable you to adapt their offensive or defensive postures on the fly, set them free to follow semi-autonomous guidance, break them into smaller flights each with their own sub-missions and targets..." – Kovacs was talking quickly – "... a single pilot, flying a hex of aircraft, together more lethal than any F-35, even with a BATS wingman."

"A hex."

"What I'm calling a flight of six F-47s. In a hot war, the losing side rarely runs out of airframes. Pilot attrition is the killer. You kill one plane, you kill or capture one pilot. Pretty soon the losing side is running out of pilots and morale is shot. But with a single pilot controlling six fighters, and that pilot safe and sound behind friendly lines, you might lose a fighter or two, but you have no pilot attrition, no POWs being paraded in front of the cameras on network news, you save on pilots, training..."

Bunny was listening now, biting her lip in thought. "You could plan a broader range of missions, be bolder, take more risks."

"Exactly! We're in combat testing phase, conducting some Red Flag missions against the Jordanians. But I don't have a pilot on the team with your combat experience or your ... creativity," Kovacs said, and then grinned. "Of course, if you'd prefer to sit at a desk in Nicosia behind a laptop..."

"You could get me assigned to this DARPA project?"

"I'm pretty sure. Your CO didn't sound exactly unhappy when I raised the idea with him."

"I bet he didn't."

"So? Can I tell my Program Manager you're in?"

Bunny held out her hand and shook with Kovacs. "With bells on, mate."

US Pentagon, May 14

"Mister Secretary, I think we need to go to DEFCON 2," Chairman of the US Joint Chiefs of Staff, Admiral Austin Clarke, said with barely disguised urgency as the US Secretary of Defense, Harold McDonald, walked into the National Military Command Center Emergency Conference Room sixty feet under a Pentagon parking lot.

"Easy, Admiral," McDonald said, sitting down heavily at the mahogany table ringed by the other members of the Joint Chiefs, who had already been in session for several hours. "It's only 48 hours since I agreed to take Navy and Air Force in Central Command to DEFCON 3. That used up just about all the credit I had with the President. I'm about tapped out, unless you've got something dramatically different to tell me."

Clarke had prepared for exactly this response. He knew McDonald well after nearly two years in which they had both been in the same chairs. He was never quick to act, never made a move without confirming it with President Henderson first, and he had a tendency to meddle at the operational level, instead of leaving the war fighting to his generals and admirals.

Across the back of the room, specialist operations officers were arrayed behind communication screens and Clarke motioned to the Assistant Deputy Director for Operations to bring up the first map on the ceiling-to-floor screen at the other end of the room.

"Force dispositions, current at..." he looked at his watch, "... 2300 hours local, 0600 in the Eastern Med. Syrian Daraa military district on the border of Lebanon and the Golan Heights UN Demilitarized Zone or DMZ. So far we have positively identified units including the Russian trained and armed Syrian 4th Assault Corps, 4th Armored Republic Guards Battalion and an Iranian Revolutionary Guards Corps 'Quds' special forces battalion. What's changed since yesterday, they've now been reinforced by 60 T-14 *Armata* tanks and personnel belonging to the Russian Strauss Security Group, but our intelligence indicates all tanks and support personnel were drawn directly from the Russian 2nd Guards Motor Rifle Division…"

"A private security company fielding Russia's most advanced main battle tank? They expect us to buy that?" McDonald scowled. A fifty-eight-year-old former four-star Marine General, he still dragged his 220lb. frame around a running track twice a week and his scowl had been known to wreck lesser careers than Clarke's.

"I don't think they worry overly much what we think, sir," Clarke said in his mild South Carolina drawl. He shifted his pointer to the Israeli side of the border. "Israel has mobilized every unit in its Northern Command facing Lebanon and Syria. Last night it pulled a heavyweight unit out of Gaza, the 1st Golani Brigade, and moved it into defensive positions near the Golan, just outside the UN DMZ."

"Defensive. They're not planning a pre-emptive strike?"

"It's possible, though we'd expect to see the tanks of the Israeli 7th and 36th Armor Divisions moving up to the ceasefire line if that was the case. They're still inside their bases."

"So Russia has beefed up its ground support. Any change in Russian air operations?"

"No, sir. Still primarily the *Felons*, *Flankers* and *Okhotniks* of their 7th Air Group, 7000th Air Base running patrols inside Syrian air space, along the coast over their airfield at Latakia and the Russian navy base at Tartus."

"Something's got you antsy, Admiral, get to it."

"Sir. We just got a report the USS *Canberra*, patrolling here…" he indicated for a new map to be thrown up, showing the Red Sea between Saudi Arabia and Egypt, "… picked up a contact from an unidentified submarine."

McDonald was looking through a briefing folder he'd brought with him. "Well, that's its mission, isn't it? It's been sent to monitor exercises between the Egyptian navy and an Iranian sub."

"Yes, the *Fateh*. This was not the *Fateh*, Secretary. We believe it was their newest and largest submarine, the IRIN *Besat*."

McDonald frowned. "And so? It's a different submarine, but why is that so interesting?"

Clarke's team of specialist intelligence officers excelled at their jobs. Even as the Secretary was talking, one of them pulled up a slide detailing everything they knew about the *Besat* and threw it up on a split screen.

"IRIN *Besat*. Launched 2028, 1,220 tons displacement. It's similar in design to the 500-ton *Fateh* class, but the Iranians upgraded its missile capability. It has four vertical launchers for longer-range *Yakhont* anti-ship cruise missiles."

"As long as it stays in the Red Sea, I don't see the problem."

"A *Yakhont-ER* missile fired by the *Besat* from the top of the Red Sea would have the range to hit Tel Aviv."

"Their Iron Dome air defense system would take it out."

"Iron Dome is designed to intercept ballistic missiles or short-range rockets. The *Yakhont-ER* isn't ballistic, it's terrain-following. Designed to hug the ground and fly under Israeli radar and hit its target at twice the speed of sound."

"I'm not taking our forces to DEFCON 2 just because Iran has sailed a submarine into the Red Sea which *could* fire four missiles at Tel Aviv."

"I'm not asking you to, sir." He nodded to the back of the room.

A series of grainy photographs came into focus, showing what looked like the deck of a large tractor trailer parked by a dock. The shots were taken from ground level, alongside the dock, and showed what looked like a large missile being lifted off the tractor trailer by crane.

"We got these photographs from a human source two weeks ago. Our people escalated these to our attention when the *Canberra*'s report on the *Besat* hit their desks. They show a single sub-launched cruise missile being offloaded from a transporter at Bandar Abbas port, with the *Besat* at its berth in the background." Clarke had his team zoom the photographs to show the missile in close up. "That is not a *Yakhont-ER* missile."

"What is it, then?"

"We are pretty certain it is a Russian *Kalibr*-M two-stage missile. The second stage is supersonic, flies at Mach 3. It can hit any target in Israel and it can be armed with a nuclear warhead. With the *Besat* so far up the Red Sea, that announcement about the *Fateh* exercising with the Egyptians was probably intended to draw us off. They wanted us chasing the *Fateh*, they even showed us the *Fateh*. But the real question is what they are doing with the *Besat*, with at least one Russian *Kalibr*-M onboard." Clarke looked grave. "A nuclear-armed *Kalibr*-M missile fired from the top of the Red Sea gives Iran the ability to strike any target in Israel, almost without warning."

"Tel Aviv?"

"Flying time, ten minutes."

McDonald was suddenly very, very quiet.

Six months earlier, the Director of National Intelligence, Carmine Lewis, had delivered a very troubling briefing to himself and the other members of the National Security Council. Ten years of covert efforts in the cyber domain, targeted assassinations of Iranian nuclear scientists and several desperate air strikes by Israel had, the US thought, stalled the Iranian effort to build its own nuclear bomb. Then, in 2028, a team of North Korean strategic rocket force personnel and scientists was seen disembarking from a North Korean merchant vessel in the remote southern Iranian port of Chabahar, together with crated 'seismological monitoring equipment'. Over the next year, more reports arrived of North Korean personnel being sighted at the Iranian underground nuclear facility buried under a mountain range at Fordo. In early 2030 the evidence gathered had become overwhelming.

North Korea had supplied six nuclear warheads to Iran, and that country was in the process of testing their ability to be fitted to its indigenous arsenal of ballistic and cruise missiles.

The US had made both subtle and none too subtle threats to North Korea, demanding it withdraw the warheads from Iran, but the North Korean regime denied it was engaged in anything but peaceful seismological research there.

US intelligence had cried wolf before, and an underground 'test' of a nuclear weapon had been declared imminent on several occasions, which was to be expected if Iran was to announce to the world that it had joined the nuclear club. But as time went by and no announcement was forthcoming, doubts began to form about the reliability of the intelligence. Israel's Mossad confirmed the presence of the North Korean nuclear specialists, but said it had so far not been able to confirm US reports that nuclear weapons had been transferred to Iran.

"The warhead on that missile? Can we…"

"We can confirm the dimensions are identical to the *Kalibr*-M tactical nuclear warhead, capable of a 5- to 150-kiloton yield."

"But we don't know for sure it's carrying a nuke?"

"Dammit, man," came a voice from down the table. "If it walks like a duck and quacks like a duck…" All eyes turned to the speaker, Marine Corps Commandant, General Charles Garrett. "Forget Tel Aviv. That Iranian sub could hit our fleet at Bahrain from anywhere in the Red Sea or eastern Med with a tactical nuke and take out a whole carrier strike group. Doesn't that make it a damn duck?"

If the outburst was intended to cow the former US Senator, McDonald, it had the opposite effect. He set his jaw. "If Iran *has* put a nuke on that sub, that's enough to take us to DEFCON 2. But I'm not taking us to DEFCON 2 unless someone here can confirm beyond doubt that it has." He glared around the table, landing a particularly hard look on Garrett. "No one?" His question was met with silence. McDonald stood and gathered his briefing folder. "Is the USS *Canberra* still in contact?"

"They trailed it for two hours, but lost contact six hours ago,

Mr. Secretary. It appeared to be headed for the Gulf of Aqaba. It's an air breather, has to come up somewhere soon to recharge its batteries."

"Then get the *Canberra* to the Gulf of Aqaba and wait for it. I want them on that sub like fleas on a hound."

It was exactly the sort of operational micromanagement that rankled with the men around the table. But Clarke bit back his frustration. "We have that in hand, sir."

McDonald tapped his fingers on the table. "Have these photographs been shared with the Israelis?"

Clarke looked at his Ops Director, who shook his head. "We only just put them together with the earlier report, sir."

"Well, make sure they aren't. We don't want the Israelis pissing about the Red Sea in corvettes trying to sink that Iranian sub. That would be just the excuse Iran needs to kick this thing off and make it look like they are the wounded party."

"We'll lock the information down."

"Good. What is the Russian Black Sea fleet doing?"

Clarke nodded to his Ops Director again and the map refreshed, showing a series of red dots approaching the Bosphorus Strait in Turkey between the Black Sea and the Mediterranean. "The Iranians and Russians have finished their exercises and Russia announced the combined fleet is going to make a friendship call at Tartus in Syria in a week. The Turks aren't happy letting them through the Bosphorus after two years of Russian interference in the war with Syria, but they just signed a ceasefire agreement that included freedom of navigation so there's nothing they can do about it."

McDonald paused, squinting at the screen. "That's become a *sizable* force."

Clarke consulted a page in front of him. He knew McDonald liked details. "One *Slava*-class missile cruiser, two *Grigorovich*-class frigates, two corvettes, two Russian *Kilo*-class subs, with two Iranian *Safineh*-class frigates riding shotgun." He put a finger on the page. "It was just joined by a helicopter landing ship, the *Pyotr Morgunov*, which can carry up to 300 troops, 40 infantry fighting vehicles and four attack helicopters. It's not just a sizable force, sir, it's just about everything the Russians and Iranians can float. If that Iranian sub is nuclear armed, and it gets in among them, we've got no chance of getting to it. And as you know, all I've got on that side of the Suez between that fleet and Israel are the four ships and their wingmen from Destroyer Squadron 60."

"And a British submarine on attachment, correct?"

"A nuclear-powered *Astute*-class attack sub, yes, sir."

"How long before the USS *Nimitz* strike group could be ready to leave Bahrain?"

"Seventy-two hours, but with only one carrier strike group in Bahrain now, I want them in the Gulf in case we need to support operations inside Iran."

"Makes sense. If you can't draw on the *Nimitz*, what are your air options?"

Clarke checked his notes again. "The 432nd Air Expeditionary Wing has arrived at RAF Akrotiri on Crete. That's 25 F-35As. Royal Australian Air Force Akrotiri, that's another 10, they lost two in the fighting over Turkey in the summer. RAF can give us 14 *Tempests* and six *Typhoons*, they also lost two aircraft, but are reinforcing to ... 22. The *Panthers* of 63rd Fighter Squadron could also be tasked from Incirlik in Turkey, but they're needed up there to patrol the Syrian border and keep Ivan from getting any new ideas about Turkey."

The Marine General, Garrett, raised his hand. "I've got a squadron of F-47Bs buzzing around in the desert over Jordan on some DARPA project. I can order them attached to the 432nd. That will give Air Force additional stealth recon and strike capability over Syria or Israel, or you could pull them back to Bahrain if they're needed for Iran."

McDonald nodded, satisfied. Three months earlier, Coalition forces had been forced to defend the NATO base at Incirlik from a Russian-backed Syrian ground and air attack without US fighter support because a hesitant US President hadn't wanted to engage in open warfare with Russia. Russia had shown it had no such qualms, taking on Coalition fighters using its new generation Su-57 stealth fighters and setting up the first air war of stealth vs. stealth in modern history. The RAAF and RAF F-35s and *Tempests* had claimed three *Felons* for every one of their own they lost, but the deciding factor had not been their own onboard firepower or the larger radar cross-section of the Russian aircraft – it was the force multipliers they brought to the fight: fast data links to other aircraft, and radar and ground units in the theatre to help them find and engage the Russians. Plus the 'loyal wingman' drones flown by the RAAF which could be sent out hundreds of miles ahead of the stealth fighters to search for and provoke an attack by hidden Russian stealth fighters. A lot of the 'BATS' drones had been lost, but the Russian fighters had wasted a lot of missiles dealing with them, depleting their firepower and helping the Coalition pilots to get a fix on their positions. The battle for Incirlik had removed any reluctance President Henderson had about authorizing either air or ground forces to be used to defend NATO assets in Turkey.

Now, it seemed, he faced the next challenge of his resolve.

McDonald zipped up his briefing folder and addressed the room. "The Admiral and I are going back to the White House. I'll ask Carmine Lewis to get the wheels in motion to confirm the intel on that nuke." He gave Admiral Clarke a thin smile. "You may yet get your DEFCON 2, Admiral."

Mansur Azaria zipped the folder he was holding, put his pen in his pocket and turned to look at his sister. He had just finished putting a new shipment of stock into the large shed out the back of their house where his sister also had her workshop, and had come inside to find her taking her green and khaki military uniform, black t-shirts, socks, underwear and boots out of a duffel bag on her bed. Beside it was a portable military field radio.

"What are you doing?"

Amal Azaria pulled her old Jericho 941 pistol out of the bag, stopped and gave her brother a smile. "Just checking everything is here."

"You can't be called up. You have a child. You're exempt." Amal was bringing up her five-year-old child, Raza, alone. The father was a Russian émigré who hadn't been able to make Israel work, and had returned to Russia before Raza's second birthday.

"I'll tell that to the Syrian tanks when they come rolling across the ceasefire line, shall I?" She held her hands in the air. "Don't shoot! I'm exempt!"

Mansur sat on the bed and regarded the pistol balefully as Amal worked the action and checked it wasn't loaded. She would never have left it loaded, but she was a very, very careful woman and she always checked. He watched as she counted the magazines lying in the bottom of the duffel bag. She applied the same thoroughness to everything in her life, whether it was weapons design, or her service as a radio operator reservist in the IDF Golani *Gadsar* battalion. "You're overreacting," Mansur told her. "It's just another military exercise. Syria wouldn't dare try to take the Golan again."

She clucked her tongue and started putting her gear back in her go-bag. "Wouldn't dare? They just kicked the Turks out of northern Syria. They bombed Istanbul…"

"The Russians bombed Istanbul," he corrected her. "*After* the Turks attacked a Russian air base in Syria."

"Tomato *tomato*," she said. "Russia, Syria, Iran, it's all the same to me. They tried to take the Golan back in 1967, they tried in 1973 and they're going to try again. One of my colleagues has Syrian cousins just over the border in Jasim. She said they called her to tell her they're all being evacuated. That can mean only one thing."

Mansur frowned. Jasim was twenty miles across the border, as the crow flew. Forty miles and an hour away if you were in a tracked vehicle. It was surrounded by farmland. The main military base in southern Syria was at Daraa, thirty miles further south. "So, they are *big* military exercises. But that's all."

"One of the girls in my unit said they got reports of tanks moving into Quneitra, with Russian crews. Yesterday, Mansur."

"You are 36 years old and a mother. It's not your unit anymore," he said stubbornly, glaring at her. She gave him a smile, patted his knee and lifted her duffel bag onto her shoulder, carrying it out into the hallway and dumping it by their front door.

She had jet black hair with a single silver streak running through it which she tucked behind her ear. Her mother's hair had been fully grey at forty and it was the first sign Amal was going the same way. She also had her mother's dark eyebrows and long nose. People joked they both looked like the former Prime Minister Golda Meir, at different ages in her life. Amal certainly had the stateswoman's infamous stubborn streak. In the hallway she stood on her toes and reached up to the top of the cupboard in which they kept their brooms, hats and coats. She felt around with her fingers until she found what she was looking for and pulled down her X95 Bullpup assault rifle. She blew the dust off it and started wiping it down with her sleeve.

"We'll pack up. You can take Raza and go to the coast until this blows over," Mansur said, following her out.

"And who will protect the people here?"

"Let God protect the people."

"God has better things to worry about than little Buq'ata." She leaned the rifle against the wall and opened the cupboard, rummaging around on the top shelf looking for the magazines she kept there.

He walked up to her and put a hand on her shoulder. "I already lost you once. Let someone else fight this war, sister."

Amal turned and took him into her arms. She understood his pain. During her last tour as a reservist, she had been serving with the Caracal battalion in Southern Command. Her platoon had been called out to a terrorist attack on a tourist hotel at Eilat. She never got there. The terrorists had planted an explosive device on the road leading into the hotel and as their truck approached it had exploded. Flying metal had cut the femoral artery in her left leg and she nearly bled out on the side of the road. Her heart had stopped twice in the ambulance on the way to hospital. It was a day of blood and confusion and her brother, bartending at night, looking after Raza for her during the day, had seen the attack on TV and heard about Israeli soldiers among the casualties. Eilat was in the Southern District, where his sister was serving, so he had called her cell phone, and got no answer. Then he called the headquarters of the Caracals to be told she was missing. That night, a message came that she was dead. He was stricken. He gathered her baby son into his bed and lay there all night, weeping. It wasn't until lunchtime the next day a second call had come through to say she was alive and in a stable condition in hospital.

She didn't really want to be left alone in Buq'ata, and was secretly glad he was stubborn too. "If you won't go, then stay here with me. Make your beautiful furniture and I will finish my new project and when it is finished I will make my world-famous-in-Buq'ata cheesecake with blueberry crust to celebrate, and we will have a house full of guests and at that feast I will find you a wife," she said, kissing his forehead fondly. "But if war comes, you will take Raza to the coast with you. And I will be ready."

"Ready, Ehud?" Captain Binyamin Ben-Zvi asked his systems engineer and second in command.

Ehud Mofaz checked the bank of screens in front of him. "Green on all boards. We're ready."

"Bring her up to a hundred feet. Nice and slow."

Ehud spoke into his throat mike. "*Gal*: engines ahead slow, set depth 100, angle zero five."

Binyamin was nervous. He was about to make contact with the IDF Navy base at Eilat for the first time in a week and doing so meant taking his *Dolphin* III submarine, the *Gal*, close to the surface of one of the busiest seas in the world, the central Mediterranean, a hundred miles east of Crete. The *Gal* had been at sea for nearly three weeks, sailing almost entirely submerged at a near-silent 20 knots. They had sailed from Eilat in late April, but instead of taking the Suez Canal and making their voyage known to the world, Binyamin had been ordered to take his boat out of the Red Sea, down the east coast of Africa, around the Cape and through the Atlantic, past Gibraltar and into the Mediterranean, a distance of about 4,500 miles. They had refueled from an Israeli freighter off the coast of Morocco and sent a short burst transmission to Eilat updating the fleet on their progress, but apart from that, Binyamin and Ehud had not set eyes on another ship since they sailed.

Nor on another human being. Captain Binyamin Ben-Zvi and First Officer Ehud Mofaz were the only crew aboard the 2,000-ton submarine, a fact that in itself was one of Israel's best-kept secrets. But then, everything about the *Gal* was secret. She was the first and only boat in the *Dolphin* III class, an upgrade of the German-made *Dolphin* II class which had been delivered to Israel in the mid 2020s and then substantially modified in secret by the IDF Navy after delivery. The first thing Israel had done was to take the 30-person crew out of the *Gal*. By automating all systems and making them triply redundant, they were able to turn the crew space, which took up about 20 percent of the space inside the hull, into housing for a new hydrogen fuel cell air-independent propulsion system that would allow the submarine to travel submerged for several weeks at a time if needed.

Only two crew were needed to crew the *Gal* – the captain and a systems engineer/first officer whose job it was to manage the communication, environmental, propulsion, navigation and weapons systems. They could take turns sleeping if a human was needed on watch, or even grab some shuteye together, leaving the boat's AI to pilot the submarine and watch for threats. There was no helmsman or weapons officer, the AI responded to natural language commands. The *Gal*'s active and passive sensors gave the two men a 360-degree view of the water around them, out to a distance of twenty miles submerged and fifty miles above the waves when surfaced.

Israel had not announced its modifications to the world. No foreign officer had set foot aboard the *Gal*, and very few members of Israel's submarine service, and even fewer politicians, had been indoctrinated into its secrets. Israel had gone to great lengths to hide the new capabilities of the *Gal* even from friendly navies. Theoretically based at Eilat, whenever it sailed on its months-long covert missions, it was replaced in dock by a floating steel shell that mimicked its shape and size perfectly and would fool anyone who didn't actually climb into the water underneath it and rap its empty hull with a hammer. The patrol around Africa and into the western Med had been its longest operational patrol since being commissioned.

There was good reason for all the secrecy around the *Gal*. It was Israel's most potent hunter-killer submarine. In its forward section it carried four near-silent hydraulically served torpedo tubes capable of firing torpedoes armed with five-kiloton nuclear warheads, or submarine-launched *Popeye* Turbo cruise missiles armed with 20-kiloton nuclear warheads. It was not only designed to kill any enemy ship against which it deployed its weapons, it was designed to kill entire *fleets*.

That nuclear strike capability was the main reason there were two crew members aboard the *Gal*. To initiate a strike, both had to enter and validate the nuclear launch codes. Both had to verify the launch with infrared retinal and voice print identification. Only 22 officers were rated to serve on the *Gal*-class submarine, and they were not allowed to sail more than two patrols together in any three-month period, to avoid forming personal loyalties. There was an additional failsafe. Both officers' bio-signs were continually monitored and if both officers were registered as dead, all human interfaces would be locked down, the weapons systems disabled and the boat would pilot itself back to the nearest IDF naval base.

Curiously it wasn't the four nuclear weapons in his forward section that made Binyamin nervous as they rose to communication depth. It was the simple risk of detection by one of the dozen navies whose ships could be plying the waters above him. The *Gal* was not a powerful weapons platform in itself. A Russian *Laika* submarine displaced 8,000 tons to the *Gal*'s 2,000 and had 16 vertical launch missiles against the *Gal*'s 10 torpedo tubes. Fitted with multiple independently targetable reentry vehicle (MIRV) warheads, a single *Laika* could take out every major city on the US East Coast. Even an Indian *Arihant*-class sub could launch 12 ballistic missiles. But the *Laika* and *Arihant* were political weapons, supposed to act as deterrents to other powers against nuclear aggression. Their power lay in their very public existence.

The *Gal*, on the other hand, was a ghost. A cipher. The world knew Israel possessed nuclear weapons. It had hypothesized that Israel had fitted nukes to its submarine-launched cruise missiles or land-based Jericho ballistic missiles. But it had never confirmed its suspicions and while it knew Germany had built at least three new *Dolphin* II submarines for Israel, it had never confirmed that Israel had upgraded and armed any with nuclear weapons. The longer the *Gal* stayed a ghost, the more real power it had. The power to strike unexpectedly and devastatingly against any ship or submarine in any navy.

The power, at any time, to strike *deniably*.

A *Kaved* torpedo fired by the *Gal* could travel up to ten miles to its target, guided by an onboard inertial navigation system to a pre-determined point before detonating. Set to explode 150 feet below the surface, its nuclear warhead would create a wave of storm-surge height out to 6,000 feet, and a column of water 5,000 feet high. The vaporized gas 'crater' it created would be 3,000 feet in diameter. Any submarine or ship within the crater would be capsized or disabled by the shock wave. But that was not the *Kaved's* only potential use.

The scenario Binyamin and Ehud had rehearsed most often, and which they had even successfully simulated by sailing the *Gal* right into the mouth of Syrian and Egyptian naval harbors, was one in which they would use a subsurface nuclear explosion to take entire enemy harbors, and all the ships in them, out of action. If fired into a harbor, the irradiated waterspout from their five-kiloton torpedo would drown and contaminate infrastructure and ships, requiring weeks or months of destructive decontamination. As importantly, unless the *Gal* was detected and forced to surface, it would be nearly impossible to attribute the attack to Israel. Israeli politicians could claim the explosion was an accident aboard the nuclear-powered vessel of a hostile nation … Russia, for example.

The *Popeye* anti-ship cruise missiles on the *Gal* were less 'subtle'. *Gal* was not a strategic 'second-strike' boat, she was put in the world to kill other submarines and ships, and the short-range, supersonic *Popeye* could be fired with either conventional or special warheads. The conventional variant had a higher risk of being successfully intercepted but was fine against the navies of less advanced nations. Against more sophisticated adversaries and in extreme circumstances, the 20-kiloton nuclear warhead could be detonated at a greater range from the target ship or fleet and still achieve target destruction.

With great power came great responsibility. Binyamin was the only officer aboard who could authorize *Gal* to fire a special, and he could only do so with a launch code provided by his fleet and political masters, which had to be updated every two hours. Which was the main reason why, now that they had reached their patrol sector, they were coming to communication depth.

"Depth 100, Benny." Like all branches of the Israeli Defense Forces, titles were reserved for occasions that demanded them. Three weeks inside a 2,000-ton tin can sailing halfway around the globe had given Binyamin Ben-Zvi and Ehud Mofaz an easy informality.

"All stop."

"*Gal*: hold at depth 100, engines astern, slow to stop." The small creaks and groans of the boat's passage through the water went silent.

Holding steady.

"Deploy sensor buoy."

Ehud called up a utility screen and tapped an icon. "Deploying."

The Israelis had already carefully scanned for nearby submarine or surface traffic using their passive sensors, but there was still an element of uncertainty about what awaited them above. Drones or aircraft were their biggest threats right now. A single well-placed sonar buoy dropped on top of them now would uncloak them completely.

From the top of the submarine's 'sail' or conning tower, a football-shaped buoy detached and floated to the surface on optical fiber cable. It was capable of satellite, VHF and UHF radio transmission, as well as infrared and radar sensing. Even as it neared the surface of the sea, it started feeding data to the tactical display in front of Ben-Zvi. In seconds, he had a radar, electronic and infrared picture of nearby shipping which the *Gal*'s combat AI immediately began classifying by type and nationality and plotting on a 2D grid. Naval warships and surveillance drones or aircraft were flagged red, but there were thankfully none of those within detection range. The nearest vessel was a cargo ship ten miles to port, moving away from them.

"Clear to transmit."

"Transmitting, aye. Message sent. And … incoming traffic downloading. Recovering buoy." The multipurpose sensor buoy could both send and receive. It could be recovered, if time and operational conditions allowed, or fired to the surface untethered from any depth to send a one-way message, after which it would sink again and be lost. Unless that message was a mayday, in which case it would continue to float and transmit an emergency GPS locator signal.

They both checked the incoming message traffic. There

were only two messages. One reconfirming their former mission orders, and one containing the updated launch codes for their special weapons.

"Take us down again, Gal. Under the thermal layer, ahead slow, random course changes but keep us in this sector.

Aye, Captain. Ahead slow, optimize for stealth.

"Ehud, I'm going to get some food, take a shower and grab some sleep. You should too."

"No problem. I'll set it up and join you in the galley." 'Galley' was a grand term for the small eating space forward of their command center under the sail. They had a microwave oven for heating food, a kettle for tea, and a fold-down table with bench seating for two. Under the floor was enough food storage space to support a three-month patrol. Forward of that were their crew quarters and, on the other side, a shower and toilet side by side, fed by the desalination plant that also gave them their drinking water. Twenty square yards of domestic bliss; luxury by any submariner's standards.

Ehud had queued up the data for their report in a single high-frequency microburst transmission and squirted it to Eilat. It was of course encrypted, but it contained everything you might expect, from latitude, longitude, depth, speed and heading to the *Gal*'s fuel, fuel cell and backup battery state. However, it also contained a message that might have caused a little alarm if it had been intercepted by an unintended recipient.

Unit 604 is in position and awaiting attack command.

All Domain Attack: Assassination

Mount Hermonit, Golan Heights, May 16

Quds Force sniper Abdolrasoul Delavari was very, very good at waiting. He had been waiting for the order to begin executing his mission after months of reconnaissance. He had been waiting for delivery of the very unusual weapons system sitting at his feet for nearly a month. He had been waiting in the bush on the hill just inside the Syrian border in the chill of night and now the baking hot morning sun for nearly twenty-three hours.

He was waiting to fire the first shot in a new war.

It would not be a technically difficult shot. He checked the distance for the hundredth time against the glowing numbers in his telescopic rangefinder. Three miles, give or take a few yards. The difficulty would come with the fact he was using a new weapons system he had only had two weeks to train on, and the fact the target would give him only a tiny window of opportunity in which to make his kill.

He checked the time in the scope. Fifteen more minutes, if their intelligence was correct. And it seemed it was. There was a great deal of activity at the IDF observation post on the hilltop at Mount Hermonit. More importantly, there was a lot of activity overhead as well. He had so far counted one fighter patrol of three aircraft, two helicopters and one drone. The helicopters and drone sweeping the countryside around Mount Hermonit were no doubt using thermal infrared cameras to scan the ground, but he wasn't worried about them. The protective lining in his 'ghillie suit' would shield him from simple infrared. Now he could see soldiers gathering inside the bunker. From this position low on the plains in front of the bunker, he would never have been able to make a conventional shot, but today was not going to be a conventional attack.

Delavari had been preparing for this mission for two

months, scouting a half dozen possible locations based on his target's known and planned movements. Several of the other hides he'd scouted would have been better than this one if he'd been using, say, his favored *Degtyarev* rifle chambered for the new Russian *Klimovsk* smart 12.7mm ammunition. But even with *Klimovsk* rounds he could never have made a shot from three miles out. Delavari was good, but not that good.

His target on this mission was Gassan Tamir, an IDF colonel and currently the commander of the Golani Brigade. Delavari did not have an overly exaggerated idea of his own importance, nor was he impressed by the number of stars on the shoulder boards of his target. But he did believe in the influence a single person could have on the outcome of a battle, and history was full of examples of that. Not least the history of this place, which Delavari had studied with interest. The Syrians called it the Quneitra Gap: the flat plains between Mount Bental and Mount Hermonit through which the Syrians had tried to channel their invasion of the northern Golan Heights in 1973. Opposing 500 Syrian tanks had been a small force of 50 tanks led by a 29-year-old Lieutenant Colonel called Avigdor Kahalani. Two days later, Kahalani's force was down to seven tanks, but 260 Syrian tanks lay burning in the valley around them, giving the gap its Israeli name – the Valley of Tears. The Syrians withdrew, and Kahalani was called 'the savior of Israel' when he was presented with his Medal of Valor. As he had lain on his bunk reading Kahalani's story, Delavari couldn't help but wonder what might have happened if Kahalani had not been in this place, at that time.

Or how Israel would cope with what was to come, without Gassan Tamir.

Ten minutes.

Delavari had not been briefed on the bigger picture. He had no idea if Syria really intended to try to take the Golan Heights back as the rumors in his unit said, or if there was some other strategic goal. Like everyone else, he had seen the activity on the plains south of his current position, as Syria, Russia and

53

Iran maneuvered their combined ground and air forces in so-called 'training exercises'. For all he cared, the Syrian objective could be Lebanon, or Golan, both, or neither. Delavari was just a tradesman, plying his trade. If he was not here, he would be in the north, helping the Syrians deal with troublesome Kurds or Turkish commandos.

Abdolrasoul Delavari had been at war a very, very long time. He had started working with the IRGC during the Syrian war against Daesh in 2013 at the age of 30, and since that time had claimed more than 150 Daesh, Kurdish and Turkish officers. Officers were his preference. He saw little point in killing ordinary soldiers or their corporals and sergeants. He could have a squad of infantry in his sights, but he would happily wait a half day in the baking sun for an officer to appear, because he would rather cut off the head of the snake than its tail.

He had several nicknames. 'One-Man Brigade' was one of them, but he didn't acknowledge it. Another was 'Assad's Hunter', but he didn't like that one either because the Syrian leader was not his master. He served the Islamic Republic, and was in Syria only because his country wanted him there. There was one nickname he answered to. Among the Quds Force soldiers he shared a mess with, he was 'Lighvan': the name of a Persian sheep's milk cheese filled with holes. It was a nickname he had earned the hard way.

Delavari was a tailor from Isfahan. He had moved there from the provinces as a young man and his relatives had helped him find work. With the money he'd saved over several years, he'd opened a clothing store. At the time he joined the IRGC he was married, with seven children. He had learned to shoot as a young man, hunting rabbits to help feed his family, and growing up in a large family with little money, he had to make every bullet count. In Isfahan he soon learned he was a better hunter than he was a businessman. So he brought his brother in to run the clothing store and joined the IRGC because it was offering a bonus to soldiers who volunteered to serve in Syria.

His talent with a rifle was soon noticed, and he was sent to the Quds Force for sniper training. And it was during his field training, on his very first mission in Islamic State-controlled Syria, that he received his nickname. A Daesh sniper had been troubling Syrian troops trying to dislodge both Islamic State and Syrian rebels from Raqqa. After the sniper was spotted camped on the rooftop rubble of a destroyed building, Delavari had been dispatched to try to take him out.

He'd found the Syrian troops crouched on the ground floor of a villa, smoking cigarettes and talking quietly as he'd been shown in. In the corner of the room, on the floor under a curtain, he saw a dead body. A long rifle was leaned up against the wall beside the body.

He stood looking at the boots sticking out from under the curtain.

One of the Syrians walked over to Delavari and stood looking down at the body for a moment. "That was the last guy your people sent," he told Delavari in broken Persian. He gestured to Delavari to follow him into the next room, and pointed at a shoulder-high window looking out to the east. "He's out there, two o'clock. You'll see a roof with a red clay chimney. He's somewhere up there." The man nodded at the window. "You can rest your rifle on the window pane, it's a good spot to shoot from."

Delavari saw pock marks in the wall behind the window from shots the sniper had apparently already sent into the room. And a patch of not-very-well-mopped blood on the floor. "I don't think so," he told the Syrian. Lifting his *Degtyarev* onto his shoulder, he walked out of the room to the rear of the villa and found a courtyard. Pushing some barrels up against the rear wall, he crawled up onto the roof of the villa and slid forward on his stomach until he could see around a TV antenna toward the east. He quickly saw the rooftop the Syrian had talked about and, pulling the scope off his rifle, settled in to watch it.

After about twenty minutes, he saw a movement. Just the smallest of changes in light and shadow. It looked like the top third of a boot. He couldn't see the leg it belonged to, but as he watched, the boot was pulled back out of sight, and then there was nothing.

That told him a lot. The Daesh sniper was careful, he had chosen his hide well, but he was dumb, or lazy, or overconfident. A smart man with initiative and just a little humility would not still be shooting from the same position in which he had already scored one kill. No matter how comfortable he was, no matter how safe he felt. Yes, the sun was going down behind him, making his hide an even better spot to shoot from now than it had been earlier. Yes, he had a good line of sight to a position in which he knew enemy troops were located. But Delavari's Quds Force trainers had taught him never to stay too long in one place, never to assume he was invisible, never to trust that just because he couldn't see an enemy, the enemy could not see him.

Looking at the layout of the rooftop, the angle down to the window below him through which he'd shot the last sniper, the fall of the shadow in which the man must be hiding, Delavari decided he needed to be two houses further over to the north. So he climbed fences and ducked through shattered walls until he reached the position he thought would give him the best line on the Daesh shooter, and he climbed a jagged wall, a staircase of blasted bricks leading up to a second floor that wasn't there anymore. There wasn't anything to hold on to. The remaining brick wall was like a one- or two-brick staircase to nowhere, with the rubble of the house to his left, and bare ground to his right. But moving up slowly, brick by brick, he eventually got to the top and placed his rifle carefully, so carefully, up on the topmost brick where he would have a good view toward the rooftop with the red clay chimney. And with his head down below the level of his rifle, he waited for the shot to come.

But it didn't.

Delavari had learned patience, hunting rabbits. Sometimes an hour would pass before the sound of his footsteps was a distant enough memory for a rabbit in a warren to stick its head above ground again, and if that's what it took, Delavari would wait. He waited now. If the sniper across the rooftops had seen him put his rifle in place, he would shoot. He had to. Just to be sure that what he was seeing was what he thought it was. And if he didn't shoot … well, then maybe he hadn't noticed.

He was patient, but back then Delavari was also green. After what seemed like an hour, but was probably only several minutes, when there was no shot, Delavari cautiously lifted his head so that he could put his eye to his scope.

The bullet came silently. He never heard the crack of the rifle. He felt a burning sensation in his temple and jerked back, too late … his rifle fell and he grabbed for it, losing his balance and falling heavily onto the ground beside the building he'd perched himself on.

Out in the open.

He should have got up and run, immediately. But he was shocked, stunned by his fall, bleeding from the bullet that had grazed his temple, gouging a deep canal through his scalp. Before he knew it, he realized he'd been laying there for nearly a minute, and the time to flee was past. His enemy must have his scope trained squarely on him now.

He lay stock still, waiting for the kill shot to come, feeling the blood pool around his head.

His rifle had fallen beside him, within reach of his outflung arm, but he knew that the moment he reached for it, he was dead. There could be only one reason he wasn't already, and that was because the enemy sniper was waiting for help to come, either to rescue him or drag his body away – a chance for another kill.

But no one came.

By pure chance he had fallen with his head facing toward the rooftop with the red clay chimney. Lying on the ground, he could not see it so well, and certainly couldn't see the sniper's hide. But he had no doubt the sniper could see him. Through shuttered eyelashes, he tried to keep his gaze fixed on the rooftop. He couldn't be sure, but he thought he may have passed out a couple of times, because the sun overhead seemed to move in small jumps through the sky. The next time he was conscious, or at least consciously thinking about it, he realized it was starting to get dark, and the rooftop opposite was in complete shadow. The ground between buildings in which he'd fallen would soon be in shadow too. Across the city, he could hear the rattle of small arms fire, and the occasional crump of a grenade or rocket.

He thought about moving, about trying to roll away. Surely the Daesh shooter would have given up by now. If those bastard Syrians hadn't come for him already, they weren't coming now. They must have heard the shot, must have heard the thump of his body hitting the ground. But they were probably still squatting in their back room, cooking bloody lentils and rice over a gas ring, smoking and drinking coffee and arguing about whose job it was to go out there and find a wheelbarrow so they could take the dead Iranian snipers back to their Raqqa base.

He slowly tensed and released his left leg, then his right. Did the same with his arms. Trying to do so invisibly, he flexed the muscles of his shoulders. Nothing felt broken. There was just the heavy thud of a headache, probably as much from the bullet that had creased his skull as from his awkward landing. His rifle still lay about a foot from his outstretched arm. In his mind's eye, he practiced his next move. *Roll right, grab the rifle, keep rolling into the lee of the wall over there. If you are still alive, jump up and run back, out of the line of fire.*

Now? He looked up at the rooftop, and it looked back at him, just a dark, jumbled mess.

No. A dark, *moving* jumble. As he watched, one shadow detached itself from the others. A man, rising into a crouch, his day's work finished. His silhouette momentarily outlined by the sun setting behind him.

Delavari rolled right, grabbed his rifle, but he didn't keep rolling. He put his eye to his scope, steadied the barrel of the *Degtyarev* in his extended left hand and felt for the trigger with his middle finger. Delavari was a middle-finger trigger shooter, a quirk from the days he had learned to shoot as a boy and his forefinger was too short to comfortably reach the trigger of his father's old British Lee Enfield rifle. The range to the rooftop with the red clay chimney was still dialed in from the sighting he'd taken before climbing the brick wall, and there was still a round in the chamber, but he had no idea of whether the scope was still aiming true or had been knocked out of alignment. He had one chance, one shot.

He took a breath, put his sight on the dark, hunched figure, and pulled gently on the trigger.

The crack of the rifle was louder than he expected, echoing off the walls beside and ahead of him. He should have rolled immediately to his right, not waiting to see the result, using the cover of his own fire to make his escape.

But he lay still, with his eye glued to his scope. And watched as the dark silhouette froze. Then slowly rose up. And, with slow-motion stillness, toppled forward, rolling down the roof and off the guttering at the edge, to disappear from view into the street below.

Finally, Delavari scuttled backwards and away.

He'd left his first mission with a kill, and a coin-sized notch in the top of his ear from the Daesh bullet that had earned him the nickname of the Iranian cheese with holes in it: "Lighvan." He'd thought it pretty funny, but his wife hadn't.

So long ago now. So many battlefields. So many kills.

In the field opposite Mount Hermonit he looked at his watch again. Five minutes. Launch time.

From the duffel bag at his feet and screened from the bunker by the thick vegetation, he removed what was quite the most unusual weapon he'd ever deployed. He'd been given it by a Druze captain who told him it was a top-secret prototype. To Delavari it looked more like a child's toy than a weapon of war. First, he lifted out the body of a small electrically powered airplane, the fuselage no longer than his arm. Then he pulled out the wings, about the same length and two hands wide. He fixed these onto the fuselage with rubber ties and tested the battery. Green light.

He'd already fitted the payload, a quadrotor microdrone, held in place with clamps that would automatically retract and drop it on command. He pulled out the command module and put it on the ground beside him.

Facing away from the bunker, legs splayed out in front of him, he fitted the airplane into a rubber slingshot, keeping his movements slow and to a minimum. This was the most dangerous part of his mission, for Delavari. If he was spotted from the bunker, he could find himself running for his life through a rain of Israeli mortar fire. He pulled back on the slingshot and fired the plane into the air. It swooped up, and before its weight took it to the ground again, he pressed the engine starter button on the command module and the rear propeller started whirring, pushing the little drone silently higher. He left it to do what it was programmed to do – climb to about 1,000 feet and loiter, one and a half miles out from the target.

Turning around, he rolled onto his stomach and crawled back into position in the bush. He was looking at a screen on the command module now, and swiveled the camera on the drone so that it was zoomed on the wide slit that opened into the bunker. There was more movement inside. It was slowly filling, as he'd expected, for the coming inspection. More and more uniforms with shoulder boards on them, their caps tucked through them in that typical Israeli way. Delavari smiled. Unless they were in combat fatigues, the Israeli officers usually wore light green shirts, unbuttoned, decorations above their left pockets. It marked them out clearly from the enlisted men around them in khaki and green. Gassan Tamir was also notable for his observance of orthodox practices, including wearing a green-fringed light-green yarmulke cap that matched his uniform.

Commotion in the bunker now. Delavari triggered the release of the microdrone. And now, the attack was out of his hands. The mother drone would be turning back into Syria and gliding to a landing near a Syrian army outpost where a GPS signal would enable it to be recovered. The microdrone, now freed, was closing halfway to the target, almost invisible to a naked eye, totally silent at a distance of more than a couple of hundred yards. He was seeing inside the bunker through the lens of the microdrone now, and his screen showed the Israelis had set up short-range jamming equipment to block radio and drone signals during the VIP visit. But the drone no longer required commands from him.

One minute.

He could see the faces of the men inside the bunker on his screen, some standing looking through binoculars. The drone laid a green facial recognition mesh grid across each of them as they moved into view, cycling constantly between them faster than Delavari could follow. Now the soldiers at the front moved aside as a new group of four men moved up to the front of the bunker. Their deference indicated this was the group he was waiting for. He started scanning the faces of the officers himself, looking for Tamir. He wasn't there. An enlisted man was pointing, an officer next to him leaning in attentively. Not Tamir. Had their intelligence been wrong? Was Tamir not here?

The drone panned its camera across the soldiers at the front of the bunker. Left to right, right to left. Searching autonomously for its target. And then it locked and turned red. Not on an officer at all – had it misidentified the target?

Oh, you clever bastard, Tamir.

In a sergeant's uniform, standing next to the other officers, was Gassan Tamir. He had changed his uniform, but he couldn't change his facial features, and he hadn't changed the yarmulke perched atop his receding hairline.

One minute.

That's how long it would take the 100 mph drone to close the one and a half miles from where it was hovering to the entrance of the bunker. As he watched on the screen, the bunker zoomed closer with dizzying speed. The target lifted binoculars up to his face. It made no difference, the drone had locked on.

Delavari pushed the guidance unit aside and grabbed his telescope, focused on the bunker again. He saw a shadow, like a sparrow diving through the opening of the bunker, then a flash of light beside the Colonel's head.

Tamir's head snapped sideways, and he dropped. Chaos ensued inside the bunker.

With a grunt of satisfaction, Delavari quickly packed his gear. Chaos was a sniper's friend. Trusting no one would be looking his way in the moments after the attack, Delavari stood and began walking down the hill, into a gully that would hide him from observers in the Israeli outpost as he worked deeper into Syrian territory.

As he walked, he pushed the drone controller into his backpack and took a swig of water. It was a good machine, the Israeli drone. He was no romantic, wedded to his old *Degtyarev* rifle through some idiotic ideal of how the work of a sniper should be done. He knew other snipers in the Quds Force who shunned modern methods. They refused to have anything to do with laser-guided loitering missiles, remotely controlled gun stations, or drones … especially drones.

Abdolrasoul Delavari embraced them all. He'd learned one lesson lying in the dirt of Raqqa: the only successful mission was one you came back alive from. And whatever increased the chances of that was good. To hell with the souls of idiots with ideals.

Inside the bunker atop Hermonit, the hell that had broken loose was breaking around Lieutenant Colonel Zeidan Amar, Reconnaissance Battalion Commander, Golani Brigade. A blast like a shotgun going off, Tamir had fallen at his feet, his head a shattered mess, and Amar had dropped to a knee, cradling the body in his arms as others shouted for a medic, shouted orders sending out patrols to find the shooter, or just shouted in shock and fear. Amar could see there was nothing a medic could do for Tamir; the head he was cradling was missing one side of its skull and the mess that was once Tamir's brains had fallen out into Amar's lap.

It might have broken a lesser man. Might have broken Amar too, except for the fact he'd been expecting it.

For years, he'd been working for this moment. He had been twenty when Israel passed a law in 2020 declaring itself 'a Jewish State'. Most of the non-Jewish Druze in Israel shrugged and got on with life. But the twenty-year-old Zeidan Amar had not shrugged. He had been outraged. He had just signed on for officer training at the end of his compulsory service. And now his country was telling him he was a second-class citizen? He posted about his outrage on social media, and was called in by the commandant at Bahad training base to be given a lecture about his attitude. It only made him more angry. He had not grown up in the Druze settlements in the annexed Golan Heights, which still leaned toward Syria, but he joined an underground protest movement that had begun agitating for the Golan Heights settlements to declare themselves independent from Israel.

There were attacks on police stations, a bus was hijacked and burned, a water treatment plant sabotaged. Zeidan wasn't actively involved, but he was certainly sympathetic and donated as much of his salary as he could spare to their cause. He graduated from officer school and asked to be posted to the Golani brigade, where he funneled what information he could about Israeli troop and police movements to the Druze independence movement.

After one of their covert meetings, he had been approached by a man he later learned was a Syrian intelligence officer.

Under Syria, the Druze in Golan would be independent, the Syrian agent had said. Full citizens of Syria. You are an officer in the Golani brigade. Loyal to your people, not to Israel. You can serve their cause more effectively by helping us restore The

Golan to Syrian control. Not now. Not soon, but one day. Forget this amateur stuff with the buses and sewage works. Serve in the Golani brigade, rise through the ranks. We will help you, and then when the day comes, you will truly help your people.

He'd agreed to cooperate. And his Syrian contact had delivered. Based on a tip from his Syrian source, he had led his company over the UN ceasefire line into Syrian-held territory and uncovered a major arms cache. That success had been followed by others: a missile site identified and destroyed, a convoy of Iranian weapons intercepted and impounded. Then, he had been given a mission which his commanding officer, Gassam Tamir, had told him carried such a high risk, he could not order him to undertake it. All men assigned, himself included, had to volunteer, and Tamir would not judge those who refused. "If you fail and the mission becomes public," Tamir warned him, "I will have to say your action was unsanctioned, and you will be censured, probably tried in a military court."

The target was a Syrian military outpost just inside Syrian territory up against the DMZ overseen by the UN Disengagement Observer Force, UNDOF. Normally, Israel would have no compunction about demolishing such a brazen provocation, and bragging about it. But there were reported to be Russian 'advisors' stationed at the outpost too. If any Russian casualties resulted, it would be an international incident. Together with Engineering Corps commandos, they were to take control of the outpost, neutralize any Syrian or Russian troops there without causing casualties, and then destroy the outpost with explosives.

The likelihood of taking the Syrian soldiers and their Russian advisors by surprise was regarded as low to zero. The risk of casualties, either Syrian or Russian, was regarded as high. It looked like a no-win mission to Amar. If he was successful, the Syrians and Russians would complain to the UN and he'd be the obvious fall guy. If he failed or there were too many casualties, he'd end up in military court, demoted at best, jailed at worst. It smelled a lot like a test of his loyalty to the Golani commander. "I'll take it, Gassan," he'd told Tamir. "We'll get it done."

With the help of his Syrian contact, he did. When they fell upon the troops at the outpost, they found them all asleep, and at only half strength. His contact had made sure the Russians had withdrawn. The Syrian captives did a good job of looking stupid, confused and afraid as Amar's men tied them up and dragged them outside their newly built emplacement. They did an even better job of looking terrified as the Israeli explosives lit up the night sky and turned the emplacement into a crater full of rubble. One of their captives took a concrete shard in the leg, but that only helped the sense of authenticity that Amar needed.

A week later Tamir had approached him. "The Syrians have complained to the UN about your little adventure."

Amar had held his breath. "And?"

Tamir adjusted the yarmulke on his thin hair, something he only did when he was pleased with himself or making a joke. Amar relaxed. "They didn't make a big fuss. Moaning through back channels, and some noise from the Russians who tried to claim you roughed up one of their officers."

"That's nonsense. They weren't even there."

"It doesn't matter. There are no politicians talking about it in the Knesset and it didn't make the papers. Our reputation at Camp Rabin just got a big boost and I made sure everyone there knows who led the raid. I don't forget this sort of thing, Zeidan."

He'd been true to his word. Soon afterward, Amar had been called to the IDF HQ at Camp Rabin in Tel Aviv and told he was being considered as successor to Gassan Tamir, should he be moved to other duties. "Keep your nose clean and your unit sharp," he'd been told.

He'd done as he was asked by his Israeli leader, knowing his chance to do something truly important for his people would come one day. And two nights ago, that day had come much, much closer.

His contact had sent him a message through an encrypted dating app:

You are about to be promoted.
- What about Tamir?
He is moving on. You will be appointed commander of the Golani brigade this week. It is certain.
- Good news
Your time is about to come, Zeidan Amar. Lieutenant Colonel and Brigade Commander!
- I don't care about that. I live for the day the Druze in Golan are free.
Not yet. But soon. You are clear about what is expected?
- Yes

Not yet? Amar was not blind. He'd watched the Syrians build up their army over the last five years with Russian armor, aircraft and troops, and Iranian missiles. He'd watched them roll into Turkey to successfully reclaim the land along their northern border, stopping only when they over-reached and ran into the wall of harm that was the US 1st Infantry Division. He'd watched and heard the Syrian leader hold speech after speech talking about Syria reclaiming its traditional lands in northern Syria *and* in the Golan Heights.

And he'd watched the Syrians, Russians and Iranians conduct their 'exercises' in the plains south of Hermonit. He'd read the intelligence reports on what they'd moved to their Southern Military District: 2,580 main battle tanks including 60 new generation Russian T-14 *Armatas*. One thousand two hundred armored personnel carriers, 1,200 artillery pieces of 120mm or greater, 50 guided missile launchers, 200 multiple rocket launchers. Twenty thousand ground troops, including an Iranian Revolutionary Guards Corps 'Quds' special forces battalion backed by *Soumar* mobile cruise missile launchers. Flying overhead, they would have at least four squadrons of

Russian ground attack and multirole fighters, including 5th-generation *Okhotnik* and *Felon* stealth fighters.

Although he would be quickly reinforced by other units, against this Syrian and allied force the Golani Brigade could stand three battalions of heavy infantry, three companies of special forces and an electronic warfare signals company. But the IDF had learned the lessons of Yom Kippur, when it had faced 2,000 Syrian tanks with 200 in the Golan Heights, and it had already moved 500 Merkava main battle tanks and crews from its 36th and 7th Armored Divisions into depots just outside the DMZ.

Israel also had one other advantage in 2030 it had not possessed in 1973. The ability to bathe Damascus in nuclear fire. Amar doubted his commanders or the politicians in the Knesset would be willing to push the nuclear button just to defend 10,000 settlers and 1,200 square miles of 'DMZ' between Syria and Israel, but the option was there.

Your time is about to come, Zeidan.

As he kneeled on the floor of the bunker, Tamir's shattered head in his hands, Amar knew now what his Syrian contact had meant. The groundwork for his promotion had been laid beautifully. Amar was primed to step into Tamir's boots as commander of Israel's elite Golani Brigade.

And the liberation of the Druze of the Golan was at hand.

White House Situation Room, May 16

US Director of National Intelligence, Lt. General (Retired) Carmine Lewis, looked around the White House situation room with a practiced eye. She wasn't taking in the data on the banks of screens – she had already reviewed it before her staff loaded it up. She was counting the number and type of water glasses around the table. There was an entire White House staff, overseen by her own people, who prepared for these meetings of the Executive Committee of the National Security Council, or NSC ExComm. Behind every meeting there were hundreds of analysts, data scientists, aides, specialists in every kind of intelligence from cyber to human source, but it was incredible how often her peers grumbled about only having still instead of sparkling water, or the temperature of the coffee, or the firmness of the fruit in the silver bowls sitting in the middle of the table.

It was their way of letting her know they weren't enamored of this whole 'ExComm thing' and especially weren't enamored of the idea that President Henderson had appointed her by National Security Action memorandum as its vice-chair. Not since the days of President Kennedy had a President convened an 'ExComm', hand picking certain members of the broader National Security Council and excluding others.

The idea had come from a conversation they'd had returning from one of the full-day NSC meetings. One which had felt more like three days.

"How many people were in that room today?" Henderson had grumbled as he rode back to the White House with Carmine for his next meeting. Which was another unpopular affectation. Henderson took the DNI with him everywhere lately and preferred to ride with her, rather than with his Chief of Staff, Karl Allen, or any of his senior advisors. It had started more than a few rumors, especially considering Henderson was a widower and she a divorcee. But he'd never once shown that kind of interest in Carmine. Not so much as a single lingering glance at her legs or a peek at her decolletage. She'd done nothing to confirm or deny the rumors, knowing that the uncertainty gave her a modicum of additional power in DC that she might need to leverage one day. Being inside Henderson's innermost circle without people daring to question her fitness to be there was a situation she knew wouldn't last, but which she used every single opportunity to earn.

"Around the table or like, in the room, in the room?" she asked, smiling.

"Both."

"Around the table, twenty-three. Used to be twenty-two, but you went and split out the Cyber Security Directorate from NSA and appointed a Director of National Cyber Security…"

"Your idea. And Tonya was your pick…"

"And she's a fantastic pick. Or will be, as soon as she gets over the fact she's sitting at the Big Table now and starts telling us what she really thinks."

"Twenty-three? Remind me why Dick was there?"

"Special advisor on Food Security. You appointed him during the wheat dispute with China."

"We had the Secretary of Commerce there. Why do I need them both?" Henderson was drumming his fingers on the window of the limo. "You add in all the aides and hangers on, there were fifty people in the room. If we get a fast-moving situation, we can't manage it in a room with fifty people."

"You have the Principles Committee," she pointed out. "Just cabinet members, me and the Chairman of the Joint Chiefs."

"Better, but still too many. Every one of them brings their aides and we still spend half the time looking at damn slides or videos. I want the smallest group possible, no damn screens, just people I trust, who know what's going on and aren't afraid to say what they think about it."

So ExComm had been born. Or resurrected, if you wanted to look at it that way.

In Kennedy's time it had consisted of the President and his Vice President, LBJ, the Secretaries of State, Treasury, Defense, the Attorney General and Kennedy's brother, Bobby Kennedy, the National Security Advisor, Director of the CIA and the Chairman of the Joint Chiefs.

After some toing and froing, Henderson had settled on a similar group. His Vice President, Benjamin Sianni, Defense Secretary Harold McDonald, Secretary of State Kevin Shrier, Homeland Security Secretary Allan Price and his Chief of Staff, Karl Allen. The only military man in the room would be Chairman of the Joint Chiefs, Admiral Clarke. Carmine had looked over his 'final' list and raised her eyebrows.

"What?" he'd asked.

"That's a lot of old white men in one room. You planning to sit around smoking cigars and drinking whisky at these things?"

"I want people there for their ideas and opinions, not their age, gender or skin color. And you'll be there."

"If you want ideas, you want Tonya Dupré. And not for her skin color."

"I put Cyber Security in the room, every branch of the forces are going to be whining even more about being left out. Besides, I don't know her well enough."

"I vouch for her. You said you want ideas? This situation gets hot, you need someone in that room who has spent their time already fighting the next war, not the last one. It was her AI that revolutionized our All Domain Kill Chain capability."

"That was her?" The All Domain Kill Chain was a long-held US military wish for an AI-supported system that would feed targets to long-range strike systems such as missiles, rockets and drones by combining and analyzing data from land, sea, air, space and cyberspace in real time. As a young programmer, Dupré had led the team which had created the AI that finally made it possible. One of the coders on her team had named it HOLMES, short for Heuristic Ordinary Language Machine Extrapolation System. The breakthrough HOLMES had enabled was that battlefield commanders, even soldiers, could give orders to HOLMES in plain language over a radio, and HOLMES could respond to them, also in plain language.

And when ordered, it could act. Instantly, and without prejudice.

He grunted. "Alright. But she sits there with those big moon eyes just watching everyone else talk, she's out."

Tonya Dupré had been Carmine's recommendation for Director of Cyber Security, the agency newly created to coordinate the activities of the many disparate cyber defense and warfare arms of the US government – inside the National Security Agency, Homeland Security, Treasury, Defense Cyber

Command, the CIA and FBI's cyber security teams. A former white hat hacker, born of Colombian and African American parents, only 42 years old, she'd been a deputy director at NSA for eight years and no one knew cyber warfare better than she did. And she'd worked in two of the agencies her new directorate was put in the world to coordinate, NSA and US Cyber Command. But she was still a little overawed at having been pulled out of the trenches and sat at the mahogany table so quickly. Carmine was mentoring her. She'd either sink or swim, but she'd earned the chance to prove herself.

As Carmine stood fixing herself a cup of coffee at the machine on a side table, the others started filing in.

The VP, Sianni, arrived first. He'd taken the lead on the US response to the Syria-Turkey conflict, nudging President Henderson step by step into greater involvement. Defense Secretary McDonald was next, together with Admiral Clarke, fresh from a meeting with the Joint Chiefs and both looking worried. For a Defense Secretary he was more a dove than an eagle, and tended to play to Henderson's natural tendencies to caution. Right behind him was Homeland Security Secretary Price, an old college friend of Henderson's who had followed him as Governor of North Carolina before taking on Homeland Security. He had only one string to his bow, and he played it with bulldog determination and monotony, 'what's in this for the USA'? Dupré came in next, and made a beeline for Carmine without saying hello to any of the others.

She grabbed a coffee cup and Carmine was glad to see it wasn't shaking. But she wasn't pleased at her first words. "What am I doing here, Carmine?"

Carmine flashed a sideways glance at her, putting cream in her own coffee. "You're here because you need to be." She put a hand on her shoulder. "Tonya, you run an agency of 300 cyberwarriors and coordinate the cyber intelligence collection activities of NSA, US Cyber Command, Department of Homeland Security, and Federal Bureau of Investigation. You can sit and drink mineral water and chew the fat with six crabby men and this old girl. Now get your ass away from this coffee machine and work the room."

Carmine sat herself next to McDonald as he unzipped his folder and papers spilled across the desk in front of him.

"Busy morning, Harry?"

McDonald looked over at Clarke, who Carmine was glad to see was talking with Tonya. "Joint Chiefs want us to move Navy and Air Force to DEFCON 2 in the Middle East."

"That Iranian sub?"

"The *nuke* on that Iranian sub," he said. He looked up from ordering his papers and shot her a glance. "Damn, is there nothing you don't hear about before me?"

"I heard it's not definitive."

"Israel gets wind of it, it won't matter. They've already got half the Syrian army running exercises on their eastern border. They'll take no chances."

At that moment Henderson walked in with his Chief of Staff, Karl Allen. Allen was an attorney by trade and had been a Commerce undersecretary in the last government. He and Carmine had an uneasy relationship since a lot of the discussions Henderson would normally have taken with his Chief of Staff – like the composition of ExComm – he was now taking with Carmine. Uneasy, but not hostile – *yet*, she reflected.

Henderson fixed himself a coffee and sat down. "Welcome to ExComm. Before you ask, yes, we are being recorded. If that changes how freely you will speak in this room, then I don't know you as well as I thought I did and you are free to go." There were a couple of chuckles, but no one left the room. A few shot glances at Tonya Dupré, but she was looking down at her own folder of papers.

Study the faces around you, not your damn briefing notes, Carmine silently urged her.

Henderson wasted no more time on pleasantries. "To the reason we are here … this morning, I received a phone call from the Prime Minister of Israel. He was a little worked up. I thought he was probably worked up about the fact there are about five thousand Syrian tanks with their engines idling on his eastern border, but I was wrong. He was much more worked up about a few Russian and Iranian ships sailing from Sevastopol to Syria. He claims the Iranian ships bound for Syria are carrying nuclear weapons, said he had asked his agencies to provide us with the proof, and he suggested we, and I quote, 'coordinate our response to this new threat'. He's asked us to help with a naval blockade in the Mediterranean to prevent the Iranian ships reaching Syria. I told him obviously I took his request seriously, I would look into it and get back to him." He looked around the room. "Which is why you are all here. CIA has been saying for months the Iranians have North Korean nukes. It looks like the Israelis have reached the same conclusion and gone one further."

"How soon can we get this Israeli intelligence?" Carmine asked.

"He said it's on the way, via the usual channels, I assume." He looked at Admiral Clarke. "What do we know about the Iranian navy being armed with nukes, Admiral?"

Carmine looked around the room. The lack of surprise on more than a few faces told her she and McDonald weren't the only ones who'd been briefed about the Iranian submarine on their way to the ExComm meeting. But that submarine had been sighted in the Red Sea. The Israelis were saying there were nukes on the ships sailing with the Russian Black Sea fleet too?

Admiral Clarke looked at McDonald, who nodded, knowing what he was about to say. "Mister President. We just learned that Iran has sent one of its newest submarines into the Red Sea, and we believe it is armed with a North Korean nuke."

Henderson frowned. "The Red Sea?"

"Yes, Mr. President."

"Well, forgive my high school geography, but isn't the Red Sea on the opposite side of the Suez Canal to the Mediterranean? The Israeli PM definitely said the Iranians he was worried about were sailing with the Russian Black Sea fleet, into the Mediterranean."

"It's a Blitz play," Vice President Sianni muttered to himself.

"Speak up, Ben."

"It's a Blitz. A quarterback rush. They're surrounding Israel with nukes. One in the Red Sea on that sub. Another in the Med, with the Russian fleet. Probably others with the Syrian forces on Israel's Golan border. Israel is surrounded."

"They're planning to *nuke* Israel?!" the President asked.

"They would never," Secretary of State Shrier exclaimed.

"They might, as a fallback strategy," Tonya Dupré said, eyes still on her papers. "It's part of an All Domain Strike." She hesitated and looked over at Carmine.

Go on, woman, Carmine thought, nodding at her to continue.

"An all what?" Allen asked.

"All Domain," Dupré said. "It makes sense now. We've been seeing a lot of chatter from Russian and Iranian hackers about a big strike coming up. They're talking electricity grids, banking, communications…"

"But nuclear weapons? That would be mutually assured destruction … Israel would nuke Damascus to glowing green glass."

"Nukes as a *last* resort," Dupré said. "First, the cyber strike cripples Israeli comms and infrastructure. If that doesn't get them what they want, they launch a land attack through the Golan and Lebanon supported by Russian air, sea and space assets. If Iran didn't have nukes, Israel might respond by attacking Tehran and Damascus with nuclear weapons, but if Iran can place them right on their borders, then their anti-ballistic missile defenses are useless…"

"And they can't use their own nuclear weapons without dooming themselves…" Shrier nodded.

"Why? What does Iran want? Israel isn't going to just roll over and surrender," Allen exclaimed. "Iran doesn't want nuclear war. So what is in it for them?"

The room was quiet until Secretary of State Shrier coughed gently. "Survival. I know this isn't a popular view in this room, but the West and Israel have brought Iran to its knees with years of sanctions, covert operations to undermine the regime, overt assassinations. They see Israel and its nuclear weapons as an existential threat, but also as leverage. Victory for Iran would be getting Israel to the bargaining table – to strike some kind of nuclear disarmament agreement, pressure the West to lift its sanctions, resume trade and diplomatic relations…"

"And Syria gets the Golan Heights, with Russia hosting the peace negotiations no doubt. Win, Win, Win," Carmine said, completing the thought.

Dupré nodded. "It's no accident we found out about the Iranian nuclear weapons at the same time as Israel. Iran let us find their sub, just like they let us take a picture of the missile they were loading into it. They *want* us to know what they've got in play."

"That's one hell of a smoke signal," Allen muttered. "They could have just detonated a nuke underground at Fordo and achieved the same thing."

"And waste a precious warhead? They don't have that many to spare," Admiral Clarke observed.

Shrier steepled his fingers. "We have no Embassy in Tehran anymore. No trade mission. There is no hotline between us and the Ayatollah. They could reach out to us through the usual back channels – the French, the Swedes – but would we take them seriously? They're presenting us with a fait accompli and they know we'll take some time to work out what to do about it so they're giving us a few days' grace until their missiles are in place and we have to start negotiating. Maybe they're even hoping we'll open a channel now, start the negotiations before things spin out of control…"

"Well, that was their first mistake," Admiral Clarke said. "We have more than enough assets in place to put a serious wrinkle in their plans."

"What are you suggesting?" Henderson asked.

"We partner with Israel and move first. Take out the Iranian naval threat in the Red Sea and the Mediterranean, while Israeli air force and armor sends the Syrians on the Israeli border back to the stone age."

Carmine saw Dupré about to speak, then bite back her words and look down again. Maybe she'd been wrong to invite her. This was no place for shrinking violets. "Tonya? Your thoughts?" Carmine asked.

"A head-on confrontation is ... unlikely to succeed. Those Iranian ships are protected by Russia: the Russian air force will fly close air support for Syrian tanks, Russian ground-to-air missile systems are protecting the Iranian and Syrian troops," Dupré pointed out. "And even the USS *Nimitz* carrier strike group can't protect Israel from a massive cyber takedown. I'm sorry, Admiral, but you can't prevent the first phase of an All Domain Strike with tanks and airplanes."

Clarke did not look happy to be contradicted by the newest kid on the block, and the glare he gave Dupré could have melted depleted uranium armor. But she didn't quail, instead looking to Carmine for support.

"The Director is right. We need to hit pause and look at all our options here," Carmine said to the room, but with her gaze fixed on Henderson.

The President shifted awkwardly in his seat.

"Options. Right. Harry, get your people working up a potential military response, everything short of pre-emptive nuclear strikes on Damascus and Tehran."

McDonald nodded. Admiral Clarke spoke up, "Including troops, Mr. President?"

Henderson didn't hesitate. "No. I watched too many flag-draped caskets come off that airplane at Reagan National Airport, after Turkey. We saved a NATO base but we lost near forty young men and women."

"And six points in the polls," Allen said, then ducked his head as a few people shot him withering looks. "Hey. I'm just saying."

"Not material, Karl," Henderson told him. "Admiral, we need cyber attack options, anything that can make life hard for

Iranian and Syrian land and naval forces, the Syrian regime. I also want cyber warfare options for disruptive strikes on the Syrian and Iranian regimes and Tonya, get warning of this 'chatter' to the Israelis so they can harden their cyber defenses."

"Yes, Mr. President," Dupré said. "I'd recommend including Russia in that targeting. As I said, the chatter we've been hearing has been among both Iranian *and* Russian black hats."

"Dammit, alright." Henderson sighed. "We reconvene in six hours. I need to know how a naval blockade might work or alternative ideas for how to take those Iranian nukes out of the equation and stop this situation in its tracks, *before* we lose control."

As he finished speaking the door to the situation room opened and an aide stepped inside, then looked around the room, his eyes landing on Carmine. He walked over and handed her a message, then beat a hasty retreat, ten pairs of eyes following him out.

Carmine unfolded the message in silence. "Things may already be accelerating out of control," she said, looking up. "There have been coordinated assassination attempts on Israeli military leaders at brigade and battalion level across the IDF. Several blue on blue incidents, at least four senior officers dead, including the commander of the Israeli Golani Brigade. And one third of the personnel in their 7th Armored brigade just mutinied."

"Mutiny? In the Israeli armed forces?" Sianni asked. "How is that even possible?"

"Apparently a populist right-wing rabbi told them to refuse to serve, in protest at women soldiers being allowed to sing."

"Women ... to *sing* ... are you kidding?"

"No. The whole men and women serving in the IDF together thing has been a heated issue for the last couple of years." Carmine read down the intelligence summary. "They're worried the protest will spread to other units. This rabbi apparently has a lot of clout."

"And he chose today to call on people to lay down their

arms?" Sianni shook his head. "That's no coincidence."

"None of this is," Carmine said. "I briefed this group on it back in February. It's called *Operation Butterfly* and it's probably been in planning since 1974."

Mount Hermonit, Golan Heights, May 16

"Telephone, Zeidan," said the young female Lieutenant standing beside Zeidan Amar's *Storm* all-wheel-drive vehicle. She held a handset out to him. He went to sit down on the passenger seat, and then remembered his trousers were still wet with blood. "I'll get you some new gear," the Lieutenant said, running quickly back into the bunker he'd just left. The compound outside the bunker was full of soldiers milling around, in panic, fear and confusion, looking to him for guidance. He could be ordering them out to comb the countryside for the shooter, but he had been told to try to delay the search for at least thirty minutes. He left them to mill about.

He looked at the telephone. The number had a Tel Aviv military prefix but wasn't one he recognized. "Amar," he said.

"*Parpar,*" the voice at the other end said.

"Understood."

The line went dead.

Butterfly.

So, his time had come.

Reaching for the radio inside the vehicle, he dialed the frequency for Camp Rabin, then picked up the code book from the dashboard under the windscreen.

"This is Lieutenant Colonel Amar, Golani Brigade. Authentication code … alpha golf romeo one three nine."

"Go ahead."

"Put me onto General Weinberg."

"He's in conference."

Pulling the Commander of the IDF Army out of a meeting was not something the poor corporal at the other end of the radio would do lightly, Amar knew that. "Get him out. I'll take the blame."

"Colonel Amar, you said?"

"Zeidan Amar."

"Wait please."

Amar wondered if news of the shooting had made it to Tel Aviv yet. As he watched, the ambulance carrying Tamir pulled slowly out of the compound atop Mount Hermonit, weaving between soldiers suddenly silent.

"Weinberg."

"Zeidan Amar, Golani Brigade." He'd only met the General twice before, but the People's Army didn't stand on formalities.

"What is it, Zeidan?"

"Colonel Tamir is dead. Drone attack. I have dispatched patrols to search for the launch site but it could be anywhere in a range of twenty miles."

"Yes. I got the report. Peace be upon Gassan Tamir."

"Your orders?"

There was a long pause at the other end. "You just got promoted a year earlier than I planned, Zeidan."

"Very well."

"This is not a coincidence. I've ordered the callup of the national reserve. As to the Golani Brigade, I want every drone in the air, every set of eyeballs on that border trained to the east, I want observation reports flowing like the Jordan in spring…"

"Yes, Moshe."

"Get your military police out on the roads, I want civilians evacuated, civilian traffic into the Golan turned around. Keep people on their toes. While we mobilize our reserves, I'm moving 460th Brigade over from Central Command. I want you ready to roll your APCs out of those outposts and into Syria the moment I give you the call."

"We're going with Plan Typhoon?"

"If I have anything to do with it. I don't want us to get caught with our pants down again. You get your boys and girls ready. And try to contain the news about Tamir. The last thing we need right now is for word of this assassination to get out. Dammit to hell."

Amar nodded. "Yes, Moshe. Amar out."

He swallowed hard. *Typhoon.* A pre-emptive strike into Syria intended to disrupt Syrian preparations for war. His special forces reconnaissance battalion would be at the spearhead of the IDF strike, their armored personnel carriers rolling at high speed deep into Syrian territory to hit Syrian outposts, while Israeli Air Force jets hammered surface-to-air missile defenses, tank parks, arms dumps and artillery positions. *If* Israel's politicians gave the green light.

Well, he knew what was expected of him, and it wasn't what General Moshe Weinberg had just ordered him to do.

His aide came running back to him, carrying clean trousers and a shirt. He stripped his bloodied shirt from his torso and pulled the clean shirt on.

"Was that Camp Rabin?" she asked, taking the soiled shirt and holding out the trousers for him.

"Yes."

"What is happening, Zeidan?" she asked. "Is this it?" She looked and sounded scared. "I thought … it was supposed to happen at Shavuot. June 6 … all the reports said June 6."

"This isn't it, Nadia," he said, unlacing his boots and taking them off. "Syria would not dare take on Israel, even with Iran and Russia at its back. This is something else. A provocation of some sort."

He couldn't watch as the hope spread from her eyes to the rest of her face. "Oh, thank God. What are our orders?"

"I've been appointed acting brigade commander," he told her as he pulled on the new trousers and slipped into his boots again. "I was just on the line with Moshe Weinberg. He told me to start evacuating civilians and prepare the brigade to pull back to Camp Shraga." Shraga was the headquarters of the Golani Brigade.

Thirty miles to the west.

"Pull *back*?!"

"Yes, 460th Brigade is taking over. Pass the word down the line to all Golani battalion commanders, will you?" He looked at the Israeli flag flying above the central bunker. "And have the flag taken to half-mast. Let them all know about the assassination of Gassan Tamir too. They are to take their orders from me."

He watched her go, then pulled out his phone, opening the dating app. The person at the other end was a member of the Druze resistance in the biggest Druze town in Israeli-occupied Golan, Buq'ata.

My darling it is time to light the candles
- I have only been waiting for your message beloved
I will arrive soon
- I wait with joy in my heart

Hanging up, he dropped the phone, pulled out its sim card and crushed it beneath his boot before flinging it into nearby grass. He didn't want anyone in his brigade calling him, or tracking him, from here on in. Climbing into the *Storm*, he spent a moment enjoying the burn of the hot seat on his back before he started the engine and pulled out of the compound. Camp Shraga was thirty miles west. Zeidan wound down the hill from the outpost, paused at the crossroad at the base of the hill, then turned *north*, toward the Druze stronghold of Buq'ata.

West Wing, the White House, Washington, May 16

If ExComm was a subset of the National Security Council, then the group meeting that morning in the Oval Office was a subset of a subset. Defense Secretary Harry McDonald and Director of National Intelligence Carmine Lewis sat drinking lukewarm coffee and poring over briefs from their agencies on tablets as they waited for President Henderson to return from his breakfast appointment. With the ExComm meetings being recorded for posterity, Henderson apparently wanted a 'safe space' where he could talk with his closest confidants, and decide himself what was recorded and what not.

McDonald paused his reading and looked across at Lewis. Silver-haired, in her late fifties, he figured she still hit the gym several times a week and was probably wearing the same size uniform today as she had five years ago when she was Lt. Gen. Carmine Lewis, deputy chief of staff for intelligence, surveillance, reconnaissance and cyber effects operations in the US Air Force. If she had one weakness, it was an over-reliance on signals and cyber intelligence, which she'd shown in her insistence on muscling the new Director of Cyber Security into the ExComm group. McDonald was old school and proud of it, he'd back a report from a human source over a signals intercept any day.

But Lewis was pretty much bullet proof in all other respects, including her relationship with President Henderson. There was a lot of beltway blarney about the two of them being in a tryst, but McDonald had spent enough time around both of them to see that was nonsense. If anything, they were more like brother and sister. More than once, watching them joke or bicker, McDonald had been reminded of books he'd read about the relationship between the Kennedy brothers, John and Bobby. Henderson was good at canvassing for opinions, but there was only one person who could speak truth to him without fear or favor, and that was Carmine Lewis.

"We can't let that Iranian sub roam around the Red Sea unhindered," Lewis said, looking up. She caught him staring at her and he looked quickly down at his tablet.

"USS *Canberra* has reacquired it, headed for the Gulf of Aqaba, possibly Israel's southern coast. If they patrol just outside Israeli waters that would give a missile 30 *seconds* flying time to the Israeli port of Eilat, four minutes to Tel Aviv. You got confirmation on that nuke?"

"All but. Our North Korean friends were sighted at the

dock when that missile was being loaded. They weren't there because they needed some sea air. There's no reason for them to be there unless it's a nuke."

"It's still not proof. Not a smoking gun."

"We may never get a smoking gun, Harry," she said, sounding exasperated. "And while I'm sure the crew on the *Canberra* are on top of their game, like I said, losing and then finding that sub again feels to me like a deliberate attempt to keep our attention."

"We should get *their* attention. Sink the damn thing."

"Sink what where?" President Henderson said, walking in. He looked tired, which McDonald reflected was not a good sign. They were only at the start of what could be a long and trying crisis.

"I was telling Harry, we have even stronger indications the missile on that Iranian sub in the Red Sea is a nuke. North Korean 'seismologists' were present for the loading."

Henderson looked at McDonald. "And you want to sink it?!"

"Not if we don't have to. But we don't want to have to run operations in the Red Sea and the Med. The USS *Canberra* carries EMP torpedoes. One of those would disable it without destroying it, and…"

"They hear a Mark 48 torpedo coming at them, they just might launch their damn nuke," Henderson said, focusing on McDonald. "I don't like it. Harry, I assume your people have given you multiple options. Find me one that won't immediately kick off World War Three."

McDonald consulted his tablet. "There is a stealth vector," he replied. "*Swarmdiver…*"

"*Swarmdiver* mines would sink it," Carmine pointed out. "That's pretty much a declaration of open warfare. We want to go that far?"

"No. I'm thinking of fouling the screw. Just put it out of commission."

The newly deployed *Swarmdiver* underwater swarming drones

on the USS *Canberra* were fired from its anti-submarine rocket launchers in swarms of twenty. Each drone weighed only four pounds, was 30 inches long, and could dive to depths of about 500 feet. In its standard configuration it was intended to scatter a cloud of mines in the path of an enemy warship or submarine. But it could be fitted with warheads of various kinds, including a propeller fouling net that was particularly effective at stopping single-screw ships or submarines dead in the water.

"Could work," Lewis admitted. "They won't see it coming at least."

"Divers can't cut the screw free while it's at sea, they'd have no option but to tow the thing back to port and put it in dry dock."

"And if you knock out its screw and accidentally send it to the bottom of the Red Sea?" Henderson asked.

"Then we offer our help with a rescue," McDonald said. "But the more likely scenario is they surface so they can be towed, rather than risk drifting."

"Blowback?" Henderson asked.

"Iran, of course. Russia. The usual suspects. But the good thing about a *Swarmdiver* attack is we can engage from miles out and keep our distance. It will look like they snagged a fishing net. Pretty much totally deniable."

"And the latest on Syria?"

"Syria has more than 2,000 tanks and 10,000 troops parked up along the ceasefire line. Looks like a full court press, just as Dupré described." McDonald grimaced.

Henderson motioned to Lewis. "Get her on a line, will you, Carmine?"

Lewis got up and went to the door to find an aide.

"Helluva situation, Harry," Henderson said, wiping his face. "How did we get here? Iranian nukes?"

"Horse has bolted, Oliver. Did you know the USA *started* the Iranian nuclear energy program?"

"No, get out."

"Yep. Back in the 1950s, under the Shah. We called it 'Atoms for Peace'. It was a great idea, trying to take the bogeyman out of the idea of nuclear energy and show the world that it could also be used for peace, not just war."

"Genius."

"Yeah, until 1979 when the good guys became the bad guys and we were the ones who gave them the means to refine weapons-grade uranium. Now you and I are the ones left holding the barn door."

Lewis returned as a telephone on the Resolute desk rang. She walked over to pick up the call, putting it on speaker and turning the screen to face Henderson before sitting down again.

"Tonya Dupré for you, Mr. President," the operator said.

The young woman came onscreen, a look of curiosity on her face. "Hello, Mr. President…"

"Tonya, walk me through this All Domain Attack scenario. Say Iran isn't looking for nuclear war and Syria and Iran want to force Israel to sit down and deal instead. How's it unfold?"

"Certainly, sir," the young woman replied. "Well, their first move would be a cyber attack on Israeli utilities – power, water, electricity, cellular phone networks. At the same time, they'd go after the Israeli economy – banks, big businesses, factories, logistic and distribution centers. Israel has been preparing for this sort of thing for a long time, so most of their systems are hardened against cyber attack, but either Iran or Russia must think they have a solid attack vector, from what we've been hearing. That's the cyber domain. If Russia is fully behind them, they will also act in the space domain in the first wave. Israel currently has ten *Amos* civilian and military communications and *Eros* reconnaissance satellites in orbit. Russia has multiple options for blinding, jamming or even destroying the Israeli satellite network. If the cyber and space attacks succeed, they can bring the Israeli economy to a halt for at least a few days, costing them billions, and cripple their military communications network."

"And that's just the *first* wave?!" Henderson asked, aghast.

"Yes, sir. I'd expect Iran or Syria at that point to deny any responsibility, but at the same time open up some sort of negotiations, probably territorial or trade. They might try to pile on pressure through some proxies, provoke civil unrest..."

"And if Israel tells them to take a hike?"

"Then they move to the land, sea and air domain. More traditional warfare: the cyber and space domain attack continues, but you will see Syrian and Iranian ground forces move into the Golan Heights, with Russian aircraft and naval forces providing air cover. In a traditional war against Syria, even with Russian anti-air support, Israel would quickly have the upper hand due to defensive advantage and massive air superiority. But remember, because this is a Russian-sponsored All Domain Attack, their recon satellites are down, their comms are compromised – if not completely knocked out – radar is compromised by electronic warfare and cyber attack, electricity is out, their civilian population is panicking, there's uprisings in Palestine, Hezbollah making trouble from Lebanon, the roads are jammed..."

"Okay, okay, I get the picture. So why the nuclear posturing? Why have they shown their hand and let us see they're moving nukes close to Israel's border?"

"Because they know an All Domain Attack will send the Israeli politicians to their fallout shelters – they see Syrian tanks rolling into the Golan and they're feeling like the end of the world is nigh. Israeli ballistic missile systems are isolated from cyber attack to protect them, so they would probably still be operational and Israel's leadership may be tempted to use them. Iran and Syria want us and Israel to know, or to think, that any nuclear attack will just provoke an equal and opposite reaction from Iran. I agree with Secretary Shrier – it's all intended to bring Israel to the negotiating table, in a position of vulnerability. As to why that, and why now, the CIA and State department would know better than me."

"Guess."

There was silence. Come on, girl. He's asking because he

wants your view, Carmine urged her silently. Don't pike on me.

Tonya cleared her throat. "Sir, every data point we have tells us Iran is at the point of economic collapse. They probably guaranteed North Korea a lifetime supply of free oil to buy those nukes. This is their last roll of the dice. They need an arms agreement with Israel, they need détente, if not mutual recognition, and they need sanctions lifted, or the regime is finished…"

Henderson picked up on her tone of voice. "Finish that thought, Director."

"Mr. President. I was just thinking, a failed State in possession of nuclear weapons, that's a lose-lose for everyone."

"Alright. Thanks, Tonya. No, cancel that. Thanks isn't the word I'm looking for, but you know what I mean. Have a good day."

"I know, Mr. President. Good day to you, sir."

President Henderson sat looking at the telepresence screen. "Is that really how we negotiate today? We bring a nation to its knees, threaten it with nuclear destruction and then hope it wants to meet with us in Geneva over canapés and mineral water?"

"It is when the nations involved are suddenly nuclear powers like Israel and Iran and superpowers like the US and Russia are pulling the strings," Carmine said.

"God. Damn." Henderson ran a hand through his thin hair. "I promised to reply to the Israeli PM in the morning."

"We don't have a defense treaty with Israel," Lewis reminded him. "This would be the first All Domain Attack we've seen in modern times. We can let it play through, learn from it, decide what to do about it when the dust settles. Keep our focus on China."

"And if that dust is radioactive?" McDonald asked.

"There's that risk," she admitted.

Henderson was up and pacing behind his desk now. "Look. If we take the Iranian nukes off the board, we level the playing field, right?" he said. "How do we do that?"

McDonald leaned forward on the couch. "Like I said. USS *Canberra* takes out that Iranian sub in the Red Sea. Deniably. Meanwhile, we announce a blockade of Iranian ships in the Mediterranean to prevent them approaching Israeli waters. We park our Aegis destroyers and persuade the Brits to put their nuclear attack submarine between the Russian fleet and the Israeli coast. We let the Russian ships through, but anything Iranian gets stopped and turned around. Russia talks tough, but they don't have the hardware to back their bluff. I doubt either Russia or Iran will risk trying to force the issue."

"If they do?" Carmine asked.

"Well, then, Iran might decide it could launch a nuclear cruise missile at Israel from outside the blockade, but our destroyer screen has a pretty good chance of knocking it down."

"That only takes care of the threat from the sea," Lewis pointed out. "The rest of those warheads are probably mounted on ground-based mobile ballistic or medium-range cruise missiles inside Syria."

"Can't Israel take care of them?" Henderson asked. "Jesus, it's *their* back yard."

"I'm betting Israel will need all the help it can get if we reach the point where we're discussing attacking Syrian or Iranian missile launchers inside Syria," Lewis said. "And we'll need a plausible rationale for even having US aircraft on readiness for operations inside Syria. We haven't conducted operations inside Syria since 2021."

The room was suddenly quiet. McDonald clicked his fingers. "The UN troops inside the Golan DMZ," he said. "Given the current situation, we could set up a no-fly zone – like we did over Kosovo in Albania or the Korean DMZ in 2028 – to protect the UN troops in the Golan Heights. But it would help if we had even a handful of US blue helmets on the ground as part of the UNDOF observer corps. That would give us the narrative we need to put the assets in place without it looking like we are directly assisting Israel in its standoff against Syria."

"A platoon, no more. Not *one* pair of boots more, is that clear?" Henderson said.

"Yes, sir."

"And another thing. That border area is going to be bristling with anti-air missile systems and Russian fighters. I'm not risking US pilots getting shot down, captured and paraded on Syrian TV," Henderson said.

"You won't have to," McDonald told him. "The Marines have unmanned combat aircraft in the theatre. General Garrett has already ordered them attached to the USAF 432nd Air Wing on Cyprus."

"Drones I can live with. Not manned aircraft, understood?"

"Message received."

"Harry, tell the Admiral he's got his DEFCON 2 and ask Navy to deal with that Iranian sub in the Red Sea as discreetly as they can. Anything short of sinking it. Set the wheels in motion for that blockade. Will four destroyers and a sub do it? Can't we get some assets up from Guam?"

"Move too much firepower into the Mediterranean when you announce that blockade and it will look like you are planning to take on the whole Russian Black Sea fleet," Lewis warned. "You increase the chances of something unforeseen happening, and Wall Street will get even more jittery."

"We can leave the war fighting to Admiral Clarke and the Joint Chiefs, Oliver. They just need to know the broad strokes," McDonald assured him.

Henderson had stopped pacing. "Alright. Carmine, I want proof those damn nukes are on those damn Iranian ships."

"We're on it, Mr. President."

"What time is ExComm tomorrow morning?" Henderson asked.

"Eleven hundred," Lewis replied.

"I'll get Karl Allen to bring it forward. I'll call the Israeli PM, let him know about the blockade and the no-fly zone. Then I need to call the House and Senate minority and majority leaders…" He had bent over his desk and was writing an aide-mémoire. "Then ExComm to iron out any wrinkles, and we go with an address to the nation at … what?" He had seen that both McDonald and Lewis were smiling at him.

"It took near on a year to get you to recognize the Syrian situation was serious and commit a single anti-air battalion to the defense of that NATO base at Incirlik. But in the last week you've taken us to DEFCON 3, now DEFCON 2, authorized a naval blockade and a no-fly zone," Lewis told him. "That's all."

Henderson colored and turned back to his notepad. "Yeah, well, you hear enough 21-gun salutes, it tends to focus the mind. You realize that if you'd taken a few more risks a whole lot earlier, you might have saved a whole lot of lives later."

All Domain Attack: Diversion

Al Azraq Air Base, Jordan, May 17

"OK, so, we had a momentary loss of control situation," Bunny O'Hare had told Shelly Kovacs.

"A 'loss of control situation'?" Kovacs had repeated. "You nearly let one of my precious F-47s fly itself into the ground."

They were standing on the tarmac outside the DARPA hangar at the northeast corner of Al Azraq Air Base, inspecting the damage to the wing of one of Kovacs' precious drones. A wingtip had clipped a powerline as Bunny had stress-tested the low-level formation-keeping routines on a flight of six of the machines.

"The problem isn't me, it's you," O'Hare told her equably. She looked up at the baking sun. Al Azraq was not a big multinational base like Incirlik in Turkey, but it had better facilities than the RAF base at Akrotiri. The first thing Bunny had done when she landed was go to the base's USO grill and order a ridiculously huge burger, sweet potato fries and a bottomless cola. After forty days of mystery meat and boiled vegetables in detention, she had been starving. But as soon as that was done, she'd started familiarizing herself with her new babies. Kovacs already had a team of pilots who had been taking them through their paces, and O'Hare immediately alienated them by ignoring just about everything they'd told her about how to fly the F-47B *Fantom*.

Most were former pilots of the Navy's *Triton* or Air Force *Sentinel* unarmed recon aircraft, used to sending their birds on long missions at high altitude where the most dangerous part of any mission was the takeoff and landing. They'd been doing a lot of testing of the *Fantom*'s sensor suite – essentially the same as the one Bunny was familiar with from the F-35 – and testing systems in Red Flag exercises with Royal Jordanian Air Force F-16s. Those had gone reasonably well, so they had moved onto Red Flag exercises against US Air Force F-22 *Raptors* based at Al Azraq to find out how easy the *Fantom* was for the F-22 to detect, and how good the *Fantom* was at picking up the nearly 25-year-old US stealth fighters.

The answer as far as Bunny could see was that the *Fantom* was too easy for the *Raptors* to detect, and not very good at hunting them. If the F-47 was going to be a threat against piloted stealth aircraft, it would need to be flown very, very differently.

"What do you mean, the problem is me?" Kovacs asked.

"Tell me why your *Fantoms* keep getting killed by those F-22 pilots."

"The algorithms are still crude, they..."

"They're not crude, but you're not giving them a chance," Bunny interrupted. "You still have a human pilot at the stick of those *Fantoms* ... he's sitting on the ground instead of in a cockpit in the sky, but you've still got him calling all the shots with the AI there as a backup. You need to set the AI free."

"We will never get permission to send those *Fantoms* out in full autonomous mode. Semi-autonomous maybe."

"I can live with that. I've got the hang of these birds now..."

Kovacs raised her eyebrows and nodded toward the shattered wingtip of the *Fantom*.

"Pretty much," Bunny continued, ignoring the look. "Let *me* fly this next two-on-two Red Flag. I'll fly lead, and let me put my wingman in semi-autonomous mode, flying defense unless I tell it otherwise. If I don't have to worry about my back, I can be more focused on finding and killing those F-22s."

Kovacs thought about it. "We can try that."

"And another thing. Your pilots are flying the *Fantom* like it's any other stealth fighter, staying fifty miles from where they think the target is and sending missiles at it."

Kovacs frowned. "That's stealth doctrine. Stay invisible, strike from afar."

"Yeah, but the *Fantom* isn't as capable as an F-35 or F-22. A

Raptor or *Panther* can pick it up at anywhere from forty to sixty miles out. Even a Russian *Felon* will see them at thirty miles. Your data shows you aren't getting a ping off those F-22s at anything over twenty miles, so your pilots have spent most of their time firing blind or circling around waiting to be killed."

"That's why I've been looking for someone with more combat experience."

"Combat experience isn't going to help unless we change tactics. We need to be using the *Fantom* the way Ivan uses his *Okhotniks*. Down low and personal, pounding air defenses, or right up in the faces of those *Raptor* pilots, dodging missiles and blasting so much radiation at them that even a 5th-gen fighter with the radar cross-section of a ball bearing can't hide."

"Alright. You can get behind the stick this afternoon," Kovacs said. "With a wingman in semi-autonomous defensive mode."

"With pilot override."

"With … alright. You can take control of it in flight but if you release it, it will go defensive again."

"I can live with that," Bunny grinned. "Wouldn't want it getting ideas of its own now, would we?"

There was a damn good reason Shelly Kovacs didn't like the idea of giving any remotely piloted system too much autonomy, but it wasn't one she shared with many people.

MIT Senior Ball, 2025.

Or the fact she never got there. Shelly was ahead of the curve on a lot of things. She'd asked Erik Jensen to be her date, after getting tired of waiting for him to ask her even though she'd known for weeks he was planning to. And she organized their ride, because ever since a certain motor company had launched its totally autonomous self-driving SUV, she'd wanted to ride in one. So she'd rented the latest model from a hire company, which was another bonus of self-driving cars because any adult, any age, could rent one. And it was much cheaper than hiring a limo with a driver.

It had been as awesome as she'd hoped it would be. She'd told Erik she would collect him, and the car had driven itself to Erik's place and picked him up, then piloted itself over to her place. He was seated in the back, freaking out over the fact *there was no one in the driver seat.* Shelly tried to be cool about it herself, making out she thought it was no big deal, but inside she was totally geeking out. She punched in the address of the hotel where the ball was being held and sat back to enjoy the ride. She'd already decided, even back then, she was going to specialize in robotics AI, and that conviction only got stronger for every mile the driverless car drove them.

She'd bought a bottle of champagne and some strawberries and the two of them were swigging it down, getting bubbles up their noses and laughing as they pulled onto the Massachusetts Turnpike, heading toward the MIT campus for the pre-ball photo session at Killian Court. Which was when the deer jumped the guard rail on the side of Interstate 90, dodged three lanes of traffic, then freaked out as it landed right in front of Shelly's hire car and planted itself stock still in the middle of their lane.

With cars to their left and cars to their right, and no chance of braking before it hit the deer, the AI on the SUV had to make a decision. It was a decision that had already been made by the National Highway Traffic Safety Administration in 2022 actually, when it approved the safety protocols for self-piloted vehicles. And in a nutshell, it said that in a situation where the AI pilot was forced to choose between an action that would endanger a human and an action that would endanger an animal, it should avoid endangering the human.

So Shelly's amazing autonomous SUV plowed straight into the deer, the deer flew through their windscreen, the car put on its emergency indicators and kept going down the highway, only slowing to a stop once it was sure it wouldn't be tail-ended, while Shelly fought off a thrashing, half-gutted deer which gave Erik Jensen a solid kick in the head that knocked him out and earned him six stitches and way too much sympathy from a good-looking student nurse in the emergency department. Who he later went on to marry, which you could safely add to her post-incident trauma list.

But you might think it was a pretty acceptable outcome, all things considered. Both she and Erik survived a potentially fatal collision, no one else except the deer was injured, and theirs was the only car that got damaged. The hire car insurance company was pretty pleased, that's for sure.

Except Shelly was convinced a human driver would have taken a bigger risk and tried to nail the gap between the two cars in the lane beside them, expecting those drivers might also react, and maybe they could have got out of it without anyone hitting anything or anyone too badly. Not to mention a human driver would have stopped the car quicker, and yeah, maybe they would have gotten tail-ended, but she would have swallowed a lot less deer blood.

So, the idea of giving an aircraft AI full control over guns and missiles in a hot combat zone?

She'd rather have a human in the loop.

Bunny had spent the next four hours deep in study, poring over the *Fantom*'s defensive algorithms. Even in 'semi-autonomous mode' the drone was responding to commands from the human pilot in control of it. Rather than flying it, she or he used a playbook to provide it with scenarios and the drone's onboard AI flew itself and deployed its sensor and weapons systems based on the scenario the pilot programmed. Bunny found the defensive playbook included everything from just keeping formation and avoiding incoming missiles to being able to automatically seek out an attacker and return fire if fired on.

She saw with satisfaction that there was a *lot* of wiggle room in Kovacs' definition of 'semi-autonomous'.

Her cockpit was a lot more roomy than the one she'd grown

used to in the F-35. Built inside a transportable trailer, it featured a large, curved screen that gave her a simulated view from the center of her *Fantom* that followed her head as she moved her helmet, allowing her to see 360 degrees around and 'through' the drones' airframes. The same view from her wingman was shown as a window inside her own view. She had no physical instrument panels, just a series of heads-up display panels for both aircraft that she could swipe through with a gesture, and command sequences she could invoke with a tap of the fingers on her left hand on a touch pad beside her throttle. It was a workspace designed for someone like her ... a former computer gamer with a talent for continuous partial attention. As the trailers were patterned on the designs used for older drones which had required a human pilot and systems officer sitting side by side, there was also room for an observer or manufacturer's engineer. Today, the jump seat was taken up by Kovacs.

And she didn't actually fly the *Fantoms* ... not really *fly* them. The inputs from her flight stick, pedals and throttle had to be squirted into space, bounced off a satellite and back down to the aircraft she was controlling. Which all happened at the speed of light, and was fine for controlling a drone doing lazy circles over a target halfway across the globe taking photos, but not for a combat aircraft. So though she kept her hands on her stick and throttle out of habit, most of the work was being done by Bunny's fingers tapping the keypad, as she thought herself into the future and issued commands to her aircraft that would put them where she wanted them, when she wanted them, doing what she wanted. The *Fantom*'s AI took care of the 'routine' business, like making sure they didn't fly into each other, or the ground ... or a missile.

As she guided her two *Fantoms* out of Al Azraq toward the exercise range over Jordan's rugged mountains to the south, she had already decided she was going to approach the challenge without subtlety or elegance. The scenario called for the opposing forces to enter the 100-mile by 60-mile exercise area at opposite corners of the diagonal at an altitude of 20,000 feet, any time inside a two-minute window. Their mission was simply to find and kill each other, which the F-22s had managed to do 23 times so far, to the *Fantom* pilots three. The 'hard deck' for the exercise – the altitude pilots weren't allowed to go below or their aircraft would be deemed destroyed – was five thousand feet, which meant Bunny wasn't going to be able to make use of the *Fantom*'s excellent terrain-following capabilities.

Studying previous engagements, Bunny had learned the US *Raptor* pilots liked to fight like an old tennis player facing a younger opponent – slug it out from the baseline and wait for their opponent to show themselves and make a mistake. They usually took up a staggered position in a corner of the range, somewhere between 30 and 40,000 feet, which meant they could cover the entire range with their passive radar detection system, waiting for an electronic squeak from their adversaries.

As soon as a *Raptor* picked up a radio or radar signal from a target, it had a bearing down which it could conduct a narrow beam radar search, get a lock, and shoot.

One advantage of the *Fantom* should have been that its pilots didn't need to use radio signals to communicate with each other and coordinate their actions. They were ground based, their trailers parked next to each other in the sandy soil of Al Azraq, talking over optical fiber cable. But they were controlled by satellite and shared data with each other – radar, position and targeting data – that they squirted to each other through the ether. They'd tried blanking as much of that energy as they could, but it hadn't helped. Bunny had a theory that something in the satellite comms link was giving away the *Fantom*'s positions to the F-22s, and she was about to test it.

For the benefit of Kovacs and the DARPA team monitoring the engagement, she kept up a running commentary.

"*Fantom* 1 approaching Red Flag entry point. Heading one niner three, altitude 20, speed six seven zero, setting *Fantom* 2 to low-follow, emissions dark." Her wingman would enter the exercise area at the same altitude as her, but then immediately dive for the hard deck and stay low, ten miles behind her, its radio and radar shut down.

"Going high," Bunny said, sending her *Fantom* through 30,000 feet to 40,000. "And dark." With a tap of her fingers she fed navigation and posture data to the lead *Fantom* and cut its satellite link.

"What are you doing?!" Kovacs asked, shocked. "Both of those aircraft are now inside the Red Flag range and out of our control!"

Bunny gave her a smile and sat back. "I know. Terrifying, isn't it?"

"We have no idea what they're doing!"

"Wrong. They're doing exactly what you programmed them to do, and exactly what I told them to do. One of them is weaving across the exercise area at 40,000 feet, sniffing for electronic signals. The other is following it, down low, doing the same. If either of them gets a target, they'll phone home to momma. In the meantime they are as close to invisible as I can make them."

Kovacs was used to seeing data flood across her screen – avionics, engine state, fuel state, radar data – but for the next few long minutes, all she had were the voices of her team back in the DARPA hangar asking her what the hell was going on.

Five minutes went by.

Kovacs was biting her thumbnail, staring at her empty displays. "I can't stand this," she said.

"You think you've got it bad?" O'Hare asked. "It's worse for those *Raptor* pilots. This just might be the first time they're feeling a little worried. By now, they've usually picked up telemetry signals from at least one of your *Fantoms* on their passive arrays. I'm guessing they've got your satellite comms frequency dialed in and every time they go out there, they're looking for it. So, no sat-comms, no *Fantom*."

"It's not a game of hide and seek," Kovacs said. "It's a combat air engagement. You can't just hide from them, you have to kill them to win."

"To kill them, I have to get into knife fighting range," O'Hare told her. She pulled up a tactical screen showing the Red Flag area and drew a line across it with her joystick. "Our girls will be about here by now. Halfway across the ops area. How many times have you gotten this deep into their territory?"

"Three," Kovacs said tightly. "Out of about twenty."

"Right. And each time, you got a kill."

"We got a kill, but we lost our aircraft anyway, to one of the other *Raptors*."

"Not today," Bunny said, with a confidence she didn't quite feel. "Today it's going to be two for zero."

As she finished talking there was a chime inside the trailer and a red dot with a line behind it appeared on the tactical display. "Contact!" Bunny said. "Radio energy. Right where I thought, high and deep."

The red dot disappeared as quickly as it appeared.

"We lost it," Kovacs said. "Why didn't you engage the *Fantom*'s phased-array radar, get a target lock, send a missile at it?"

"Because that would get us killed," Bunny told her. "*Fantom* 1 phoned home, sent the targeting data to its wingman and then hung up the phone straight away. If that *Raptor* saw anything, it saw a blip of radio energy that disappeared as quickly as it appeared. *Fantom* 1 has changed heading now. It's still working the target on its passive sensors. It'll be circling around to flank its target from the east while its wingman down low flanks from the west. They'll be arming their missiles. I've set engagement range for 15 miles."

"It can't engage autonomously!" Kovacs said.

"It won't." Bunny looked at her watch. "Give it thirty seconds."

Thirty seconds came, and went. Bunny was starting to feel a little less confident.

"They're dead," Kovacs said in a flat voice. "But because we don't have a sat link, we can't *see* it yet. I am deeply uncomfortable with this."

"If they were dead, you'd hear *Raptor* pilots jeering," Bunny said, fingers drumming on her keyboard. "Get ready. This could get a little crazy."

As she finished speaking, several things happened at once. The 270-degree screens mounted on the walls around the trailer flashed to life, showing the sky around the lead *Fantom*. High on the starboard quarter, a red box was drawn around a tiny black dot. Bunny's heads-up display showed a target locked and missiles armed. Without hesitating she jabbed her finger on the missile trigger on her flight stick.

"Fox 1, Fox 1," she intoned as she launched two simulated *Peregrine* hit-to-kill missiles at the F-22 which had just been locked up by the *Fantom*'s targeting radar. "Splash one!" Bunny called in delight seconds later as the red box on the screen turned into a red cross, the Red Flag umpires marking it as a kill. "Oh, shit." Her fingers flew across her keyboard. "Enemy radar lock. Missile! Evading."

A simulated *Peregrine* fired by the second *Raptor* was spearing toward her *Fantom* at a nominal 2.5 times the speed of sound. No human pilot could have reacted in time to evade it, but the combat AI aboard the *Fantom* was no human AI. Firing tinfoil chaff and infrared countermeasures, blasting radio energy at the missile to disrupt any targeting data it was getting from the aircraft that fired it, the *Fantom* spun on its axis and dived for the hard deck in a maneuver that would have broken the neck of any human unlucky enough to be sitting in a cockpit inside it.

As it did, its wingman down low got a lock on the second *Raptor*. Bunny's fingers flew, enlarging the view from the second *Fantom*, which showed another small black dot, also low on the horizon, framed in a red box.

"*Fantom* 2, Fox 1," Bunny said. "*Fantom* 1 maneuvering, reacquiring." Her right hand gripped her flight stick, twitching it involuntarily, fingers on her left hand dancing like a pianist's as she bullied the first drone around so it was pointed at the *Raptor* that had just ambushed it. *"Fantom* 1, Fox 1. *Splash two*! He's toast." The second red square turned into a cross. Bunny jumped from her seat, startling Kovacs as she leaped in the air and punched the ceiling of the trailer. "Yeah baby! What I'm talking about!" She collapsed into her seat and pulled the helmet from her head, turning to Kovacs with a sheepish expression. "Sorry about that. Got a bit of history with bloody *Raptors.*"

"I guessed," Kovacs said.

Bunny looked up and saw she had put a small dent in the roof of the trailer. She rubbed her knuckles. No, nothing broken. Kovacs was looking at her like she was one die short in a game of Trouble. "What?"

"Nothing. I guess I'm just used to a little more … calm in the cockpit … kind of thing."

Bunny was still rubbing her knuckles. "This is combat, Shelly. Kill, or be killed. Literally. Not algorithms, not computer code. It's bloody, horrible, undignified death and dying. Screw being calm. If you don't get a bit emotional about that, you aren't wired right." O'Hare had flown with pilots who did their jobs like it was another day at the office. Who delivered precision munitions on command, able to abstract themselves from the thought of who or what lay in the crosshairs of their cruise missiles. She admired and respected them. Truly. But she was not one of those. "So now you see what your babies can do. Are you a little less uncomfortable now?"

"Not really. You didn't break the Rules of Engagement, but you bent the definition of semi-autonomous to breaking point, O'Hare," Kovacs said. "You gave those aircraft their orders and then cut their sat links. For all intents and purposes, they were *fully* autonomous at that point. That's not standard procedure."

"Those sat links were getting you killed – I just proved that. Standard procedure might be fine against 4th-generation fighters, but against a 5th-gen fighter like the *Raptor*, or a Russian *Felon*, you have to use every trick you've got if you want to win, and to hell with 'procedure'."

Kovacs spun her chair around, deep in thought. When she stopped, she leaned forward, elbows on her knees. "I wasn't sure whether bringing you into this program was the right idea, O'Hare," she said. "But while you were prepping for this exercise, I got word that our field trials are being terminated anyway, so I guess we'll never know."

O'Hare felt her small victory turn to ashes. She had a sudden vision of herself parked behind a desk on Cyprus. "Sorry, what?"

"I just got told that our aircraft are being assigned to the USAF 432nd Air Expeditionary Wing, based out of your favorite airfield, Akrotiri."

"Marines aren't going to like that."

"General Garrett authorized it."

Bunny's shoulders slumped. "Oh well, at least I'll be able to get a lift back to Cyprus."

Kovacs smiled. "Oh, I can guarantee that. We still need pilots to fly them. I can see if I can get you reassigned to the 432nd, if you're interested."

"Are you going?"

"I have to. These experimental aircraft are still DARPA assets until there is an official handover to Marine Corps Aviation. Assuming the Air Force doesn't trash them all."

Bunny nodded. "Alright. I'm in. On one condition."

Kovacs laughed. "Condition? I already got you out of a jail cell and now I'm saving you from death-by-desk-job, how can you have *conditions?*"

"You promised me a hex. You definitely said I'd be flying six birds at a time and now you've seen what I can do with two. I'm not going back to Cyprus unless we're putting six birds in the air at a time." She gave Kovacs a conciliatory wink. "*Semi*-autonomous, I promise."

Kobani, Kurdish-Controlled Syria, May 17

"You saved a lot of lives down there, Bell," said 'Gunner' James Jensen, Marine Gunnery Sergeant, 1st Battalion, 3rd Marines, to the Marine combat corpsman sitting opposite him in the belly of the Bell-Boeing *Big Boy* twin rotor as they lifted up and away from Combat Outpost Meyer in the Kurdish-held northern Syrian city of Kobani. Bell-Boeing had originally envisaged an entirely new quadrotor design for the *Big Boy* but it had proven easier for the manufacturer to take the pilots out of their piloted V-22C *Osprey* design than build an entirely new aircraft. The V-22DU *Big Boy* could carry 20,000lb. of cargo, or 24 troops, and it flew with only a single crewman, an airman who functioned as both comms operator and loadmaster.

The young ginger-haired corpsman sitting next to Jensen had his duffel bag stowed above his head, his ever-present medical pack slung over his shoulder and resting in his lap, and his M27 rifle upright, butt on the ground between his boots. He too was watching the hilltop base that had been their home for nearly six bloody months drop away and, if anything, he showed even less regret in his bloodshot eyes than Jensen felt.

"Maybe I did, Sarge," Bell acknowledged. "But there were plenty I didn't."

After several months of siege, the hundred remaining 'Lava Dogs' of 1st Battalion, 3rd Marines had faced a battalion-level assault by Syrian forces which had included a barrage by thermobaric rockets, and by the time the smoke had cleared and the Syrian ground troops had been beaten back, although they still held the hilltop, they'd lost around thirty Marines.

It hadn't felt like a victory.

Over the following weeks they'd evacuated first their wounded, and then their dead. Following the ceasefire between Syria and Turkey, Jensen had stayed on as part of a small force to complete the closure and handover of the US outpost to Kurdish forces at Kobani. The Second Lieutenant in charge of their company and most of the remaining men had been lifted out a couple of days earlier, and Jensen and the platoon-sized remnant he was attached to had packed up the last of the equipment and put it on transport rotors.

Among the last items to be shipped out was one of the two Legged Squad Support System LS3 *Hunter* units that he'd been sent to Syria to put through their combat trial paces. His two semi-autonomous 'dogs' as he called them – armed with a variety of projectile weapons and utility attachments – had acquitted themselves well, but only one of them had made it through. One had fallen in combat during the assault on the outpost. But the data they had collected in Syria had impressed the team back at Marine Combat Development and Integration enough for them to recommend the *Hunter* systems transition into full-scale production and deployment phase; so his job was done.

All that had remained were their personal effects, and a minimum of weapons and ammunition they'd kept for themselves in case of 'unforeseen events'. For Jensen that meant his sidearm and an M27 carbine. He soon learned they each had a different understanding of the concept 'minimum'. Corporal Patel, for example, had lugged three duffel bags of hardware out of the bunker, including a 15lb. Barrett Mark 22 MRAD sniper rifle with accompanying swappable barrels, bolts and assorted .308 Winchester, .300 and .338 Norma Magnum ammunition.

"Where in hell did you get that beast, Lance Corporal?" Jensen had asked Patel as he swung his duffel bags into the chopper and laid the heavy rifle on top of them.

"Card game, Gunny," he said. "Won it off a CIA contractor didn't know the butt from the barrel. But I was allowed to keep it because I am the best damn marksman in the 3rd Battalion. Get back Stateside, I'm booked into Camp Pendleton, training for Scout Sniper."

Each of the several Marines on the chopper had their own plans for what they were going to do when they got out of

Kobani. Jensen was looking forward to some liberty at Joint Base Eagle in Kuwait before heading back to Quantico Station, Virginia and his next weapons development assignment. He had no idea yet what that might be, but after his tour in Syria he sincerely hoped it involved something much, much less interesting than testing robot combat dogs in a Middle Eastern war zone. He'd heard there was a project evaluating which powder to use in the newest .338 rounds for the Marines' new Mark 13 sniper rifles. That sounded perfect.

"Where are you headed after Kuwait?" Jensen asked Bell.

"Kaneohe Bay, Sarge."

"Got family?"

"Parents are dead, but I got a brother in the Navy. He's in the Red Sea right now but being sent to Pearl once he's finished the patrol he's on now. Got some catching up to do, you know…"

"I bet."

"How about you, Sarge? Anyone waiting?"

Yeah. How about you, Jensen? There was a reason he'd re-upped and gotten himself sent to Syria. And not one he felt like discussing with Bell. After twelve years, and a final promotion to Gunnery Sergeant, James Jensen had been ready to get out. He'd put a little money away, had a wife and two kids he wanted to spend more time with, who didn't seem to mind the sight of him too much, and a buddy back in Indiana who could get him a job as a crew boss on a team installing wind turbines. He'd even had the interview and made it through that and their damn psych test, which was worse than the interview itself.

He'd been two weeks from his pre-separation counseling session when he got word that his wife and kids had been walking a trail to Manoa Fall on Oahu when a rockslide had killed them and four other hikers. After burying his family he walked into the pre-separation interview still in a daze, and came out having re-upped instead of getting out. He'd just lost his wife and kids, he couldn't stand the thought of saying goodbye to the only other family he had left in this world, the

Corps. There were times – especially under fire – he felt he'd been too hasty, and others, like now, he knew he'd done exactly the right thing. Sure, Bell wasn't going home to a wife and kids, but going home to the noise and smells of K-Bay was better than going home to a dark, empty house.

James Jensen was pretty damn sure if he hadn't re-upped, he'd probably have shot himself by now. So every day he spent above the ground was a win, even if he'd spent it in Syria.

"No one special, kid. Envy you." He leaned his head back against the column behind him and closed his eyes. Man, he was tired.

Bell had been watching the sandy dirt and scrub flowing along a few thousand feet beneath them, and he frowned. "Kuwait is south-east, isn't it, Sarge?"

"Two hours, son, settle in," Jensen told him, without opening his eyes. He could feel he was about two minutes from a well-deserved nap.

"That's what I thought. But unless I'm going crazy, we're headed west, is all."

Sighing, Jensen opened his eyes reluctantly and focused on the shadows on the ground below them. He frowned. The kid was right. Their machine was pointed west.

Freaking typical. Another screw-up.

Their quadrotor was pilotless. It had a Marine Corps Aviation crewman, but only for loading and unloading personnel and equipment.

"Hang tight," Jensen told Bell, unbuckling himself and heading forward past a small group of men and women already either sleeping in their metal bucket seats, or well on the way.

Jensen tapped the shoulder of the aviator, a corporal. The man was also dozing.

He started awake. "Sorry. Yes, Sergeant?"

"Something's up. We're supposed to be headed for Kuwait. South-east. We're headed west, across Turkey."

The man leaned to his right, looking at a panel display at the front of the crew compartment. "You're right. Must be a detour for operational reasons, that's not unusual. Let me get onto the sector controller, Sergeant."

"You do that."

The airman reached for a radio headset and jammed it on his head, then tapped some icons on the flat screen panel on his right. He spoke for a few minutes and then pulled the headset off his head. "Someone to speak to you, Sergeant," the man said.

Jensen fitted the headset over his head. "Jensen."

"Gunnery Sergeant, this is Captain Fernandez…"

Jensen frowned. Fernandez was a Lava Dogs company commander, but as far as Jensen knew, he was back on Hawaii, not in Syria. "Yes, Captain."

"I want to confirm something first. The personnel you have with you … I have a list here … just let me get it. Alright, Johnson, B.; Patel, R.; Stevens, D.; Buckland, R.; Wallace, B.; Lopez, M.; Bell, C. And yourself. Did I miss anyone?"

Jensen had been checking off the faces inside the drone as Fernandez had read them off. "Just the airman we're flying with, Captain. You want his name?"

"No. Look, here's the deal. We're rerouting your aircraft. Your liberty will have to wait. We urgently need to put some boots on the ground on the ceasefire line between Israel and Syria in the Golan Heights and…"

"Sorry, sir, did you say Golan Heights?"

"That's right, Sergeant. You'll be joining the United Nations Disengagement Observer Force, UNDOF, to supplement the observers already there."

Jensen lowered his voice and turned toward the empty front of the quadrotor. "Captain, with all respect, the Marines on this aircraft have just come off the line after six *months* of continuous combat operations. I'm not sure they're capable of…"

"It's peacekeeping duty, not combat duty, Sergeant," Fernandez said. "We're already working on a plan to relieve you within the week. But the order for this came from the highest level, and I mean the highest. We had to find a platoon-sized force that could deploy in the Golan yesterday, and your aircraft was already airborne. So it's you. Is that understood?"

"Yes, sir." Jensen felt the fatigue in his bones flow down and into his boots at the thought of even a single day longer in Syria. Let alone a week.

"Good. You'll put down at a town called Buq'ata. UNDOF will meet you there with transport and drive you about ten miles north-east to an observation post on Ceasefire Line Alpha where you'll join a Dutch unit manning the OP. You'll get your blue helmets and take your orders from the Dutch Lieutenant there, Willem Cort, C-O-R-T. You got that?"

"Yes, Captain."

"Sorry for the bad news, Gunny," Fernandez said. "Trust me, we're working on getting you out of there as quickly as we can."

That's what they said about Kobani, Jensen thought, but kept the thought to himself. "Appreciate it, sir."

"Fernandez out."

Jensen peeled the headset off his head and handed it back to the airman. "You pull up a map on that thing?" he asked, pointing at the multifunction panel on the wall beside the aviator.

"Sure," the man said. He switched the screen to show a map of the border region between Turkey and Syria that they were currently crossing. "Just pinch and zoom, or you can tap this icon…" the man pointed at the screen, "… to show our new route and follow it to our destination."

He vacated his seat and Jensen sat in front of the screen. He zoomed it out a little and then hit the icon that showed the route they were taking. West across southern Turkey to the Turkish coast and then south out of Turkey, down the coast of Lebanon, past Beirut to Sidon on the coast and then south-east across Lebanon, the northern tip of Israel and into the Golan Heights and Buq'ata. Three hundred and fifty-seven miles, two hours left to run.

He turned to see everyone in the compartment was awake again and seven pairs of eyes were trained on him. A Marine pretty quickly developed a bad news detector, and could usually see The Suck coming a mile away. After six months under siege in Kobani, which was pretty much all suck, the men and women inside the quadrotor didn't even need Jensen to open his mouth before they reacted. They just needed to look into his eyes.

"Ah, man," Bell said, spitting into the space between his rifle butt and his boot. "Seriously?"

LCS-30 USS *Canberra*, The Red Sea, May 17

"No, seriously, tell me what you really think, Ears," Watch Supervisor, Chief Petty Officer Goldmann asked with undisguised sarcasm, pulling a chair up beside Bell's sonar station.

"Sorry, Chief, but if we fall any further back, we are going to break contact and I can't see us catching this guy again if he makes it through the Straits of Tiran and into deeper water."

It had been a fraught couple of days. Bell and the other sonar operators had found and then lost the small submarine several times in the warm and flukey waters of the Red Sea. Whoever was driving the Iranian boat was either very lucky, or very skilled, at playing with the thermocline – the shifting plane deep in the sea where warm water met cold and sonar waves bounced back to the surface without revealing the submarine beneath it. But a thermocline was neither reliable, nor predictable, and the USS *Canberra* had gotten lucky itself a few times as the *Besat* had broken above the thermocline and shown itself to its pursuer again.

The *Besat* wasn't headed for the upper reaches of the Red Sea, that much was obvious. After passing the *Canberra* it had sailed north toward the mouth of the Gulf of Aqaba, with Egypt to the west, Saudi Arabia to the east, and Israel dead ahead. To get into the Gulf, it had to make a run through the only deep-water channel, at the entrance of the Gulf. A channel that was only two miles across, at a point called the Straits of Tiran.

The Straits of Tiran were the ideal place for the USS *Canberra* to either put itself, or a quadrotor with dipping sonar, so that they were right on top of the *Besat* when it hit the deeper water on the other side. Instead, they had reduced speed and were now trailing the Iranian sub by nearly ten miles. They had pulled their aerial assets back, recalled their *Sea Hunter* unmanned surface vehicle, and the only system still tracking the *Besat* was Bell's towed array sonar.

"Don't worry, son. We have our reasons. Just tell me what he's doing."

"He's heading three two three, depth three hundred, fifteen knots steady as a rock, Chief," Bell told him. "Not even bothering to change depth or course now, engine note is steady, no extraneous noises … with us falling back like this, I'd say he probably thinks we're giving up the chase, and right now he's settling down to a nice glass of mint tea."

"Well, we're about to spill his tea," Goldmann warned Bell. "We're going to general quarters in a few. Stay sharp." The Chief patted his shoulder, got up and went along to the next man in the circle.

Bell swallowed hard. An exercise? It had to be an exercise. There was no apparent reason to…

"General quarters, general quarters. All hands man your battle stations. The route of travel is forward and up to starboard, down and aft to port. Set material condition 'Zebra' throughout the ship. Hostile subsurface contact. This is not a drill. Repeat, this is not a drill."

Bell jammed his headset on tighter and adjusted his throat mike. *Hostile subsurface contact?* There was nothing hostile about the Iranian submarine's posture, unless sailing under the water in a straight line was suddenly defined as a hostile act.

Drysdale was wide awake this time. The general quarters call on the loudspeaker had barely finished ringing around the CIC before the Tactical Action Officer's voice came over Bell's headset. "Target is contact Charlie one one. Air Detection Tracker, I want a UAV five hundred feet over the target, optical tracking only please. Weapons, ASROC, load *Swarmdiver*, warhead ASFN, prepare to engage." He took an audible breath. "Ladies and gentlemen, our objective is simple. We have been ordered to disable that Iranian boat. You're aware, I trust, how rare such an action is ... in fact I can't remember the last time a US warship stopped any Iranian warship at sea in this way, let alone a submarine. This is a high-risk operation and I need you all a hundred and twenty percent on your game."

Ears checked his screen. There was nothing more he could do. He still had contact with the *Besat* on passive sonar and it was as solid as it was going to get at this range. The attack had been timed for the window when the submarine was preparing to squeeze through the Straits of Tiran. As the swarm of undersea drones caught up with them, they would have nowhere to run, nowhere to hide.

If they even detected them before it was too late.

ASFN warheads... wow. Usually if you wanted a sub to surface, you'd drop a few Sound Underwater Signal charges into its path to rattle the crew's eardrums and start jackhammering the boat's hull with sonar as Ears was already doing. But of course, they could choose to ignore you. Firing a *Swarmdiver* salvo at the Iranian boat and attacking it with Anti-Screw Fouling Nets was taking the situation to a whole other level. Ears opened a channel to Goldmann. "Chief Goldmann, Sonar."

"Go ahead, Ears."

"You want me to prep for a Gertrude call?" 'Gertrude' was one of the only ways for a surface ship to communicate directly with a submarine, by dropping an underwater 'telephone' near the target and hailing it on voice or morse.

"Not needed. We won't be moving any closer than we are now unless we need to effect a rescue. But stay alert, Ears. If the Captain of that boat decides it was us who fouled his screw he may just decide to send a missile our way. You'll hear it before we see it."

"Understood, Sonar out."

Ears heard other stations report in, including the ASW officer reporting his ASROC loaded and ready to fire, and Drysdale conferring quickly with the Captain on the bridge. "TAO, Weapons, ASROC *Swarmdiver* salvo, target Charlie one one, match generated solution and shoot."

"TAO, ASROC, shot away!"

Deep inside the superstructure of the ship, ears glued to his headphones, Bell heard and felt nothing as the ASROC launcher punched ten rockets into the air forward of the ship's bow. The 30-inch munitions inside were in essence small, dolphin-headed torpedoes that used their own onboard sonar to hold formation with each other and guide themselves to the target programmed at the time of their launch. With the Iranian boat ten miles ahead of the *Canberra* and three hundred feet down, the launch and splashdown were almost simultaneous, and should have been near indetectable to the submarine. Even if the Iranian had picked up the splashes of the *Swarmdiver* rockets hitting the water five miles behind him, he would have almost no chance of picking up the sound of their small electric motors over the noise of his own engine and churning screw.

Almost, but not none. "TAO, Sonar, change in screw revolutions, target is slowing…"

They'd heard the splashdown.

Bell had to give it to the Iranian Captain, he had reacted instantly to the sound of the *Swarmdiver* shoal striking the water behind him. In less than a second he'd cut propulsion and started to drift, to give his sonar operator the best possible chance of hearing what was happening behind him.

Which was a strategy that would have made sense against conventional torpedoes, turbines powering them loudly through the water at 55 miles an hour. The Iranian had no room to maneuver, but he would have had a good chance of picking up a Mark 48 torpedo in time to be able to change his depth, fire noisemaker and magnetic decoys, even try to jam the attacker's active-passive acoustic homing system. The much smaller electric engines of the *Swarmdiver* shoal were nearly inaudible. Ironically, his best strategy would have been to try to outrun the tiny torpedoes, as the *Besat* had a top speed underwater that was higher than a *Swarmdiver* shoal. In a straight-line footrace, it could have outpaced them.

But the Captain of the *Besat* didn't fear and couldn't outrun what he couldn't hear.

One mile from the Iranian submarine, the shoal picked up the sound of the boat powering up again, its screw beginning to churn the water, its Captain and crew anxious to keep moving and put the narrow Straits of Tiran behind them. Forming into a long snake-like line astern formation, with a hundred yards separation, the shoal aimed itself at the distinctive sound of the seven-bladed screw of the *Besat*.

The first *Swarmdiver* got to within ten feet of the screw and the compressed air in its warhead fired, shooting a continuous carbon fiber reinforced net at the twenty-foot-wide screw. It caught onto two of the blades and began winding around them as the screw turned. Seconds later, the next *Swarmdiver* approached and fired its net. And the next … and the next …

At ten miles distant, Bell couldn't hear the sound of the warheads firing, but he could hear the *Besat*'s screw begin to slow again. And stop.

Bell could only imagine the chaos and confusion unfolding inside the Iranian boat. Engine hammering, screw fouled in near unbreakable carbon fiber netting, propulsion system still pouring power into the shaft, the whole boat shaking until someone hit the emergency stop … Three hundred feet down, at that point in the Strait, they had only two hundred feet under their keel. It was not the kind of place you'd want to suddenly find yourself adrift without steerage way.

"TAO, Sonar. Screw is no longer turning." He checked the data on the target's speed and ran it out a few minutes at a constant rate of change. "She's adrift."

As the submarine coasted to a halt, Bell bent to his screen, straining eyes and ears, looking and listening for any indication of the *Besat*'s response to their new situation. The sound of a torpedo tube door opening, of its engine restarting, or, god forbid, a torpedo or missile headed back toward the *Canberra*. Wait. Was that the sound of metal scraping rock? Screw fouled, unable to control its drift, had the Iranian hit a reef or rock shelf?

"TAO, Sonar, main ballast blow! Repeat, main ballast blow. She's making an emergency ascent!" Bell said, as calmly as he could, the sound in his headphones automatically dampened as the *Besat* fired thousands of cubic meters of compressed air into its ballast tanks and forced the water out, sending the boat rocketing toward the surface.

On the bridge, they were monitoring the chatter and the data coming from the CIC and Bell immediately felt the *Canberra* swing to port and cut its engines so that it wouldn't appear to be approaching the surfacing submarine.

"Surface Watch, forward camera onscreen, orient on the target bearing, now!" Goldmann ordered, and the target tracking screen that had filled the 360-degree wall switched instantly to show the view ahead of the *Canberra*. Better than the best seat in the house, Ears was about to be ringside for an iMax-sized view of a sight every anti-submarine warfare seaman hoped to see at least once in their career … a submarine conducting an emergency ascent.

Thar she blows! he thought, as the bow of the *Besat* broke the water and the metal monster kept rising, higher and higher, like a whale breaching, before its weight overcame its momentum and it came crashing down again, sending a wave through the air higher than a five-story building. The watch officer kept the camera trained on the *Besat* as the *Canberra* kept up its slow turn to port, away from the surfaced submarine. Bell saw motion at the top of the submarine's sail, the large fin-like structure which housed aerials, radar masts and periscopes. It was also the fastest way out of the boat for officers and ratings in the submarine's control room. He saw a hatch swing open … and two heads appear. They'd no doubt checked on radar to see if there were any ships nearby, and now Bell could see as they swung binoculars toward the *Canberra*. It couldn't have been comfortable up at the top of the sail, swaying in the waves washing across the deck of the becalmed submarine. From the deck of the boat, aft of the sail, a second hatch opened as two more crew members appeared and moved aft along the deck of the submarine, peering into the water behind them. The *Besat*'s screw would have been a good fifty feet down. Bell doubted they would be able to see anything. They'd have to put divers in the water for that, and all they would find would be a strange tangle of netting, wound around their screw. Netting that would take more than a simple oxyacetylene torch to cut through.

There was more commotion atop the submarine's sail as the submarine's watch officers noticed what Bell had already seen – they were drifting closer to the rocky shelf of the Egyptian shoreline to their west.

Two rows inward from his station, a comms operator spoke up. "*Mayday* from the IRIN *Besat*. They report they are without power and adrift in the Straits of Tiran. Requesting immediate assistance."

Even as the man finished speaking, Bell felt the thrum of the *Canberra*'s turbines spooling up beneath his feet and he was pushed gently into the back of his chair as she swung around and began accelerating toward the Iranian submarine.

Well, we did it, he told himself. Now what?

White House Situation Room, May 17

"Now to an unfolding situation in the Red Sea. The US Defense Department has just advised that one of its ships has gone to the aid of an Iranian submarine experiencing an emergency off the coast of Egypt. We're taking images from Egyptian television. I'm here with our Defense Correspondent, Katy Warner. Katy, tell us what we are looking at here."

"Yes, thank you, Dan. The images you can see are coming from an Egyptian television helicopter circling around the site of the incident. We can see what looks like a surfaced submarine. That warship near it is, we believe, an *Independence*-class US warship, probably deployed to the Middle East with the 5th Fleet. If I had to guess, I'd say it's the USS *Kingsville*, or *Canberra…*"

"The DoD communique says the submarine is Iranian, Katy. Did the ships collide, were there shots exchanged, what do we know?"

"Defense is being tight lipped at this stage, Dan. Egyptian television is reporting that the submarine issued a mayday call a couple of hours ago. I just got off the line to a source in the Pentagon who told me on condition of anonymity that this is a rescue operation, and US forces are rendering assistance to the Iranian vessel by towing it away from shore and into deeper waters to await repair or rescue by an Iranian navy vessel. Looking at the images, I can't see any damage to either ship, so there's nothing to indicate what might have caused the submarine emergency, though of course, anything could have happened under the waterline…"

In the situation room under the White House, President Henderson turned away from the screen and faced the room. Nearly four tense hours had passed since he'd ordered the *Canberra* to try to take the Iranian sub out of play and despite what he was seeing, he was having a hard time feeling jubilant about the outcome. "Where are they headed?" he asked.

"The *Canberra* is towing the disabled submarine to safety," Admiral Clarke told him. "When they got clear of the Straits of Tiran, the Iranian Captain demanded the *Canberra* cut the tow line so that they could try to effect repairs, but this request was denied, due to the risk of the submarine drifting into shipping lanes. They then requested they be towed to the Egyptian port of Berenice, which is unfortunately also not possible since the US does not have an agreement to berth military vessels at Berenice."

"So where are we taking it? Saudi Arabia?"

"We can't tow a nuclear-armed Iranian submarine to a Saudi seaport," Clarke said. "That wouldn't exactly enhance relations with the Saudis."

"Not to mention Iran would raise holy hell if we deliver their most advanced submarine into the bosom of their Sunni Islam foes."

"Should have thought of that before they put a nuke aboard," Karl Allen muttered.

"Port Sudan," Clarke continued, "is the best option. We drop the *Besat* off in Sudan. They're allies of Iran, though not close. Port facilities are pretty limited, so if we're lucky and the *Swarmdiver* attack damaged the sub's shaft or propulsion system, repairs will take longer. Plus it puts an extra few hundred miles between that sub and Tel Aviv. If they launch from Port Sudan, a *Kalibr*-M would have a twenty-minute flight time. We'll make sure we have surveillance overhead to detect any launch and give the Israelis plenty of time for an attempted intercept."

"But we still don't know if the damn thing is even carrying a nuke!" Henderson exclaimed. "None of you here is willing to put your hand on your heart and swear you're certain. We don't know if this sub is carrying a nuke, we don't know if their mobile ballistic missile units in Syria are armed with nukes, we don't know which, if any, of the ships sailing with the Russian Black Sea fleet is carrying nukes!"

Secretary McDonald let the explosion land and then raised his hand before theatrically putting it over his heart. "If that's what you need, Mr. President, I'll be that guy," he said. "Iran isn't playing poker, it's laying its cards on the table where we can see them. It showed us that missile being loaded, it let us photograph its North Korean A-team on the docks, and we have to be ready to admit the reason we were able to find and track that Iranian sub all the way up the Red Sea and into the mouth of the Gulf of Aqaba is because they let us."

"Well, that was just dumb," Homeland Security Secretary Allan Price said. "Did they think we would do nothing about it?"

"Short of us sinking their boat, which we were never likely to do, what did they have to lose?" Secretary Shrier asked. "Even if we tow them all the way back to the Persian Gulf, that missile of theirs still has the range to strike Israel, doesn't it, Admiral?"

"Yes. The further the launch point, the better the chance we or Israel have of an intercept, but you're right."

"If I can continue," McDonald interrupted. "We weren't able to board and inspect the *Besat*, but the *Canberra* got radiation readings off its hull that were higher than the expected background radiation, so hand on my heart, I'm willing to say they have a nuke aboard."

All eyes turned to the President.

"Alright. I'm a simple guy. Here's how I see it. Our goal, believe it or not, is pretty much the same as Iran's. Since fifty years of sanctions and covert action have apparently failed to stop Iran acquiring nukes, we want to get Iran and Israel sitting down together, talking nuclear arms control. This is not an insurmountable challenge, people. What were you telling me, Harry? India and Pakistan were on the brink of nuclear war and they did it in '88, right?" McDonald nodded. "South Africa, Cuba and Angola in '89. Israel has peace treaties with most of the nations of the Middle East now bar Iran and Syria. If we can get a deal between Iran and Israel out of this, under our auspices, and on our terms, that leaves Syria on its own and Russia with its ass twisting in the wind."

Henderson gave Carmine a quick *back me up here?* glance and she nodded to him as subtly as she could. He'd come a long way since the dithering, indecisive Commander in Chief who had kept the USA out of the conflict between Turkey and Russian-backed Syrian forces until it was almost too late. But she believed him when he said that standing on the tarmac at

All Domain Attack: Cyber and Space

The Black Sea, 150 miles north-west
of the Bosphorus Strait, May 17

Captain Hossein Rostami of the Islamic Republic of Iran Navy stood at a window of his bridge looking out at a very dark Black Sea, about halfway between the Russian port of Sevastopol and Turkey's Bosphorus Strait, gateway to the Mediterranean. It was not where he had expected to be. By this time he should have been entering the Bosphorus, a cowed Istanbul gliding past his ship on either side.

"We have been asked to stand by the radio at 1200 hours tomorrow, Captain," a communications officer told him.

Rostami nodded. "Good, get back to your station." He turned to his executive officer. "Salari, tell the Russian Captain the transfer needs to be completed and this ship on its way back to the fleet within the hour. We cannot have more delays."

"Aye Captain," his XO, Lieutenant Salari, said and headed off the bridge for about the fifth time that evening. Rostami sighed. Yes, the seas were rough and uncooperative. There had been a problem with the crane aboard the Russian freighter. One of the North Korean specialists had been sick and refused to come up from his berth until 'persuaded' to do so. But the clock was ticking, dammit.

He looked down over the vertical launch missile cells on the foredeck of the *Safineh*-class frigate, IRIN *Sinjan*, the newest and most potent surface warship in the Iranian fleet. A 3,000-ton trimaran with capabilities similar to the US *Independence*-class littoral combat ships, it had just completed a transit of the Volga-Don Canal waterway connecting Iran to the Black Sea, followed by two weeks of exercises with the Russian Black Sea fleet, and had been making for the Bosphorus together with the rest of the fleet when it had made a planned detour to rendezvous with the Russian freighter now bobbing off its starboard side.

He watched as a crane with hooded lights swung a large cylindrical object out of a forward hold on the freighter and began gently lowering it toward the men on the deck of the *Sinjan*, including the very unsteady-looking North Korean.

The crane's cargo looked for all the world like a single oil barrel. Which, of course, it was supposed to.

One of the missile hatches on the *Sinjan* was being levered up by two men on the deck and Rostami couldn't help a shiver of pride as he looked down on the open nose cone of the *Yakhont* supersonic cruise missile nestled inside it. His ship could fire 36 of the deadly long-range missiles at targets up to 200 miles away.

"So many missiles, Captain, but only one is needed to change the course of history."

Rostami turned and saw his 'guest' for this voyage, Rear Admiral Karim Daei, walk onto his bridge. "Admiral on the Bridge!" he said quickly, as the rest of the officers on the *Sinjan*'s bridge also straightened to attention.

"Continue, gentlemen," the Admiral said. He joined Rostami to watch the loading operation. "One day soon, Rostami, such subterfuge will not be needed. Iran will take its place among the great powers of the world and be treated as an equal, not as a pariah."

"Yes, Admiral," Rostami said. He was a military man, not a politician, and not comfortable indulging in any conversation involving opinions beyond his pay grade. Unlike the Admiral, a former cleric who had connections inside the Assembly of Experts, the Guardian Council and the Presidential Executive. "We should be underway inside two hours and back with the rest of the fleet in six."

"Step outside with me, would you, Captain?" Daei asked. The *Sinjan* had no external watch stations, but a stairway led up out of the bridge to the external superstructure where radar and communication equipment was mounted, along with the eight-tube anti-submarine rocket launcher. Officers on the bridge were allowed to use the upper level to grab a quick cigarette when circumstances allowed, but Rostami was relieved to see none were doing so as he followed the Admiral up and into the night air. He was even more relieved when the Admiral pulled out a packet of cigarettes himself and offered one to Rostami. Rostami pulled out his lighter and lit them both.

"She is a fine ship, with a fine crew, Captain," Daei said. He had thick grey hair under his white peaked cap, and an equally thick salt and pepper beard. He also had a habit of wearing dark aviator sunglasses, even at night, making his eyes impossible to read. The rumor was that he'd developed cataracts from long service in the harsh daylight of the Persian Gulf, but Rostami was just as sure that it was an affectation intended to intimidate junior officers, like himself.

"Thank you, Admiral, but there is always room to improve," Rostami said guardedly.

"Perhaps, but the time for training is over. The time for action is upon us."

"My crew are ready," Rostami assured him.

"Yes. Are you, I wonder?"

Rostami felt his gut tighten. "Admiral?"

Daei flicked ash from his cigarette and looked up at the flag flying on the superstructure above him. "Six men in the Republic have been entrusted with the most powerful weapons Allah has seen fit to supply us with. Two of those weapons are under the command of the Revolutionary Guard Corps. Two are under the command of our Aerospace Force. Two have been allocated to the Navy and one of those..." he pointed with his cigarette at the activity on the deck below, "... is under *your* command."

"It requires the assent of the two most senior officers aboard to fire it, and only on the express order of the Supreme Commander," Rostami said carefully. "With the Admiral's flag on the *Sinjan*, I could not use the weapon without your assent."

"Yes, yes. I am less worried about what you would do while

I am here than what you would do if I was not. Or if I was, for some reason, 'incapacitated'."

"Inshallah, that will never be the case," Rostami said quickly.

"Inshallah. But tell me, when you look in your heart, is there any doubt that if the order came, you would do what was needed?"

Rostami answered immediately. "None, Admiral."

Daei drew thoughtfully on his cigarette, the tip glowing red in the darkness. "Really? None at all?"

"No, Admiral, I will do my duty, as will every man aboard."

Daei dropped his cigarette and ground it under his boot. "That is disappointing, Captain. It is a terrible responsibility our Leader has placed on your shoulders. The power to take thousands, maybe even millions of lives. It should never be exercised lightly, blindly, or unquestioningly, is that clear?"

Rostami blanched, surprised at the rebuke. "Yes, Admiral. But as you know, neither I nor any of the men on this ship have been briefed on what warhead is being loaded on that missile. Whether it is conventional, chemical, biological or nuclear … it is just another missile to us."

Daei put his hand on Rostami's shoulder and squeezed it. "If I, or anyone else, gives you the order to use that particular weapon, I want you to question me. I want you to look in your heart and ask yourself if there is any other option, *any* other alternative we have not considered. I want you to find that option, or that alternative, and present it to me. And if I insist upon using that weapon nonetheless, I want you to look into your heart and do what is right. Is that clear?"

"Admiral, I … I'm sorry," Rostami stuttered. "Are you proposing I should *disobey* your order?"

"The Quran teaches there are two kinds of leader, Rostami," Admiral Daei said gently. "Those who call people to do what is good, and those who call them to do what is bad. On resurrection day, those who call men to do bad deeds will not be saved." He patted Rostami's back before turning back toward the stairs. "You and I do not want to be among them."

Mississippi Road, Russett, Maryland, May 17

People who didn't know the Director of National Cyber Security expected Tonya Dupré to work out of the Directorate's offices inside the Fort Meade NSA campus. But you'd be disappointed if you looked for her there. Unless she was forced to, Tonya never even left her apartment overlooking the Little Patuxent River.

Because the thought terrified her.

Tonya Dupré lived her life on the spectrum, balancing the job of running a key government agency with managing her social anxiety disorder symptoms as best she could, by hiding them from the world around her. And she was very, very good at that. Raw talent had only gotten her so far in her career, and she'd quickly learned that only those with connections and networks were promoted into the jobs she coveted. Jobs where she could have control and influence, where what she did had *impact*. But those jobs went to the men and women with the easy smiles, the warm handshakes and the amusing stories. If Tonya Dupré found herself unexpectedly in a group of people without an agenda in front of her – a *party*, for example – she started trembling, got palpitations and felt physically ill.

Six months into her second job, she'd realized that she was going to begin and end her working life assigned to obscure corners of the NSA where skills in human relations were optional, unless she did something radical to bend the world to her needs. This realization coincided with another. Her anxiety only manifested when she was physically together with other people. Seated in a teleconference with a dozen people, she felt no anxiety at all. Called on to stand in for her manager and address a virtual global conference of hundreds of the world's leading cyber security professionals, she was praised in feedback for being both informative, charming and amusing. In real life, Tonya sucked the life out of a room, creating a vacuum of social energy around herself that caused people to edge away or leave her alone, which was in fact what she deeply desired. On screen, though, Tonya had *presence*.

She thought hard about how to turn her disability into a strength. As a ten-year-old child she'd had Guillain-Barré syndrome, a rare disorder in which the body's autoimmune system aggressively attacks the nervous system. She'd been mocked by her 'friends' at school when the tingling and numbness had first manifested and had started skipping school to avoid them, which was probably either the root cause or the first sign of her anxiety disorder. Three weeks later, getting worse by the day, she was sitting at her school desk, numb and having difficulty breathing, the children around her throwing balls of paper at her trying to get a reaction, laughing at and teasing her, when she collapsed. She was immediately hospitalized. She was given high-dose immunoglobulin therapy, which interrupted the attack on her nervous system, and was soon transferred to a rehab unit and, six months later, released.

She refused to go back to school and had been home tutored for the rest of her schooling.

She decided to leverage that history to create a narrative around herself that could play to her few social strengths. Early in her NSA career she told her manager about the Guillain-Barré episode and asked for permission to work from home more. Remote working had become much more commonplace following the COVID-19 pandemic, and her request was granted. She paid from her own pocket to have a hardened optic fiber landline laid into her apartment so that she couldn't be denied any opportunities to work on secret projects due to her work situation. She told colleagues around her she had to be careful to minimize physical contact with friends and colleagues because she was scared of a relapse of Guillain-Barré. Most accepted the story without question.

Overcompensating for her physical absence, she was hyper-present in the virtual space at NSA. She never sent a message if she could facetime a colleague. She attended ninety percent of meetings virtually and a therapist gave her the coping skills to attend the meetings she needed to attend in person.

And she was very, very good at her job. She led a series of matrix teams on small projects and then a breakthrough project landed in her lap. One of the roles of the Directorate of National Cyber Security was to support the US Warfighting effort. The US Defense forces had been pursuing the concept of All Domain Kill Chain capabilities – the ability for everyone from a general to a Marine company commander in the field to be able to pull on the combined resources of land, sea, air, cyber and space commands if needed to complete their mission.

But they lacked the AI needed to take a request from a commander in the field, assess what was needed to fulfill it, find and allocate the available resources and then focus them in support of that commander. Tonya was assigned to a project that failed, and decided that the problem was that they were trying to teach new skills to commanders in the field that were simply too complex; even the best of them were drowning in command sequences and data overload. Their mistake, Tonya felt, was that they were thinking of the AI as a tool a commander would carry with them, like a radio or infrared scope.

Tonya asked her new team to try to make the AI less like a tool and more like another member of a combat squad. A grunt, just like the other grunts the officer commanded. That meant you had to be able to give it orders in the same way, and it had to be able to reply to you in the same simple way – yes sir, no can do, sir, or how about we try this instead, sir.

The Heuristic Ordinary Language Machine Extrapolation System – HOLMES – was born. Unlike some of their earlier laptop-based concepts, HOLMES wasn't something physical you carried around with you. It was a cloud-based system that was always with you, everywhere you needed it. If you had a radio link, a satellite link, a wifi or cell phone connection, HOLMES was with you.

Tonya's team realized they'd met the project requirements when they'd been monitoring a field trial of HOLMES in South Korean military exercises. A US Army platoon had been pinned down by a heavily fortified South Korean position and was unable to move to flank it without taking heavy losses. Seven thousand miles away they'd heard the following exchange from the platoon leader.

"HOLMES! What the hell is that in front of us?"

"Captain, my analysis indicates the enemy position comprises about twenty entrenched troops, two fifty-caliber machine guns and an 80mm field mortar."

"Options?"

"I recommend a long-range precision fire strike with antipersonnel munitions. When the strike hits, I will give you the signal to move out and flank. Your orders, Captain?"

The Cyber Security team could hear the sound of heavy machine gun fire and the crump of a mortar smoke round landing nearby. Even though they were just exercises, they sounded terrifying.

"Call it in, HOLMES!"

"Yes, sir. Precision strike ordered. Fifteen seconds to impact. Ten seconds. Five…"

"Fox platoon, get ready to move!" the Army Captain called.

"Strike," HOLMES announced. He then consulted with the exercise referee, also an AI. "On target. Enemy suppressed."

"Move out!"

The Korean position had been taken with minimal 'casualties'. In her apartment in Russett, Tonya had done a little dance. In a matter of seconds, and based on a couple of verbal commands, HOLMES had pulled down data from satellites and orbiting drones, analyzed the audio feed coming from the platoon commander and other troops in his unit, together with audio feeds up and down the line of engagement, to determine the size and nature of the force opposing the platoon. It had cued several options for fire support and proposed the one with the highest probability of success to the Captain – the long-range precision missile – but it had also identified options such as a drone or other air strike, which would have taken longer to effect, or a mortar barrage which may not have been as accurate. Though it all happened in the background, HOLMES had negotiated available fire support options and was ready to go with whatever the Captain ordered if he rejected HOLMES' first suggestion. Again pulling on overhead surveillance, HOLMES had conducted an instantaneous strike damage assessment to be sure the target had been hit, and relayed this to the Captain so his platoon could break out and flank the enemy position.

All of this had been done in less than a minute, and with four entirely verbal interactions.

NSA personnel policy didn't stretch to paying for gifts for government employees, so Tonya had immediately gone online and with her personal credit card ordered a bottle of champagne delivered to every one of the twenty or so members of her development team.

She'd been given the task of ensuring the NSA-wide implementation of the HOLMES platform, and her team had grown from twenty to nearly a hundred before she was promoted, then promoted again. HOLMES was now being used for everything from All Domain Kill Chain support on the battlefield to intelligence analysis within the NSA and even strategic decision support at the level of the Joint Chiefs.

And Tonya Dupré, the woman most of her staff had met only over a telepresence link, was now Director of National Cyber Security and a member of ExComm.

She still kept up a high volume of interaction with all of her leadership team, with her network in other agencies and in government, and made sure she had face time with every single one of her 300 or so employees as part of their onboarding. And she still had HOLMES.

Putting her feet up on her desk and looking out of her apartment window over the forested verge of the Little Patuxent River, she spoke to the seemingly empty room.

"HOLMES, update your estimate of the timeframe for the possible cyber attack phase of an All Domain Attack on Israel, and report."

Yes, Director. Updating. Do you have a specific question?

"Your latest estimate regarding the initiation of cyber and space-based hostilities against Israel?"

Yes, Director. Space-based operations first. Russia has moved the Kirov-class cruiser Pyotr Velikiy into the eastern Mediterranean. It is now in position to launch blinding anti-satellite laser and Nudol missile attacks on the Israeli geostationary satellite network at short notice. It and its escorting missile destroyers are also able to provide potent anti-air and electronic warfare cover of the airspace over Israel if needed.

"So the space assault assets are in place."

Yes. Cyber chatter has dropped to a very low level. As you know, this is indicative of either one of two states: the attack has been aborted, or the attack is imminent. Given all other indicators, I believe the second to be the case. The phase 1 space and cyber attack is imminent.

"Imminent meaning?"

Four to six hours, Director.

"Confidence?"

High.

"Damn. Is Mossad reacting yet?"

At your request, NSA and Cybercom have already been in communication with the Israeli Defense and Security services. I do however suggest a one to one between yourself and the head of Israel's SIGINT National Unit, Unit 8200, to ensure they understand the urgency of the intelligence they've been provided.

"Can you get him on the line now please?"

Certainly, Director.

Tonya picked up her laptop and walked out to her kitchen, pulling open a cupboard and pouring herself a neat bourbon as she opened a secure comms window. Moments later the face of the head of Israel's Unit 8200, Colonel Ari Zuckerman, appeared as a pixelated blob on her screen that quickly resolved itself into the image of a narrow-faced man with dark swept-back hair and a black beard with a single grey stripe down the chin. He was wearing a suit, not his army uniform, which indicated she'd pulled him out of a meeting, probably with civilian contractors.

"Madam Director," he said. "Your assistant said it was something urgent? This is about the expected attack on our cyber infrastructure, I assume?"

"Hello, Ari, yes, I'm afraid. You've been briefed?"

"I have, and our preparations are well advanced, but I appreciate the courtesy call. I never know how much weight to put on such interservice briefings. The fact you called in person tells me we need to increase our preparations. How much time do we have?"

"Four to six hours is our best estimate," she told him. "They'll be going after your cellular comms, internet, air traffic control, utilities, international data traffic like banking, military and civilian satellite networks, recon assets … a coordinated, brute force, multiple vector space and cyber strike."

"I can be honest with you, Tonya. If this *is* an All Domain Attack, we could be screwed. Our command and control systems rely on military satellite comms. Our backup in case our satellite links go down is cell phone and landline. If they successfully take out both satellite and telecommunications, we will be back in the stone age. And I mean radio and motorbike courier style stone age. We've wargamed it, sure, and I've been screaming about it to the high heavens ever since we got our first reports about this *Operation Butterfly*, but no one up the chain here really believed Russia would support such an attack. This is feeling like it could be our Pearl Harbor."

"I know. All I can say is, plan for the worst. No one else has ever faced what you are about to face. Call me if you can see any way we can help, any way at all."

"Unless you can book us bandwidth on the US mil-sat network, I can't think of anything more right now."

"Good luck, Ari." Tonya cut the call. "HOLMES, what is your damage estimate?"

Would you like the estimate in US dollars or Israeli shekels?

"Dollars, and lives."

The space and cyber phase of the All Domain Attack will see a hit of eight to eleven percent of Israeli GDP or 30 to 36 billion US dollars next year alone. Excluding any lives lost in a military conflict scenario, between 2,000 and 5,000 deaths will result due to compromise of the Israeli healthcare and hospital system, cellular networks, joblessness, collapse of small and medium-sized businesses and related mental health issues. The range in these estimates is dependent on the success of the Israeli defense.

Tonya felt her gut tighten. No wonder her opposite number, Ari, had sounded so forlorn. Even with their best efforts, Israel was facing an economic wipeout that would impact it for years.

"HOLMES, you still assign a high probability to the likelihood this is an All Domain Attack? Not just a limited cyber and space-based operation?" Tonya had gone into the recent ExComm meeting armed not only with her own theories around what Iran, Syria and Russia were planning, but with a conviction based on the analysis provided to her by HOLMES. She still hoped beyond hope that the AI was wrong, or had revised its conclusions. Her heart fell as soon as the AI spoke. She'd given her personal version of HOLMES a comforting Southern accent. It didn't help.

Yes, Madam Director, that is still the scenario with the highest level of probability. I have the following assumptions at high probability. Syria hopes to regain control of the Golan Heights from Israel and is willing to use military force to do so. Iran hopes to force Israel to negotiate a peace treaty involving curbs on nuclear weapons and missile systems. Russia hopes to reduce what it sees as the destabilizing military power imbalance between Israel and its neighbors and cement its role as the pre-eminent regional superpower. The confluence of these ambitions, combined with the observed and reported cyber, space, air, land and sea military activity centered around Israel, support the high likelihood of the planned operation, dubbed Operation Butterfly in Syrian intercepts, being a full-scale All Domain Attack.

"What is your latest estimate for the phase timeline?"

Phase one, cyber and space, will be initiated in the next four to six hours. This will be followed by an initial attempt to begin diplomatic

132

negotiations. If this attempt fails, ground operations could be initiated within one to three days. Ground operations would likely begin with small-scale commando or insurgency activities as a precursor to full-scale war. I predict attempts to provoke civil unrest in key Israeli population centers, in the Palestinian territories, on the border with Lebanon and within the Golan Heights, combined with increased diplomatic activity. If this is not successful in provoking peace negotiations, then a full-scale invasion of the Golan Heights would be initiated and would likely succeed in the first few days due to the massive disruption still being experienced by Israeli command, control and intelligence systems.

"Is there any updated intelligence on the existence of Iranian nuclear weapons in the area of operations?" HOLMES had real-time access to CIA, DIA, NSA, FBI, DoD, SPACECOM and CYBERCOM intelligence reporting and could update and pull down intelligence community-wide information faster than any of her own analysts.

Updating. Naval intelligence reports indicate the USS Canberra is currently conducting a seizure and search operation of the IRIN vessel Besat. No further information. Satellite and aerial surveillance data indicates the Iranian Quds battalion located near Quneitra on the Syrian border with Israel includes a battery of Shahab-3 medium-range ballistic missiles capable of being fitted with tactical nuclear warheads and with a range that would easily allow a strike on any target in Israel. The satellite data indicates the missiles have already been fitted to their launchers and could be fueled and fired within 30 minutes if needed. Five launchers have been identified but their current locations are unknown as they are both camouflaged and believed to have been hidden inside buildings or subsurface revetments.

"Is there even a single recent report confirming Iran possesses North Korean weapons and has fitted them to its battlefield platforms on land or sea?"

No new reporting, Madam Director.

Tonya reached for her laptop and pulled up the list of people she wanted to facetime with today. She made the week's list every Sunday night, to make sure she regularly and meticulously covered her entire network, making up for not meeting people in the real. It was still a very long list and she might only have four hours to make the calls, so she drained the last of her bourbon and tapped the icon for the next person on the list. She put the glass down and looked at it. *Yes, I am an alcoholic. I am a social misfit. I shouldn't be in charge of a kindergarten fundraising drive, let alone coordinating America's cyber warfare capabilities. But here we are.*

LCS-30 USS *Canberra*, The Red Sea, May 17

'Ears' Bell's watch was over, and like every other sailor on the *Canberra* who didn't have somewhere he or she was supposed to be, he was loitering on the warship's aft deck. Unlike frigates of old, the *Canberra*'s stealth design allowed for very little deck space on which the crew could grab some sea air. The superstructure ran down flush to the sides of the hull, and the forward deck was taken up with the housing for its 2-inch gun, recently modified to take a GPS-guided artillery round. There was limited space for lounging around on the foredeck.

In any case, the aft helicopter deck was where the action was right now. And then some. They had been joined by one of the newest *Arleigh Burke*-class ships in the fleet, the USS *Sam Nunn*, which was steaming watchfully about a mile behind the Iranian sub. If, for some crazy reason, the crew of the *Besat* were ordered to fire a torpedo or missile either at their rescuers or at a target in Israel, it would be a very short-lived attack.

A braided steel tow cable was fixed to a cleat on the stern of the *Canberra*, and they were pulling the disabled Iranian submarine through the water at a slow and safe ten knots. Ears had still been in the CIC when a message had been sent to the Captain of the *Besat*, inside his submarine, to advise him his request to be released from the tow had been agreed. With the *Besat* still unable to engage its own propulsion system, the maneuver was not a simple one as it involved the submarine crew manually releasing the tow cable from its bow at the same time as the *Canberra* began to accelerate and turn to take it out of the path of the submarine as its momentum continued to carry it through the water. But the conditions for the maneuver were perfect – the Red Sea was cooperating today, and its waters were calm, with only slight swells – and it was agreed the operation would take place in two hours. Which suited Bell perfectly. He could come off watch, get a shower and some food, and still make it down to the helo deck to watch the show.

Along with the seventy other off-watch members of the *Canberra*'s complement. Bell arrived to find all the best places along the stern rail taken and so he went forward to the helo hangars. The hangar doors were closed – no doubt so that the Iranians couldn't get a view inside – but there was a service ladder to the navigation radar housing above the hangar and Bell climbed up there, sat down on the deck a good distance from the small rotating radar, and pulled out a sandwich.

He frowned. There was something wrong with the picture he was looking at, but he couldn't immediately see what it was. The Iranian officers had spent most of the morning standing in the sail of their submarine, watching the *Canberra* through binos or taking photos of it. On the big screen inside the CIC he'd even clearly seen them taking selfies of themselves with the *Canberra* in the background. He guessed it was as rare an event for them as it was for the crew of the US warship.

Right now, though, the top of the sail was vacant as the officers and crew no doubt prepared for the coming maneuver. The *Canberra*'s signals interception unit had also detected outgoing radio energy from the submarine, which was no doubt coordinating with nearby friendly naval units to come and provide assistance. According to the intel Bell had seen, the nearest Iranian naval unit capable of providing a tow to a 1,200-ton boat like the *Besat* was the *Moudge*-class light frigate, the IRIN *Sahand*, currently steaming at flank speed on an intercept course, but still at least three hours away, in the Gulf of Aden. All of this seemed perfectly normal to Bell.

What was not normal was the complement of Marines on Zodiac raiding craft who were making their way from the aft port quarter of the *Canberra* and toward the hulking metal hull of the Iranian submarine. The *Canberra* had sailed with a platoon-sized detachment of Marines who were on a training rotation, and Bell and the rest of the crew had gotten used to working around them, and their constant bitching. They bitched about the gym timeslots they were given (green side hours) and were constantly trying to sneak in during Navy timeslots (blue side hours). They bitched about any duty that involved cleaning or trash removal or any of the hundreds of other menial tasks aboard a ship, which, admittedly, they were probably given more than their fair share of. They bitched about having to salute Navy officers who generally showed them zero respect. They bitched about having to take their turn at 'breakouts', moving supplies out of storage, because there weren't enough of them to do it efficiently, so it involved more work for the few Marines when it was their turn on breakouts or replenishment duty. And they resented Navy ratings reacting to their moaning by remarking, "SITFU dude."

The men in the two Zodiacs drifting slowly back toward the *Besat* weren't complaining right now. They were dressed in dark blue Navy coveralls, rather than their own Marine working uniforms, which made no sense. He scanned the faces again. OK, maybe a couple of the men in the Zodiacs were Navy, but the rest were definitely Marines. Bell could also clearly see that each of them was carrying a sidearm on holsters strapped to their left thighs. Also, very weird. As he watched, Bell saw one of them check a duffel bag lying in the bottom of the boat, unzipping it to reveal what looked very much to him like a Benelli M4 Super 90 semi-auto shotgun, which the man quickly pushed to the bottom of the bag under some ropes, before zipping it up again.

That was no Navy working party.

Bell realized he still had a mouthful of sandwich hanging out of his open mouth and he quickly chewed and swallowed. He decided he and the rest of the crew assembled on the helo deck were about to be ringside to a boarding operation.

Sure enough, the Zodiacs bumped alongside the portside hull of the submarine and grabbed a handhold just aft of its fifty-foot-high sail. Three Navy ratings and a chief petty officer climbed out of the rubber boats – real Navy ratings – and made their way forward so that they would be visible to anyone on watch atop the sail. The Marines in Navy coveralls climbed out of the Zodiacs too, but took up positions aft of the sail, out of view. Bell counted ten. He had no idea how many crew members an Iranian sub like the *Besat* carried but guessed it would be at least twenty, maybe thirty. It seemed like a pretty underpowered boarding force, but hey, he was no expert.

He watched with fascination as the Navy crewmen took out a wrench and hammered on the sail of the submarine to indicate they were aboard and ready to begin the tow cable release work. As they did so, Bell saw at least four Marines climbing a ladder at the back of the sail and hang on it, just below the lip of the access hatches. The four Navy personnel also walked casually toward the bow to wait by a forward access hatch on the *Besat*'s foredeck.

Bell noticed they all had gas masks on their belts, which was not normal equipment for sailors about to cast off a tow line.

A moment later, the hatch was pushed open and a head appeared. Bell was a good 200 yards away and couldn't hear what was said, but he heard laughing. The US sailors took a couple of steps back, and a couple of Iranian seamen hoisted themselves out of the hatch and onto the deck. They all began shaking hands. Up on the *Besat*'s sail, another hatch opened and an officer began climbing out. Bell had seen the submarine's Captain enough times to recognize it was him climbing out of the conning tower to check on the operation.

What happened next took only seconds. Three US sailors grabbed their counterparts by their forearms, turning handshakes into a grapple as they swung the Iranians around and, putting a boot into their chests or guts, kicked them off the side of the sub and into the sea. Stepping around the fray, a fourth US sailor pulled what looked like grenades from the utility pockets of his coveralls and dropped them through the hatch the Iranians had just climbed out of. Bell couldn't hear any explosions, but white smoke came streaming out of the hatch and the four Navy sailors on the foredeck pulled on gas masks and jumped into the open hatch. Tear gas? Or worse?

Up on the conning tower, there was another struggle underway. The Marines on the ladder going up the sail had jumped up behind the officers emerging onto the submarine's watch deck and were fighting with the two Iranian officers there. They quickly overwhelmed them and pinned them against a railing with their arms behind their back. In moments, the remaining eight Marines also dropped gas grenades into the open conning tower hatch, pulled on gas masks and disappeared inside the submarine. The first and last ones through were carrying the shotguns Bell had seen.

He could only imagine the mayhem inside the submarine as the Navy and Marine boarding party entered in a cloud of what was probably tear gas. Surely the crew would slam internal hatches shut at the first sign of a boarding party, seal the raiders in and isolate themselves? But if the boarders could get control of the command center under the conning tower, that might be enough. It would depend on what they wanted to do: take the crew hostage, take control of the submarine, or just prevent them from taking hostile action?

There was visible consternation among the watching crew of the *Canberra* on the helo deck at what they'd just witnessed, and a few officers were ordering people below decks. If they hadn't been there watching, it would have looked suspicious, but spectators were clearly not needed anymore. After the brief rush of action, there was nothing to see anymore anyway. The decks of the submarine were clear. The officers and Marines, and their captives, atop the sail had either ducked out of sight or descended into the sub. The only activity was the two Zodiacs, which had fallen behind the sub now, their crews pulling three sodden Iranian sailors out of the water at pistol point.

Bell finished the last mouthful of his sandwich and decided he might as well climb down under his own steam, before he was ordered down. *Holy crap.* He'd never heard of the successful capture of an enemy submarine at sea.

Perhaps he'd just seen the first one!

White House Briefing Room, May 17

Carmine Lewis stood by impatiently watching the circus around Oliver Henderson as he prepared for his address. He'd been bunkered down with his speech writers all afternoon, he'd been through the final draft line by line with Carmine and his National Security Advisor, he'd taken a briefing on preparations for the naval blockade and no-fly zone from the Joint Chiefs, and he'd made calls to the Senate and House majority and minority leaders to let them know what was coming. Most had their own sources inside the administration, even inside ExComm, but they'd appreciated the gesture, Carmine was sure, even if they had their own opinions about the direction Henderson was taking.

Pro-Israel congressmen of course wanted him to go further. Anything less than a full-blooded commitment to the defense of Israel would not satisfy their donors. Isolationists thought he was going too far. The USA had bigger issues to worry about, right here at home. A third faction, being pushed by the House minority leader, was forming around the opinion this was the wrong fight altogether, and the USA could not afford to waste lives and materiel in the Middle East, again, when it was facing even greater challenges in Asia from China.

"I wish the crises would get in line and we could deal with them in priority order, Alexandria, I really do. But the world doesn't work that way," he'd told her.

After finishing with his makeup, he'd stolen a moment to

walk to the corner where Carmine was standing waiting her turn.

"Any word from the Red Sea?" he'd asked her immediately, sipping on a glass of water. She was glad to see his hand was steady.

"We've taken the *Besat*'s command center and penetrated to the forward missile hold. Half of the crew has been taken hostage and is being held on the *Canberra*. The other half has sealed itself behind watertight doors and isn't coming out. One Marine was wounded, and two Iranians. None seriously. It seems the missile launch systems are all controlled from the command center, so the danger of them launching any *Kalibr*-M missiles at Israel has been nullified." Carmine tried to sound upbeat, but there was no avoiding his next question.

"And the nuke?"

"We checked the radiation levels on the missiles in the tubes. There are radiation levels that are above normal. But there are no nuclear missiles on her now."

His shoulders sagged. "God damn it, Carmine."

"No. This changes nothing. Maybe those photos show a test loading operation, and they took the nukes off again before she sailed. Maybe they're playing cat and mouse with us and were worried the mouse would get caught. Your speech was written to cover any outcome. The reality doesn't change. Iran has nuclear weapons. Policy response: we want Israel and Iran negotiating a nuclear arms treaty instead of dragging us and the region into another endless war, right? You have two audiences tonight, one in the USA, one in the Middle East."

He straightened. "Yes. You're right."

Carmine leaned close, her mouth to his ear so no one nearby could hear. "This is your Kennedy moment, Oliver. But remember. Kennedy and Khrushchev both went into the missile crisis with the possibility that a single wrong move could trigger Armageddon. We aren't quite there, yet."

He gave a short laugh. "Yet? Thanks for the pep talk, Carmine," he said and turned away.

OK, she could have handled that better. But Henderson settled behind the Resolute desk with a resolute demeanor and before she knew it, the cameras were rolling.

"Good evening, my fellow citizens. Six months ago, American troops took part in a battle with Russian-backed Syrian forces to protect a NATO base in Turkey. This Government, as promised, has maintained the closest surveillance of foreign interference in the affairs of Syria and its neighbors and we have worked tirelessly against the efforts of Iran, another close ally of Syria, to develop atomic weapons.

Within the past few days, we have obtained unmistakable evidence that Iran has procured nuclear weapons and is attempting to deploy them on its ships at sea. The purpose of these efforts can be none other than to provide themselves with a nuclear strike capability against their perceived enemies, the United States and Israel."

Carmine could sense a ripple of tension, even shock, among those in the room. Not all of the audio and video technicians, nor even all of the aides, had seen the content of the President's address in advance. Many were hearing it for the first time, just like the rest of the nation. She heard a collective intake of breath.

Henderson continued. "Yesterday, you may have seen news reports about a US vessel going to the aid of an Iranian submarine in the Red Sea, which is just off the coast of Israel. The brave men and women of the US Navy will always stand ready to assist seafarers in distress, no matter what nation they belong to. But while working to rescue the Iranian sailors aboard the submarine, our medical teams detected traces of nuclear radiation aboard the Iranian vessel. This provoked us to review satellite intelligence of the Iranian submarine as it prepared to take to sea, and our intelligence analysts discovered these grave images."

The camera cut to grainy photos of the *Besat* being loaded with the *Kalibr*-M cruise missile.

"These are images of a nuclear-capable *Kalibr*-M cruise

141

missile being placed into a missile launch tube on the Iranian submarine, the *Besat*. The same submarine that got into difficulties off the coast of Israel yesterday."

Nuclear-capable? That was true. And they had been careful not to definitively say nuclear-armed. But 'off the coast of Israel' ... well, that was a bit of creative license, Carmine had pointed out to the speech writers. It was closer to the coast of Egypt. *Ah, but only a hundred miles from the port of Eilat in Israel as the crow – or cruise missile – flew*, they'd replied.

"We also have evidence that the nuclear warheads we believe are now being fielded by Iran were provided to it by North Korea, with the knowledge of, if not support from, technical experts from Russia. As many as six warheads have been tracked from North Korea into Iranian hands. Any claim by Iran that these weapons are intended only for the defense of Iran is given the lie by its decision to place them aboard warships or submarines such as the *Besat* and sail it into foreign waters from where it could strike US bases across the Middle East – from Saudi Arabia, to Qatar, Bahrain, Jordan, Iraq or, if it so chose, even to strike US bases and capital cities in Europe.

"These offensive acts constitute an explicit threat to the peace and security of the USA and our allies in NATO, and are a deliberate breach of the Nuclear Non-Proliferation Treaty, to which Iran has been a party since 1970. This action also contradicts the repeated assurances of the Iranian regime, both publicly and privately delivered, that in return for reopening of trade relations with the USA and treaty signatories, they would cease research into the development of nuclear weapons. The advanced nature of the weapons placed aboard this submarine shows years of research and planning, and thus years of deceit.

"Neither the United States of America nor the world community of nations can tolerate deliberate deception and offensive threats on the part of any nation, large or small. We no longer live in a world where only the actual firing of weapons represents a sufficient challenge to a nation's security to constitute maximum peril. Nuclear weapons are so destructive and supersonic cruise missiles are so swift that any substantially increased possibility of their use or any sudden change in their deployment may well be regarded as a definite threat to peace. Our unswerving objective, therefore, must be to prevent the use of these missiles against US forces, or those of any other country, and to secure their withdrawal or elimination from this world."

Henderson paused, making sure of himself as the teleprompter changed to show one of two sets of sentences that had been prepared for him – one in the case of the submarine capture going right, the other if it went wrong.

He read a few words ahead, and then continued smoothly. "Therefore, today I gave our Navy orders to board and take control of the Iranian submarine in the Red Sea to prevent any likelihood its weapons can be used against US or allied bases, cities or citizens. This has been achieved, and the Iranian submarine will be placed in quarantine in Port Sudan. Its crew are unharmed, and will all be returned to Iran in due course."

Henderson paused and made a show of changing the speaking cards in front of him to signal he was making a slight change of topic.

"This is not the only matter of grave concern I have to share with you tonight. Earlier this morning, we received word that a large Russian and Iranian naval fleet is currently moving out of the Black Sea and into the Mediterranean Sea with the stated intention of making port in Latakia, Syria – putting it within cruise missile attack range of Israel. As you may have also seen, and as we have watched with concern, Syrian armored forces, backed again by Iran and Russia, have marshaled on the western borders of Israel.

"Since 1974, United Nations peacekeeping troops have been monitoring a ceasefire between Syria and Israel in the Golan Heights. The United States has voted numerous times in the United Nations to continue this important mission, as recently as in May of this year. US troops are currently stationed with the UN peacekeeping force."

Carmine looked at her watch. The Marine chopper should have touched down by now. So, yes, technically another 'just-in-time' truth.

"The decision by Syria, Iran and Russia to conduct military operations in the area of the Golan Heights poses a grave threat to the peace of this region, and we cannot be so blind as to think these events, the entrance of the Iranian and Russian fleet into the Mediterranean, Syrian tanks on the Israeli border, and the discovery of nuclear-capable missiles aboard an Iranian warship, are unrelated.

"Our policy has been one of patience and restraint, as befits a peaceful and powerful nation that leads a worldwide alliance. We have been determined not to be diverted from our central concerns by mere irritants and fanatics. But now further action is required, it is underway, and these actions may only be the beginning. We will not hesitate to act in defense of our own security and of the entire Western Hemisphere, and under the authority entrusted to me by the Constitution as endorsed by the resolution of the Congress on the prevention of proliferation of nuclear weapons, I have directed that the following initial steps be taken immediately…"

You could have heard a mouse fart in the room at that moment. Even Carmine found she was holding her breath, even though she knew what was coming.

"First: To prevent the deployment by Iran of nuclear weapons at sea, a strict quarantine on certain Iranian naval shipping is being initiated. *All* Iranian shipping, commercial or naval, entering the Mediterranean Sea or the Red Sea from whatever route may be subject to search and, if found to contain nuclear weapons, will be escorted back to Iranian territorial waters. If it refuses to be searched, it will be regarded as hostile and may be destroyed.

"Second: I have directed the United States Navy, Air Force and the Aviation Wing of the US Marines to provide such support to US and UN peacekeeping forces in the Golan Heights as is necessary to secure the continuation of their

144

important duties. Any hostile action by any nation, which in any way threatens the safety of US or UN troops or the peaceful conduct of their duties, will be regarded as an act hostile to the United States and will result in a retaliatory response by our air and naval forces.

"Third: It shall be the policy of this Nation to regard any nuclear weapon launched by Iran against any member of the United Nations as an attack by Iran on the United States, requiring a full retaliatory response.

"Fourth: We are calling tonight for an immediate meeting of the Signatories to the Iran Nuclear Arms Control Agreement, including the Governments of Iran and Russia, to resume discussions as part of a special session of the United Nations Security Council, to be convened immediately.

"My fellow citizens: let no one doubt that this is a difficult and dangerous time. No one can see precisely what course it will take or what costs or casualties will be incurred. In the days and weeks ahead our patience and our resolve will be tested – you will hear threats and denials from those opposed to peace which will only serve to reinforce the dangers we face. But the greatest danger of all would be to do nothing.

"The cost of freedom is always high – and Americans have always paid it. And one path we shall never choose is the path of passive submission in the face of evil. To paraphrase US President John Kennedy's words at a similar time in our history, *Our goal is not the victory of might, but the vindication of right – not peace at the expense of freedom, but both peace and freedom, in that far hemisphere, and, we hope, around the world.* God willing, that goal will be achieved.

"Thank you and good night."

As Henderson finished speaking and waited for the cue to look away from the camera, Carmine's telephone started buzzing. She pulled it out of her jacket pocket and looked at it, expecting it to be one of the ExComm members with a view on what Henderson had done right or wrong … but she frowned when she saw the message from Tonya Dupré.

Contact lost with US Embassy Jerusalem and consulate Tel Aviv. Nudol anti-satellite missiles fired by Russian cruiser in Mediterranean. All Domain Attack Phase 1 has started.

All Domain Attack: Ground

Iranian Quds Force base, Damascus, Syria, May 17

"Thanks for the lift. Good night," Abdolrasoul Delavari told the commandos dropping him back at the Iranian Quds Force base outside Damascus. Delavari was berthed with an IRGC infantry officer who was the best company Delavari had shared a tent with in any war in his long military career. Advi Yazd was a Zoroastrian, a member of an ancient religion that predated Islam, and he surprised Abdolrasoul by explaining his religion was not only still alive in Iran, but also officially recognized, with its adherents even guaranteed a seat in the Iranian parliament. He was educated, literate, worldly and, like Delavari, had strong family values. He was a mechanical engineer who had started his career after university working for the Iranian Defense Industries Organization on a project to update its *Saher* 14.5mm anti-materiel rifle to make it suitable for Russian-made smart munitions. It was a given, then, that he would be put in a tent with Delavari, the only shooter in the Quds Force certified to use the new *Klimovsk* smart rounds. He had been trying to persuade Delavari to take a modified *Saher* into the field, and Delavari had promised Yazd he'd try it out on a routine mission, if he was ever given one.

As he walked into their tent and dumped his gear on his bunk, Delavari saw the Iranian hastily close down a program he'd been watching on his cell phone and shove the phone under his pillow. He turned eagerly to Delavari. "So, how did it perform?"

"The Israeli microdrone? Like a damn guided missile. The army will no longer need us specialists if all you have to do is shoot a hobby plane into the air with a picture of the target in its memory." He sat on the bunk.

"A shame it was the only example we have. I would have liked the chance to reverse engineer it."

"I still have the guidance unit," Delavari said, taking the remote out of his bag and handing it to the engineer.

"Thank you. It's something, at least." He turned it over in his hands, flipping up the viewing screen. "I would like to see their faces when they realize it was their own weapon that was used against them."

"I suppose that was the whole point." Delavari nodded at the man's pillow. "What were you watching? Video from home?"

"No. We are close enough here to pick up Lebanese news services. I was watching the US President address his people."

"Ah. And what did the Great Satan have to say?"

Yazd flinched. "There are no evil nations, only evil men," he said.

"I was joking, Advi. What did he announce?"

"He asserted that Iran has nuclear weapons and announced a naval quarantine. Any Iranian ship in the Red Sea or Mediterranean approaching Israel will be stopped and searched. If it is found to carry nuclear weapons, it will be escorted to Iranian waters."

Delavari slapped his thigh. "That is a laugh. And how will they enforce it? With a strongly worded press release? They would not dare try to stop an Iranian warship on the high seas."

"They already did. They have boarded one of our submarines in the Red Sea and taken control of it."

"My God, that's an act of war," Delavari found himself saying before he stopped his line of thought. *And what was your last mission if not the same, Abdolrasoul?* Delavari had seen the huge 12-wheeler tractor trailers with their ballistic missile launchers moving into and then out of the Quds Force base. He leaned forward and lowered his voice. "Do we ... have you heard any talk of nuclear weapons?"

"No. If the famous 'Lighvan' doesn't know, then there's no reason they'd tell a shitkicker like me."

"But you believe it."

148

"I hope … with all my heart … that it is true. We are lambs living in a forest full of wolves. The Israelis have nuclear weapons and the Americans sail their nuclear-armed warships along our shores, fly their nuclear-armed bombers close to our borders. We will never be safe until we can meet force with force."

"You surprise me, Advi. You are a weapons engineer, but in your heart I had you down as a man of peace."

"Zoroaster teaches that war and courage have done more great things than charity," Yazd said. "Danger must be defeated, it cannot be wished away."

Delavari pointed at the *Saher* rifle Yazd had standing against the wall next to his cot. "Well, you and I may not have nuclear weapons but we have 14.5mm *Klimovsk* smart rounds. How about tomorrow morning you take me out and show me what your guided missile rifle can do?"

Buq'ata township, the Golan Heights, May 18

"Yozam, do me a favor? Check the 9G router?" Amal Azaria called out to her brother's shop assistant.

Her workshop was behind their two-story house on the outskirts of Buq'ata, but she preferred to use the airconditioned office in the back of her brother's furniture repair shop in town when she was working with her design software. The wifi connection there was much faster. Mansur had not been happy when she'd told him she was going into town alone, but he was still in bed and Raza was sleeping. He'd become even more protective of her, and she knew why. The drums of war were beating louder by the day, as evidenced by the military traffic moving through Buq'ata at all hours of the day and night. Many Israeli citizens had already evacuated to the west, but the majority of the population of Buq'ata was made up of Druze like themselves, so they had stayed put.

She had tried to calm Mansur, telling him she would only be

a couple of hours, and she could help his assistant Yozam open the store.

Speaking of Yozam, where was the man? When there was no response, she called out again. She was working on a new design for a mother drone that could lift a heavier payload. She just wanted to send the latest project update to DRD, attach her new drawings, then get back home, get some breakfast into her and go out into the early morning sunshine to play with Raza before it got too warm. But her computer was telling her she had no wifi connection. Suddenly her computer monitor died and the lights in the furniture shop cut out completely. OK, so, it was more than a wifi problem.

"Yozam?! Can you check the fuses?"

Still no answer. She sighed and walked out of the office to the stairs leading down to the shop. She could hear the radio on downstairs. "Amal, get in here!" Yozam yelled.

The old Druze carpenter was hunched over the radio in the shop's small kitchen. "What's up?" she asked.

"Quiet! Listen…" he said, looking at her wide-eyed.

"… civil emergency broadcast. The government has declared a national emergency. Stay indoors unless ordered to leave by police, armed forces or emergency services. All armed forces personnel or reservists are to report in person to their base immediately. This is not an exercise, this is not a rehearsal. This is a government of Israel civil defense emergency broadcast…" They stood, stunned, listening as the message repeated. Mansur changed the radio channel. It was the same message being played on every single Israeli radio channel.

"The power is out," Amal told him. "The internet is down."

"We should leave," Yozam said, looking around himself wildly. "I'll lock up here, you get back to your house. Grab whatever we can and…"

Amal heard car horns outside on the main road that went past their window. Their shop was in Buq'ata's central shopping district, an intersection with a war memorial commemorating the fallen in the 1973 conflict. As she pulled the curtain aside, she saw that traffic was already jammed, and people were standing outside their cars yelling at each other.

"I'll call Mansur." She dialed and held the phone to her ear. It returned a busy tone. She frowned and looked at the display. "No coverage? The cell phone network is down too?"

"It's why I turned the radio on," Yozam explained. "I was on the phone to a supplier. The line went dead. I tried to call him on the message app, but there was no wifi either. I turned on the television, but there was no signal on any of the channels, just a message saying 'signal failure'. Like the transmitter wasn't there anymore. Then the power went out. Then that message on the radio."

"I need to get home, get my bag, get to my unit," Amal said again. Next to the shop door on a coat rack was her handbag, the green IDF jacket and X95 rifle she'd started taking with her everywhere. Yozam had moved past her to the door, and stood watching people arguing outside. "Look at this idiot, stopped right in the middle of the intersection."

She heard shouting and walked to join him at the door.

With a heat like the doors of hell had been thrown open, a blinding flash lit the street outside and they were thrown back into the shop in a hail of glass.

Acting Golani Brigade Brigadier General, Zeidan Amar, had only managed to get about a mile from Mount Hermonit to the village at the foot of the hillside, El-Rum, before he ran into the first military convoy, stopped at the crossroad as a platoon leader, a captain, stood in front of his truck, arguing with someone on the radio. As he couldn't pass in his *Storm* utility vehicle, he climbed out, the small crowd of soldiers parting as they saw who he was. The captain looked up and paused his conversation as Zeidan approached. Zeidan didn't recognize him. He was from a different battalion, but he was Golani Brigade.

"What's going on?" he asked the man.

"We were supposed to move up to the outpost at Hermonit. Now we're being told to return to Camp Shraga."

"That's right," Zeidan told him. "I am Colonel Amar, Reconnaissance Battalion. General Weinberg has ordered the entire brigade to pull back to Shraga."

"But…" the man frowned. "Is it true? Colonel Tamir?"

"Is dead. Yes. Peace on his soul. Now turn your men around. We are needed on the border with Lebanon. Not here."

The man frowned again. "We overtook tanks from the 7th Armored on the road outside Kfar Blum, five miles back. They were blocking the crossroads, refusing to let traffic pass, so we went around them."

"Why?"

"Some religious dispute. We heard they ordered all female personnel in the unit to hand in their uniforms and weapons and go home!"

Zeidan suppressed a smile. He'd been ordered to sow as much confusion as he could and, at the very least, order his own battalion to withdraw from its positions in the Golan Heights. He'd heard a rumor there would be other attempts to disrupt the Israeli mobilization. Iran and Syria had spent many, many years getting all of their agents in place for exactly this day.

Agents like Zeidan Amar.

"Ignore that. We have been ordered to urgently reinforce Northern Command. Find a way around Kfar Blum. Other units will take up our positions in the Golan. Clear?"

"Yes, Colonel." The man put the handset back on the radio. He signaled to his men. "All right, mount up! Turn it around!"

Zeidan had returned to his vehicle and sat watching in silence as the trucks reversed, painfully slowly, inching around on the narrow road until finally they were pointed west and began moving off again. Once the junction was clear, he pulled onto the road and headed north. He crawled along, passing military and civilian traffic going in both directions, and stopped at a farmhouse outside Buq'ata where he'd arranged to meet with his men – Druze loyalists who shared his vision of an independent Druze homeland.

They'd worked into the night and through the next day, finalizing their plans, and then dispersed. In the morning he'd risen, set a pot of coffee to boil on a gas ring and then heard the civilian emergency alarm on their radio. *"...has declared a national emergency. Stay indoors unless ordered to leave by police, armed forces or emergency services. All armed forces personnel or reservists are to report in person to their base immediately. This is not an exercise, this is not a rehearsal. This is a government of Israel civil defense emergency broadcast..."*

He smiled. *Operation Butterfly.* It had begun.

He poured himself a mug of scalding hot coffee and went outside to take a deep breath of fresh early morning air. It was so quiet here. The search for him would be well underway by now, his disappearance so soon after the death of Colonel Tamir sowing maximum confusion and doubt among the remaining commanders of the Golani Brigade. All over the Golan, the Brigade would have been packing up and moving out, only to be challenged about what the hell they were doing by other units moving west. The roads would be jammed with military traffic going in every direction. And at the peak of all that confusion, a nationwide cyber attack of a scale the world had never seen.

Not his main concern right now, however.

Throwing his coffee mug on the ground, he climbed into his *Storm*, turned on the emergency hazard lights, and pulled out onto the road. Traffic was light, but he sounded his horn at any car or truck too slow to get out of his way.

After about five hundred yards, he heard a large explosion, then saw a column of white smoke rise into the air from the center of town, still a mile ahead. Their drivers startled, three cars in front of him slammed into each other, blocking the narrow road. He was still a mile out of town.

Damn, he thought to himself, pulling to the side of the road and jumping out. He grabbed his sidearm from the car and broke into a jog. *Too soon! They were to wait for me!*

"Orders, Sergeant?"

"Park your butts while I see where our ride is, Private."

Gunner James Jensen had just alighted from the quadcopter and was standing in a field next to Highway 98 outside Buq'ata, watching the *Big Boy* copter lift off into the air again in a storm of dust and scrap paper. He ducked his head to avoid the flying gravel and surveyed their situation.

He'd seen no troop transport trucks or buses on the road as they'd come in to land. And most definitely none that looked like they were in white and blue UN livery. The roads were strangely deserted, especially given it was early morning and farmers were usually early risers. Walking to the vine-lined wire fence at the edge of the field bordering the highway, he saw the outskirts of the township, roughly built two-story houses of concrete slab and tile making up the bulk of the dwellings. Across the highway were two couches that had been dumped by the side of the road under a road sign with Hebrew characters on top and 'Buq'ata Center' underneath, pointing to a narrow road that led between two-story civilian houses.

It was starting to get warm. And he was thirsty, and hungry, so he assumed his squad was too. 'His squad'. He turned and looked at them, squatted on their haunches in the dirt field. Seven exhausted men and women, comprising a medical corpsman, four riflemen, privates, and two corporals, both of whom were communications techs who had stayed behind at the outpost at Kobani to ensure no sensitive equipment was left behind.

Jensen guessed why the dilapidated couches had been dumped under the road sign. It was an informal pick-up point and people needed somewhere to sit while they were waiting. It was as good as any place. He decided he'd leave most of the squad by the road sign in the shade of a very weird white concrete sculpture that looked like an upended bowl with a chickpea in it, and take a man into town with him to find some water and food.

He had just turned to call out to the Marines to form up on him when he heard a loud crack followed by a booming echo, car alarms started beeping all over the town, and a column of white smoke rose up into the sky. Birds scattered into the air in all directions.

Seriously?

He crouched down and turned to look at the Marines behind him again. Like himself they had reacted instantly to the now familiar sound of a mortar round or improvised explosive device and had cautiously lowered themselves to the ground, rifles cradled in front of them, fanned outward to cover all approaches with overlapping fields of fire. After six months on a Syrian hilltop facing daily mortar fire and a final battle against Syrian troops which they'd fought hand to hand inside their perimeter, it wasn't so much training anymore as hard-wired instinct.

An open field in the baking sun was no place for seven US Marines in combat fatigues and their piles of personal gear. Directly across the highway from him was a two-story house, still under construction, no windows or doors yet installed. It would do.

"Everyone up!" he called out, running back to them. "Grab the gear. On me."

When they were all ready, duffel bags over their shoulders, rifles in hand, he pointed to the construction site on the other side of the suddenly empty highway. "We're moving to that building. Set up inside and stay alert. I'm taking Bell and going into town to find out what the hell is going on." The cloud of smoke was boiling up into the air now, something burning underneath it. He grabbed the most senior of his corporals, Patel. "Probably just a house demolition or something, you stay here, stay cool, and for Chrissake don't shoot anyone unless they start shooting at you. Got that? Now go."

He watched them run across the road and pile into the vacant house, then clapped Bell on the back. "Alright, Corpsman, let's move out."

"Aye aye, Sergeant."

Both had their rifles and helmets, ballistic vests and field gear, Bell also carrying his medical pack and the standard M27 automatic rifle, Jensen the 6.8mm bullpup next-gen squad weapon and accessories that he'd taken to Kobani for field trials. It had already been adopted by the US Army, but the Marines of course wanted to run their own evaluations.

Strange. There was no traffic on the highway at all now. Like a tap had been turned off either side of the town. Car alarms were still sounding up ahead, but a few people had started emerging from their homes and onto the street, looking terrified. Jensen couldn't help notice that a lot of the houses appeared deserted, but that at least made some sense. With 2,000 Syrian tanks parading up and down the border a few miles away, he'd probably have gotten his family as far away as he could too.

There were a few people walking or running toward the source of the explosion though, others gathered in small groups at their fences to talk. They shot suspicious or worried glances at Jensen and Bell, but no one stopped them. Though he would never have worn it inside Syria, Jensen pulled his US flag patch out of a pocket and slapped it onto the Velcro tape across his right breast where it was easy to see. He indicated to Bell to do the same.

After winding through a couple of narrow streets, they emerged at an intersection shrouded in dust, smoke and the sadly familiar smell of violent death. Jensen saw immediately what had happened. A pickup parked outside a shop on a corner had detonated, destroying the shops behind it and the cars that had been driving past it, which were burning furiously too, adding to the smoke. Civilian casualties lay strewn across the road, a few shocked casualties were still crawling around.

"Get to it, Bell," Jensen said, but Bell needed no direction, he had already run to help a man pumping the chest of a woman who lay unconscious and bleeding on the road in front of them. Looking around himself, Jensen saw a woman in a military jacket and jeans, leaning inside a doorway, with a hand to her bleeding forehead. There was a rifle, bag and utility vest at her feet. She looked like she was still in shock.

He ran over to her. "Hey, are you alright?"

She stared at him uncomprehending, then took her hand down and saw the blood.

"Do you speak English?" he asked.

She focused on him for the first time. "Yes, of course." Then she spun around. "Yozam!" She ran back into the ruined shop. Jensen followed her in and found her crouching behind a tumble of shattered furniture. She was speaking frantically in Arabic, shaking the shoulder of an old man who lay in a crumpled ball against the back wall.

Jensen didn't need to be a medic to see he was dead.

Jensen crouched beside her. "Ma'am?"

She ignored him, trying to turn the old man over.

"Ma'am, he's dead, and you're bleeding. You need to get help."

She put a hand up to her face and it came away covered in blood. She had a gash just under her hairline, but as far as he could see it wasn't too deep. She put her bloodied hand on the shoulder of the dead man.

"Yozam. Poor Yozam."

"Yes, ma'am. Come with me. My corpsman is outside."

"Corpsman? You're American?"

"Yes. American."

He helped her rise to her feet, but before they could start moving toward the door again, Jensen heard the crackle of small arms fire as an automatic weapon opened up outside. There was screaming and yelling, and more automatic fire, somewhere outside and to their right. The woman reacted instantly, running to the front door and scrabbling under fallen furniture and glass. From underneath it she pulled what was clearly a military assault rifle. Putting the strap over her head and shoulder, she flattened herself against the door frame and peered around it. Jensen crouched down at knee height behind her, doing the same.

"I can't see him," she said. "The shots are coming from down by the café."

Jensen's mind was racing. It was a classic terrorist action. Detonate an improvised explosive device to cause carnage and confusion. Wait until first responders arrive or the scene is packed with civilians trying to evacuate the dead and wounded, then open fire on the crowd. There would be more than one shooter. He looked for Bell and found the Marine sheltering behind another white concrete statue, this one in the middle of the roundabout, a big blocky structure with what looked like an arm extended into the air, holding a crown. Bell signaled with his hands. *Two shooters.* One at his ten o'clock, the other at his four o'clock, opposite sides of the street. When he saw that Jensen had seen him, Bell swung out of cover, sent four quick rounds toward one of the shooters, and then rolled back behind the statue.

Jensen tapped the woman's leg. "There. Behind the blue metal sign."

As he watched, the shooter stood up from his crouch and returned fire at Bell. Further down the street, where he had no view, he heard the second shooter, also firing. Chips flew off the sculpture Bell was hiding behind. He was pinned.

"Is that weapon loaded?" he asked the woman.

"Yes, of course," she said. "I am an IDF reservist."

"When I tap your leg, can you fire at the shooter behind that sign? Keep his head down. I'm going to get further down the street, try to flank. Yes?"

"Yes."

Jensen gathered himself, trying to remember the layout of the street outside. He couldn't. He had no idea what he was running out into.

He thumped her calf. "Go!"

With calm, methodic discipline, the woman swung out and began firing at the shooter down the road behind the sign, in short, two-shot groups. If she was shocked or angry, she was good at controlling it. He ducked behind cover, then signaled to Bell, who also rolled out of cover and began firing.

Jensen ran out the doorway, hugging the wall to his right. Beside the clinic a small alleyway led away from the roundabout. Without hesitating, he legged it down the alley, away from the shooting, looking for a path or road that would parallel the main street and allow him to get around or behind the two shooters. He ran twenty yards, got to the corner of the next building, saw a path into a yard strewn with building rubble, a fence on the other side of it he could vault, and went that way. He was moving through the back yards of the houses and shops that lined the main street, under washing hanging on lines in the sunshine, scaring cats into cover, bolting past a small child standing in a yard alone, crying.

Tumbling over a corrugated iron fence he gathered his breath, trying to work out how far he had come. Fifty yards? Seventy?

He heard rifle fire again, but this time it was close.

Very close.

Looking up at the building into whose yard he'd fallen, he saw it looked like a shop of some sort. An air conditioner in a rear window thumped noisily, and the back door was open.

On the tiled floor inside the door, he saw a body, unmoving.

As quietly as he could, he approached the door, flattened himself against the rear wall and looked inside. It was a hairdressing salon. A woman lay on the floor in front of him in a pool of blood. Dead.

Further down, another person. Face down. Not moving.

He heard automatic rifle fire at the front of the building, then saw a shadow, crouched, move across the front of the salon. The sound of glass, shattering as the shooter fired through the front window at something or someone. When he stopped firing, Jensen heard return fire from up by the

159

roundabout, the Israeli woman and Bell no doubt, but they didn't have a shot on this guy, they were still engaged with his friend across the road.

Come on, JJ, get in there! Without thinking, he pulled the magazine out of his bullpup, checked it, and eased it back in. *OK, go time. Easy, boy.*

Stepping inside the door on the balls of his feet, he nearly slipped in the blood of the woman in the hallway. Crouched low, he waddled slowly up the hall as the shooter fired again, around to his right, out of sight. Now he heard movement again and steadied himself, waiting for the man to move across the front of the salon into a new shooting position. He sighted at the gap at the end of the hallway.

A silhouette crouched low and running. He fired.

Before the sound of his shots had died away he was up and running. The shooter was down, spreadeagled on the floor, reaching for the rifle he'd dropped when he fell.

Jensen put two more shots into his back, ran over and kicked the rifle away.

He was dead.

Moving past him to the salon window, Jensen looked out onto the street. The roundabout was about sixty yards back up the road. The café with the blue metal sign was about twenty yards further up, across the road from him.

He had a clear line on the man crouched behind the metal sign, sheltering from the suppressing fire still being generated by Bell and the Israeli woman and looking about himself as though considering his options. Sighting through his scope, Jensen put his crosshairs on the middle of the man's back and fired.

All Domain Attack: Air

RAF Akrotiri Air Base, Cyprus, May 18

Bunny O'Hare was starting to like Shelly Kovacs. Beyond the fact she'd saved her from death by a thousand paper cuts, and got her back to active duty at RAF Akrotiri base, she was delivering on all her promises. Together with the other five pilots of the DARPA Marine F-47B unit she'd been attached to the US 432nd Air Expeditionary Wing at Akrotiri and within a half a day of their arrival, she'd been airborne with a 'hex' of six *Fantom* drones training in protocols and procedures for coordinating operations with Israeli Defense Force air controllers. As the only unmanned combat aircraft in the theatre, the 12 aircraft of the Marine Experimental Wing were taking point on the newly declared no-fly zone over the Golan. To reach it, they had to fly south-east from Cyprus, avoiding Syrian ground-based military radar at Tartus, and enter via southern Israel near Tel Aviv, one of the heaviest air traffic corridors in the Middle East.

"Why not here, at Haifa?" Bunny had asked. "Why detour all the way south to Tel Aviv and mix with all that commercial flight traffic?"

"China," Kovacs had shrugged. "Israel and a Chinese venture capital fund built a port at Haifa in the early 2020s and we haven't been allowed to inspect it. No one is comfortable with the idea of letting them get a close look at our *Fantoms* flying to and from the Golan."

"China has a port in *Israel?*"

"Yep. So you have to factor in ingress and egress via Tel Aviv for every mission. We've set up a dedicated liaison in IDF Air Force air traffic control, and an open channel between RAF Akrotiri control and Tel Aviv, but run a few sorties to smooth out any bumps. The no-fly zone comes into effect tomorrow," Kovacs had told her.

Smooth out any bumps? They were going to be flying experimental unmanned combat aircraft, up to two or three times a day, through a civilian and military air corridor. What could possibly go wrong? Luckily given the tensions in the theatre and the US President's announcement of a blockade and no-fly zone, most commercial airlines had cancelled their flights into and out of Israel. But there were still hundreds of light aircraft and Israel's own airline, El Al, which refused to ground its aircraft for something as trivial as a 'border dispute'.

The dog-legged route added an extra 260 miles to every mission, reducing the *Fantom*'s time on station by almost exactly thirty minutes. But it still gave Bunny's hex nearly four hours over the Golan Heights on every patrol. She would be the only one piloting the six-plane formation. When her flight retired, it would be replaced with two pilots each flying two-plane formations.

The briefing the DARPA Marine pilots got from the Colonel in command of the 432nd Air Expeditionary Wing had been blunt. "Gentlemen and ladies, you will be providing close air support to United Nations observers in an area of only 700 square miles. To your north and east, you will be facing aircraft of the Russian 7th Air Group and if you cross into Syrian or Lebanese airspace, they *will* shoot your aircraft down. If they cross into your airspace, you can only return fire if fired upon first, and we believe they *will* try to provoke you. If the Syrian army enters the Golan Heights, putting UN troops in danger, you will fly missions to protect those troops if needed, in which case Russian aircraft will almost *certainly* attempt to shoot you down. You may only engage hostile aircraft if you are attacked, and only to allow yourself to withdraw. If the missiles start flying, my staff calculate your likely attrition per sortie at thirty percent. At that rate, your small unit will be non-mission capable within about three days, which is why we are *not* committing manned aircraft to this operation."

Bunny had noticed Kovacs had looked pale at the idea of her precious airframes being turned into smoking holes in the ground across the Golan Heights. "If that's the case, Colonel, what is our plan for continuing the no-fly zone beyond that period?"

"If that happens, then Syria will be well and truly at war with Israel, and we will be organizing a rescue operation for those UN observers, not close air support." He had seen the expression on Kovacs' face and gave her a wan smile. "Cheer up, DARPA; consider this the ultimate 'proof of concept' trial."

That had all happened yesterday. And overnight, things had gotten batshit crazy in Israel.

The first reports came over radio and television, indicating that all telephone and internet links to Israel had apparently been cut. Russian media had put out a statement from its Ministry of Defense saying that an anti-satellite missile test conducted by its cruiser, the *Pyotr Morgunov*, may have 'inadvertently' shot down an Israeli communications satellite. Rumors around the base at Akrotiri said a massive space and cyberspace attack on Israel was underway. Commercial air traffic into Israel was in chaos, with pilots receiving no response from air traffic controllers and having to divert their aircraft to Lebanon, Egypt or Jordan. Two light aircraft collided over Haifa, the wreckage coming down in a residential suburb.

Bunny and the other pilots had been glued to the TV screen in their mess. *'Inadvertently shot down' my ass*, Bunny decided. The timing with the cyber attack was too much of a coincidence. The TV was also showing images of Israel taken by Egyptian news helicopters showing large parts of southern Israel completely blacked out, except for the headlights of cars traveling slowly down dark roads and motorways. And she was willing to bet that more than one Israeli satellite had been hit. You didn't lose all communication with the outside world, your air traffic control system, and your power generation network, just because a Russian missile flew wild and took out a single satellite.

Sure enough, the *Fantom* pilots were called to readiness, and by 0400 Bunny was in her trailer, with Kovacs in the jump seat again. As she approached Israeli air space, she switched her radio to a Bombardier Global 6000 aircraft which was at 30,000 feet over Cyprus, acting as 'quarterback' for US air operations over the eastern Mediterranean. Unlike the older E-3 Sentry AWACS aircraft, the Bombardier didn't have its own onboard radar systems. Instead, it was a part of the recently introduced 'Advanced Battle Management System' adopted by the US and acted as both a controller and an aggregator of data from multiple inputs: unmanned drones in the air over the Middle East, satellites, ground radars at US bases in the region, data from ships at sea and from aircraft like the *Fantoms* Bunny was flying into the Golan Heights.

It had a pretty good picture of the chaos over Israeli airspace and gave her a new ingress route that would take her over Lebanese rather than Israeli airspace. Checking the situation along the route, Bunny quickly saw why. Israel had managed to get one of its three Gulfstream G550 *Eitam* AWACS aircraft into the air to try to coordinate military air traffic, and the IDF was busy scrambling its fighter defenses. How that would help them fight a cyber warfare strike, Bunny couldn't quite see. But the US air controllers were in contact with the IDF Gulfstream, and the IDF had told them in no uncertain terms to keep US fighters out of Israeli airspace. That suited Bunny fine, she had no desire to fly her six *Fantoms* into a fraught environment filled with Israeli fighter pilots who were no doubt on edge and looking out for anything unusual to shoot at.

Like six bat-winged drones crossing Lebanon from west to east, just outside Israeli airspace.

"Leaving international airspace, entering Lebanon," Bunny told Kovacs. "We're going to hit Golani airspace from southeastern Lebanon. I'm picking up Syrian anti-air radar. Classification … S-400 *Growler*. Not good. That thing has teeth. Range is about twenty miles: they've put it right on the border. Pretty certain they can already see us. There's no Lebanese air force to worry about, but Russia might get nosy, since their definition of Syrian airspace is pretty fluid."

"We want them to see us, correct? This is not a combat patrol," Kovacs reminded her. "*Peace*keeping. Right?"

"Sure. I'll be trying to keep your *Fantoms* in one piece, if that's what you mean?"

"Not funny. I've got a bad feeling about this."

"You should have," Bunny told her. "Russia hasn't acknowledged the US no-fly zone. They might decide our presence is both illegitimate and inconvenient. Besides, one twitch of the stick in the wrong direction and we are in Syria, with that *Growler* throwing missiles at us at five times the speed of sound."

Kovacs looked pained. Bunny decided to try a little misplaced optimism.

"Look. I'll do my best to make it hard for them. Yes, we want them to see us, but I'll only have two aircraft at 30,000 feet, and the rest are going to be down in the weeds. They call it the Golan Heights for a reason. There is plenty of terrain I can use to make life difficult for that *Growler*. I'll have four of our machines down low, back inside Israeli airspace as a kind of ready reserve, if things get hot."

"I signed off on your latest additions to the combat AI routines. You really think you can manage a complex engagement with a single set of *ten* commands?"

"No," Bunny shook her head. "But your AI can. What's been holding you back is, none of your pilots trust it. Your AI can fly those machines better, closer to the edge of the envelope, than any human pilot. It can react faster to changes in the tactical environment. It doesn't get target fixation. It won't freak out or get scared. And it *learns*. Every time it makes a mistake, gets outmaneuvered, gets locked up by an enemy radar, or god forbid gets shot down, it gets smarter and knows what not to do next time. A human pilot would be dead, but your AI lives to fight the next fight, and the next…"

"Yes, but you can't just set it loose up there and expect to be able to direct the actions of six separate AIs," she warned.

"Three," Bunny reminded her. "I am only directing three.

The other three are flying wingman unless their lead is destroyed. In which case I am still only directing three. Your AI is directing the others. And I'm not flying them, my ten commands just tell them what *postures* to adopt — attack or defense, long or short range, passive or active sensor profiles, high altitude or low, aggressive or conservative ... combining those ten routines in different ways means I can give over 100 different orders. Which is more control than I would have over a human wingman who would probably forget what I told them the moment they entered combat."

Bunny hoped she sounded more convincing than she felt. She'd taken on US F-22s in a Red Flag with two *Fantoms* and won. Having faced off against the Russian 7th Air Group before over Turkey, she knew the real thing was going to be even more of a challenge.

Syrian Airspace, East of the Golan Heights, May 18

As his flight of two Su-57s got within engagement range of the Golan Heights, Lieutenant Sergei 'Rap' Tchakov of the Russian 7th Air Group was coming up against Bunny O'Hare for the second time in his short fighter pilot career, though he didn't know it.

All he knew was that the US had declared a no-fly zone over the Golan Heights and the Russian Aerospace Force inside Syria had no intention of recognizing it. Two US aircraft, probably unmanned drones judging by their electronic signatures, had just been spotted on radar over the Golan Heights and he'd been vectored to intercept them with orders to challenge whoever was flying them. Six months earlier, he'd traded missiles with an F-35 over Turkey and had barely made it home on one engine after the Coalition pilot had followed him into international airspace and then attacked him, *illegally*, after he'd made the clearly peaceful gesture of joining formation with the Coalition pilot and even waving to them, pilot to pilot. He was still smarting over that confrontation. The Coalition pilot had made a fool of him, ignoring his gesture and attacking him without warning.

Rap Tchakov was not the kind of guy who let himself be made a fool of twice. He'd even gotten a photograph of that Coalition pilot as they'd flown side by side for several minutes … a woman. She'd taken advantage of his gallantry, his chivalry. But he'd lived, and learned. He had no compassion any more for the pilots of the Coalition, and even less for the drones they sent to police their illegal, unsanctioned 'no-fly zone'. Was there a UN resolution authorizing the no-fly zone over the Golan? The hell there was. Were they brave enough to send their own human pilots to do their dirty work? The hell they were. They sent robots instead. *Robots.* It was the strategy of cowards, of men without honor.

But not of Russia. Thirty miles back from the UNDOF border, Rap set up a figure eight patrol pattern, ordering his wingman to watch his six while he worked the two drone contacts. Newly promoted to Lieutenant because of his performance in combat over Turkey, Lieutenant Sergei 'Rap' Tchakov was so named because of the music that blared through his earbuds whenever he wasn't flying. But he also liked to think it was because of the way he carried himself. Gangsta, sure, but with a code of his own. Lines he would cross, and those he wouldn't. Like attacking a foreign aircraft in international airspace who had openly declared their intention not to seek combat. For example.

Let it go, Rap, he told himself. He turned back to the task at hand. His *Felon* was pulling data from both a Syrian S-400 *Growler* ground radar unit and a *Beriev* A100 AWACS orbiting over Damascus. Of the two, the S-400 had the best lock, so close it was able to bathe the American aircraft in enough radiation to get a solid return despite the fact they were both physically small, and had an even smaller radar cross-section. Thanks to the US Presidential address, Russia's 7th Air Group had known American fighters were coming, almost to the hour.

And they'd had plenty of time to prepare.

Rap didn't need to use his own targeting radar, and doubted the Americans would even know he was hunting their aircraft. He zoomed out his tactical display, looking at all the activity over Israel. The sky was swarming with Israeli fighters – old F-15s and F-16s, and so many F-35s that even a few of the normally difficult to detect stealth fighters were visible. There was only so much airspace in which to hide over the tiny nation of Israel. Zooming out again, Rap locked the two drones up and switched his radio to the Guard frequency. "Attention US aircraft over the Golan Heights, this is Captain Ali Assad of the Syrian Arab Air Force." He smiled. Using the surname of the Syrian President was his own invention. It would make the US controllers wet their pants to think a relative of the Assad family was behind the stick of his *Felon*. He checked his knee pad and continued. "You are acting in breach of UN Security Council Resolution three three eight, which prohibits any nation from positioning military forces inside the borders of ceasefire lines in the area of the Golan Heights. Please withdraw immediately."

There was no immediate answer. Rap prepared to broadcast again. He'd asked his CO exactly *who* was expected to respond, given that there was no pilot in the American aircraft, and the actual pilot could be as far away as Nevada in the USA for all they knew. So many elements of war in the air over Syria were being explored for the first time. It gave Rap the sense he was making history with every contact with the enemy.

Still no answer. Time to escalate. "American aircraft over the Golan Heights, this is Captain Ali Assad of the Syrian Arab Air Force … I repeat, you are in breach of UN Resolution, uh … three, three, eight. If you do not withdraw immediately, you will be fired upon."

Bunny opened a channel to the controller in the US Bombardier Global 6000 aircraft. "Falcon Control, Valor flight leader. We are being hailed on Guard, do you copy?"

"Valor, Falcon, we have received the hail. Please ignore, continue your mission."

"Falcon, do you have the Russian aircraft on radar? There's nothing on my display…"

"Negative, Valor. It might also be a ground-based radio, we don't have a fix. We're working on it. Maintain patrol, Falcon out."

Ground-based my fat backside, Bunny thought to herself. "Strap in," she told Kovacs. "Metaphorically, I mean. This is how it starts."

"You really think the Russians will fire on our drones?"

"Would we?"

"I suppose so."

"Exactly."

Rap's rules of engagement, or ROEs, were very simple. He was to close to a range at which he could lock up the US aircraft on his phased-array radar – probably about twenty miles, since he already had a good fix on their position. If they did not respond to the targeting lock by withdrawing their aircraft from the airspace over the border DMZ, he was authorized to engage them with missiles, from within *Syrian* airspace. Diplomats could then argue for months about whether Syria or Russia had actually broken the terms of the ceasefire or not, but he would be sending a very clear message to the US that its 'no-fly zone' was not being recognized.

"Kogot leader to Control, I have no response on Guard, moving to engage. Please confirm?"

"Kogot, Control. You are cleared to engage, out."

"Kogot two, Kogot leader, watch my back, keep separation, keep targeting on passive systems only."

"Kogot leader, acknowledged. Happy hunting."

Rap swung his aircraft around to point its nose west and sent a high-powered beam of narrow-band radar waves down the bearing to the two US drones. "This is Kogot leader, lighting up the targets. I have a lock. Missiles armed, data synched."

A warning chime sounded inside Bunny's trailer. "Targeting radar," she said for Kovacs' benefit. "Not the *Growler*. AI is calling it a *Felon*." Her fingers danced on her keyboard, one hand on her flight stick out of habit, just in case she needed to assume manual control for any reason – like a totally random AI maneuver. "I can't see him, yet. Moving the two top cover units to aggressive-defense posture, radar active and searching, weapons safed. Bringing our reserve online, moving them into missile range." To herself she added, *Come on, Ivan, get curious, come and have a look. Cross that UNDOF line…*

The two *Fantoms* on Rap's heads-up display moved apart and as he looked down at his targeting screen he saw them each taking up station at the far northern and far southern extremes of the UN zone, forty miles apart. It made the engagement slightly more difficult, but only slightly. The important thing was that they showed no sign of withdrawing into Israeli airspace. As he watched, both of the American aircraft started radiating, searching for him with their radars. They didn't have the same long-range passive detection systems that a true stealth fighter like the F-22 or F-35 possessed, so he wasn't too worried about using his own radar, but there was always a chance that another radar system such as the Israeli ULTRA Active Electronically Scanned Array atop Mount Hermon would get a return off him or his wingman. He had to assume that the Israelis and Americans were sharing data.

"US aircraft illegally occupying the Golan demilitarized zone, this is your last warning," he said on Guard, his finger hovering over the launch button for his two K-77M missiles. "Depart the demilitarized zone immediately or you will be fired upon."

He checked his position. His K-77M traveled at Mach 5 or five times the speed of sound. At twenty miles distance, it would only take thirty *seconds* to reach its target. Taking its targeting data from his own radar, it would give almost no warning before it struck.

There was no further reaction from the American drones: they stayed anchored to their waypoints at each end of the demilitarized zone, 30,000 feet altitude. Nor was there any communication from the pilots controlling them. So be it then. *Goodbye, robots.*

He pressed the stud on the front of his flight stick with his forefinger, felt the K-77 missiles drop from his weapons bay and saw them streak out ahead of him before veering toward their targets to the north and south. In a second, the burst of flame from their rocket engines was gone, leaving just a faintly glowing smoky trail against the night sky to show where they had been.

"This is going to happen too quickly for us to follow," Bunny predicted. "I'm betting there are already missiles inbound."

"Why can't we see them on the threat warning?" Kovacs asked.

"Too close, with too many radars locked on. They won't even need to go active…"

As she was talking, a missile detection alert sounded in the trailer. Two missile detection alerts. In the millisecond before the Russian 'hit to kill' missile struck, the two *Fantoms* reacted with a speed no human could have matched, firing radar and infrared decoys behind them, rolling onto their backs and diving at the ground at a rate that would have snapped the neck of a human pilot.

The Russian missiles were not fitted with proximity warheads – they relied on sheer speed, maneuverability and surprise, and had to hit their targets to kill them. If they had the ability to be shocked, as they flew through the holes in the air where the *Fantoms* had been just a millisecond before, they would probably have cursed. As it was, they tried maneuvering to reacquire the diving *Fantoms*, but they were traveling too fast to make the turn and ended up slamming into the earth ten thousand feet below the American drones as the *Fantoms* reversed their dive and began climbing back up to altitude.

"That's my girls!" Bunny growled. "Still no target. Come on, Ivan, that all you got?"

Rap watched on his heads-up display in disbelief as his missiles flew wide, arced into a Mach 5 dive and buried themselves into the earth before they could complete their loop and reacquire the enemy drones.

"Control, Kogot leader, missiles failed to acquire. Firing with end-stage active homing. Out."

Rap wasn't worried. The American drones had evaded, but they hadn't returned his fire and he had no indication they had a radar lock on his or his wingman's aircraft. He could see the signal from the Mount Hermon Israeli radar, but it was sweeping over him without staying fixed on his position.

He was invisible and, against the faceless, pilotless aircraft, felt invulnerable. It was possible they weren't even armed. That would make sense ... the American commanders probably didn't even trust the men back on the ground in their trailers not to screw up and cause an international incident by shooting down a foreign aircraft inside Syrian airspace. He still had four air-to-air missiles in his weapons bay, and only two targets to worry about. His wingman had another six missiles.

They could keep this up all night.

"Kogot leader, I still have a target lock. Missiles armed. Firing one, firing .... two," he grunted, watching his missiles arc away into the night again. He'd fired them in terminal self-guidance mode this time ... they'd guide themselves to their targets using the data from his aircraft and the *Growler* below, but then about five miles out from their targets they would switch on their own homing radar. It would give the enemy aircraft slightly more warning, but it would also give the missiles a dramatically higher chance of scoring a kill.

Bunny O'Hare had pulled a screen on a flexible arm closer to her face and was busy with a mouse setting new navigation waypoints for the four F-47s she had skimming the ground inside Israeli airspace, about ten miles back from the Golan Heights ceasefire line.

"What are you doing?" Kovacs asked her.

"Sending in the cavalry," O'Hare told her.

Kovacs stood up and looked over her shoulder at the navigation plot. "Those waypoints are inside Syrian airspace."

"Yup." Bunny hit a key and the four F-47s began following the track she'd just laid out, spearing east from Israel, across the Golan Heights and into Syria.

"That's outside our ROE."

"Nope, operational exigency, it's called. We were fired on by an aircraft inside Syria. We are allowed to return fire in order to facilitate a withdrawal. That's what I'm doing."

"Flying into Syrian airspace is not withdrawing."

"Nuance, Kovacs," Bunny said. "That Russian will shoot again. We'll have a brief window in which to get a reverse bearing on his missiles. Watch and learn."

Sure enough, seconds later, her two high-altitude drones picked up targeting radar from incoming missiles. They punched out decoys and dived for the ground again, but they had a fix on the missiles that had been fired on them and Bunny's combat AI calculated a point of origin.

Which turned out to be 20,000 feet directly *above* the four *Fantoms* she had sent into Syria at sand dune height. With a tickle on her flight stick and tapping her keyboard with her left hand, she sent the four F-47s into a vertical power climb straight up, at the same time as she engaged the search radar on all four machines.

Floating through the sky directly above them, their fat radar-reflecting underbellies and hot rear exhaust ports exposed perfectly to Bunny's drones, were the two enemy *Felons*.

"Locking targets," Bunny told Kovacs. "Arming missiles."

A radar threat warning screamed in Rap's ears. His eyes had been glued to his tactical display, waiting for confirmation of the kills on the American drones.

What the...

As seconds elapsed without him reacting, his combat AI took control of his *Felon*, rolled it onto its back and powered into a diving turn that would give the enemy below the lowest likelihood of a good shot. His wingman had already done the same, grabbing his stick, shoving his throttle forward and following the autosteer cue in his helmet visor that told him where to point his plane to minimize the chance he'd be swatted from the sky.

Rap panted, shoved back in his seat by the acceleration, pushed up against the side of the cockpit by the force of his aircraft's turn. In his ears he registered the tone that marked one of his missiles striking home, but his vision was starting to grey out and he was waiting for the higher-pitched warbling tone telling him an enemy missile was arrowing toward him.

When it didn't come, Rap quickly decided an American drone kill was not worth dying for and pulled his machine into a high-g turn back into Syria.

"Damn," O'Hare muttered. "We lost one of our top cover birds. But we spooked those *Felons*, they're bugging out."

"You didn't engage," Kovacs observed. "You had them dead to rights."

"Don't sound so surprised," O'Hare said. "I can actually

follow orders, you know. The CO said not to engage from outside Israeli or Golani airspace, and I didn't. I'm pulling back the low-level element now. Keeping the remaining high-level element on station over the Golan so Ivan can see we aren't abandoning the high ground." She opened a channel to the US Bombardier Global 6000 AWACS. "Falcon Control, Valor flight leader, did you copy that engagement?"

"Valor leader, Falcon copies. We registered four missiles fired by hostile aircraft, one Valor bird lost."

"Valor confirms. You want us to stay on station, Falcon?"

"Affirmative, Valor leader. Losses are within acceptable parameters. Continue your patrol."

Kovacs kicked the footplate in front of her seat. "Acceptable parameters? Acceptable to who?"

"Thirty percent expected attrition per sortie, right?" O'Hare reminded her. "We're only at fifteen percent so far."

After the adrenaline-fueled few minutes they had just been through, the quiet inside the trailer felt strained, unreal.

"That engagement was a success, you realize that, right?" O'Hare asked Kovacs. "An unseen enemy got four missiles away at us, and we lost only one machine. We spooked them so badly it looks like they've pulled back. And we still hold the skies over the operations area."

"When one of your babies is dead, it's hard to celebrate the other five still being alive," Kovacs told her.

"Maybe you shouldn't be sitting in this trailer, then," O'Hare said, not without feeling. "I mean, if you're that invested? These aircraft are built to fly, fight and die. That's what they do. Sometimes we'll win, sometimes we'll lose. It may not feel like it to you, but that was a win."

"I know, I know," Kovacs said. She ran a hand through her hair. "But I can learn more sitting here watching you fly my machines in the real than I would from a thousand hours of reviewing flight data and video recordings. I never in my wildest dreams thought we would get to a state where one pilot could fly six aircraft in a combat engagement, but it just happened."

Bunny was running her eyes across her displays and reached out her hand to tap a few keys before responding. "Still happening. We're still on patrol."

Kovacs sighed and fell back in her chair. "What are the Russians doing now, do you think?"

Bunny scratched her cheek, thinking about it. "They made their point, they scored a kill. They got spooked though. Those pilots are checking with their commander, getting orders, like we did. They can still see our aircraft patrolling over the Golan Heights, but now they know we have more aircraft in the operational area than they can see."

"You think they'll attack again."

"For sure. In strength. But they have to know it would be like punching a wall made of Jello. It might make you feel good, but you aren't going to get rid of it just by punching. Aircraft can't take and hold ground, so at some point they'll either need to back off or transition to kinetic ground operations."

"But today?"

"My guess? They'll start sending ground-to-air missiles at anything they can get a lock on. Why risk piloted aircraft like they just did when they can sit on the ground and try to swat us from the sky that way?"

As though it had heard her speaking, a warbling tone filled the trailer.

Bunny pulled up her threat warning screen. "Annnnnd here it comes. That's their *Growler.*" She twitched her stick, and the simulated cockpit view showed their top cover aircraft rolling onto its back and diving for the ground.

"For controlling a single aircraft I've programmed the stick with a range of standard flight maneuvers," she told Kovacs. "So I'm not actually flying it, I'm sending it commands telling it what I want it to do. Eight directions on the gimbal, three buttons on the stick gives 32 standard maneuvers. Each pilot can program their own favorites. For me a clean down and left means execute an evasive maneuver to port and head for the dirt." They watched as an infrared image of the ground below grew larger in their sights until the aircraft leveled itself out and started skimming across the dunes. "*Growler* takes 9 to 10 seconds to get a lock and launch a missile. Plenty of time for us to pull our bird down to dune level, reposition and then pop up again," Bunny said. She reached out her arms and cracked her knuckles. "I call this tactic *Fantom* whack-a-mole." She twitched her stick again, sending her *Fantom* back up to altitude. "A few hours of this, they are *reeeeeally* going to hate us."

All Domain Attack: Insurrection

Buq'ata, Golan Heights, May 18

"Somebody really hates you," Jensen told the Israeli woman whose forehead wound Bell was cleaning as she leaned back against the wall in her hallway. After dealing with the two shooters, Jensen had left Bell to help tend to the wounded while he fetched his squad from down on the highway. There was still no sign of their UNDOF connection. They had tried their cell phones, but the network was down. At a house near the highway they'd asked to use a landline but were told that both telephone lines and electricity were down, which Jensen did not take to be a coincidence.

It was turning into a Bad Day in multiple ways.

The Israeli military had moved into the town and set up down by the highway. It had looked like they were waiting for orders before moving in, so Jensen and his squad skirted around them without attracting attention – he was not in the mood for explaining their presence, not yet, anyway. He'd put his people to work helping the walking wounded and shifting the bodies.

"Yes. There have been incidents," the woman said, wincing as Bell dabbed her wound with disinfectant. "Since the Syrian civil war. Bad feeling between pro- and anti-Assad factions, and lately, between the Syrian Druze and Israeli settlers. Around 2020 the government declared that Israel was a Jewish State, which didn't help relations." She gestured at the people around. "But there has been nothing like this." She gestured at the ruined buildings around the intersection. "These are Druze businesses. Syrian Arabic. But Israeli settlers would not do this."

Bell finished working on her wound. "Best I can do for now, ma'am," he said. "You should get antibiotics soon as you can." Bell pointed at himself, then Jensen. "Corporal Calvin

Bell, US Marine Corps, and the big ugly one is Gunnery Sergeant James Jensen."

The woman held out her hand to shake. "My name is Amal Azaria," she said. "I am a Corporal in the IDF. This is…" she looked out the shattered doorway at the street beyond where cars were still smoldering, "… this *was* my brother's furniture shop. I need to get in touch with my unit to report this. Can you stay and help the wounded?" she asked Bell.

Jensen nodded to him.

"Sure, ma'am."

Jensen sized her up, taking a real look at her for the first time. She was about five ten or eleven, wearing jeans, a black t-shirt and a military-style jacket, looked to be in her mid-thirties, had raven black hair and olive skin, with a spray of freckles across her nose. And she didn't appear at all fussed that her face was still covered with her own dried blood.

"I saw some IDF troops gathered at the outskirts of town, looked like they were waiting for orders to push in."

"They will have a radio," she said, standing. "Where?"

"I'll show you," he said. "I need a radio too, to get in touch with our UN contact."

They walked around a line of bodies and past the still smoking wreck of a car. "You have no idea who did this?" he asked.

"No. Feelings have been running high but there has never been this kind of violence between Israeli settlers and Druze Syrians," she said.

"Druze Syrians? Buq'ata is not Israeli and Jewish?"

She looked at him curiously. "Who are you, that you do not know this?"

"Ma'am," he said tersely, "we literally stepped straight off a flight from Kobani and into your firefight, so you'll excuse my ignorance."

"I'm sorry. But I'm glad you were here today."

"You are pretty handy with an assault rifle yourself, for a shop owner," he observed.

She gave him a slight smile. "Every Israeli serves three years in the People's Army. I am a communications reservist in Golani Brigade, *Palhik* Signals Company. But the shop is my brother's. In real life I'm a robotics engineer."

"In that case, you are pretty handy with an assault rifle, for a robotics engineer." Jensen pointed. "The roadblock was down here," he said.

She frowned and followed as he led the way back down the main road to the south. "Why have they not come in to help?"

He shrugged. "How many Israelis live here?" he asked.

"Most of the population are Syrian Druze," she said as they walked. "The Druze are a separate religious group, not Jewish, not Muslim. Buq'ata became part of Israel in the 1980s and about ten percent of the population is Israeli now. The other ninety percent still think of themselves as Syrian. They accept Israeli resident status, but most won't take citizenship or carry an Israeli passport."

"Doesn't exactly sound like a friendly neighborhood."

"We have lived in peace most of the time," she said. "The Druze religion has much in common with Judaism. We say there is Covenant of Blood between us…"

"I saw that today," Jensen said wryly.

"Not usually bad blood," Amal replied. "Today was … something different. Something new."

They turned a corner and saw the roadblock that Jensen and his Marines had bypassed – two military vehicles drawn up across the road, and several soldiers in dark green uniforms – but he noticed immediately that there was an officer with them now. Although they were still about thirty yards away he could tell from the number of stripes on the man's shoulders that he was a colonel.

Which seemed to be a very high rank for a guy manning a roadblock. The officer saw Jensen and Amal at about the same time. He also saw that both of them were carrying assault rifles. Reaching behind himself he motioned for a bullhorn and called out something in Hebrew.

Amal took her rifle from her shoulder. "He says we should lay down our rifles and approach." She bent to put her rifle on the ground. "It is standard procedure until we identify ourselves."

There was something wrong with the picture. Jensen's blood was still pumped full of adrenaline, so maybe he was overreacting, paranoid … but shouldn't that colonel and his men have been in the center of the town, checking on the situation, trying to restore order, as Amal had expected? Why were they back here, manning a *roadblock*? "Wait," Jensen said, going down to one knee beside her as though putting his rifle down too. "Do you recognize him? The officer?"

She looked up quickly. "No. The uniform is Golani Brigade. Recon Battalion, I think. Why?"

Jensen nodded at the troops behind the colonel, all of whom had stopped lounging around and were now standing with weapons at the ready.

"And those men?"

She squinted. "Those are … not Golani. They're Sword Battalion, Druze soldiers. But the Sword Battalion was disbanded. I haven't seen those uniforms for years. That's strange."

Strange. That was all Jensen needed to hear. "Pick up your rifle."

"What?"

"Get up slowly. Pick. Up. Your. Rifle."

As she rose to her feet again, Jensen raised both hands in the air, one of them holding his rifle high so they could see it. "American! United Nations!" he yelled. "I want to speak with your commanding officer."

"What are you doing?" Amal asked.

The officer lifted his bullhorn again. "I am commander here. Put down your weapons and approach," he repeated.

"Get behind me," Jensen told her. He looked over his shoulder. The street corner was about ten yards behind them.

"Why?"

"When did you ever see a full colonel in charge of a damn roadblock?" he asked her in a low voice. "He must have seen or heard that blast. Or even heard the gunfire from here. These men should have moved up by now. Something isn't right here."

Jensen raised his voice again, calling out to the troops on the roadblock. "We need medical help, in town! Come with us!" Jensen waved his free arm, pointing back the way they had come.

The Israeli colonel turned and handed the bullhorn to a man behind him, and barked an order. Walking out from the barricade, he moved quickly toward Jensen and Amal, exuding calm and confidence. Behind him, though, Jensen could see his men had taken up firing positions and were covering him.

As he approached, Jensen could see him weighing them both up. He was almost a carbon copy of the Marine Gunnery Sergeant in height and age, but about 20lbs. lighter and five ranks his senior. If he was expecting Jensen to salute him, he was about to be disappointed. Jensen stood at ease, with his rifle crossed casually across his chest.

"American?" the man asked as he stopped in front of them.

"First Battalion, 3rd Marines, attached to the UNDOF," Jensen told him.

"I wasn't aware there were any Americans stationed with UNDOF. And you seem to be missing your blue helmet, *Sergeant*," the man said, emphasizing his rank. He turned to Amal and spoke in Hebrew. "And you?"

"Corporal Azaria, *Palhik* Company, *Gadsar* Battalion," she replied. "I need to contact my unit."

"What did you say about needing help?" the colonel asked, turning to Jensen again.

"There was a terrorist attack. There are dead and wounded in the town center. An IED exploded and then they started shooting civilians with automatic weapons."

"Where are the two shooters now?" he asked.

Jensen tensed. He had not told him there were *two* shooters.

"They are dead too," Amal told him.

The colonel's eyes narrowed briefly, but he nodded. "Join my men. There is a civil emergency across Israel, not just here. We have established a perimeter around the town. I was about to send my men in to secure it."

Amal shot a look at Jensen, her eyes telling him all he needed to know. *This is not normal.* "I live here. I can guide them," she offered.

He smirked. "Thank you, *Corporal,* and you, *Sergeant.* But your help is not needed. My men can take it from here."

Jensen pointed with his chin over the man's shoulder and laughed. "Those goofballs?"

The colonel turned to see what he was referring to, and Jensen moved. He swung his rifle around and brought the stock up under the man's throat, hauling him backwards into a chokehold that put the officer between Jensen and the soldiers on the roadblock. They shouted, raising their rifles and training them on Jensen and Amal as they started to back away, dragging the IDF colonel with them.

He was choking and spluttering, grabbing the barrel of Jensen's rifle in both hands as he tried to relieve the pressure on his throat, but Jensen kept him moving, heels dragging as he backed away from the roadblock toward the corner just behind them. Without anyone telling them what to do, the soldiers behind the vehicles were limited to yelling and pointing with their rifles, but they made no move to pursue. As they reached the corner, Amal ran around it and Jensen moved out of the line of fire, but left the colonel's thrashing legs out in full view so that his men could see he was still being held.

"Get on this corner, watch both ways. If anyone on that roadblock moves out, put a round into one of the vehicles and keep their heads down."

Amal moved up and trained her rifle around the corner. "Alright."

The officer was still kicking and grunting, trying to wrench himself free, but Jensen had him in an iron grip and pulled it tighter. "I can choke you dead, or you can stop struggling, your choice, Colonel," Jensen said through gritted teeth.

The man stopped struggling and Jensen eased his grip, just enough to let him draw breath, making sure the troops at the roadblock could still see at least his shins and boots and see he was alive.

"Your name?"

"Screw ... you ..." the colonel said.

"Amal, his pockets."

She pulled back, put down her rifle and quickly went through the pockets of his uniform, finding cigarettes, a wallet, and an ID card.

"Lieutenant Colonel Zeidan Amar, Reconnaissance Battalion, Golani Brigade," she said, showing Jensen the card. "I know the name. He is Druze."

"Druze in the Golani Brigade?" Jensen asked, surprised.

"I told you, a Covenant of Blood," she said. "There are many Druze in the IDF. But those other men are not Golani Brigade. This is something else."

"Tell me, Zeidan Amar, what is a Golani Brigade Lieutenant Colonel doing at a roadblock in Buq'ata with a bunch of Druze militia?"

"Screw you," the colonel spat. "American."

"There was a terrorist attack here, you know anything about that?"

"If there is ... a terrorist here ... it is you," the man said.

"Not a lot of sympathy for his fellow citizens, Amal."

"No."

"Take his pistol, check him for other weapons."

She pulled a pistol from a holster on his belt, then continued searching him, patting down his legs. From his boot she pulled a serrated hunting knife and threw it onto the street behind them.

"Rifle, Amal."

She put the pistol into her own belt, picked up her X-95 bullpup and crouched at the corner again, barrel trained on the

184

roadblock.

"There are fewer men now," she said.

"They're trying to flank us. We need to pull back," Jensen grunted. "Alright, Colonel," he said. "I'm going to release you. If you don't start running back to that roadblock, I'll put a 6.8mm round in your ass. Understood?" He tightened his grip on the man's throat.

"Screw ... you."

"You need to learn more English," Jensen said. "Amal? Cover our rear."

"Yes." She spun and sighted down her rifle at the street behind them.

Jensen released his left hand, stepping back and putting a boot into the colonel's back as he tried to rise. The man stumbled forward and fell on his face, trying to scrabble to his feet.

Jensen lifted his rifle, sighting on the man's back, and tapped Amal's shoulder. "Alright, we go back to the roundabout. Nice and easy, understood? Check your corners. You take point, I'll watch behind us. Warning shots if any civilians get in our way. But anything that looks like armed Druze military opening up on us, return fire."

She nodded and started moving. The Israeli colonel wasn't running. He was standing in the street, glaring at them. The last Jensen saw of him as they rounded the next corner was him shrugging off the hands of one of his soldiers as they ran up to him, trying to pull him back into cover.

In about two minutes they'd made it back to the roundabout. The burned-out cars were still smoking, scattered in a circle in front of the roundabout. There were still a few civilians milling around. Some of the wounded were being loaded into pickups to be driven to hospital. One shopkeeper was already out with a broom, sweeping shattered glass out of his shop and into the street. He saw Bell was also treating a number of walking wounded, most with cuts from flying metal and glass. There was a lot of blood, and Bell had set two of the others to tearing up bandages.

Jensen ran through their situation in his mind's eye. That officer back at that roadblock had probably been waiting for his two shooters to report back, which was why he hadn't come in to check for himself. That indicated he was the cautious type – and right now he had no idea how many or few Marines there were in Buq'ata town center. A cautious man would send a couple of scouts in, or send a drone over to scope out the tactical situation ... which gave them precious minutes. "Buckland, Stevens, behind that car," Jensen ordered. "Cover the street we just came in on. Anyone military approaches, fire a warning shot." He walked over to Bell, keeping his voice low and calm. "We need to get moving. You about done here?"

Bell nodded to a small group of people standing on the curb nearby, watching fearfully. "Those guys were begging us not to leave them before. They're Jewish, say the Druze are going to blame them for this attack and kill them all."

"Hell they are." He called Amal over. "We need to bug out before that colonel gets his act together and moves on us. You know those people?"

"Yes."

"Bell says they're scared of the Druze."

"Well..."

"Is it possible that colonel and his men will come in here and start rounding up the Jewish residents?"

"Possible, yes, I guess so. To question them. And Israeli citizens would make good leverage in case the IDF tries to intervene here."

"Leverage? That's all I needed to hear. Corporal Azaria, we need to keep moving. We need a more defensible position, and we need to get a message out about what is happening here."

"We should go to my house. That way," she said, pointing.

"With respect, Corporal, is your house the most defensible position in this town?"

She nodded. "It backs onto a quarry. If they have put roadblocks on the main entry and exit roads, it would be in between them. It's a two-story concrete home with a rooftop terrace and high walls."

Jensen considered it. "Well, that sounds…"

"And the workshop in my backyard is full of military ordnance."

"… sounds pretty much perfect, I guess," Jensen said.

"Plus, my IDF tactical radio is at home."

"I'm sold. Go get those settlers organized to follow us." Jensen moved to the base of the sculpture in the middle of the roundabout. He started bellowing as soon as he reached it. "LAVA DOGS! Form up. Grab your gear. On me, now!"

There were no questions, just the sound of running boots, hardware and bags being lifted off the ground. In minutes seven bodies were crowded around him. After a short discussion with Amal, about ten civilians joined them too. Several were wounded.

"Situation," Jensen yelled over the top of their heads. "The target of this attack appears to have been the local Druze population. The identity of the attackers is not known. What I do know, a hostile force has surrounded this town, they have roadblocks at the main entrances and exits. They are commanded by an IDF colonel, and they include armed Druze militia. Dark green uniforms. They may attempt to either capture or kill us. Do any of you Devil Dogs feel like being killed or captured today?"

"Sergeant, no Sergeant!!" the Marines replied as one. There were no questions, only resigned looks. It was Kobani again, just written smaller. Same shit, different country. A Marine's fate. Jensen took Amal's arm and pulled her forward. "This is Corporal Azaria of the Israeli Defense Forces Golani Brigade. She is going to lead us to a place where we can establish a defensive position and attempt to radio for help."

Bell stepped out of her way. "Lead on, ma'am."

West Wing, Washington, DC, May 18

President Henderson had morphed from resolute to wracked with doubt in the space of an hour. The consequences of his speech to the nation – to the world – had been immediate. World leaders, Congressmen and Senators were queued to speak with him, the Dow Jones stock market index had dived eight percent, the partisan news media had lost its collective mind, either in a fervor of patriotic flag waving or in doomsday sensationalism.

And then the news had broken that Israel had experienced, was still experiencing, a massive cyber attack by 'unknown actors'. Following on the heels of the announcement of the US blockade and no-fly zone, aimed at Iran, Syria and Russia, the media had quickly decided who the 'unknown actors' were, even if Henderson declined to name them. But leading the headlines on the bulletins was the news, the apparent confirmation, that Iran had joined the ever-growing club of nuclear armed nations. Coupled with the cyber attack – the media hadn't yet been briefed on the scale of the Russian anti-satellite offensive – pundits were predicting either a full-scale military assault on Israel at any moment, or a full-scale Israeli air assault on Iran, Syria or both.

The 24-hour news channels were also showing 'real-time' plots of the progress of the Russian-Iranian fleet as it made its way out of the Bosphorus Strait and through the Sea of Marmara into the Greek Aegean Sea, which led into the Mediterranean. Henderson had deliberately and, unfortunately for those who liked a little dramatic tension, annoyingly not painted a clear 'red line in the sea' for the news anchors to draw viewers' attention to. But that didn't stop them from reaching a pretty accurate consensus based on his declaration that any Iranian ship 'entering the Mediterranean' would be subject to the blockade. That put the Mediterranean red line at the southeastern edge of the Aegean Sea, just outside the Greek Dodecanese islands of Crete, Karpathos and Rhodes.

Henderson had retired to the West Wing with VP Ben Sianni, Carmine Lewis and Defense Secretary Harry McDonald and turned off the TV they had been watching. They were killing time, waiting on a call from the Russian President. "How accurate is that picture they're painting?" he asked McDonald.

"Not too far off. I can get a screen brought up with a feed from the situation room if you want, but it won't change the basics. The Aegis destroyers *Donald Cook*, *Porter* and *Roosevelt* are with the fast combat support ship *Supply* and the British sub *Agincourt* just east of Rhodes. They'll be joined by USS *Canberra*, which is transiting the Suez Canal as we speak. The *Sam Nunn* has taken over the job of towing the *Besat* to Port Sudan. The captured Iranian crew will be released once it gets to port."

"We don't seriously expect the Russians to allow us to sail into the middle of their formation to stop and search those Iranian warships, right?" Sianni asked. He had an abiding distrust of Russia going back to the time his father had fled Chechnya to escape marauding Russian troops who had wiped out most of his extended family. "If they want to force the issue, they'll put a ring of destroyers and cruisers around them and dare us to try."

"No, Ben," Henderson said, running his hand across his tired face. "We're leaving the specifics to the Joint Chiefs, but the basics are that we'll hail the fleet as soon as it gets in range. We've already identified the Iranian ships among them, and we'll demand they stop so they can be searched. If they don't, and they proceed into the Med with the Russians, the Brits could put a torpedo in one of them, but let's hope it doesn't come to that."

"Britain has agreed to that?" Sianni asked, surprised.

Carmen nodded. "The RAF had more than a few casualties over Turkey. It didn't enhance their love for Russia."

"The British PM actually volunteered the support of their sub, the *Agincourt*," Henderson added. "It's a pretty safe move – any sub attacks an Iranian ship, the world will assume it's American. But we don't have a boat in position right now. The

British sub was already there on exercises."

Sianni was still playing it through in his mind. "And if Russia responds by finding and sinking the *Agincourt*? How do we stop this from escalating into a shooting war between our destroyers and the Russians?"

"That's the reason for my next call," Henderson said. As though on cue, an aide stepped into the office.

"President Navalniy on the telephone for you, Mr. President."

The world had yet to get the measure of the new Russian President, who had won the recent Russian elections in a landslide following the sudden death by heart attack of Vladimir Putin while riding his horse bare-shirted across a frozen river. Never much interested in anointing a successor while he'd been alive, Putin had left the perfect vacuum for the populist Alexei Navalniy to step into, walking Nelson Mandela-like directly from his prison cell into the Kremlin.

Russia's support for Syria in the Turkish conflict had been set in motion by Putin, but Navalniy had shown no inclination to stop. To the contrary, he had poured even more men and equipment into Syria since. It clearly suited him to show his people that its true enemy was outside its borders, not within, and that he would continue Putin's work of expanding Russia's footprint in the world once again. Nelson Mandela he was not.

Henderson walked to his desk as the others reached for earpieces so that they could follow the conversation without it having to be put on speakerphone. Henderson had wanted to give the impression of a person-to-person call, even though both men knew there would be people listening in on both sides. They had met face to face at a number of economic summits, but were not on what you might call first-name terms.

"President Navalniy, thank you for calling," Henderson began.

The Russian President preferred to speak Russian in media interviews, giving the impression that he was not fluent in English, which he had become after a year at Yale University.

confidence."

"Israel can deal with Syria alone, Mr. President, we both know that. All I am suggesting is the withdrawal of Iran's naval and missile forces. In return, we can perhaps achieve a new era of peace and stability in the Middle East together."

"You make it sound so easy, President Henderson. I fear the devil will be in the detail, as you Americans like to say. But I will discuss your proposal with my cabinet and our allies."

"Thank you, Mr. President, and may I suggest that while you do so, you ask Admiral Gromyko of your Black Sea fleet to sail a little slower through the Aegean?"

Navalniy chuckled. "I think you have not met Admiral Gromyko, Mr. President? I would no sooner tell him how to sail his ships than you would tell me how to run my country. Good evening to you, sir."

"And to you, President Navalniy."

Sianni didn't even wait for the phone to hit the cradle on the Resolute desk. "The bastard is going to test us. There is not a chance in hell those Russian ships will back off."

Lewis' phone started buzzing, but she silenced it. She could get to her messages when they were finished debriefing on the call. She couldn't disagree with the VP's analysis. Still… "All that matters is that it looks like Tonya was right. Iran wants a deal with Israel and Russia is behind them. Syria wants the Golan Heights, and Navalniy threw that into the pot too, but I suspect they'll pull back on that if they can get the credit for inking a missile treaty between Iran and Israel."

"Did you hear him denying Russia is behind the cyber attack? 'We stand ready to help' my wrinkled ass," Sianni muttered. "And you never mentioned the fact their missile cruiser just swatted ten Israeli satellites from the sky while they say they shot down one, 'by accident'."

"They know we know, Ben. They know Israel knows. What matters is, he all but admitted the goal is a treaty between Israel and Iran and Golan is a sideshow."

"A treaty with Navalniy as the peacemaker? What a joke. We

give him that, we give Russia the Middle East from Lebanon to Iran."

"I'd be happy to hear the Vice President's alternate strategy," Lewis said carefully.

Sianni didn't hesitate. "It's the same as the Joint Chiefs are advocating outside this room. Get right in behind Israel and smack this gorilla in the face. A massive air assault on Syrian forces launched from Israel, Cyprus and the *Nimitz* in the Gulf. Knock out their air defense, communications and control and destroy every damn tank and missile on the ground, whether it's Syrian, Russian or Iranian. Stop firing fishing nets at Iranian warships and put mines or torpedoes in their hulls if they try to enter the Red Sea or the Med. Send a battalion of US infantry to reinforce Israeli outposts up and down the border."

Carmine listened respectfully. She knew well what the belligerent generals of the Joint Chiefs were advocating behind closed doors in Washington, and she knew their view was gaining traction not least because it played perfectly to the hearts and minds of the Jewish lobby.

"The Joint Chiefs, for all their words about modernization, still think putting ordnance on targets is the solution to everything," she responded. "Say we do all that? Will that stop the cyber attacks? Covert anti-satellite activities? Or will it just expose us to a massive retaliatory attack on US space and cyber infrastructure? If we defang a nuclear-armed Iran without destroying all of its nuclear weapons, will that make it more or less likely they'll use a nuke? Even this massive air assault – how does that even work? It isn't a Syrian or Iranian air force in the skies over Syria. It is Russian. US forces didn't shoot down a single Russian aircraft in Turkey, only Turkish Coalition Forces were engaged – for a reason. So how will Russia react if US aircraft start smacking Russian aircraft out of the sky over Syria? Do the Joint Chiefs really think Russia will just pack up and go home, or are they looking for a bare-knuckle fist fight with Russia that can only end one way?"

Sianni wasn't backing off. "No one ever got what they

wanted by playing nice with Russia. If we keep going down the non-confrontation path, they will win. You'll see."

Henderson, who had been listening to them both, reached for the TV remote and turned the TV on again. It was still showing a map in a small window on the news feed of the Russian-Iranian fleet in red, US warships in blue, and a dashed white line across the Aegean Sea marking the entry into the Mediterranean, with the Russian fleet getting closer by the minute.

"I may be a simple man, Ben, but this particular scenario does not appear non-confrontational to me."

Buq'ata, Golan Heights, May 18

As the Marines jogged up a winding driveway to the IDF corporal's house, a worried man appeared in the doorway with a small child. He looked past Jensen to the Marines and townsfolk behind, some bandaged, some – like Amal – still bleeding. "Amal?" She ran to him, took what was apparently her child and pulled him inside the house. Jensen could see he still had a lot to learn about Amal Azaria.

While she was gone Jensen walked the yard, and the more he walked, the more he liked what he saw. He even wondered if the IDF reservist had picked it with this day in mind. Like the other houses in Buq'ata, it was made of double-walled aerated concrete blocks. A green painted chest-high concrete wall ran around the front and sides of the house. At the rear of the house, flanked by the walls, was a large metal shed, and at the rear of the shed, the ground to the east fell steeply away into a gravel quarry. It was scalable, but no one would be rushing them from that direction. The walls around the house gave open fields of fire for at least a hundred yards to the west, south and north.

"Gear in the house, let the corporal direct you," Jensen said. "Then get back out here with weapons and ammunition."

He stood surveying the ground. When the squad was assembled again, Jensen gave them positions on the perimeter. "Buckland and Stevens, the wall to the west, Wallace and Lopez, south, Johnson, north with me." He turned and looked up at the roof of the house. He could see a sun umbrella up there. "Patel, on the roof with that Mk22 MRAD, alright?" Patel grinned; he wasn't about to let anyone else play with his new toy anyway. "Bell, you are his spotter, keep an eye on that quarry to the east too. Anyone sees anything in a green uniform, call it out."

Jensen waited until everyone was in position, and made some adjustments to ensure his people on the perimeter had overlapping fields of fire, then went inside to check the layout of the house. The civilians were huddled in the downstairs living room, which he didn't like, so he had them move upstairs where there were bedrooms and a bathroom. While he was upstairs, he heard a blazing argument start downstairs. A man and a woman, shouting in Arabic. He walked cautiously down the stairs. Immediately, the man he had assumed was Amal's husband came stomping out of the kitchen with a child in his arms, and a backpack over his back. He pulled a set of keys off the wall and, without a backward look, pushed past Jensen and stormed out of the house.

Amal came out behind him, looking pained. "My brother. We have an aunt at Qiryat Shemona, about fifteen miles west. I sent him there with my son. He was not happy, but I do not want Raza here."

"What about the Druze roadblocks?"

"We grew up here. He knows the back roads."

"You could go too," Jensen told her. "Leave us the radio, go with your brother."

Amal looked at him like he had insulted her. "This town is my home. These people are my people. I am staying."

He nodded. "Your call, Corporal. Now, someone needs to look after those people upstairs, and you are too valuable to be babysitting them."

"I will see to it." She went up the stairs and in a few moments was back again with a grey-haired old lady who looked to be at least seventy. She had a bandage over a burn on her arm.

Amal pulled her forward. "This is Gadeer. She used to be a nurse. She will take care of the townsfolk, keep an eye on the injured."

The old lady reached out her hand and Jensen thought she meant to shake it, but she grabbed his hand in both of her own and gripped it tight. She spoke quickly in Arabic for a couple of minutes, then waited for Amal to translate.

"She wants to say 'thank you'."

"All that for thank you? She's welcome."

"She also said to tell you that it was not anyone from Buq'ata who did this. Jewish and Druze have lived here for decades without problems. This is outsiders."

"I understand."

The old woman shook his hand firmly one more time, then climbed back up the stairs.

The IDF corporal leaned on the stairs watching her go. She looked thoughtful, no doubt reflecting on her decision to send her son and brother away. Jensen put a hand on her shoulder gently. "Corporal, I desperately need to contact the UN unit at Merom Golan. Your radio?"

She pulled her hair back over her ears. "Yes. Of course. It is upstairs. Follow." She took the stairs two at a time. In a few moments she appeared from a bedroom with a small digital transceiver unit on a shoulder strap which she slung over her shoulder. She pulled up the long rubberized whip antenna. "We should go up to the terrace," she said.

He followed her upstairs to where a spiral staircase led from a small passageway up to the roof. He saw with satisfaction that Bell and Patel had moved some concrete planter boxes into a rough square in the middle of the terrace to give themselves some additional cover, though the rooftop appeared to be the highest point for about a mile around. He looked up at the sun.

Mid-morning already. It was going to be hot up here, umbrella or not. "Bell, go fill some bottles with drinking water, bring them up here and stay hydrated."

"Aye aye, Sarge."

"All clear so far, Sarge. Civilian foot traffic is all," Patel told him.

"Thanks, Corporal." Jensen knelt down next to Amal, who had sat herself on the rooftop with her legs crossed and the radio in front of her. "Call your unit first. Tell them the situation here. See if they can send help."

"Yes." She turned on the radio and pulled a handset from its cradle. In a few minutes she was talking rapidly in Hebrew. Jensen couldn't follow what was being said, and didn't even know enough Hebrew to know if she was sounding glad or mad. But he didn't like the look on her face when she put the handset back in its cradle.

"Bad news?"

"The commanding officer of the Golani Brigade was assassinated. Colonel Zeidan Amar was appointed acting commander."

"That guy we tackled?! A brigade commander? So what in hell is he doing at a roadblock in Buq'ata during a civil emergency?"

"That is the question. My friend in *Palhik* Company said Colonel Amar has been reported missing. He left Mount Hermonit after the assassination and has not been seen since. My friend doubted that this man could be Colonel Amar."

"You saw his ID card. Did it look genuine?"

"Yes. I don't understand."

"We don't have to understand. We just need to get ourselves out of this cluster. Is your unit able to send someone in to get us?"

"No. My CO was told what is happening here, but said he has no one to spare. The whole country is in chaos. I was ordered to join my unit at our unit base in Mas'ade if I can. The Brigade is pulling out, heading west to our headquarters at

Camp Shraga."

"West? I thought the whole Syrian army was lined up on the border to the east?"

"So did I."

"By whose orders are they withdrawing?"

"Colonel Zeidan Amar."

Jensen scratched his jaw. "My folks were South Bend Irish. We have a saying: 'Don't be breaking your shin on a stool that's not in your way.'"

Amal frowned. "I don't understand."

"It means that whether that officer was Colonel Zeidan Amar, why he is here and if he ordered your Golani Brigade to pull back to base, is not our problem right now."

"Not your problem, perhaps, but it is mine, and a problem for the people of Buq'ata," she said with fire in her eyes. "Many of whom are now mourning their dead."

Jensen flinched. "I'm sorry. That was stupid. Let's see if we can get help from somewhere else. You know what frequencies UNDOF uses? Because I don't."

"Yes, we have a coordination channel. They will be able to put you through to their base at Merom Golan."

Jensen felt his hopes lift. At last, something was going right.

Zeidan Amar surveyed the damage in the center of Buq'ata. There was no sign of the Americans, or the IDF corporal. He saw a woman kneeling by the body of an old man on a sidewalk, keening, a small crowd gathered around her. Some shopkeepers were already starting to sweep glass and debris out of their shops. He motioned to a local police officer. "Get the bodies off the street. What about the seriously wounded?"

"We sent them to the hospital at Mas'ade."

Amar pointed at the wrecked vehicles. "Get a truck and have these towed away."

"Yes, Colonel." The man walked over to the small group around the body and started speaking with them.

Zeidan motioned to one of his men and took the bullhorn once more, climbing up onto the roof of his *Storm* utility vehicle. "Israeli citizens of Buq'ata! You are not safe here. We cannot protect you. All Israeli citizens should evacuate, now. It is not safe in Buq'ata. You must leave, now." Fearful, confused faces stared back at him. He handed the bullhorn back to the corporal. "Start moving around town, repeat what I said. If anyone asks you, we are evacuating all Israeli citizens, by my order. They are to leave *immediately*. Understood?"

"Yes, Zeidan. And if they do not?"

"If they do not leave by lunchtime, then they will become guests of the armed forces of Syrian Golan."

Zeidan walked over to a shopkeeper who had returned to pulling broken glass from a window frame. "Your name, friend?" he asked in Arabic.

The man had his back to him and jumped. "You scared me. Labib Hanifes," he replied, also in Arabic.

Druze. Good. "This is your shop?"

"It is."

"My men will help you clean up. The people who did this will be found."

"Thank you."

Zeidan gestured around him. "This was a parting gift from the Zionists."

"Perhaps. Someone said the men with guns were Druze. They recognized one of them."

"*Someone* was wrong. Tell me, friend, there was a young woman here, an IDF corporal. She fought back against the terrorists. Her last name is Azaria. Did you see her?"

"With the Americans, yes." The man turned and nodded at a wrecked shopfront across the road. "That was their store."

"Yes. I wish to thank her. Where did they go?"

The old man pointed. "The east road. She has a house near the quarry. Perhaps there."

Zeidan shouted to two of his men loitering near the roundabout and ordered them to help the old man, then stood

200

looking up the east road.

The loss of two of his men in the 'terrorist' attack was an inconvenience. But the presence of a squad of Marines and that damn IDF corporal were more than that. Amar's timetable was now being sorely tested. By now he should have been in full control of Buq'ata. This was supposed to be the first and easiest phase of the operation. Having achieved control of the largest Druze township in the Golan Heights, he was then to make a declaration over local radio in his own name of its provisional independence from Israel, and alliance with the Syrian regime. The third phase of the operation – at a time and date to be agreed with his Syrian contacts – would be to invite the Syrian government to send troops into Buq'ata to protect it from Israeli reoccupation.

By that time, he was supposed to be well dug in and to have been joined by Russian 'advisors' – false-flagged troops waiting just across the border in the ruins of the old town of Quneitra in Syria. The Russian unit was made up of a platoon of T-14 *Armata* tanks and crews operated by a private security company – Strauss Security – but his information was its personnel had been drawn from the Russian 2nd Guards Motor Rifle Division.

Knowing what little he did about Syria's ambitions for the Golan Heights, he felt it was a sound strategy. Provoke a security situation in Druze-held Buq'ata during a nationwide civil emergency. Refuse any help from the IDF and accept the help offered by Syria. Reinforce Buq'ata with battle-hardened troops and the latest in Russian main battle tanks, more than a match for anything Israel could throw against them. And from this position of strength, negotiate for the return of the Golan Heights to Syrian rule.

With Colonel Zeidan Amar as the Provincial Governor.

There was only one problem with this elegant plan, and that was the handful of US Marines currently unaccounted for in Buq'ata. He had no concerns about the toothless UN force five miles away, but the one thing he didn't need was the US conducting a major attack on his position to free their trapped Marines.

The humiliation of his earlier capture burned in his gut. But that was nothing in the greater scheme of things. He called out to one of his men, his best scout.

"Abdullah, you have your map?"

"Yes, here."

Zeidan unfolded the map on the hood of a still warm wrecked car. He was relatively familiar with Buq'ata from his childhood, but it had grown. *The east road ... yes, here.* He put a finger down on the map. "Do you see this road? It goes up a small hill and there is a house at the end of the road, in front of this quarry. Got it?"

"Yes."

"Make your way up there. Alone. Don't let yourself be seen. I want you to check that house, our American guests may be hiding there. Take a radio, contact me when you're there."

Fifteen minutes later, his scout called in. Six or seven Marines at least, in defensive positions inside the grounds of the house. And there were civilians in the house. "There's no easy approach, the place is built like a compound, concrete walls on three sides, big metal shed and a sheer drop at the back. They do not look like they are planning to leave soon, Colonel," the man said.

"We'll see about that."

Amal dialed in the UNDOF frequency and put the radio handset to her ear. "UNDOF duty operator, this is Corporal Azaria, Unit 351, *Palhik* Company, for the commander of UNDOF Merom Golan, come in."

She listened to the reply and then reached down and hit a button so the sound came out of the unit speaker. "... ahead, Corporal, patching you through to the duty officer at Merom Golan, please wait, UNDOF operations coordination out."

Jensen felt a tension rising in his gut. He needed to be clear about what he wanted. What he wanted? He wanted a big white UN armored personnel carrier to come rolling into town to help evacuate any wounded and take him and his squad where they were supposed to be. Merom Golan was just five miles away. How hard could that be?

"Corporal Azaria, this is Second Lieutenant van Leenan, duty officer UNDOF Merom Golan. How can I assist?"

"Lieutenant van Leenan, I have a US Marine sergeant here to speak with your commander…"

The Dutch UN officer interrupted. "Our commanding officer is not available, Corporal, ask the American to…"

Jensen grabbed the handset. "Lieutenant, this is Gunnery Sergeant James Jensen of the 1st Marines, 3rd Battalion. Myself and my squad were to report to Colonel Willem Cort of UNDOF Merom Golan today, but our transport did not arrive and…"

"Yes, Sergeant, well, as you can appreciate, with Israel declaring a national emergency, things have been a little busy around here this morning so I'm sorry you missed your ride. We aren't a bloody taxi service. Where are you? I will see if we can…"

"Lieutenant! With respect, sir, please listen. We are in Buq'ata. There was a terrorist attack. Multiple civilians have been killed and wounded. We killed two of the terrorists but we believe that local Druze militia are…"

"What? You did *what?*"

"We killed two terrorists, active shooters, in the act of defending the civilian population. We are currently holed up in a house in Buq'ata with Israeli civilians who fear for their safety. We need immediate evacuation…"

"My God, man! What have you done? We do not intervene in Israeli civil affairs!"

Jensen lifted the handset away from his ear and stared at it. He looked to Amal for a cue, but her face was blank. He put the handset back against his ear. "… created a diplomatic incident, at best. I want the name of your commanding officer back in the States. Now!"

"Lieutenant, I don't know how the UN runs its operations, but in the US Marines, if we see terrorists shooting unarmed civilians in broad daylight, yeah, we intervene. Now put me on to your commanding officer, because there is a force of Druze militia about to move on my position any time now and if you are worried about an international incident, you haven't seen anything yet."

"Hold."

Jensen put the handset against his shoulder. "What the hell? Who are these guys?"

Amal looked pained. "They are an observer force, Sergeant. Not even a peacekeeping force, not really. UN troops tend to stay out of armed conflicts: what you did today was … unconventional."

"Unconventional? What would they have done?"

"They would probably have stood and watched, and then rendered assistance to the survivors. If there had been any."

"You are shitting me, right?"

"No. We have been living alongside UNDOF all my life. How is your history?"

"Weak. Enlighten me."

"Syrian civil war, Syrian rebels made constant incursions into the Golan, captured Quneitra, took UN peacekeepers prisoner, UNDOF did nothing. Bosnia. NATO aircraft attacked Serbian troops at Vrbanja Bridge. The Serbs surrounded a nearby UN base and four hundred UN peacekeepers surrendered to numerically inferior Serbian forces without firing a shot. Then there is Srebrenica."

"I heard of that. UN troops stood by while Serbs took the local Bosnian men hostage and massacred them."

She nodded.

"Alright, I get the picture." The radio crackled and he lifted the handset to his ear again. "Gunnery Sergeant James Jensen, come in."

"Jensen, this is Colonel Willem Cort, UNDOF outpost

Merom Golan. Tell me what you just told my Lieutenant."

Jensen told the UN colonel everything that had happened from the moment they had disembarked from their quadrotor up to fleeing the Druze roadblock and regrouping at the IDF corporal's house.

"Thank you for a very clear report, Sergeant," the man at the other end said. "Now let me tell you what is happening outside Buq'ata. Israel has been subject to a suspected large-scale cyber attack. Just about all internet and cellular communications systems are down. The national electricity grid is down. The national banking system is down. A Russian missile cruiser in the Mediterranean claims to have accidentally shot down an Israeli communication satellite but that would not explain the massive cyber and space offensive we believe is currently underway. Your report of civil unrest in Buq'ata is, sadly, not inconsistent with reports we are hearing of other similar incidents throughout the Golan Heights, the Palestinian territories, and on the Lebanese border with Israel. The situation here in the Golan..."

James Jensen was a native of Indiana, in the US Midwest. He tended to tune out if he heard too many words coming at him, and tended to trust the speaker less and less the more they talked. He took in what seemed relevant to him, then interrupted. "Colonel, with respect, I just want to know, are you going to come and get us and these Israeli civilians out of here, or not?"

"No, Sergeant, we are not."

Jensen couldn't believe his ears. "Sorry, Colonel, did I misunderstand? Did you deny my request for an evacuation?"

"You heard right, Sergeant. I do not have the resources, and even if I did, I could not expend them on non-UN forces right now."

"*Non-UN forces?* We are attached to UNDOF, Merom Golan."

"Not until you officially report to me, which you have not done. Any actions you took this morning were done without the authority or protection of the United Nations, Sergeant."

"Oh for the love of …"

"Careful, Sergeant. Now I am sorry, but this conversation is done."

Jensen tried one last time. "Colonel, I am talking to you soldier to soldier," he said. "We are trapped in the middle of a Druze town, surrounded by Druze militia, following what seemed to be a Druze terrorist attack on civilians in this town. I have nearly a dozen civilians here, some of whom are wounded, all of whom fear for their lives. Your troops are *five* miles away. I am formally requesting your urgent assistance."

There was a moment of silence at the other end of the radio, then the voice of the Dutch colonel came back. "Sergeant, you have my sympathy. You are not attached to UNDOF, but you *are* a member of the greatest military power in the world, according to your own media machine. I suggest you call your Pentagon. Cort out."

Jensen handed the radio handset back to Amal, who jammed it into a pocket in the carry pack.

"Sarge! I got movement on the access road south. Infantry fighting vehicle and a squad of infantry, moving up!" Bell called out.

Jensen heard voices, but they weren't breaking through his disbelief. Less than 24 hours ago, he and his squad had been standing on a hilltop in Kobani in Syria, getting ready to say good riddance to the stinking sewer of a bunker that had been their salvation through six months of siege. He'd blown a kiss at Combat Outpost Meyer as they'd flown away, so happy at the thought he'd never have to go through *that* particular brand of shit again. Now he was crouched on a rooftop in what might still be Syria, or Israel, depending on who you asked, and he and his squad were under siege once more. Except they didn't have a nice deep bunker to weather the storm in, they were in a domestic dwelling. He didn't have an army of Kurdish Peshmerga he could call on for assistance, he had an IDF corporal still bleeding from her wounds. The UN had turned its back on them.

They were ten degrees of screwed.

Finally a voice penetrated his gloom. He realized he had frozen. "*Jensen.* What do you want us to do?" Amal was asking him.

He looked up. Bell was staring at him, imploringly. "Gunny?"

Right now, Jensen would have killed for the basic comms kit every normal Marine squad carried. Helmet-mounted radio comms so he could speak to everyone and coordinate. What a damn luxury that would be. But he'd inherited the leftovers of an outpost no one wanted to be the last to say goodbye to, which meant both the unluckiest personnel and the last of their materiel.

They would have to do.

He stood and raised his voice. "Buckland, Stevens, Johnson!"

"Sergeant!"

"Incoming, west. Watch for infiltration on the flanks."

"Sergeant!"

"Wallace, Lopez!"

"Gunny!" The two privates were either side of an iron gate in the concrete wall, which was the logical place for an enemy to try to breach the compound.

"Heads down, stay out of sight." He checked their positions again. "Stay cool, everyone. Weapons off safe but hold fire!"

The scene outside the villa had a surreal element of stillness about it for several minutes. He could see the Druze troops and their small tank through some pine trees, parked up around the bend in the road. They weren't making much effort to hide themselves, but they were staying out of easy engagement range.

He saw the white flag before he saw the man carrying it. A soldier in a green uniform edged into sight, a white flag on a stick stuck out in front of him like the universal signal for 'parlay' was a shield that would protect him from American bullets. He stopped as soon as he reached the open ground in front of the compound.

Behind him, out of sight for now, Jensen heard a voice he recognized. "American Marines! Let me approach."

Jensen had been lying on his stomach and rolled over to the access stairs, dropping through and making his way to the ground floor, then out to the wall near the gate. As he approached, Lopez looked over the wall at the man with the flag.

"Sarge, I think they want to…"

"I heard, Private, keep your damn head down! A sniper in those trees and you'd be dead now."

Lopez crouched lower, looking abashed.

"I'm listening!" Jensen called through the small gap between the gate and the wall.

Zeidan Amar took a deep breath and stepped out from behind the man with the flag.

He needed to resolve this situation quickly, with the minimum of fuss. Get these damn Americans out of here and take control of Buq'ata before the IDF intervened. That damn corporal had probably already radioed for help.

Americans? What in the hell were US Marines doing in Buq'ata?

Like everyone else in the world, he had heard the US President's address on the radio, including his declaration of a no-fly zone over the Golan Heights. Had he mentioned something about US troops? Amar vaguely recalled he had, but the fact had gone right over his head as he'd driven from Mount Hermonit to Buq'ata. He had a million other problems to worry about, chief among them securing the town of nearly 10,000 Druze people and preparing it for its coming status as the capital of an Independent Druze Homeland in the restored Syrian province of Golan.

As he'd surveyed the compound for himself from the safety

208

of the trees, he had toyed with the idea of rushing their position, but for that he needed their *Namer* infantry fighting vehicle or IFV, with its 30mm autocannon, and it had been slow reaching Buq'ata from the IDF unit in Mas'ade that had been persuaded to defect to the Druze cause. Built on the chassis of a Merkava Mark IV main battle tank, it had shown in combat it could withstand RPG and even Russian *Kornet* anti-tank guided missiles. It would be able to smash through that metal gate and into the yard with ease.

He hoped his opponents would see that and come to their senses. His scout had reported more than a squad, less than a platoon of Marines. But also some civilians. Eyewitnesses in the town gave inconsistent information: some said there were ten Marines, some at least twenty. If he'd been operating with his usual resources, he could have put up infrared sensing drones and got a better count. But even standing back in the trees as he was, he could see at least three Marines peering out occasionally from behind the walls. Maybe one on the roof? That would make sense.

He rubbed his bruised throat. Whatever transpired, that Marine Sergeant was going to rue this day.

"Give me the flag," he said to the private he'd sent out front. Taking the flag, he hoisted it over his head and walked forward until he was standing in the open twenty yards from the gate. His scout had been right, it was more of a compound than a normal house. Probably an old farm overtaken as Buq'ata had expanded.

"Close enough, Colonel!" the Marine Sergeant called out. He stayed in cover, which was annoying. Amar had a rifleman in a good position with orders to take him down if he showed himself. "Talk."

"Sergeant, I assume you have contacted your UN superiors at Merom Golan. I am more than happy to allow free passage for UN vehicles to evacuate you, or for your men to walk out to the outpost." Either option would suit Amar. It certainly wouldn't hurt to have a brace of UN blue helmets as hostages for leverage when the IDF inevitably came to call.

"We have civilians under our protection. Some are wounded."

"The seriously wounded have already been evacuated to the hospital at Mas'ade." That much was true. Dead townsfolk were of no use to him, either Jewish or Druze. "If you have anyone inside who needs medical attention, you should send them out, we will get them to Mas'ade too."

"Why should I believe the guy who wounded them in the first place?"

"Sergeant, you have blundered into the middle of a situation that is beyond your pay grade. UNDOF is an observer force, not a peacekeeping force, certainly not an intervention force. Your presence here is only making a difficult situation worse, for you and your men. I will give you thirty minutes to consider your position. At the very least, send out the civilians."

"Or what?" Jensen asked.

"Or we will free them by force. I have several hundred men at my disposal. Many Marines will die – possibly civilians too – and it will be on your head. You can still resolve this situation peacefully."

After watching the Druze colonel and his man withdraw, Jensen scuttled back into the house and up to the rooftop.

"You heard that?" Jensen asked Amal.

"Yes."

"What is that armored vehicle?"

"An IDF *Namer* IFV. That one has a 30mm autocannon and 40mm grenade launcher."

"Patel? We bring anything with us that can dent the hide of that thing?"

"No, sir. I mean, Buckland had a few M-14 thermite grenades left over from the equipment she was destroying in Kobani, but they aren't going to burn through *Namer* armor. That tank rolls in here, we'll get squashed like bugs."

Amal nodded. "We will need to take it out before it gets moving. I may have an idea."

"You have a Javelin anti-tank missile launcher downstairs by any chance?"

"No, something else."

As she led the way down from the roof, Jensen remembered she had mentioned having an ordnance store back at her house. She led him through her back door and out into the rear yard where a large metal shed backed onto the quarry. She put her thumb to the print reader on a padlock on the doors. Heaving on a sliding door, she pulled it open.

Jensen stepped inside, and whistled. "What. The. Hell?"

"I told you," Amal said, turning on the lights. "I am a robotics engineer."

"Well, this explains why the place is built like a small fortress."

"Yes, the DRD insisted on that. Not that it was supposed to withstand a siege, just maybe buy me enough time to destroy any sensitive equipment in my workshop. They built those walls to withstand RPG rounds, but they looked so military, I painted them bright green."

"This is more than a one-woman operation."

"Yes. I usually have three junior engineers working with me. They have an apartment in town. But they were pulled back to DRD in Tel Aviv when the security situation got worse."

Jensen looked around him at racks of parts, computers and technical equipment. "Aren't you worried about the Syrians rolling in here and just taking all this stuff?"

"No. There is…" she reached for the door to close it behind them, "… a, how you say, contingency plan."

The shed was nothing less than a sophisticated weapons manufacturing plant. In the center of the floor stood a piece of equipment that Jensen immediately recognized. But it was five times the size of anything he had seen.

"That's a 3D printer?"

"Yes. I keep the feedstock in barrels under the floor."

It was a huge metal and glass cube, with computer terminals down one of the support pillars that controlled it.

"You could print a tank with this damn thing," he said admiringly.

"Actually, I could. If you gave me the plans, enough steel alloy powder ... and about three years."

"What else have you got in here?" he asked. The side and rear walls were lined with heavy metal cabinets, all with combination locks. There was Hebrew writing on the front of them.

She pointed to each in turn. "Small arms, pistol parts and ammunition. Drone parts, engines, propellers, batteries, cameras. Explosives, fragmentation and stun grenades, miniature air-to-ground rockets, unguided ... no Javelin missiles, sorry." On workbenches around the 3D printer were drones in various states of construction, or deconstruction.

"Holy hell."

"My specialty is tactical drones for IDF Army use. Surveillance, counterinsurgency, tactical precision fire support..." Amal shrugged. "In the DRD they call me The Toymaker."

"Yeah? If Santa delivered his presents in a B-21 bomber. You said you had an idea for that tank out there?"

"Yes!" she said, skipping over to a bench and lifting a quadcopter drone. "You said you had thermite grenades?"

"Yes. Couldn't be many. And I should be chewing out Buckland for taking them aboard the flight with her."

"These drones can carry two 40mm grenades. They are designed to provide a crude but effective anti-defilade weapon to our troops if they are faced with an enemy firing from cover." She showed a small digital display on the drone. "It's pretty simple. You enter the distance to the target, and this display shows you how many seconds to dial into the grenade timer. You guide it to the target with the onboard camera, or if the enemy is jamming, it can home on the spot from a laser target designator. The camera is low light, and infrared. I call it the *Nightwalker*." She stood on her toes and held the drone over his head. "Boom. You're dead."

"Cute. And how does this…"

She turned it upside down, where a small payload bay was nestled. "We mount thermite grenades. I'm thinking you fly them into the tracks, they melt the rollers, destroy the tracks. The *Namer* can't move."

"But it can still shoot. Could you land a drone on the turret and burn through that?"

"No. The *Namer* is built on a Merkava main battle tank chassis. Very tough reactive armor, even on top."

Jensen thought about it, picturing the tank in his mind's eye. "Have you ever been inside a *Namer*?" he asked her.

"Yes, why?"

"How do the troops get in and out?"

"By a ramp at the back. Hydraulic; it can be raised and lowered by the driver, or from the outside of the vehicle. What are you thinking?"

Jensen reached out and took the drone, inspecting it carefully. "I'm thinking we're going to find out just how good a drone pilot you are."

Zeidan Amar looked at his watch. Twenty-five minutes, and no word from his lookouts that the Americans were showing any signs of forming up and pulling out. No signs of civilians being prepared for release. If it hadn't happened by now, it wasn't going to.

He turned to the squad lined up behind the *Namer*, twirling his finger in the air, leaning inside the rear ramp door as he yelled forward to the driver and gunner. "Alright, start up and mount up!"

With a throaty bellow, the engine on the IFV burst to life. The driver sat up front on the left, the gunner on his right, both controlling their systems via large flat panel screens, so that the crew and troops inside the IFV could be completely sealed off from attacking projectiles or chemical weapons. There were yellow metal seats around the inside of the IFV for eight troops. Other variants of the *Namer* could seat nine troops, but the 30mm cannon required an autofeed magazine that took up one seat place.

The plan for overwhelming the Marine position was simple enough. The *Namer* would charge through the gate and lay down suppressing fire, taking out any ground-level resistance. Then it would throw out a barrage of smoke grenades and the troops inside would spill out and move into the house to flush out any Marines on higher floors. He had a second squad in reserve if extra support was needed to clear the compound, but he doubted it would be. Some civilians would die, that was inevitable, but his Druze troops were veterans of house-to-house combat in Lebanon, including hostage rescue operations. As the Americans liked to say, 'this wasn't their first rodeo'.

As the last man stepped inside and took his seat, Amar looked at his watch again, then thumped the side of the vehicle. "Alright, move out!" He stepped back as the hydraulic ramp at the rear of the IFV juddered and began to rise.

With the noise of the engine and the ramp hydraulics, he never heard the two drones approaching. The first flew past him at chest height and right over the ramp into the front of the IFV interior. It was so unexpected that he stood there like a fool looking at it as it crashed to the floor of the tank between the driver and the gunner, its engine still whining and propellers drumming on the deck.

Then there was a hiss and brilliant light filled the interior of the IFV.

Men started screaming. Two or three jumped for the ramp door, but it was closing fast, sealing everyone inside.

Amar threw himself to the ground and saw the second drone approach, aiming for the shrinking gap between the ramp door and the top of the IFV as it closed. With an evil whine, the drone slipped through the last thirty centimeters at the top of the ramp before it shut, and Amar heard another hiss of molten fire triggering inside the vehicle.

Getting to his feet, he staggered backwards and then, as the 30mm cannon ammunition inside the IFV started exploding, he ran.

Thermite grenades are not effective anti-personnel weapons. Producing a white-hot torrent of fire that can melt metal, they are usually used for destroying equipment so that it cannot be used by an enemy – like cannon barrels, vehicle engines or computers. That had been Corporal Buckland's job back at Kobani – to ensure there was nothing left behind that could be used by the Syrian army if their hilltop outpost was ever abandoned by the Kurdish militia who would be taking it over from the departing Marines.

But almost anything that wasn't bolted down had been given to the Kurdish forces in Kobani for their own use, including most of the tools and equipment in the outpost's machine workshop. She had used the thermite to destroy the 3D printer for which the Kurdish troops had no use, because it required a constant supply of raw materials they didn't have access to. She also used the thermite charges to destroy the outpost's small rack of communication computer servers because they had been left in place for use right up until the last Marine was lifted out. By the time the thermite charges burned out and the smoke had cleared, they were nothing but melted metal and silica.

The remaining M-14 THT grenades Buckland took with her out of Kobani were triggered in a two-step process – first the operator set the fuse delay, for anything from three to thirty seconds. Then they removed the safety pull ring, and finally the secondary pull ring. Then they got into cover.

Mounting two M-14 grenades on Azaria's *Nightwalker* quadcopters was simple enough; she just had to swap out the recon pack in the belly of the drone for a 'freight pod' and fit the two grenades in place with heavy-duty rubber ties. They used the Leopold scope on Patel's Mk22 MRAD marksman rifle to measure the distance to the rear of the IFV and allowed a few extra yards for the drones to overfly the vehicle and make a handbrake turn.

And then, with only the drone's low-resolution wide-angle forward-looking camera to steer by, Amal set the timers, pulled the pins on the grenades and sent them on their way to the target in quick succession. She only had to actually 'fly' one of the drones. One of the features she had added to their guidance software was that they could be placed in a crude 'swarm' mode so that one just followed the other at a set distance, which was useful if delivering small packages to troops in difficult to access locations, because multiple drones could be chained together. Six drones could quickly deliver 20lbs. of ammunition or equipment.

Or two drones, like the ones she sent down from the terrace atop her house, could deliver 8lbs. of thermite into the interior of a *Namer* IFV loaded with ammunition.

Up on the terrace roof, Amal saw the second of her drones follow the first into a maw of incandescent flame and then the vision went down. In the distance, they could hear muffled explosions.

My god, what did I just do? Amal thought to herself. She'd expected to be flying the grenades into an open, empty IFV. But the last image she'd seen from her first drone was the shocked expression of the *Namer*'s driver, looking down at the drone that had just landed beside his chair.

As though reading her mind, Jensen leaned over and pushed down the screen on her command unit, putting his hand on her shoulder. "They were coming to kill us, Corporal. Kill us, and do god knows what to you and those civilians. Remember that every time you think about today, alright?"

"Yes, Sergeant."

"Now take five, get some water and start cranking out the

rest of the drones we discussed." He patted her shoulder.

"Right. Yes."

Jensen went down the stairs to the gates, joining Wallace and Lopez. He was glad to see they were letting Bell up on the roof of the house do most of the watching, sticking their heads up only occasionally to check the situation in front of the wall. As he reached the wall, the sound of high-explosive rounds cooking off inside the *Namer* died away.

"That racket was the Druze tank?" Wallace asked him. "The drones nailed it?"

"They did."

"Freaking *ace*," Lopez said.

"They're going to be pissed, looking to hit back," Jensen warned them. "They may try to rush us. If you see us losing the walls, get back to the house. We don't have radio comms, so use your own judgment, don't wait for my order. They get inside this compound, you pull back to the house, got it?"

"Yes, Sergeant," they replied in unison.

He gave the same message to Johnson, Buckland and Stevens, then ran into the house. Amal had opened the windows but pulled the drapes across to hide their movement, and he leaned up against a wall looking out the front of the house. The IFV was smoking, but the troops that had been around it had evaporated. Pulled back, he guessed. There was no movement. For now. There was a telephone on her sideboard, and he automatically picked it up. It was still dead.

Amal came in through the back door, joining him at the window, X-95 rifle over her shoulder again. She put a bag at her feet. "I have prepared two reconnaissance drones, and four loaded with anti-personnel grenades. I have also distributed grenades to all of your people. We have parts for four more drones – after that, I will need to start printing parts. But power for the printer is the problem."

"You only have mains power?"

"No, I have an old diesel generator as backup. The power supply to Buq'ata has never been that reliable. But it makes a racket. If we start it up, our enemies will become curious about what we have in that shed." She lifted a drape aside. "How long, do you think?"

"Before they regroup and attack? They'll probably be tending to the dead or wounded from that IFV. The pressure to counterattack immediately will be high. It depends how cool the head on your Colonel is. If it's him, if he's really the kind of guy who would be made an acting Brigade Commander, he's not going to be the hot-headed type. He's got some kind of plan for this place, and we weren't part of it. He needs to work that through." Jensen nodded at the radio she was lifting off her shoulder and sitting on the ground. "But we can't sit here waiting for him to make the next move. We have to keep the initiative."

"What are you thinking?" she asked, sitting down against a wall.

"IDF can't help us, I get that. UN doesn't *want* to help us. I don't get that, but it is what it is. I need somehow to get in touch with US forces."

"The only US base I know of in Israel is the Hatzerim Air Base in the Negev Desert."

"Is that near here?"

She laughed. "It's one hundred and eighty miles from here. My radio has a range of about *ten* miles. If I'm on high ground."

"But your unit could get a message to them."

"Perhaps."

"Call in the intel on that latest engagement. Druze militia attacking US Marines? That has to make them realize this situation is six kinds of wrong."

She didn't look optimistic. "I was told there is a national emergency. That's one step short of full-scale war. What is happening here today is happening precisely to sow confusion, to divert attention and distract our armed forces. Should I contribute to that?"

"You're telling me to suck it the hell up."

At that moment, he heard the boom of a jet aircraft flying

overhead and some cheering outside.

"What the hell?" Jensen said, looking up. Keeping low, he ran to the doorway and saw Johnson pointing. As he watched, a bat-winged drone banked onto its left wing, flattened out and then zoomed into the clouds overhead.

"Johnson, what was that?"

"I don't know, Sarge," the man called back. "But it had US markings!"

Amal had joined him in the doorway. Jensen grabbed her by a shirt sleeve and pulled her toward the stairs. "Get on the roof! We need to try to contact the pilot of that aircraft!"

All Domain Attack: Political

5,000 feet over Buq'ata, Golan Heights, May 18

Bunny O'Hare was nearing the end of her patrol. For the last two hours she'd been playing whack-a-mole over the Golan with the Syrian *Growler* and had nearly had her *Fantom* shot down twice as a reward for her efforts, but she was still showing only one loss for the mission, which was a victory in her books. Russia had also held back from sending more aircraft to challenge the US no-fly zone, for now.

Like any close air support aircraft, her *Fantom* was equipped with an onboard radio transceiver that monitored local radio frequencies so that she could coordinate ground strikes directly with a joint terminal air controller or JTAC, embedded with troops on the line if needed. She immediately noticed a new icon blinking in her heads-up display to show that someone was hailing her on a US JTAC frequency. But it was unencrypted, meaning that the radio hailing her was *not* a US military unit.

She put the hail through to the speakers inside the trailer. "… of the IDF Unit 351, *Palhik* Company, hailing US aircraft over Buq'ata, I am with US Marines of 1st Battalion and we are in urgent need of air support, over. This is IDF Corporal Amal Azaria, Unit 351, *Palhik* Company …"

She quickly patched the call through to the US Bombardier Global 6000 aircraft. "Falcon Control, Valor flight leader. We are being hailed in the open on UHF 243 megahertz by a unit claiming to be IDF. Patching through to you now." As she spoke, she dropped a waypoint over the town of Buq'ata in the Golan and peeled two of her reserve aircraft away from their holding pattern, sending them to circle the town at low level so they'd be hard for the Syrian *Growler* to detect, but within range of whoever was hailing them down there.

"Thank you, Valor leader, we have your signal. Analyzing

now. We need to run this back through ops intel at Akrotiri. Please maintain contact with the sender but do not respond. Supporting Israeli forces is not in our Operations Order."

"Valor confirms, out." Bunny turned to Kovacs. "Weird. The whole damn Israeli Air Force is airborne right now, why isn't she calling in air support from them?"

"Because it's the Golan? Or maybe the cyber strike knocked out their comms?"

"I guess. She is using UHF ... but this feels like something else." Bunny pulled up the waypoint for Buq'ata and fine-tuned it. "I'm bringing down our decoy bird and sending it to reserve. I'll get the two *Fantoms* circling Buq'ata to do a recon pass, give us a look at what is happening down there, let whoever is down there know we're still in the neighborhood."

"What if it's not IDF? What if it's Syrians, trying to lure you in so they can take a shot at you with low-level anti-air missiles or guns?"

Bunny raised her eyebrows. "Kovacs, where is your trust in human nature?" She prepped her decoy flares and chaff though, because of course the DARPA engineer was right. It could be a trap.

"No response," Amal said, putting the handset back in its cradle. "Are you sure about the frequency?" she asked Patel.

"UHF 243 megahertz," he said. "It's the international air emergency frequency. You want me to try? That radio is pretty much the same as the ones I was trained on."

"It's like I can still hear a jet though, Sarge," Bell said. "Moving east to west."

"If it's out there, it isn't hearing us, or it isn't responding," Jensen agreed. He turned to Amal. "Can we try another frequency? Is there an IDF Air Force frequency you can use? Maybe it's one of yours."

"I mean it, Sergeant, I can hear it, and I think it's coming over again," Bell said. "Listen!"

He was right. Low and to the east was a growing roar. On the horizon he saw two small dots, approaching fast. He had no flares or even flags to signal the aircraft with. "Bell, what's the signal for a 'require assistance'?"

"To an aircraft? Capital V."

"Good enough. Quick, down and flat!"

Amal watched mystified as both Marines put their rifles down and stretched out across the roof with their arms straight up along the ground behind them, their legs meeting at the feet so that their bodies formed a V.

Jensen, staring straight up, heard the two jets screaming toward them and saw only shadows before they blasted past. He rolled up onto a knee and saw one aircraft breaking right, the other breaking left, pumping out flares and chaff as they turned. There was cheering from the yard below again, so Johnson or Buckland were still convinced they were American.

"Get on that handset again," Jensen said.

In her trailer on Cyprus, O'Hare was paging through the vision from the two *Fantoms*. She didn't have a recon camera package on either of them, but she had the wide-angle cameras used to simulate cockpit views and as she'd overflown the small town, she'd banked the aircraft onto their wings so that they would capture a wide-angle view of the ground below. She jumped through it frame by frame, seeing nothing unusual as they crossed a highway empty of traffic on the outskirts of the town, some seemingly empty fields, a few houses and ...

"Wait, what's that?" Kovacs said, pointing at the screen. "Something burning?"

O'Hare went back a couple of frames and zoomed in on the object.

"That's an armored personnel carrier, maybe a small scout vehicle, on fire," O'Hare said. "Three, maybe four people on the ground a couple hundred yards back, more standing around. Can't see their uniforms with this crappy resolution."

She paged back and forth, but the image they had was about as clear as it would get. She copied it and kept moving the vision forward. "OK, look here," she said. "Center of town. I've got what looks like four, five wrecked vehicles in a circle around this intersection. These here … troops, in cover." She went forward two frames. "And on this rooftop outside town, three more."

"Why are they laid out like that?" Kovacs asked, seeing two figures stretched out on the rooftop. "Are they dead?"

"Not yet, but that's the international ground to air signal for 'need assistance'," Bunny told her. She compared the images of the burning tank and the troops on the outskirts of the town. "Different uniforms, see," she said. "These guys down from the burning vehicle, dark uniforms, these guys on the roof, desert camouflage. If I was a betting girl, I'd bet the guys on the roof are the US Marines that IDF corporal was talking about." She made a copy of all the imagery and sent it through to the AWACS aircraft.

"Falcon, Valor. We have some recon imagery for you. We think it shows a firefight in the town of Buq'ata in the Golan Heights. The troops below appear to be US Marines, signaling for assistance."

"Valor, Falcon copies. Maintain contact, but do not respond yet. Still waiting on Akrotiri."

"Let me try, Sarge. Maybe they just need to hear an American accent?" Patel suggested.

Jensen nodded. Patel was the only one among the squad trained to work with close air support aircraft.

Amal passed the radio over to him. "The Druze troops will be using the same radio system as me. They can listen in on every word you say."

Jensen pulled Patel close. "Don't use your own name. We want an evac, alright. Ask them to find a landing zone east of here so we don't have to go through town. Depending how long it takes, we're going to need rations, ammunition…"

Patel nodded and kneeled by the radio. "Map, you have a map?"

Amal carried a map of the Golan Heights in the pack with her radio and pulled it out, unfolding it and showing him their location and the map reference. Patel put his finger on it.

"US aircraft over Buq'ata, this is 1st Marines, 3rd Battalion JTAC, attached to UNDOF forces Merom Golan. Friendlies are at coordinates 33.198, 35.787, a large domestic dwelling. Under assault by a company-sized force of Druze militia following a terrorist attack in the town. Enemy in various positions around town, closest enemy troop concentration is 200 yards distant at 33.198, 35.786, bearing … uh … 272 degrees our position. Estimated size, 20 pax. We require immediate evacuation…"

A new voice broke in over the radio. "US aircraft over Buq'ata, please disregard. Terrorist elements have stolen an IDF radio. Repeat, terrorist elements have stolen an IDF radio and are holding civilians as human shields in the town center. We have initiated an operation to free the civilians, please ignore all radio calls. IDF ground forces out."

Jensen recognized the voice immediately. It was their friend, the colonel.

"How can we tell who is who down there?" Kovacs asked. "That last caller could be telling the truth."

"Except terrorists don't dress in Marine combat uniforms and lie flat on a roof using JTAC protocols to task air assets, where I come from," O'Hare said. "OK, time to take a risk."

"Oh no. What…"

"Not with your precious aircraft. We need to get that Marine unit down there, if that's who it is, speaking to us on an encrypted frequency so that no one else can butt in. That means I need to send them the encryption key code, but I can't call it down to them on the radio because anyone else listening in would get it too."

"Then how…"

"Creative thinking, Shelly," O'Hare said. "Let's hope there's someone down there who thinks like me."

Jensen had no desire to play radio tag with the Druze colonel. That would only further confuse whoever was listening in. They needed a visual signal that the pilot would recognize as uniquely US forces, but what?

"Jets coming back around," Bell said. His hearing was good, but maybe that ran in the family. Jensen had heard his brother was a sonar operator in the Navy.

They looked up and saw the aircraft approaching again, this time in line astern formation, one behind the other. A little higher this time, and further to the east. It occurred to Jensen that this put them out of line of sight of the Druze troops in town, probably to reduce the chances of getting attacked by ground-to-air missiles. But as they crossed from left to right, each jet fired four flares and then spat out a cloud of tinfoil chaff that glittered in the sunshine before they banked away.

"Doing more recon," Jensen decided. "Worried about ground-to-air missiles."

"Maybe, Sarge," Patel said, frowning. "Just…"

"Just what, Corporal?"

"Nothing." Patel turned his head to one side, then the other. "They're coming back around."

In a carbon copy of their last run, the two jets crossed the town from left to right. Each machine fired off exactly the same decoys as it blasted past, four flares and a cloud of chaff.

"What are they *doing*?" Jensen asked, frustrated. Amal had her ear to her radio handset. "Anything on radio?"

"No. They have not responded."

Bell had scratched something in the dirt, and suddenly looked up. "Morse! It's morse, for the number two. Four dots and a dash."

"Two what?"

Over the next five minutes they saw the two US fighters flash past several more times. The second time they fired five flares. The third time, five clouds of chaff.

Bell was busily scratching in the dirt on top of the roof. "Two, five, zero." On their fourth run, they dropped three flares. "Sierra. That's two, five, zero, Sierra."

"It's a four-digit encryption code!" Amal said, lifting her radio onto her lap and flipping open the cover for the keypad. "Two..."

"Five, zero, Sierra..."

She punched in the code. "Handshake! That was it. You're online with the pilot and encrypted." She gave the handset to Patel.

"US aircraft, this is Corporal Ravi Patel, 1st Marines, 3rd Battalion JTAC, attached to UNDOF forces Merom Golan..."

As the voice came in loud and clear over the speakers in the trailer, O'Hare gave Kovacs a wink. "*Someone* down there can think out of the box." She flipped on her mike. "US aircraft to unidentified ground unit, we copy your transmission. We are awaiting confirmation of your identity."

"You want my goddamn social security number, pilot?" Patel asked, exasperated.

"Stay cool, Corporal," O'Hare told him. "I understand your situation. I am awaiting orders. Out."

O'Hare could imagine the stream of invective that probably followed her cutting transmission, but what could she do? She switched to the AWACS frequency. "Falcon, Valor leader. We have a confirmed handshake with the unit on the ground at Buq'ata now. Encrypted comms link established, what am I doing here?"

"Valor, we can confirm a Marine squad from 1st Battalion, 3rd Marines was dropped at Buq'ata earlier today. They have not made contact with 1st Battalion headquarters and we are

above rooftop height. "Let's send him a little message."

Zeidan Amar had opened a hatch into the *Namer* IFV and then backed away again as a thick cloud of smoke boiled out of it, along with a smell he would remember for the rest of his days. Cordite and burned human flesh. He tried to open the ramp, but there was no response to the release button on the outside of the hull. He had no hope that any of the men inside would have survived that inferno. But a vague hope the turret might still be repaired, yes, why not?

That had been just before the first US aircraft had passed overhead. Coincidence? He didn't believe in that kind of coincidence. His radio operator had come running over with the message that the US Marines were broadcasting in the clear … a mistake under pressure, probably. He'd gone on the radio to try to muddy the waters, but then the broadcasts had stopped. They'd probably realized their mistake and switched to an encrypted channel, but he could still hear the damn jets buzzing around to their east, making several passes, no doubt to map the position of his troops. He had squads on the highway and the four main roads out of Buq'ata, a total of about fifty men, not counting the ten he'd lost in the attack on the *Namer* IFV. He was just ordering his men to get under cover, inside houses or under trees, when the radio crackled to life.

"This is US Marine Air Wing for Colonel Zeidan Amar of IDF Golani Brigade, do you read?" a female voice said, then repeated the hail.

He considered not replying. But if the American on the radio knew his name, there was no point hiding anymore. She would pass it on to IDF liaison sooner or later and the questions would start, just as he had expected they would. He was prepared.

His operator held out the radio handset and he took it. "This is Colonel Amar, come in."

"Colonel, our JTAC has advised that you and your troops have killed and wounded civilians in Buq'ata and threatened to attack our Marines. We have a message for you. US reinforcements are on their way to Buq'ata and you do *not* want to be there when they arrive. Marine Air Wing out."

"Whoever you are..."

"Duck, Colonel."

The radio operator held out his hand for the handset. "They have cut transmission, Colonel."

At that moment he heard a growing roar and stepped out into the middle of the street, staring up at the sky. Sweeping in low over the fields to the west of Buq'ata he saw one, two ... *five* low-flying dart-shaped aircraft headed straight toward him.

"Into cover!" he yelled.

O'Hare slid her mouse pointer a couple of millimeters across her targeting screen and put a crosshair on the burning IFV near the center of the town.

"Lava Dogs JTAC, Lava Dogs JTAC, Marine Air."

"Marine Air, go for JTAC."

"I am inbound that IFV. Want to make double sure it won't trouble you."

Patel rolled to a gap in the small wall around the terrace and checked there were no civilians near the still-burning tank. He could see a few Druze soldiers hovering nearby, but no townspeople. "Good copy, Marine Air. You are cleared hot."

"Roger, JTAC, Marine Air coming in hot."

She had air-to-ground JAGM missiles in her weapons bays but no authority to use them, so she slaved the five four-barrel rotary cannons of her *Fantoms* onto the target she'd painted with the laser of her lead aircraft and then tied them to the trigger on her flight stick. Five hundred yards out from the rising column of smoke over the burning vehicle, she pressed the trigger and held it down.

One hundred and eighty-nine miles away from her trailer,

five streams of supersonic 25mm high-explosive rounds slammed into the *Namer* IFV at the rate of 3,300 rounds a minute.

The three Americans and the Israeli on the rooftop terrace watched as the five *Fantoms* hammered toward Buq'ata and then opened fire on the IFV with a tearing, shredding noise that only hit their eardrums after the jets were already pulling around to the north in perfect formation.

Bell whistled, watching them go. "If that *Namer* wasn't dead before, it's dead now. Way to send a message."

The five jets turned into small dots and then disappeared, the sound of their engines fading as it rolled across the hills either side of the town.

"Did that drone pilot sound to you like she had an *English* accent?" Jensen asked Patel thoughtfully. "Or Irish maybe?"

"Australian," Bell said. "I've got an ear for accents. She was Australian."

"Makes sense. Never met an Australian I didn't like."

As O'Hare leaned back in her chair, she rolled her head around on her neck, easing out the tension.

Kovacs, however, was only getting more tense. "You weren't authorized for a close air support action!"

"That was a guns test," O'Hare said.

"On an infantry fighting vehicle!"

"Guns test, on a *wrecked* vehicle," O'Hare corrected her. "I wrote a routine that slaves the guns of multiple *Fantoms* to a single target. You can put the birds into formation – line abreast, delta V, just not line astern – and they'll open fire simultaneously on the target the lead aircraft is painting with its laser. It seems to work pretty well, right? And for the record, that JTAC cleared us in."

"They…" Kovacs protested. "That attack is going to be

logged, O'Hare. You can't just call it a 'guns test' and expect it to be ignored."

"Aren't you the one who pulls those logs?"

"Yes, but…"

"Are you going to write me up?"

"No. Those Marines are in big trouble, I get that, but…"

"Guns test, Shelly."

Sheer luck had seen all of his men survive the onslaught of HE rounds that had poured into the road around the already burning *Namer* IFV. It rocked and bucked with hundreds of impacts, shrapnel ricocheting into nearby walls, splintering almond trees and wooden power poles. The earlier drone attack and destruction of the IFV had driven any remaining townsfolk out of the nearby area, but anyone who had been unlucky enough to have been caught out in the open would have been shredded.

When the jets had first appeared, he had almost dismissed them, assuming they would not dare attack targets near a densely populated civil district. He'd revisited that assumption.

What kind of Army was this that dealt such destruction so casually?

One to be taken seriously. He'd become too used to the passivity of the UNDOF troops. These Marines were not cut from the same pale blue cloth.

He had been smoking a cigarette, but he stopped and threw it on the ground. He looked around for the radio operator, mind working at a mile a minute. He may just have come upon a way to neutralize the American presence in Buq'ata *and* make them pay for what they had done here today.

"Get me Iranian liaison on the radio."

Iranian Quds Force base, Damascus, Syria, May 18

Abdolrasoul Delavari relished calls such as the one he had

232

just received from the Syrian captain in charge of Quds Force support for *Operation Butterfly*.

The man had laid a map on a table and pointed to a small town sixty miles south-west of Damascus. Buq'ata.

"This is the situation. An allied Syrian Druze unit has been engaged with US Marines at this position…"

"US Marines? In the Golan?"

"You heard the US President's speech? We think these are the US UNDOF troops he was talking about. As far as we can tell, they were not here a week ago, but they are here now."

"Convenient."

"Not for them. They got into a firefight with our Druze allies and are holed up in a villa on the outskirts of town here using some residents as human shields. The Druze tried to free the civilians but were driven back. They took casualties."

Delavari raised his eyebrows. "And?"

"And we need to win the hearts and minds of the Druze in Buq'ata. If we can free those civilians it will be a major coup. We will transport you to Buq'ata by chopper. You are to reconnoiter the area and despatch their commander…"

Delavari smiled. "Ah. Thank you. Just the kind of mission I like."

"Sorry to disappoint you. He's just a Sergeant, apparently. If that is not enough to persuade them to abandon the civilians and flee for the UN outpost, then take down a couple more. They'll soon see their situation is hopeless."

Delavari smiled. "They are with the UN observer force, you say?"

"Why do you ask?"

"I'm surprised they even know how to use a rifle. UN troops are usually more proficient at waving white flags."

He'd left the briefing in the best of moods. Even a Sergeant was a worthy target, if he was commanding this American force. Cut the head off the snake, it was always the quickest way. Just like his hit on the Golani Brigade commander, Tamir. His was just one of a series of coordinated decapitation attempts all along the Golan ceasefire line. If even half of the attacks he'd been briefed about had been successful, the Golani Brigade would now be rudderless, floundering in a leaderless vacuum. Israel itself was in chaos thanks to cyber attacks. Syrian media said Israeli spy satellites had been brought down too by 'Syrian strategic missile forces'. Syria and Iran had no anti-satellite missile capability, so he assumed that had been done with Russian assistance.

Operation Butterfly was proceeding nicely, as far as he could see.

And he had a new mission. A mission that befitted his skills. A mission he could tell his children about one day. The time he freed ten innocent civilians from the brutish Americans. Fifty civilians, perhaps, by the time he was finished telling the story.

He'd been given GPS coordinates for the target dwelling and gone back to his tent and studied his own maps. Over the last three months he'd just about walked every single mile of the ceasefire line from the slopes of Mount Hermon in the north to Al Asbah, thirty miles to the south. He knew all the routes into Buq'ata, from roads a car could travel, to narrow paths barely suitable for goats.

Hmm. The Americans had chosen well. The house was isolated, with a clear field of fire for about two hundred yards around. It was on a small rise with forest at the bottom. He had shot from nests in trees before, but these would probably be too low. He checked satellite imagery of the town to the south of the target. Most of the houses there were two-story, too low. But … here. Someone was building a three-story house by the look of it. With a water tank on the roof. That might give him the elevation he needed. He got out an old wooden divider he'd had since he was a recruit and measured the distance to the target. One and a quarter miles.

Well, it seemed the Zoroastrian engineer was about to get his wish. It wasn't a shot he could make with his *Degtyarev*. But with a *Saher* anti-materiel rifle and a few *Klimovsk* 14.5mm smart rounds, he'd be able to sight on just about anyone on the western side of the compound silly enough to expose themselves above the walls … maybe even get an angle into the windows of the house. Depending on the thickness of the walls, the heavy-caliber *Saher* might even be able to punch through them to any troops hiding inside. He would explore other sites, but it was good to have somewhere to start.

Something caught his eye on the satellite photos. Aha. A rooftop terrace. He wouldn't be able to get up high enough for that. A drone with a frag could do it, if he could scrounge one up. But if the Marines put a shooter up there…

If Delavari had been the kind of man who licked his lips, he'd have been licking them right then. A worthy cause, and the chance of an opponent, in a superior position, looking for him. But he was going to battle with a new weapon in his hands that tipped the balance cleanly in his favor.

What more could a lowly tailor-turned-sniper ask for?

After she got out of her trailer and wrote up her mission report, O'Hare went back to her barracks and spent two hours on the telephone from RAF Akrotiri to multiple officers at the Lava Dogs headquarters in Kaneohe Station, Hawaii. She spoke with a lot of people who had no idea how to help Jensen, several who had no idea what a country-wide civil emergency meant and told her she should be calling UNDOF headquarters in Israel, and several others who insisted she should call the IDF commander responsible for the Golan Heights and speak with him.

After that last piece of advice she slammed her cell phone down on the table and screamed. "Oh, right, just call the guy trying to *kill* your Marines?! Because that makes sense!" She had one more lead. A second lieutenant called Gudinski who had served in COP Meyer in Kobani with the 1st Marines 3rd Battalion but who had been wounded and evacuated before the rest of the unit.

"Yeah, I heard," the man said. "The Corpsman who patched

me up is with them, Bell. Helluva thing. He owes me money from a card game."

"Well, if you ever want to collect, you're going to have to work for it because right now he's in a tough spot, out of luck and out of friends."

"Let me make some calls."

Post-adrenaline fatigue hit O'Hare as she put the phone down, and when it started buzzing again she found herself fast asleep at the small desk in her quarters, face stuck by sweat to a piece of paper under her cheek. She pulled it off and grabbed the phone. "Ow, bloody hell."

"Sorry, is that Flying Officer O'Hare?"

"Yes, in person. You have news I hope, Lieutenant Gudinski?"

"Not so good. There is a reason you were getting the runaround. Those troops are supposed to be there, and they have to stay there. There are reasons we can't pull them out."

"What bloody reasons?"

"Well, if you're a pilot patrolling the no-fly zone, you're the reason. It's a political thing. That no-fly zone is supposed to be for their protection. If we pull them out, there's no one to protect."

"Tell your Air Force that. I was overhead, guns hot, and they pulled me out."

"That just ain't right."

"No, it ain't, Gudinski."

"I'll get back to you, O'Hare."

She decided a shower and cup of tea and some toast would be the trick. Luckily Akrotiri was an RAF station, so they had decent tea in the NAAFI canteen, but the only spread they had for toast was an evil black goo called Marmite. She was just about dozing off again, though, when Gudinski called back. She looked at her watch in panic … 1930 hours! She was due back on the flight line in an hour. The Marine officer had good news.

"Alright. Our CO has put a rocket up the commander for

the 432nd Air Wing. You'll find them being a little more assertive from here in. The bad news, the nearest US presence to you is at Hatzerim Israeli Air Force Base. There's a Marine company there from the 1st Battalion, 24th Marines, but they're a hundred eighty miles from Buq'ata."

"That's not a factor if they can get troops onto a *Big Boy*. They could be in Buq'ata inside an hour."

"Not going to happen. President's orders, the CO said. No more US boots on the ground in the Golan. But they're standing by to send supplies."

"Do they do cheese crust pizza?"

"Ma'am?"

"Don't worry. I've got a list for you. Ammunition first: 5.56mm for M27 carbines, .338 for a Barrett sniper rifle, 40mm grenades…"

West Wing, Washington, DC, May 19

Carmine Lewis' biorhythms were all screwed up. Henderson had kept them talking through the various scenarios until so late in the night/early morning that they'd ordered coffee and omelettes to keep themselves going at about 0300.

Now it was 0930 and she was back in the situation room for an ExComm meeting and craving pizza. Her biorhythms weren't the only thing that was messed up. So was the news from Israel as it headed into its first full day of unrelenting cyber warfare.

"Israel is one of the most digitally connected countries in the world," Tonya Dupré was explaining to the group around the meeting table. "Small population, high tech, one of the first on board with the internet of everything. The attackers went after their medical system first – every Israeli has a digital patient journal, every hospital, clinic and surgery sends and receives health data and payment information to and from about three major health insurance funds. Knock out the

HMOs, you bring the healthcare system to its knees, and that's what they did." She had a map onscreen of key data hubs across Israel, with spider lines of connections showing how interdependent they were. "The HMOs were their attack vector into the banking system. Israeli banks process about 27 million transactions with the HMOs hourly – the attackers spiked the data flowing between the HMOs and the banks and brought the bank networks down. From the bank networks the attack spread to the stock market." Hubs across the map of Israel started going blood red.

"Nothing military?" McDonald asked. "I thought they'd also lost air traffic control, radar, communications?"

"They went after the civilian infrastructure first," Tonya replied. "Which included civil airports. Since most airports in Israel are dual purpose – civil/military – they were pretty hard targets, but knocking out air traffic control compromised both civilian and military operations. It was the satellite attack that was the vector to Israel's military communication network. Somehow, the attackers were able to insert attack code into an older communication satellite network Israel launched in the 1990s and kept functional mainly as a backup for other, better defended networks. That Kirov cruiser took down just enough of the newer satellites that Israel had to bring their old network online. The minute they did, the attack code was downloaded and started spreading through their land-based comms network." Two thirds of the map turned red. "We still don't know how they penetrated the control stations for the electricity grid. We think that attack was Iranian, so it could have been through human agents working inside the utilities, rather than a digital attack vector, but seventy percent of the grid was knocked out within the first four hours." The map went almost entirely red.

Henderson turned to Carmine. "What is the status now, Director?"

"As bad as it can get, Mr. President. Stock exchange was up for about an hour last night, back down again. Queues a mile long outside every bank as people try to pull their cash out, but the government has announced a $100 daily withdrawal limit. No money is moving into the country since international trades are in chaos. Half the electricity grid is back up, but only intermittent since the damage was both physical and cyber. That side of things is a total cluster. The Russians and Iranians must have been preparing this for months, even years. The Israeli military is recovering fast, though. Tel Aviv air traffic control is being managed by mobile military radar, emergency and military traffic only. Haifa the same. Israel's air defense capacity will be the first to recover, ground and naval will take a little longer."

Defense Secretary McDonald saw all eyes turn to him. "The Israeli Air Force is still combat capable. They've got their major air bases back up with mobile radar and AWACS units providing command and control and have doubled their already high level of airborne patrols. We understand the Navy is having trouble contacting ships at sea since their satellites went down … they've asked for our help and we're looking into it. Might be able to use our Aegis destroyers to relay their messages but Israel would need to trust us with their comms and intel and they aren't there yet. Army is able to fight in place, but large-scale maneuvers will be hard to coordinate. They issued a general callup of all reserves, but they don't have an overview of who is reporting in where. Radio comms are running on diesel backup generators and the cell phone network is down so C3i systems are compromised. They're estimating another 12 to 24 hours to get everything back on line, assuming the attack doesn't morph."

Tonya had been reading an intel report on her tablet and interrupted. "I don't think the attack is over yet, Mr. Secretary. Israel is one of the most internet connected nations on the planet. Eight out of ten homes are what you'd call 'smart homes'; devices connected to the internet, personal digital assistants in every room for ordering groceries and telemedicine appointments, you name it. The hackers got into the personal assistant software – every damn device in every connected home in Israel has just started broadcasting this message, in Hebrew, Arabic and English." She tapped a voice file and the broadcast filled the room. After a few moments of Hebrew, it switched to English. "This is an Israeli Government announcement. False messages are being broadcast on radio and television calling on reservists to report to their units. These messages should be ignored. All reservists should remain in their homes and await further instruction. Repeating, this is an Israeli Government announcement…"

McDonald pulled a paper out of the folder in front of him. "Great. And if that weren't enough, you remember the commander of their Golani Brigade was assassinated? Well, his replacement is missing now."

"Who?"

"The *acting* commander of the Golani Brigade. Dropped off the grid yesterday morning, not seen since. Israeli brass is worried he's either been assassinated too or abducted." McDonald put the report down. "Another two Israeli battalions in their Northern Command have mutinied, refusing to serve alongside women. If Syria was going to move on the Golan, now would be the time to do it."

"So what's holding them back?"

Secretary of State Shrier held up his hand. "I believe I may have the answer to that, Mr. President. After your call to the Russian President, Iranian diplomats approached the Swedes in Tehran. They admitted nothing regarding the ongoing cyber offensive, but said they would be interested in Sweden working with Russia to broker discussions with Israel regarding…" He picked up a note of his own, "… uh, 'improving bilateral relations, particularly with regard to limits on strategic missile systems'."

"No mention of a seat at that table for the USA," VP Sianni remarked. "What a surprise."

At that moment Karl Allen, the President's Chief of Staff, looked up from checking his telephone. "Sorry to break in. Can we turn on the TV? We need to see this."

Henderson waved to an aide and as he brought the TV news feed up on the big screen at the end of the boardroom table, Carmine snatched up her telephone and saw a stream of messages had come in since the start of the meeting. The one at the top was the latest from her people and she opened it first.

Ignore earlier messages. Here is latest. Israeli Air Force 0900 Eastern launched a massive air offensive against targets inside Syria and Iran. Air-to-air and air-to-ground attacks underway against Syria and Iran. Israeli aircraft also attacking Iran through Turkey. Targets in Syria confined to Syrian and Iranian ground and missile forces and military targets in Damascus. Targets in Iran including suspected missile launch sites and nuclear facilities at Fordo, Bushehr, Natanz, Arak. Russian and Israeli aircraft engaged over Syria. Israel ground forces still in place, no sign of Israeli armor movement, yet.

The TV screen snapped to life, showing a breathless reporter in nighttime Damascus yelling into a microphone as ground-to-air missiles and cannon tracer lit the sky behind him and a cloud of smoke from a recent ground strike rolled into the air. Tickertape rolling across the bottom of the screen said: *Israeli PM blames Iran for cyber attack chaos. Announces retaliatory airstrikes are underway on Iranian forces in Syria and nuclear facilities inside Iran.*

Henderson waved a finger at Karl. "This is what he calls 'coordinating our responses?'"

Karl gave a shrug of resignation. "The situation Israel finds itself in, he probably figures a press announcement counts as coordination."

"Get him on the line."

Syrian Airspace, East of the Golan Heights, May 19

"Kot leader, Control, acknowledged, I have two IAF *Heron* unmanned aircraft for you, targets marked, please confirm."

Lieutenant Yevgeny Bondarev, of the Russian 7th Air Group, had been circling his formation of four Su-57 *Felon* fighters a few miles inside Syrian airspace, behind the point on the map where the Israeli, Lebanese and Syrian borders met in the northern Golan Heights.

He checked his tactical display, seeing the sector controller had called the new contacts as Israeli drones. Easy prey. Except that he'd already fallen for that trap before in Turkey, going after a couple of surveillance drones only to find they were flying under an umbrella of stealthy F-35 *Panthers*. That mistake had cost him an aircraft.

Bondarev checked his targeting display. The two unarmed Israeli drones were just where he would expect them to be, one circling at about 20,000 feet over Israel's northern border with Lebanon, the other over Lebanon's eastern border with Syria, no doubt monitoring traffic on the Damascus to Beirut motorway. Both were inside Lebanese airspace. Bondarev checked quickly for civilian aircraft in the sector, but saw none on his display.

Two sides could play the stealth game.

"Targets confirmed, Control, Kot flight will prosecute, out." He switched channels and called up his number four. "Kot four, the first two are yours, guns only please, take your targeting from the AWACS, radar off, save your missiles."

"Understood, Kot leader, four committing." His number four didn't sound disappointed. A kill was a kill, armed or unarmed. Bondarev watched as the aircraft peeled away, his eyes flicking from screen to screen in his cockpit, checking the flight instruments in his heads-up helmet-mounted display, checking the relative positions of his three remaining wingmen, checking the sky around him for the telltale exhaust signatures that might signal an aircraft nearby that his infrared detectors hadn't picked up.

Then the radio had exploded to life. "Kot four. *Missile!* Evading…"

Just as he'd thought. His number four had been jumped!

Bondarev's eyes had desperately scanned the threat screen in front of him, but it remained stubbornly empty.

"Hold station, Kot flight," he ordered his other aircraft. "Eyes on sky and sensors."

Helplessly, he watched the icon for his number four spin as it plummeted toward the ground, maneuvering to avoid the missile fired at it from an unknown quarter. With relief Bondarev saw his man recover.

"Kot four, rejoin. Disengage, repeat, disengage."

There was strength in numbers, and they would be safest against the enemy stealth fighters if they stayed inside Syrian airspace and let the Israelis come to them. It wasn't worth losing a man just to claim a damn surveillance drone, that was for sure.

"Kot four rejoining," his pilot said, panting from the exertion of dodging the enemy missile.

The Russian aircraft patrolling over Syria hadn't been taken by surprise. They'd seen the Israeli buildup all through the evening in response to the cyber chaos on the ground below. The *Beriev* A100 AWACS through which Bondarev was receiving data and interception orders had been tracking no fewer than 175 separate aircraft in the air over Israel at one point, before about thirty split north and south, headed for tankers over either Turkey or Saudi Arabia, of that he'd been in no doubt. Added to the 175 the *Beriev* and Syrian ground radar could 'see', Bondarev knew there would be at least another 50 F-35 stealth fighters they could not.

That much was confirmed moments later as all hell broke loose on the ground beneath them and flashes of white and red began lighting up the ground as the first wave of Israeli strikes rolled in. Soon the air was filled with tracer fire from 30mm anti-air cannons, the burst of fire and smoke that marked ground-to-air missile launches all along the two-hundred-mile border with Israel. Bondarev's tactical screen had been showing two older Syrian S-300 radar systems active in his sector, and both of them stopped transmitting at the same time, disappearing from his screen.

Stealth aircraft, taking down the air defenses with homing anti-radiation missiles, he guessed. Now comes the real harm.

Air war fighting tactics in the modern age were relatively simple. You sent in your most sophisticated aircraft to knock out the enemy air defenses and take down its air patrols, preferably from long range. If you succeeded, then you sent in your older, slower, ground-pounding aircraft or cruise missiles to attack ground targets. But first, you had to account for the enemy's defenses, on the ground and in the air.

The aircraft that had just fired at his wingman knew there were Russian fighters over the border with Syria. Their mission now would be to find and kill them. Bondarev's mission was to make them pay for trying.

Simple, yes. For the strategist. Not for the pilot.

"War is simple only for Generals, Yevgeny," his grandfather, former General of the Russian Aerospace Command, Viktor Bondarev, had once told him. "For the common soldier, or pilot, it is a confusing, messy, bloody affair and your job is not to make sense of it. Your job is to *fight* it."

He had no doubt the fighting had well and truly begun tonight. Seconds later his number two, Lieutenant Tchakov, broke the silence.

"Kot leader, Kot two. I am picking up search radar on my passive arrays. US type AN/APG-81. AI classification, F-35. Bearing 198 degrees, altitude 25,000, range 13 miles."

Bondarev felt a tightening in his chest. *Panthers.* As he'd expected. But they couldn't see the Israeli fighters on radar yet, just the ghostly radiation from their radars as they searched for the Russian *Felons.* Bitter experience over Turkey had taught Bondarev that the *Panthers* were likely to find him before he could lock onto them. But he did not plan to wait for that moment. His number four was still making his way back to them. He couldn't wait for that either.

He contacted the other two pilots. "Kot two, Kot three, arm K-77 missiles, autonomous target-seeking mode, prepare to fire down the bearing to the radar contact." Bondarev's eyes flicked to his weapons display, checking his own K-77 missiles were armed and ready to fire down the bearing to the Israeli search radar, which had closed to within fifteen miles. He could wait no longer.

"Kot flight, engage and hit the deck!" Bondarev told his pilots. "Missile one, *launch*." Bondarev felt the supersonic air-to-air missile drop from his weapons bay and he hauled his machine around and pointed it for the nap of the earth. As he did so, he angled his machine so he hid his engine exhaust from the Israeli fighters, slightly increasing his radar cross-section but minimizing his infrared signature.

Three K-77 missiles speared toward the source of the Israeli radar signature. They had no specific target, but had been fired at relatively short range, in 'target-seeking mode'. They immediately switched on their own onboard radar and optical infrared seekers and began scanning the sky ahead of them for targets.

They very quickly found the Israeli F-35 *Panther* of a rather self-confident Lieutenant Tal Goren, who had just minutes ago identified one of the Russian *Felons* on his optical Distributed Aperture System (DAS), apparently stalking an IDF drone. He had fired on it and watched with satisfaction as it spiraled to the earth and then disappeared from his radar. He was going to chalk that up as a kill and was looking for his next when Yevgeny Bondarev's K-77 missile slammed into the nose of his *Panther* and detonated before his warning receiver even had time to chime in his ears. He died with a hungry smile on his face.

Bondarev leveled out just above the ground and checked his situational display again. The *Beriev* was showing possible contacts in Syrian airspace, but very few on which it had a solid lock. That was to be expected.

"Kot flight, join on me, maintain five-mile separation, climb to 20,000." All four aircraft fell into formation around him, giving the flight a thirty-mile span of sky they could monitor on passive optical and infrared sensors without giving away their positions. "Sector control, Kot leader, splash one *Panther*. Kot flight available for tasking."

"Kot leader, stand by."

Bondarev had learned in Turkey that war came at you fast, and disappeared just as quickly. Fifteen minutes ago he'd been circling over Syria. Five minutes ago they'd claimed their first Israeli fighter. Now, five minutes later, he was circling in apparently clear skies east of Lebanon again, his radar warning receiver silent, his tactical display showing no hostile aircraft in his sector. It was a situation that couldn't last given what he was seeing up and down the border, he knew that.

His radio crackled. "All aircraft in the sector, we are picking up multiple hostile fast movers launching from Israeli airfields, types F-16 and F-15 – expect also stealth aircraft. Sector control out."

It seemed the Israelis were either impatient, or overconfident. The Israeli Air Force could field F-35 fighters, 4th-generation F-15E strike fighters, F-15 multirole fighters and a large force of older but recently upgraded F-16C/D fighters. Against this, for border patrol duties Russia was standing two squadrons of Su-57 *Felons* and four of unmanned *Okhotnik* strike fighters. In reserve deeper inside Syria were two squadrons each of 4th-generation Mig-29 and Sukhoi-30 fighter aircraft. In crude terms, it meant the Israeli force of up to 300 fighters outnumbered the Russians more than two to one. They were not odds Bondarev had enjoyed thinking about and they apparently gave the Israeli mission planners confidence.

But Israel had never faced a modern air opponent like Russia, equipped with stealth fighters, sophisticated early warning aircraft, supported by satellite and ground radar data, and fresh from battle in the skies over Turkey. Israeli pilots were used to being able to roam with near impunity over the skies of Lebanon, or strike targets near the border with Syria without being challenged.

Bondarev watched as the newly revitalized city of Damascus

slid below his wing, lights still burning brightly even though he could see streams of tracer fire from anti-air fire lacing the sky and the occasional flash of a missile launch. As though to underscore the wrongness of the sight, there was a massive explosion on the outskirts of the city and half of the lights went out immediately. Israel was paying Syria back for the attack on its infrastructure by targeting the Syrian power grid.

"Kot flight, echelon left, begin scan and track pilots," he said, ordering his pilots to begin actively scanning the skies with their phased-array radars. They no longer had the luxury of total stealth if the enemy was hitting targets below them.

"Good call, Comrade Captain," Rap replied. He was one of many younger pilots who still enjoyed using the old Communist habit of calling fellow officers 'tovarisch' or comrade. In fact, it had never died out. Bondarev still referred to his grandfather as 'Comrade General'.

Immediately, the four *Felon* fighters began scanning the air and ground around them, and Bondarev's situational display lit up with potential targets as they synchronized data with each other. The *Beriev* was already tracking a large number of Israeli fighters, mostly 4th-generation F-16s or F-15s, moving out from their bases across Israel.

The fact Bondarev could see the Israeli F-16s and F-15s moving toward him did not reassure him. He did not fear them, or their missiles. He had faced upgraded Turkish F-16s in the north and found his *Felon* could almost always see and engage them long before it was seen by them. The problem was those bloody *Panthers*, and he was painfully aware that for every F-35 *Panther* Russia had destroyed over Turkey, it had lost three *Felons*. His own *Felon* had been one of them, and his leg still ached at night from hitting the ground after he ejected.

On his tac screen he watched as unmanned Russian *Okhotnik* fighters swept in beneath him and began engaging the Israeli 4th-generation aircraft at long range. He saw a blizzard of 16 missiles spray across the border and at least six Israeli aircraft icons wink out before the small, stealthy *Okhotnik*s turned back into Syria, unscathed.

"Kot leader, Kot three, I have two targets on infrared. Bearing zero niner three, altitude 5,000, range 20 klicks. Refining. Synchronizing."

Instantly, the targets picked up by his wingman were shared with the other three *Felons*. At that range, and visible only on passive sensors, Bondarev's combat AI was not able to classify the targets. Bondarev didn't want to waste missiles on unmanned or lightly armed drones. But as his pilot worked the target, sending a tight beam of high-frequency radar energy down its bearing, the targets sprung into clarity.

"Kot flight, *Panthers* low to starboard. Take your targeting from Kot three, home on data. Engage!"

Four missiles dropped from the *Felon* flight's weapons bays, tipped toward the ground and accelerated toward their targets at more than twice the speed of sound. The Israeli pilots had detected the targeting radar of Bondarev's pilot, and reacted immediately. Two missiles fired from the *Panthers* down low speared up toward him. He would either have to maneuver to break their radar lock, or stay on the target and take his chances.

Bondarev decided neither was a good option. He took over the targeting, locking up the two *Panthers* below with his own radar. "Kot three, I have a lock. Evade, evade, evade."

The Russian missiles switched from taking their targets from his number three to taking their targets from him. No doubt with relief, his pilot rolled his *Felon* onto its back and began diving toward the earth, forcing the rising enemy missiles to radically adjust their flight paths to try to intercept him as he fired decoy after decoy into the air behind him.

But now the *Panthers* could see Bondarev too.

"Splash one!" Rap called as their missiles speared into one of the *Panthers*. The second managed to get a new missile away in the direction of Bondarev before it too was...

"Splash two!" Rap called again.

But Yevgeny Bondarev wasn't listening. At the first sound

of the missile launch tone inside his helmet, he had pushed his throttle forward, rolled his *Felon* onto a wingtip and begun steering toward the missile evasion cue in his heads-up helmet display. He grunted with the effort, his flight suit inflating as it tried to keep the blood from flowing out of his head and into his boots from the brutal gravitational forces he was subjecting himself to. Spiraling downward, he desperately tried to keep the steering cue inside the circle on his visor that his AI calculated might, could – no, *bloody well should* – keep him safe.

His world went black-tinged grey, his head lolled helplessly on his shoulders, his hand dropped from the flight stick…

The moment it did, the *Felon*'s AI took over. Ignoring the plight of its pilot, it pulled the aircraft into an even tighter turn as the Israeli missile screamed past its wing and detonated in a cloud of decoy chaff. At the same time, it scanned for new threats, found none, and leveled the *Felon* out, jinking the nose gently down to force blood back to its pilot's head as it increased the percentage of pure oxygen flowing to his mask. Bondarev had never fully lost consciousness, and he came around slowly, taking the flight stick again and guiding his machine back up to join the others at altitude.

He checked his ordnance level. Two missiles fired, four remaining. Plus cannons, of course. Swiping across the weapons stores on the other aircraft in his flight he saw a similar picture, with the exception of his number four, who had expended one fewer missile. *Good.* All of his pilots alive, his aircraft still in the fight and still able to bite. Three enemy *Panthers* down.

"Kot leader, Sector control, four Israeli F-15s moving toward your sector. Bearing two ten two degrees, altitude 30,000, range forty miles. Pushing targeting to you. Commit."

Four new red icons appeared on Bondarev's screen. Pulling a lungful of oxygen through his mask, he dialed back the oxygen level and focused on the intercept. "Sector control, Kot leader. Targets received, Kot flight vectoring for intercept."

"Let's get some, Kot pilots!" Rap called. The kid was

irrepressible, but had grown into a reliable hand after a few harsh lessons over Turkey. Bondarev let him have his moment.

As Bondarev laid a waypoint on his screen for his pilots to follow, he zoomed his screen out and momentarily stared, stunned, at what it was telling him. There were at least seventy Israeli aircraft being tracked over Israel and Syria. He could see only thirty Russian aircraft, manned and unmanned, opposing them. Most of the Syrian ground air defense systems were down, though a few of the more sophisticated S-400 *Growler* radars in central Syria were still operational. For now. They had the ability to jam and decoy attacking missiles and had apparently survived the first wave of the Israeli assault.

He almost wished they hadn't. They were showing him an Israeli air assault that was beyond anything he'd seen in his lifetime.

He choked down his shock, his dismay and, yes, his fear. Focus, Yevgeny. Working the target that was the four Israeli F-15i Strike Eagle fighters, he allocated a total of eight missiles across the flight to them. He and his pilots were only six miles from optimal launch range for the K-77M, which Yevgeny and his pilots had learned with pride was a bloody good missile indeed. The F-15 pilots had only minutes to live, but were already as good as dead. Why was Israel being so reckless?

Focus, Yevgeny. Your job is not to make sense of the war. Your job is to fight it.

All Domain Attack: Silicon

10 miles south-east of US demarcation line,
Mediterranean Sea

"Focus, Ehud, there has to be a way."

Aboard the Israeli Navy *Dolphin* III class submarine, *Gal*, the atmosphere was getting thick in several senses. For the last twelve hours, they had been unable to contact their fleet base in Eilat. They had tried the tethered sensor buoy several hours earlier, and successfully sent a status report by encrypted burst transmission, and received only a brief confirmation before they had to dive again. Heavy civilian shipping over their position south of Rhodes had forced them deeper, to a depth that exceeded the reach of the tether cable. So for their last check-in, they'd been forced to burn a buoy, sending it to the surface untethered, which meant they could get a message out but not receive. The buoy presumably sent its message, then flooded its tanks and sank to the bottom of the Med. They had no way of knowing.

They only carried one backup.

Now they had risen to sensor depth again and deployed the buoy to update their picture of the battlesphere above the water around them, which supplemented what their onboard AI was able to glean from sonar.

Something strange was happening.

The shipping lane leading from the Aegean Sea into the Mediterranean south of the Greek island of Rhodes was one of the busiest in the world, feeding traffic from the Black Sea, Turkey and Greece into the Mediterranean and onwards to Europe, the Middle East and Africa. At their previous check-in with the tethered buoy, they'd seen normal levels of shipping, both on sonar and radar. But in the period since, their sonar had detected declining levels of traffic, unusually low for the time of day and year.

As their radar scanned the sea around the buoy, it picked up almost no civilian shipping, just a few coastal freighters. No oil supertankers, no bulk carriers or container ships. And now, about ten miles off their starboard side, they were picking up an active sonar search signal. Military. Their AI had classified it as coming from a US *Arleigh Burke*-class Aegis destroyer, and the sonic signature from its screws and engine identified it as the USS *Porter*.

It was clearly searching for something and that worried Binyamin Ben-Zvi because the chances were that the *Porter* was searching for the same thing that the INS *Gal* was trying to avoid … the 4,000-ton Russian *Kilo*-class submarine pickets that would be traveling out of the Aegean Sea ahead of the Russian-Iranian fleet. The newest variants in the class, which were known to have been assigned to the Black Sea fleet, were both silent and deadly.

To hide themselves from sonar, their hulls were covered in rubberized anechoic tiles. Even the internal surfaces were rubberized to prevent sounds from inside the hull – like engine mounts or even tools dropped by its fifty-man crew – reverberating through the hull and into the surrounding water. Their double-skinned hull was lined with passive acoustic sensors that Russian admirals had bragged could 'hear a dolphin burp at a range of twenty miles', and active decoy systems designed specifically to defeat the most common US anti-submarine weapon, the Mark 48 homing torpedo.

Most importantly, it was designed to hunt and kill enemy submarines, like the INS *Gal*.

The fact that a US *Arleigh Burke*-class destroyer was combing the waters near them for what could only be the Russian pickets was like being a surfer out on the lineup and hearing the lifesavers sound the 'shark warning' siren. You couldn't do much except roll onto your stomach and paddle as quietly as you could toward shore, hoping the shark ate someone else.

Their problem right now, however, was not a Russian *Kilo*, or the USS *Porter*. Their problem was that they still had no link with Eilat and had no idea whether the strategic environment around them had changed along with the tactical environment, which clearly had. Their latest inbound communication from fleet command had updated them on the known position, bearing, speed and composition of the Russian-Iranian fleet, along with the news that the US President had ordered a blockade as hoped. The communique also confirmed that their orders were the same as when they had sailed; in that respect, there had been no change to their mission.

"Well, we can try to increase the reception range. The drone on top of the buoy can lift the aerial a hundred feet into the air. That will give us about another hundred miles range but I'm not even picking up Tel Aviv, so I don't see how…"

Subsurface contact on passive sensors. Screw in the water, bearing three five zero, depth 200, range five point three miles, speed sixteen knots relative.

The voice of their AI-assisted sensor system broke into their conversation exactly as a human sonar operator would have done, though with much more calm in its artificial voice. Five miles! And directly ahead of them. A single screw … it could only be another sub, hunting them.

"*Gal*: all engines stop, pull in the buoy, turn to zero four zero and glide," Binyamin ordered. They were bobbing about just under the surface of the sea, the submarine equivalent of being in plain sight to any boat coasting below them.

All engines powering down, turning to zero four zero, gliding, the AI repeated. I recommend arming aft torpedoes.

"Confirmed, *Gal*. Arm aft torpedoes. Prepare for emergency evasion. And analyze that screw signature."

Arming aft torpedoes. Emergency evasion routines prioritized. Analysis already underway.

If it was a Russian *Kilo* and it saw the Israeli *Dolphin* as a threat to its fleet, it may just decide to fire, in which case the *Gal* had to be ready to respond.

Target is changing heading to an intercept course. I calculate a high probability we have been detected. No active sonar registering.

"Damn," Ehud said. "They caught us sleeping, Benji." Just because the unidentified sub wasn't pinging them on sonar didn't mean it didn't have a good enough lock on their position to be able to take the shot.

"Well, more fool them. *Gal*, engines ahead one third. Turn to an intercept bearing. Take us down to 250 feet. Do you have an ID on the target?"

Insufficient data. Analyzing. The AI confirmed his orders and the boat accelerated again, turning more tightly so that it came around and pointed directly at the unidentified contact.

"Playing chicken?" Ehud asked with a grin, checking his instrument display. "We're back at twelve knots relative, increasing."

"Let me know when we hit twenty." They were pointed directly ahead of the contact and accelerating their dive so that they would cross directly aft of it. A Russian *Kilo* was twice the weight and half as nimble as the *Gal*, a supertanker to a speedboat, and Binyamin planned to take advantage of that. If they lived long enough.

"He's not deviating," Ehud observed. "Fifteen knots relative."

"Good, take steerage control."

"*Gal*, first officer assuming manual steering control."

AI pilot deactivated. You have the helm, Officer Mofaz.

The *Gal*'s AI painted a laser-generated 3D holographic image of the water around their sub and projected it into the air between their two chairs. It showed a generic image of the contact in yellow, since it was still unidentified, gliding through the water straight and level below them and to starboard, and, in blue, the *Gal*, in an angled dive that would bring it across the contact's stern. It was a maneuver intended to make a torpedo shot almost impossible, and if the enemy did get one away, to close the range so dramatically there was a chance it wouldn't arm before striking because the *Gal* would be inside their minimum safe distance.

"*Gal*: sound collision alarm at 100 feet."

Collision alarm set for 100 feet.

Binyamin scratched the back of his neck, and his hand came away covered in sweat. "When you get underneath him, turn hard starboard, put us in his baffles and glide again. Unless he fires on us, I want to try to increase separation and play the thermocline, got that?"

"Yes, Benji."

The throb of their engines and the tick, tick, tick of their hull compressing as they dived down toward the unidentified submarine was background noise. The only sound they were interested in was the inappropriately gentle chime that would signal an enemy torpedo launch.

A loud sonar ping sounded through their hull as the contact at last engaged its active sonar to get a precise fix on the Israeli boat. It provoked an immediate and drastic reaction.

Contact decelerating. They appear to be executing an emergency stop. Engine noise. Analysis indicates screw has reversed. Acoustic analysis complete. Contact identified as the Astute-class submarine HMS Agincourt.

"Oh shit. It's a Brit attack sub," Binyamin said under his breath. He had put them on a collision course for an 8,000-ton British nuclear submarine. "*Gal*: engines back full!"

"Speed eighteen knots relative. Falling, but not slow enough," Ehud said. "We'll have to push through with it."

"Port ten degrees," Binyamin said. "Cross their stern and level out at 200 feet. Engage active sonar and match speed and bearing."

"Aye aye. I'll pass ahead of them and then pull around on their portside inside Aqua-fi range. Let's hope they've also worked out who we are or we are going to give them a perfect shot into our starboard side as we pass. *Gal*: engage active sonar."

Active sonar engaged. Sounding. Contact acquired.

If it was a game of chicken, it was being conducted in the dark, with their eyes shut. Neither of the leviathans rushing toward each other under the sea could actually 'see' the other, but now both were using their sonar at least they had a fix on each other, and with both of them chopping back their speed, a collision was less likely.

Using the hologram as a visual cue, supplemented by the bearing, speed, depth and range data on his own display, Ehud tightened his hand on the submarine's 'flight stick' and as the *Gal* crossed close behind the *Agincourt*, he twisted it to full right rudder and pulled back on the stick to angle the dive planes upward. Steering a 2,500-ton submarine was not like steering an airplane, and he had to allow for the momentum of the boat and the lag in response to its controls, but he was pleased to see the *Gal* swing around the bigger British sub and then drop in alongside it, on a parallel track. It was helped, of course, by the fact the British captain had known to keep his own boat sailing straight and level, but as he leveled out and applied a touch of portside rudder, Ehud couldn't help feeling a little like a Top Gun pilot on a fighter range.

Just for a moment.

"*Gal*: cut sonar, use acoustic sensors to match depth and bearing and hold separation," Binyamin ordered, clapping Ehud on the shoulder. "Nice work, Ehud. *Gal*: hail the contact on Aqua-fi."

For nearly a century, the only way submarines could contact each other while submerged was via 'Gertrude', an acoustic system that fired soundwaves through the water between transceivers on the hull and allowed voice-to-voice contact at short range. While the range hadn't improved much – both boats still needed to be within a hundred yards of each other – contact was possible now using boosted wifi signals that allowed both voice and data transmission between boats. It took only moments for the *Gal*'s hail to be answered, and the thickly accented voice of a very perturbed British captain to come over the command room loudspeakers.

"*Agincourt* to INS *Gal*, what in the bloody hell kind of suicidal stunt was that?!"

Binyamin felt his cheeks redden. "Apologies, *Agincourt*, we were unsure of your identity until we had committed to the maneuver. As soon as we identified who you were, we adjusted course. I am sorry for the scare."

"We had you identified twenty minutes ago, *Gal*, your boat needs a bloody good sensor upgrade. I know a firm in Bremen that could do it for you at 'mates' rates'."

Whether that was true or not, Binyamin was grateful the British commander hadn't overreacted to their aggressive maneuvering. "Uh, thank you, *Agincourt*. I will pass that offer on to my Admiral."

"Good, that's the bollicking out of the way then. I assume that we both have a similar mission out here, *Gal*?"

I very much doubt that, Binyamin thought to himself. But he kept his reply neutral. "I can't confirm that, *Agincourt*, but I am happy to listen to your ideas for avoiding another incident. I assume also that you are in contact with that US destroyer to the north?"

"We have been, and I can tell you, they already know you are in the neighborhood, *Gal*. Given that all our friends know, I think it reasonable to suspect that our enemies know as well. Whatever your mission is here, as they say in the clandestine services, it would seem your cover is blown, old girl."

Again, Binyamin had no way of knowing if what the British captain was saying was true, but then, what reason would he have for lying? Their trip via the Cape of Good Hope, their efforts to avoid detection on entering the Mediterranean, had they really been for nothing? No. He had exercised with both the British and US navies, and he and his former crew, in their older, noisier, slower *Dolphin* II boat, had scored more than their share of 'kills' against their NATO partners. And racked up more than a few simulated kills against Russian warships too. If their presence in the Mediterranean had been betrayed, it was by other actors in the IDF, not himself and Ehud.

He ignored the jibe. "What intelligence can you share about the estimated position of the Russian subsurface pickets?"

Binyamin asked. "We have made no contact to date."

"Happy to share, *Gal*. We're all on the same side in this little stoush, and all that. Our friend the USS *Porter* is prosecuting a contact twenty miles north of our current position," the British captain said. "*Kilo* class, probably the *Yakutsk*. We think the Russians have two *Kilos* with them, so if they follow their usual pattern, the other will be trailing the fleet to guard against a rear approach. If their picket is already well into the Med, it rather looks like they intend to force the issue, don't you think?"

Binyamin could see the British and their allies did not have a full picture of what they were facing. Should he share? He raised an eyebrow to Ehud. Aqua-fi communications weren't recorded or logged, there would be no blowback for disclosing confidential information. Ehud nodded at Binyamin, reading his mind.

"Yes, it seems like it, *Agincourt*. Look, I said we have had no contact with the Russian-Iranian fleet since we started our patrol, but you should know it is accompanied by *more* than two *Kilo*-class submarines. Our intelligence service says an Iranian *Fateh*-class submarine sailed from Latakia in Syria last night. We estimate that at submerged cruising speed, it would currently be approximately 250 miles east, and likely to be in position off Rhodes to support the incoming fleet in about ten hours. If the Russians and Iranians plan to force the blockade, it would make sense for that *Fateh* to be in position to engage the US destroyers just before they clash. Do you understand what I am saying?"

Binyamin heard voices confer at the other end of the connection before the British captain replied. "I suspect you are saying, *Gal*, that we have a maximum of ten hours before all hell breaks loose in the Mediterranean."

Binyamin and Ehud exchanged glances. "That is a good way to put it, *Agincourt*."

"Very good. Look, we will continue our patrol in support of the US destroyer squadron. For coordination purposes, you will find the five of them strung out in a hundred-mile line between

Rhodes and Lefkos. That may sound like they are spread thin, but each of them fields helos with dipping sonar, plus unmanned aerial and surface surveillance vehicles, so nothing is going to get past them unchallenged." The British captain paused. "And that includes you, *Gal*. Our American cousins do not take kindly to either enemies or friends 'pissing in their pool' as they put it. Your presence would be considered … inconvenient."

Ehud gave Binyamin a sour look and seemed to be about to say something aloud, but Binyamin put a finger to his lips to silence him. "Message understood, *Agincourt*. At the next opportunity, can you please advise the commander of the US destroyer squadron that we can see you have the exit routes from the Aegean well covered. We will withdraw to a position … let me see … at MGRS coordinate 4QFJ12345678, between Cyprus and Turkey on the most likely route for the Russian-Iranian fleet to approach Tartus. That particular part of the world we regard as 'our pool', as you delicately put it."

There was a chuckle at the other end. "Touché, sir. I can't promise I'll be able to keep our cousins out of your pool, but they can hardly be surprised to find you lounging about in it. Very good. Well, bon voyage and good hunting, *Gal*."

"And to you, *Agincourt*," Binyamin said. He cut the contact, pulled up his navigation screen and put new waypoints on it. "*Gal*: steer to waypoints please, optimize depth and speed for stealth." They both sat quietly and watched the holograph sphere as the two submarines separated, the *Gal* headed north and the *Agincourt* east.

Navigation order confirmed and onscreen. Stealth cruise routines prioritized.

Ehud leaned over, looking at the waypoints. He raised an eyebrow. "That course will put us nicely behind that Russian *Kilo* and in a position to intercept their fleet. You don't intend to pull back to Cyprus at all?"

"No."

Ehud settled back in his chair. "Our allies may find that

'inconvenient', Binyamin."

"Israel has no allies, you know that, Ehud. Only enemies it has not made yet."

RAF Akrotiri Air Base, Cyprus, May 19

Shelly Kovacs had trust issues. She knew that. She'd put eight years of her life into the Marine F-47B *Fantom* project, and she'd fought like a wildcat to prevent her precious prototypes being suborned to the Air Force 432nd Air Expeditionary Wing, but she'd been told it would be good for fostering Marine Corps Aviation-USAF joint operations, good for DARPA and good for her project.

"You will get more data in a few weeks of real combat than you could possibly get in a year of exercises and simulations, Shelly," her program manager had told her, as she called to bitch again.

"Yeah, except they don't expect my babies to last *one* week, let alone a few," she'd replied. "I've lost two machines already. They aren't ready for combat and you know it. I have five pilots who fly them like they're hobby drones and one pilot, *one*, Matt, who flies them like she's possessed and none of the other pilots can come close to matching her skills. She's a coder, a hacker, a gamer, a fighter pilot and frankly, she's either the worst or the most inspired recruitment I've ever made."

"She's the one who rewrote your aggressor routines? It doesn't matter the others you've already got can't do what she can do, we'll find more like her."

"Not sure that's even vaguely possible, Matt." She hung up.

They were flying into a literal shitstorm. As the last no-fly zone mission had been withdrawing from the UNDOF DMZ, Israel had launched a full-scale air offensive into Syria. There had already been dozens of aircraft in the air over Israel, but O'Hare had been forced to find a way through what seemed like the entire Israeli Air Force for her six *Fantoms*, avoiding the ire of Israeli military air traffic controllers who no longer seemed to care that she was on a mission to protect UN troops in the Golan. After repeated orders to withdraw her aircraft or be shot down, O'Hare had pushed them down to ground level to get them off Israeli radar and barged across the countryside following river valleys and highways in southern Lebanon to the Golan.

Kovacs watched from the jump seat as the woman in the pilot's chair beside her in the trailer scratched the stubble on her close-shaven head and reached for an energy drink at the same time as she plugged in the coordinates that would keep her six-plane hex of *Fantoms* hugging the nap of the earth over the Golan Heights as soon as they got on station. O'Hare was wearing her headset and heads-up display eyepiece and noticed that Kovacs was looking at her. She pulled an earbud out of her right ear. "Sorry, you talking to me?"

"No, I was on the phone."

"Cool, because I was just getting in the zone, you know. You want to say something, just tap me on the shoulder or get on comms." O'Hare pointed at a tactical map that showed their aircraft approaching the UNDOF DMZ. "We'll be going live in five." With that, she put her earbud back in. "Lava Dogs, Lava Dogs, this is Marine Air aka the Golani Angel, do you read?"

"That's *not* your call sign," Kovacs pointed out. "And technically you aren't Marine Air, you're USAF."

"They don't want to hear that," O'Hare said, putting her hand over her throat mike. "It's a morale thing." She released the mike again. "Come in, Lava Dogs. I got that pizza for you."

"Uh, Golani Angel, this is Corporal Patel. You got good news for us? Because ma'am, we need it."

"Depends what you call good news, Patel. I got rations, bottled water, enhanced combat helmets with inbuilt headsets, ammunition and medical supplies coming your way by tilt rotor, courtesy your friends at Hatzerim Air Base. ETA 0400."

"Awww. No pizza?"

"Nope. SITFU, Corporal. And the bad news, no cavalry

coming to the rescue. The message is 'do what you can, where you are, with what you have'."

"We expected that, ma'am. But we got civilians here. Israeli citizens, mostly. My Sergeant wants to know, do the IDF know that? Maybe they can break through here."

Bunny looked across at Kovacs. "How much you think we should tell them?"

Kovacs didn't hesitate. "They deserve the full picture."

O'Hare nodded. "Not happening, Corporal. Whole of Israel is under intensive cyber attack. IDF ground forces are in disarray. Infantry pulling out of the Golan for no apparent reason, while armor tries to push in. Reserves being called up and stood down at the same time, no one can tell them where to report. Roads are chaos. No one seems to be in charge. In the air, it's the opposite. Any thunder you might hear is Israeli Air Force jets pounding Syrian positions to your east, or Israeli jets plowing dirt as they get hammered by Russian and Syrian air defenses. It's a much more even fight than Israel is used to and it isn't going to plan." She looked across at Kovacs and covered her mike again. "I forget anything?"

"Navy."

"Oh yeah. And the US President drew a line in the Mediterranean over the Iranian nukes and challenged the Iranians to cross it. They're protected by some heavyweight Russian missile cruisers, so it looks like they're going to call his bluff. You got anti-radiation pills, Corporal?"

"Not unless you included them in our Walmart order, ma'am."

"Oh well, you're a Marine, you probably don't need hair anyway."

"I do like it nice and short, ma'am."

O'Hare's voice softened. Kovacs could tell that for all her banter, O'Hare was full of feeling for the men on the ground below her. "Just like me, Corporal. I'm overhead now. Those Druze boys give you any trouble, you let me know, alright mate?"

he suggested they could be brought down to Buq'ata, to mortar the roof. Mortar the compound too. But Delavari didn't like that option. A mortar on a suburban roof could crash through and kill the hostages immediately below it. A mortar intended for the compound, poorly aimed, could hit the building's façade, killing anyone near a window.

"I've been sent here to save those civilians, not massacre them," he told the officer.

The man had looked bemused. "You are the specialist," he'd replied. "But do it quickly. Or I will bring that mortar crew here and get it done."

Delavari looked at the sky. "It will be dusk soon. I will have the setting sun behind me. That is my window. US Marines have excellent night vision equipment. If we wait too long, they will have the advantage." He already had his ammunition belt and water bottle in his webbing, so he lifted his rifle, holding it across his chest. "It will be done by nightfall, or it will have to wait until daylight. I make the shot. God determines the outcome."

James Jensen had learned in the siege of Kobani that if you wait for the enemy to come to you, he will oblige; at the time of his choosing, in ways unexpected, and usually with overwhelming force. He had no intention of allowing the Druze colonel that luxury.

Lying flat on the rooftop terrace behind his sniper team, Jensen and Amal Azaria had been guiding a recon drone around the town, mapping the Druze roadblocks, troop concentrations, garrisons and what seemed to be their base of operations in a high walled villa near the center of town. They found two marksmen on nearby roofs with radios, keeping an eye on their compound and reinforcing the need for the Marines to keep their heads down and the civilians to stay away from the front and side windows. Luckily the second-floor bathroom was at the rear of the house. And thankfully, they hadn't seen any other armored vehicles, just jeeps and trucks, so another armored assault seemed unlikely, for now. Jensen and his few Marines couldn't take on an entire Druze garrison, but he could reduce the threat to his squad and the civilians by persuading the Druze colonel to pull his marksmen further back.

Having marked the GPS coordinates of the two Druze riflemen, they crawled down from the roof and went out to Amal's workshop. Jensen watched, fascinated, as she pulled drone parts off shelves and started building a small drone about a third the size of those they had used to take the *Namer* apart. Not satisfied with the rotors she had on hand, Amal started her generator, moved to the 3D printer, called up the specs for slightly larger propellers and quickly printed them before fitting them to the drone and powering down the generator again. After a quick test flight with a dummy weight, she fitted cameras, a miniaturized guidance system and a battery pack.

All this she did while whistling absently to herself. Jensen decided not to disturb her with questions.

She turned the drone on its back, belly up, and opened a compartment about the size of a teacup, with two studs visible inside it. From a locker in the floor protected with a thumbprint coded lock, she pulled something that looked like a half baseball, studded with ball bearings. It fitted exactly into the teacup-shaped compartment and she pushed a detonator into the soft half-ball, connected the detonator wires to the studs inside the compartment and closed the compartment door, screwing it shut.

Letting out a big breath, she turned the drone the right way up and stepped back.

"Always happy I don't kill myself when I'm doing that," she said with a smile, pushing a black lock behind her ear.

"That was explosive?" Jensen asked. "C4?"

"BCHMX bonded C4," she told him. "Higher detonation velocity and blast heat." Putting the first drone aside she picked a second drone frame from off a shelf. "Unfortunately, also slightly more sensitive. Don't sneeze."

Jensen was about to pick the drone up to examine it, but stopped in his stride.

She looked over her shoulder. "Just joking, Sergeant. It *is* more sensitive, but feel free to sneeze. Gently."

As he watched from behind her, she went to her workbench and repeated the process, building a second identical drone.

The entire job had taken under thirty minutes.

She sat the second drone on her bench next to the first, and then went to the door of the shed, pulling it wide. Late afternoon light spilled in, highlighting her silhouette, and he saw her straighten her back, roll her shoulders. She returned to the bench, leaning on it with arms wide, either side of her drones.

"What is easier?" Jensen asked. "We want to hit them in daylight or dark?"

"The cameras have both daylight and infrared modes," she explained. She picked up the same control unit she had used to send the first wave of drones against the *Namer* IFV. "But it will be better to attack now, in low light, while we can still see to fly around any obstructions."

"How loud is it?"

"In here, it will sound louder because this is a large open space with metal walls. In the open air it is no louder than a small battery-powered hand fan. The Druze riflemen won't hear it coming until it's too late." She fished in a cabinet and brought out another control unit. "Are any of your men qualified to fly these sorts of drones? It would be better to attack the two riflemen simultaneously."

Jensen considered. "Patel is, but I want him on overwatch while we do this. It may flush out other shooters we haven't spotted." He held out his hand and took the control unit, looking it over. "This looks a lot like the controls I used to command the Legged Squad Support Systems I was testing in Kobani. This one here is direction, these are…?"

She pointed at the various controls on the unit. "Altitude,

attitude, speed, power on/off – don't touch that – and trigger."

"I can work this."

"Good. You take the control units, I will carry the drones," she said, implicitly not trusting him not to blow them both up. He was fine with that.

He followed her out of the shed and she put the drones on the ground in the middle of the concrete apron in front of the shed, sliding the shed door closed behind her and locking it. He watched as she crouched to move the drones further apart, wincing as she thoughtlessly scratched the wound on her forehead, making it bleed again.

"'Toymaker'. How did you ... you know?"

"Get my nickname, or how did I get into this line of work?"

"Well, the first one is kind of obvious. The second one."

She stood, taking a control unit from him. "In the movie they make about this war, this is where I would tell you about how my family was killed by terrorists and this is the best way I found to use my talents to avenge their deaths..."

"I'm sorry to hear that."

"Don't be. They weren't." She hit a switch on the drones and their rotors started spinning. "I do this because the IDF paid for my university degree, and I was recruited by the Defense Research Directorate based on a paper I wrote about the potential military applications of facial recognition technologies. My obsession with drones and robotics came later. I tell myself that my work will one day save Israeli soldiers' lives, because instead of sending them out on potentially life-threatening patrols, we'll be sending out my drones instead."

"We could have used these in Kobani, that's for sure," Jensen said.

"Yes. But that's just what I tell myself. Between you and me, Sergeant, I do this because I just love building little winged messengers of death." She winked at him and bent down again to fuss with one of the units.

"I'll go topside and tell Patel what's about to go down. Bell

268

can let the others know."

"Don't be long, we only have another thirty minutes of light."

Little winged messengers of death? OK, she was messing with him. Wasn't she?

Delavari settled on his stomach on the platform of the water tower. He'd brought two wooden boxes up with him and placed them in front of him to hide his silhouette, laying the muzzle of his *Saher* between them. Using a small laser rangefinder no larger than a pencil torch, he measured the distances to the rooftop, the surrounding walls, the front gate, and the front door of the house, and dialed them as presets on his scope so he could quickly flip between them if the Sergeant showed himself.

Around two thousand, two hundred yards. At one and a quarter miles into an elevated target, probably one of the longest shots he'd ever attempted. It would be an almost impossible shot with the *Degtyarev*'s normal 12.7mm rounds, but a *Saher* with 14.5mm *Klimovsk* smart rounds had a maximum range of nearly two miles, the bullets able to artificially sustain their trajectory by flying high and then gliding toward their target for longer-range strikes before a final burst of acceleration. His bullets would take around two and a half seconds to cross the distance between himself and the villa and all he had to do was keep his crosshairs on the man's torso.

The *Saher* could be magazine-fed if chambered for standard 12.7mm rounds, but not when fitted with the barrel and bolt needed for the *Klimovsk* smart rounds. With those it was a single-shot weapon. Reaching to the pouch by his right hand, he took out a round, inspected it and loaded the rifle.

He estimated he had thirty, maybe forty minutes of light. A very small window in which to strike. But he didn't like being out in the cold Buq'ata night. In an environment like this, even a heat signature-reducing ghillie suit wouldn't make him invisible to the Marines' night vision.

But Abdolrasoul Delavari had a secret talisman, one that had kept him safe on battlefields from Chechnya to Syria. Around his neck, on a gold chain, was a rabbit foot from a rabbit he had shot in a field near his home as a boy. As he settled in, he touched it once, for luck.

Movement, on the target rooftop.

He leaned to his sight, pulling the stock in against his cheek, the forestock resting on a folding bipod. He had definitely seen movement, but now, nothing. They were very disciplined, these Marines. It suggested to him that they had been under fire before. Learned the hard way.

No. If someone was there, they were keeping low. He had no shot. He quickly scanned the walls of the compound. A possible shot on a man near the eastern wall, but in a private's uniform. Not a sergeant. He ran his scope over the doors and windows to the house. Civilians only, second floor, rear, no uniforms. He scanned over the rooftops between himself and the villa. The Druze officer had told him he had two marksmen already in place, keeping an eye on the Marines, but they weren't visible to him. He'd arranged that they would hold their fire while he got into position even if they had a target, but if he had not taken his shot before 1930 hours, they would start firing into the compound and try to provoke return fire and movement.

It was 1904. He settled in to wait.

Delavari did not work with a spotter. He preferred to reduce the risk he would be seen and one man was always safer in that respect than two. He also preferred hides that made unlikely attack vectors because they were small, high, narrow … things that often precluded taking a second man along.

If he had worked with a spotter, though, he may have seen the two small drones lift off from behind the target villa, rise high in the air above it, and then zoom south and west. And he may have wondered why.

Jensen and Amal were seated in the rear courtyard, butts on the concrete apron, backs against the metal shed, eyes fixed on the small screens in front of them. The drones automatically steered to the GPS coordinates Amal had fed them based on the observations they'd made of the Druze shooters' positions. Once there, they hovered a hundred feet overhead.

Amal had also sent a surveillance drone to loiter between the two shooters, even higher, and watch for any other movement in the streets below. Its wide-angle vision showed in a small window in the corner of the control units' main screens.

"Contact. I have my target, seated behind a laundry line. Looks half asleep," Jensen said.

"Mine is … I'm going to infrared," Amal said. "Mine is a little more careful. Lying down behind a planter box. There is a roof overhang partially obscuring him. I will need to make an angled approach."

"Clear to engage?"

"Yes. Watch your speed, don't approach too quickly. Trigger the bomb at about four feet for best effect."

"Roger." Jensen watched the zoomed image of the man below him. The guy was very relaxed. Reaching for what looked like cigarettes now.

Amal nodded to Jensen. "On three. One, two, *three…*"

Jensen kept the crosshairs of his camera centered on the man's head and shoulders and gently pulled back on the altitude control from the drone. Amal was right, it responded immediately, diving straight down, covering fifty feet in milliseconds. *Easy, JJ!* He eased off the stick a little and slowed the descent … twenty feet, ten, five…

Now!

Delavari jerked his cheek from his rifle as the first explosion briefly lit the sky directly ahead of him, about halfway between himself and the target villa. It was high, somewhere on a rooftop. A grenade, it sounded like.

Then a second, further west. The same small bright explosion, the same sharp grenade-like report.

What... he bent to his scope, watched the compound carefully, thought he saw someone behind the wall pump a fist in the air and pull it down again.

No small arms fire. No movement.

From the street below he heard a car moving in the direction of one of the blasts and then saw it pass between buildings. Shouts of alarm. A jeep, going to check what had happened, perhaps. A few faces appeared at windows around the area of the explosions, but they were only a few because it seemed most of the townsfolk knew to keep their heads down and their curiosity in check right now.

Delavari didn't like to speculate without data, but right now he was willing to speculate that the Druze officer had just lost his two forward scouts.

The frustration with blowing up their drones was that as soon as they did, they were blind. But Amal switched her screen to the surveillance drone and took control of it with her unit as soon as she had triggered her bomb.

Jensen leaned over to watch as she maneuvered the drone over the Druze rifleman's position to the east. It was Jensen's ... the man in the nest of laundry.

"He's down," Amal said, pointing to shredded, blood-stained sheets that obscured an unmoving body. A rifle was visible on the ground beside it, and a leg.

"Call that a kill," Jensen said dispassionately.

"Yes. Now the other."

There had been about two hundred yards between the two riflemen and the vision dipped and swayed a little as Amal steered the drone over the second site. Jensen saw the roof overhang she had been talking about, and some blasted planter boxes and furniture. A long-barreled rifle. Their target was not there.

"Here," Amal pointed at the screen. "Blood. A lot of blood."

Jensen squinted. "Looks like he dragged himself back under cover. Into a door or window maybe? Or someone came out and dragged him in."

"I tried to get in under that roof but I may have triggered it too early."

"You tagged him, that's for sure. A soldier doesn't leave his rifle behind unless he's hurt badly and can't hold it." He held out his hand for a high five.

She looked at it sadly. "I don't feel like celebrating."

He pulled his hand back. "No. But that will give them pause for thought. Force them to pull their scouts further back. The greater the distance, the harder the shot, the less accurate they'll be if we…"

As he was speaking, there was a crack of a far-off shot and a cry from the front of the house.

"Corpsman!! Bell!!"

Delavari had decided that if the Marines had taken out his fire support, as he suspected they had, then he would need to create movement inside the compound himself.

He had a shot on what looked like a man's elbow or part of an arm. Between the gatepost and the wall. A man sitting with his back to the wall, head well below the top of it, thinking himself safe. Thinking about food or sex, no doubt. Or maybe sharing a moment of celebration with his comrades over whatever had just transpired.

Delavari had put his crosshairs on the small scrap of desert-colored uniform, took a breath, held it, and pulled gently on his trigger with the tip of his right forefinger.

He kept the crosshairs on the elbow in the gap between the wall and the gate until the round slammed home and the target disappeared. Then he worked the bolt of the *Degtyarev*, ejected the spent round, reached for his ammunition pouch and loaded another, scanning the front of the villa as he did so.

Movement on the roof. No shot.

Movement in the compound, behind the walls. No shot.

Movement inside the house. A shadow by the front door. Two shadows.

Ah, good. Hello Sergeant.

Jensen stood well back inside the hallway of the house and surveyed the situation in the front yard of the compound. Lopez was curled in a ball on the ground, clutching a bloodied arm. Wallace on the other side of the gate, head down, yelling for Bell. Buckland, Stevens and Johnson on the north and west walls also had their heads down.

"Anyone hear where it came from?" Jensen yelled.

"West. A long way," Wallace yelled back.

"Lopez, talk to me!"

The private lifted her head. "Hit in the arm, Sarge. Need … a tourniquet."

They had to generate covering fire so Bell could get out to Lopez without being shot too. But unless they had a target, they would just be exposing themselves and spraying at nothing.

Bell was tucked in behind Jensen, who put a hand behind him to stop Bell moving up. "Wait." Jensen turned toward the stairs behind him. "Patel! You see anything? Look out a mile or more…"

He didn't hear the bullet, but he felt it. It slammed into his upper thigh just to the left of the dangling groin protector of his body armor. He staggered back into the hallway, collapsing onto Bell and pulling him to the floor with him.

Delavari watched with satisfaction as the Marine Sergeant was punched backwards.

Mr. Klimovsk, please take a bow, he thought to himself as he jacked the empty smart bullet casing out of the chamber and put it in a pocket in his trousers. Pushing himself backwards, he reached the rear of the water tank platform, worked his legs over the back of it and dropped the four feet to the unfinished concrete roof. He was back in cover now, no way he could be seen from the villa.

The shot had gone precisely where he'd aimed. The man had been wearing body armor and, at such extreme range, he needed a soft body part to seriously wound, but the man was in shadow and moving his upper body. The head and torso were not high probability shots. So Delavari had chosen the upper right thigh, beside the groin, where the 14.5mm copper-jacketed bullet would bury itself deep in the flesh, flattening as it struck and tearing through skin and muscle to the deep femoral artery beneath. A blood highway directly from the heart to the leg, as thick as the tip of an index finger, blood loss would be quick and massive. A tourniquet was near impossible to apply and, unless plugged, the victim could lose just about every pint of blood in their body within five minutes. Blood pressure fell dangerously low, the body tried to get blood to vital organs, and then the body's temperature dropped. Put together, it was called the 'shadow of death'.

As he reached ground level, rifle gripped across his chest again, he checked his watch. It was 1914. He would return to the Druze command center, find a bunk and sleep until dawn.

Then, unless something transpired during the night, it was time to hunt again.

Amal had heard the cry for help, but she had not run into the house. Instead, she stayed with her recon drone, sending it higher and widening the angle of the lens on its camera so that she could more quickly scan the rooftops below. She saw Druze soldiers on the streets near the buildings where they had attacked the two riflemen. Saw what looked like four men running through town with a stretcher. More soldiers loitering uneasily on street corners, speaking with civilians at a roadblock...

There!

A figure with a rifle, climbing off a water tower, about a mile and a half back. Was that him? Was a shot like that even possible?

Her drones had an optical target lock feature. As long as he stayed out in the open, it would stay high and follow him through town. If he went into or behind a building it would loiter and then try to reacquire him based on the images it had taken after being locked on. But a change of clothing, even a hat, could fool it.

If the target knew they were being followed.

She locked the drone onto the figure now walking calmly back through the streets of Buq'ata, rifle held to his chest, and carrying her control unit, thumbed the shed lock, heaved the door aside and ran back into her workshop.

She hastily pulled out a large, wide drawer that held drone bodies and selected a needle-nosed fuselage with a push propeller. From another drawer she pulled a set of wide wings and clipped them on. The motor, guidance system and battery were in a single unit and she quickly located this, sliding it into the fuselage.

Warhead.

This particular longer-range drone had a nose compartment that could be fitted with an extra camera, tear gas, forward-firing one-shot munitions or explosives. She hesitated. She could go with a shotgun payload, a 3D-printed shotgun chamber made to fit into the nose of the drone and able to hold a single shell, loaded with either birdshot, buckshot or a one-ounce slug.

But if she missed?

Instead she ran to the floor locker that held the prepared explosives and pulled up a box containing a small metal cone filled with plastic explosive. The metal cone was machined so that it would splinter into red hot metal shards or flechettes when the explosive was detonated. It had a much higher chance of killing or disabling him than if she tried to aim a shotgun blast from a moving drone.

From a box beside it she also grabbed four small cylindrical canisters, shoving them in her trouser pockets as she slammed the explosives locker shut and checked the display on her control unit which showed the surveillance feed. The shooter was still sauntering through the streets, rifle held ready but with a relaxed, almost jaunty gait.

Let's see if we can change your mood, kalba.

Running back outside again with her drone in hand, she slaved it to her controller, started its engine and threw it in the air the way a child throws a paper plane. Buzzing like a swarm of bees, it swooped, dipped and then started climbing. Amal knew the streets of the small town of Buq'ata very well. It looked to her like the sniper was headed back to the villa near her shop which they'd identified as some sort of command post, which made sense. He was going to report on his handiwork.

Rather than chase him, she aimed her explosive drone at the end of the street between the sniper and the command post. It could circle there and wait for him, to see which way he was going before she attacked. She had a couple of minutes until then. Setting a waypoint on the screen, she put the controller on the ground and ran into the back door of her house, pulling the four canisters out of her pockets.

On the roof, Patel had seen Lopez roll to one side clutching her arm before he heard the muted crack of the shot. A sniper's bullet traveled around twice the speed of sound, so it was normal for a bullet fired from a distance to strike without warning.

"Find that shooter!" Patel yelled to Bell, who was lying down beside him scanning the rooftops with binoculars.

"Medic!!" Wallace had screamed and Bell had rolled on his back, handing the binos to Patel before rising into a crouch and heading for the stairway down from the rooftop. Patel jammed the binos to his eye sockets, adjusting the focus, sweeping the roofs in front of him left to right, trying not to go too fast, looking for any sign of movement. He'd seen the two drones take out the Druze scouts and had cheered inside because he had felt impotent, with no firing solution on them. He saw a soldier on the rooftop where they'd evacuated one man, wounded, but the shot hadn't come from there. They were to the south, and the shot had definitely come from the west. He was still watching the site of the drone attack, wondering whether the shooter there had been killed or just wounded, was starting to move the binos again when...

Crack!

A second shot, and a shout from inside the house. *Dammit!* He swung the binos wildly, trying to settle, control his breathing, move methodically, taking the houses row by row. The radio chose that moment to interrupt, someone hailing him. He ignored it, tried to focus. Well back, a water tower caught his eye. It was small, not much bigger than a 55-gallon drum, sitting on a platform four feet above an unfinished roof, with a couple of wooden crates sitting on it.

Yeah, if I was good enough to set up somewhere way, way back, it would be there. He dialed up the magnification on the binos, scanning every inch of the water tower.

No one. If the shot had come from there, the shooter was gone.

With a rising sense of failure he was still scanning the rooftops to the west when he heard a shuffling sound behind him and Amal eased up alongside on her knees and elbows. She held two small cylindrical canisters out to him. "Smoke. How is the wind?"

"About three miles an hour, from the north-east."

"Alright. You drop it straight down in front of the house, north and north-east. I'll drop north, that should give your people below a chance to pull back into the house." She pulled another two canisters from her pockets.

"What's happening downstairs?" Patel asked, getting ready to throw. The radio was still crackling. Whoever it was, was persistent.

"Not sure. Your Sergeant was hit. Ready? How do you tell it?"

"We say 'popping smoke' or just 'smoke out'."

"Call it and throw."

Patel rolled on his back, one grenade in his hand, the other beside him. He took a lungful of air. "POPPING SMOKE!" he yelled, pulled the pin and tossed the first grenade back over his head and just in front of the house so the wind would take it over the heads of the men and women below. Amal did the same, but off to the east of the house.

"Give it time to spread," she said. As they saw smoke drifting up into the air over them, she rolled to her knees so she could aim her next throw better. "Again!"

Patel did the same, saw that his first throw had fallen very close to the wall of the house and was going just about straight up, so he put his second closer to the northern wall. Rolling back onto her stomach, Amal put her hands and mouth to a break in the small wall around the terrace. "Marines! Pull back into the house!"

She started edging back toward the stairs, and Patel made to follow her, but she put a hand on his back to stop him. "Not you. Stay here and watch for movement. They may take this chance to rush us. If you have air support, ask them to be ready, it may be needed."

"Can't you put a drone up?"

"I have. I will send a spotter to you when they are all inside, alright?"

He wanted to know what was happening with Jensen and Lopez, but he couldn't fault her logic. As the IDF corporal disappeared, he picked up the radio handset and checked he was on the JTAC frequency. "Golani Angel, Lava Dogs JTAC, do you read?"

No-Fly Zone, Golan Heights, May 19

Bunny had split her hex so that five birds were patrolling north-south along the length of the Golan Heights on terrain-following mode, while one was holding at around 25,000 feet over Buq'ata. She'd made sure that on this new patrol she had one bird with a recon pod in its weapons bay instead of ordnance, and it was sending her a hi-fidelity image of the whole town that she asked Kovacs to keep an eye on while she focused on trying to identify and mitigate potential air or ground threats.

The first wave of the Israeli air attack had taken down the closest *Growler* ground-to-air missile site, so she was free of the constant warbling that indicated a ground search radar was looking her way. But the S-400 *Growler* had a range of nearly 200 miles and it was possible one of the units she could still see operating further into central Syria would be able to pick up her high-flying recon drone. Not to mention any of the no doubt dozens of *Felon* and *Okhotnik* stealth aircraft Russia had patrolling the border, smacking down any Israeli jet or drone incautious enough to reveal itself.

"I've got ... I think there were some small explosions..." Kovacs said. She put her finger on the screen showing the surveillance feed. "Here, and ... here. See the smoke?"

Bunny zoomed the feed. "Could be explosions, could also be chimney smoke."

"Both chimneys starting up at the same time?" Kovacs asked. "There were flashes, and then smoke."

Bunny panned the camera up to the compound where the Marines were hunkered down, but saw nothing unusual. She switched to the JTAC frequency. "Lava Dogs, Golani Angel. All quiet down there?"

There was no reply. She tried again, panning her camera

around the town. There was some movement, hard to see in the dusk light. She switched over to infrared and picked up some bodies moving around town, a small vehicle or two, but nothing that looked like a firefight.

"More smoke," Kovacs said. "A lot more."

Bunny panned the view out to center on the Marine compound again. "Those are smoke grenades," she said. "Something is going down."

"Golani Angel, Lava Dogs, do you read?"

"Receiving, Patel. What's happening down there?"

"We're taking sniper fire. One shooter at least. We got two casualties, our Sergeant is down. I don't know how bad. I can't see the shooter ... I don't know..."

"Easy, Patel. I have a bird overhead. Let me have a look." She switched her other aircraft to AI control, weapons safe, and concentrated on the recon *Fantom*. "Do you have a bearing from your villa?"

"West, say two eighty degrees, range fifteen hundred to two thousand yards is my best guess."

"That's a *long* shot."

"Gap between the bullet strike and the sound of the shot was two Mississippi and some. One Mississippi, nine hundred yards. That's what they teach us."

"Wait one, Patel."

She switched to infrared and started panning around town looking for prone figures west of the villa with warm rifle barrels. She didn't see any, but she saw something else.

"Patel, Angel. You guys didn't happen to stir up any other trouble a few minutes before now? Two explosions?"

"Yeah, took out a couple of Druze riflemen with a drone strike."

"That might explain why I see a platoon forming up at the road junction where you had your firefight earlier." Bunny zoomed in. "I count twenty men, all carrying rifles, some carrying ... yeah, I got at least two with rocket launchers."

"We've got civilians here!"

"Then if there is a cellar, I suggest you tell them to get into it. I can't do anything for you while they're in the middle of a civilian area. I can lay down some hurt once they reach your compound, but you'll be danger close."

"Understood. Anything you can do, Angel."

"Hold this channel open. Angel out."

Huddled over her command unit again, Amal saw the sniper approaching the end of the street, and she saw something else. Men running from the command post up to the junction near her brother's shop and forming up. Armed men. The sniper had seen them too, and lifted a hand in greeting.

Amal suddenly had to choose between the greater of two evils. The deadly marksman who had just attacked them, or the platoon of regular soldiers who were very obviously preparing to. As her drone swung around and gave her a better view of the soldiers below, she saw one of them carried a rocket launcher in his arms.

Crap. That made her decision simpler.

Using a thumb joystick on her controller, she moved a crosshair into the middle of where the men were standing by the roundabout, an officer of some sort – but not, as far as she could see, the colonel they had met earlier – standing by the statue and addressing them. A pre-battle pep talk maybe.

Pep this.

She pressed a button on the controller and two miles away, her drone dropped its nose and made an unpowered dive toward the intersection. She didn't have to time the detonation, the camera in the drone's nose worked as a crude proximity sensor and would do that job for her, sending a thousand needle-sharp metal shards into the mass of bodies below.

There was no telltale shadow. No buzz of electric engines. Abdolrasoul Delavari was twenty feet from the soldiers, still with his arm in the air trying to get the attention of the Druze captain marshaling his forces at the intersection, when he saw a flash of white fall from the sky and explode right in among the troops at the intersection.

He staggered, but kept his feet. A mortar round? No, too accurate. *Drone.* As smoke from the blast cleared, he saw the ground in front of him littered with dead and wounded men. And several standing exactly where they had stood moments earlier, in the middle of bodies either horribly still, or trying to crawl away, with stunned looks on their faces, checking their arms and limbs, unable to believe they were alive, unhurt, amid all the carnage.

For a moment, Abdolrasoul Delavari thought he was one of them. Then he realized he was having a little trouble breathing. Perhaps it was the smoke. He looked down, checking to see if he'd been hit, and saw a tiny circle of blood flowering on his chest above his left tunic pocket.

His rabbit foot! He didn't want to get blood on it. Fumbling with his top button, he quickly pulled the gold chain and rabbit foot out. Then frowned at it. It was wet with blood. Looking down at his chest again, he saw the small flower of blood was starting to spread.

And it was getting harder to breathe.

Well, that was not good. He needed to find a medic.

He was still holding his rifle. It was suddenly very, very heavy. He wouldn't need it again tonight anyway, so he let it drop butt first to the ground as he walked. That was better. He could come back for it later.

He tried to put his rabbit foot into his right tunic pocket. It wouldn't get blood on it there. But the damn button was too tight or his fingers not as nimble as they usually were. Well, it was cold. Going to be a cold night.

He stepped over a man trying to crawl in front of him. Poor fellow. He was bleeding from the ears. That was probably worse than bleeding from a chest wound, wasn't it?

Delavari had to stop and lean against a shop wall. He looked up at the sign over the door, written in Arabic, Hebrew and English. "Buq'ata Furniture Repairs. While You Wait."

He looked down at his chest again and gave a coughing laugh. Well, he could certainly use a man who was handy with a needle and thread right now. He looked through the shattered window. Perhaps he was inside?

He didn't feel the rabbit foot slip from his fingers, or the shattered glass cut him as he fell through the window trying to lean on a window pane that wasn't there. Lying on the shop floor, gasping for air and unable to find any, he wasn't scared.

A wound like this, they would send him home for sure. Where he would tell his family the story of how he'd rescued a *hundred* civilians.

James Jensen was also having trouble breathing, but not because he had a hole in his chest. He was holding in his breath so that he didn't scream. Bell had a finger jammed into the hole in his thigh, right up to the top knuckle. Jensen had never been shot before. Six months under constant sniper and mortar fire in Kobani, and not so much as a scratch. When he'd seen a boot on duty, looking pale or shaky after a near miss, he'd say to the guy, hey, don't worry about it. If it kills you, you'll be dead and if it just wounds you, you won't feel it, the adrenaline kicks in, you'll just feel numb, so don't sweat. But keep your damn head down.

Numb? What a load of horseshit.

Every time Bell shifted his weight, it was like someone was pushing a hot wrecking bar further into his groin.

"God*damn*, Bell!" he grunted.

"Sergeant, I need to find out is all this blood coming from your deep femoral, or your superficial femoral artery, so lie still and stop whining."

"What's the damn difference?"

Bell was talking through gritted teeth. "The difference, Gunny, is I can use a tourniquet to clamp your superficial

284

femoral artery, pack it hard like I'm trying to do, and you *might* live. But if it's your deep femoral artery, then you'll die about a minute after I take my finger out of the hole in your leg."

Jensen lay back, resting his helmeted head on the floor. "Hell … of a bedside manner … Bell."

"Yeah, well. Probably only reason you aren't already dead is the bullet seems to be plugging the hole in whatever artery it is." The rest of the squad had come galloping in a few minutes earlier, and Bell had grabbed Buckland to help fit a tourniquet around Jensen's upper thigh. She was winding it tight with a metal rod from his medical kit. "Tighter," he told her.

"Any tighter, I'll sever his leg," she grunted.

"I don't hear him screaming. Tighter."

After pushing some more gauze into the wound and satisfying himself the tourniquet was as tight as anyone could get it, Bell looked up. "Sarge, you with us?"

"Wish … I wasn't."

"Well, depending how this goes now, you might get your wish," Bell said. "You got any last words?"

"Yeah. Tell your mother … I had a great time."

"I think you mean my grandma, Gunny." He looked over at Buckland and nodded. "Okay. Here we go. Could get bloody."

"I can take it," the corporal said.

Bell eased his finger out of the tunnel of Jensen's wound, hoping the packing would hold and the tourniquet had cut off the flow of blood. Hoping it was Jensen's superficial femoral that was bleeding, not his deep femoral too. Hoping if it still bled that it was just pulsing, not pouring out of the wound…

"Ah, jayzus…" Jensen sighed, and blacked out.

All Domain Attack: Imbalance

Situation Room, White House, May 19

"The Russian fleet is showing no signs of slowing, Mr. President," the figure onscreen was saying. The CO of the USS *Canberra*, Captain Carson Andrews, was a native of Chicago and had come up through corvettes and mine hunters to destroyers. He was now commanding a ship in what had once been the White Elephant class of the US fleet but, after ten years of upgrades and refits, was now one of the most capable surface combatants in the Navy. And, since passing through the Suez Canal and into the Mediterranean, the new flagship of Destroyer Squadron 60.

"How close are they now?" Henderson asked.

"We've already been passed by their intelligence ship, the *Yuriy Ivanov*. It's sailing south from Rhodes now, I suspect trying to map how many drones and helos we've got in play. At least one *Kilo*-class submarine was detected, but as ordered we did not prosecute the contact. The main body of ships is eighty miles back. Up front and closest are the two *Karakurt*-class corvettes, the *Mytischi* and *Sovetsk* – anti-air, anti-ship platforms. They will reach our line of control within three hours."

"And you will let them pass," Admiral Clarke confirmed.

"Yes, Admiral. We expect, though, they will choose to hold station near us and make our lives difficult. The main body of ships is four hours out. Two guided missile frigates, the *Admiral Makov* and *Admiral Essen*, sailing either side of the *Slava*-class cruiser *Moskva*."

"Where are the Iranians?" Henderson asked.

"Tucked right in behind them. The two *Safineh*-class missile destroyers, *Amol* and *Sinjan*, are more or less sailing line astern in the wake of the *Moskva*."

"Like ducks behind momma duck," Homeland Security Secretary Price quipped.

"Yes. If momma duck was an air defense cruiser able to fire eighty surface-to-air missiles at the same time as engaging sixteen surface contacts," Carmine responded.

"The *Moskva* is nearly fifty years old, but its missile and sensor systems got a 2025 refresh, so yes, it's a big momma," the *Canberra*'s captain confirmed. "Bringing up the rear are at least one more *Kilo*, and their helicopter landing ship, *Pyotr Morgunov*. It can carry a battalion of troops and a company of tanks, but we believe it sailed as a replenishment ship on this voyage."

"So Russia isn't planning to invade Israel from the sea, only from Syria – that's a blessing," VP Sianni remarked drily.

Henderson winced. "Thank you, Captain Andrews, we appreciate the job you did on that Iranian submarine, and the job you are doing now. Please let your crews know they have our total confidence."

"Thank you, Mr. President. Sir, if I may?" the captain replied. "There is one wild card we haven't discussed."

"The Israeli submarine," Admiral Clarke guessed.

"Yes, Admiral. The British sub *Agincourt* was damn near rammed by the *Gal* overnight. A clear sign they are keyed up and ready for action. It reported to the *Agincourt* it was planning to patrol west, to Cyprus, but it was last logged headed north, toward Rhodes and the Russian fleet. Given the air assault on Syria and Iran currently underway, we have to consider the possibility that…"

"Yes, Captain," Clarke interrupted him. "The possibility of pre-emptive Israeli action at sea is noted. Alert me if you make contact with the *Gal* again."

"Aye, Admiral."

The connection was cut and Clarke addressed the unasked question. "We won't be able to get near those Iranian ships without risking a collision with either them or the Russians. And it appears they have little or no intention of detaching from the fleet so we can board and inspect them. Sending a helicopter and boarding party across to board a moving vessel protected by Russian anti-air is also out of the question."

"We don't have to board and inspect them," Sianni said. "If they enter the Mediterranean, the *Agincourt* can put a torpedo into the screw of the trailing Iranian frigate and they'll stop quick enough."

Defense Secretary McDonald nodded in agreement. "Simple and clean."

"If they don't depth-charge the *Agincourt* first." It was Secretary of State Shrier who said what Carmine was thinking. "Can I remind everyone we still do not have absolute proof that Iran has deployed nuclear weapons on those ships?"

"They must have," Dupré said. "Israel's reaction is too strong. They have attacked nuclear and ballistic missile sites in seven locations in Iran. They have attacked Quds Force troops and armor inside Syria. They have not hesitated to engage Russian fighters over Syria. They have sent an attack submarine out to meet the Iranian ships. They seem willing to start an all-out war with Iran and Russia which I believe they would only do if they have intelligence that an Iranian nuclear attack is imminent."

"So because Israel has lost its collective mind, we should lose ours and ask the Brits to put a torpedo into an Iranian frigate?" Carmine asked.

Henderson rose. "I need some air. You all keep gasbagging. The situation is this. When those Iranian ships approach our blockade line…"

"In six hours, Oliver…" Sianni said gently.

"In six hours, yes, Ben … when they do, the good Captain Andrews will demand that they stop and allow themselves to be searched. And only after that will we decide our next course of action." He looked down the table. "Carmine, walk with me."

Carmine got up and followed Henderson out, ignoring the various looks that followed her out of the room, not least that from Tonya Dupré which said, *Get me out of here.*

"Goddamn, Carmine," Henderson said as they waited for the lift to ground level.

"About the tenth time you've said that this week," she noted as they stepped into the lift.

"Yeah, well ... goddamn just sums it up. Hey, any news on your mother?"

Carmine did a double take. Had she told him her mother had been hospitalized after a minor stroke? She didn't think so. She wouldn't have wanted to trouble him.

"Thanks for asking, Oliver. Uh, she's ... good, in the circumstances. Some loss of feeling in her left side but the doctors are pretty optimistic that will return. She's 84, so these things are going to happen."

"This mess is over, I want you to take some time. She's in Atlanta, right?"

"Yes."

"You go see her, alright? That's an order."

"I will. How are you holding up?"

"Had better nights, Carmine, I'll admit it. You know, when I took over this job, the outgoing President said something to me. Or their Chief of Staff, I can't remember. Did I tell you?"

The outgoing President. Henderson never referred to his predecessor by name. He couldn't abide them when they were in office, and preferred to treat their administration as a historical aberration. "Maybe," she admitted. "But remind me."

"They said, the next big war, it isn't going to be where you expect it. It isn't going to be Taiwan, or the South China Sea or Korea, or Russia invading the Baltic States. It's going to be some pissant little conflict that starts small and gets bigger and bigger and unless you say screw this and back off before you get in too deep, suddenly you're staring down the barrel of Armageddon, either political or actual."

Lewis hadn't heard that one and she thought about it. Sure, Vietnam fit that bill. Iraq, thirty years of conflict. Afghanistan, the same. Now Syria. It had started in 2013 with air support for the war against Islamic State. Seven years later the US was still there, supporting the Kurdish separatists. Fast forward another few years, we're sending AWACs aircraft to Turkey, a Marine company to support the Kurds in the north and an Army air defense battalion to the NATO air base at Incirlik. Suddenly we're putting together a Coalition to oppose a Syrian invasion of southern Turkey and the 1st Infantry Division is shipping out. Next thing, we're flying US soldiers home in caskets again.

Now Israel? "I hadn't heard that one, but I can see how it's true," she replied.

"Yeah. So maybe this is that moment."

"The moment when you say, 'screw this'?"

"Exactly. Harry and the Joint Chiefs want to torpedo Iranian frigates. The Israeli PM, that two-faced bastard, tells me he will do his best to coordinate with us, but he also has to act in the best interests of Israel. 'I trust you understand, Mr. President. You would do the same.'"

"Wouldn't you?"

"Irrelevant, I'm not the one who called the USA and begged us to set up a naval blockade we didn't want and can't enforce." They walked out into the garden. It was a cool night, mid-fifties. "Now I'm waiting on a call from the Russian President hoping he can get us out of this mess, which, by the way, he damn well created. Maybe this is where I say, 'screw this'."

Carmine couldn't help but smile.

"What? What's so damn funny?"

"Oliver, you are President of the USA, commander in chief of the most powerful military and leader of the country with the biggest economy in history. You aren't waiting for anyone to pull your ass out of the fire, the decisions are all there, you just haven't made them yet."

Henderson pulled his coat tighter around himself. "If there's a roadmap, I'm not seeing it, Carmine."

Carmine could see it. She could also see that now was the time to lay it out for the President. She didn't expect him to follow it, and she was no seer or prophet, so an unforeseen event could certainly send it sideways, but Henderson needed to see there was a clear way forward that treated the current situation as an opportunity, not a disaster.

290

"Alright. First, if the Russian President calls, you stall him…"

"And do what instead?"

"Pick up the damn phone to Tehran. Fifty years of letting the State Department run our relationship with Iran through proxies, never once in all that time sitting down face to face, President to Ayatollah – that's got to end. You know how many times a Russian President or Prime Minister has met with the Iranian leadership in that time?"

"Dozens, I suppose."

"About thirty times. And we get upset that we're dependent on Russia to get Syria and Iran to back down? That has to stop, today."

"Just call the Ayatollah of Iran?"

"That's it. No press release diplomacy, no going through back channels, call the guy. And get the VP to call his President."

"To say what exactly?" Henderson asked. As she knew he would, he was thinking about what a hard sell it was to tell Congress he had unilaterally decided to walk back a half century of policy on Iran.

"To make them an offer. You will personally bring Israel to the table to discuss an arms treaty and start talks on mutual recognition. You will walk back some sanctions in return for an immediate guarantee Iran will never station nuclear weapons on Israel's borders, either at sea, or on land."

He shook his head and smiled. "I can see you aren't a politician, Carmine. How do you think that would play in Congress? After fifty years of telling Americans Iran is our enemy, suddenly I want to kiss and hold hands?"

"Tell me why Iran is our enemy, Oliver," she asked simply.

"Well … because … hell, you know what? I don't know," he admitted.

"OK, I'll tell you." She stopped walking and began counting on her fingers. "One: because *fifty years ago* they took fifty Americans hostage during the revolution and held them for more than a year. Two: they support terrorist groups that attack US interests. Chicken and egg – maybe if we didn't treat them as the enemy, they'd be less inclined to screw us. Three: it's a totalitarian Islamic state whose values are inimical to ours. Except that doesn't stop us having normal relations with any number of similar states, so that's BS. Four: the biggest oil-producing nations in the Gulf are Sunni Muslim and at odds with the Shia Muslim regime in Iran and they wouldn't like it. Well, guess what – we don't need their damn oil anymore. Five: they are a sworn enemy of Israel so our pro-Israel voters and donors would regard it as unacceptable that we normalize relations with Iran." She stopped and took a breath. "Except the pro-Israel lobby said that about Egypt, Jordan, Saudi Arabia, Qatar and the Emirates but they've all normalized relations with Israel and now we don't hear a peep."

"Iran just joined a massive attack on the Israeli economy that's going to cost billions of dollars and probably thousands of lives. Should we reward them for that?"

"That attack was orchestrated out of Moscow. Tehran wouldn't have anywhere near the resources or capabilities to pull it off. This is going to sound heartless…"

"From you, never."

She wasn't sure if that was irony or sarcasm, but plowed on. "That attack is leverage. We can't undo it, but we can hold it against them when we get down to horse trading. And the first thing they have to trade is, to announce they are going to pull back their ships, their missiles and their support for Syria, and we'll get them a sit down with Israel."

Carmine let Henderson process what she had said as they walked a lap of the lawns in near silence.

"Harry and the Joint Chiefs will fight it. State will shit kittens."

"Tell them after it's too late to stop it."

"The pro-Israel lobby…"

"If the Israeli PM supports it, most of them will too."

"Russians are going to pop a cog if we manage to do a deal

behind their backs," he said at last.

"Yeah, another upside. Screw Russia."

"I'll sleep on it."

Carmine stopped walking and faced Henderson, taking him by the shoulders. It was a gesture with a level of familiarity no one else in the cabinet could have dared but her. "Oliver, you don't have that luxury. Inside six hours, Iranian and US ships are going to be facing off in the Mediterranean. Either you walk back inside now, ask an aide to get the Ayatollah on the telephone, or you're deciding to let the Joint Chiefs, the State Department *and* the Russian President solve this for you, which you and I know they won't."

Two miles north-west of US demarcation line, Mediterranean Sea, May 19

Surface contact delta nine now bearing three one two degrees, range 4,200, speed 30 knots. Plot ready, ship ready, weapon ready, solution ready, standing by to shoot, the Gal's AI announced. Do you want to prosecute, Captain?

"No, *Gal*," Captain Binyamin Ben-Zvi said. "Disarm anti-ship missiles." He and his second officer, Ehud Mofaz, had just been woken from two hours' sleep by the AI with the news it had identified a nearby contact as the Russian corvette the *Sovetsk* and classified it as a possible threat. The *Sovetsk* was one of the newer, smaller missile boats that Russia had begun churning out; primarily an anti-air, anti-ship platform. But the nimble *Karakurt* class had proven so successful that instead of commissioning a replacement for their aging *Grisha*-class anti-submarine corvettes, Russia had simply added a towed sonar array, depth charge racks and two RPK-8 anti-submarine rocket launchers to their *Karakurt* corvettes in place of the outmoded 100mm gun turret. The sound of the searching sonar penetrated their hull with a worryingly regular pulse, and it was strengthening.

Disarming anti-ship missiles. Chance of detection without evasive action, 54 percent.

Binyamin pulled up the tactical screen and laid in a new waypoint that would lead them away from the searching Russian. "*Gal*, steer to new waypoint, prioritize stealth."

Steering to waypoint gamma 93. Stealth algorithms prioritized.

Ehud rubbed his eyes. His two-hour nap had turned into less than one. "She woke us for that?"

"If she hadn't, you might have gotten a depth charge as an alarm clock," Binyamin pointed out. "Double check the specials are safed, will you?"

"She can't fire a special," Ehud told him. "Only you and I can do that."

"Check anyway."

The word 'nuclear' was never used in the Israeli Armed Forces, because Israel had never confirmed that it possessed nuclear weapons and thus it was not possible to refer to something that did not, officially, exist. Therefore, the weapons loaded into the four large 650mm torpedo tubes in the nose of the *Dolphin* were referred to simply as 'specials'.

And yes, Binyamin was being overcautious. The *Gal* had been through three years of sea trials but was still a new boat on its first full-fledged operational patrol, with an AI 'decision support system' that had not existed even five years earlier, and in that respect her captain was a strong believer in the principle 'trust, but verify'.

Ehud tapped a couple of screens. "All weapons safed. Logs show she's performing just as expected. Picked up the sonar from the Russian corvette, identified it as the *Sovetsk*, sounded the alarm, locked the target and armed torpedoes, ready to launch on our command. Smooth as silk." He leaned back in his chair, looking around their control room, which was little bigger than the front seat of a passenger car. "We both served on boats with crews of thirty to forty men. Now we are two. How long do you think it will be before we are zero and the

Gal is piloting herself around the Mediterranean?"

"Never, I hope," Binyamin said, with feeling. "Unless they strip the specials from her ... and even then."

"Amen to that, Benny."

Binyamin checked their sensors for signs the Russian sub hunters were using helos or drones with dipping sonar, but he found none. The Black Sea fleet was not the best equipped in the Russian navy, and had often struggled for both funds and personnel. But it was still a potent force and the newer *Karakurt* corvettes were definitely to be avoided.

"I want to get up to launch depth for the sensor buoy and use the radar to scan for that damn fleet. Get an update from Eilat fleet base. We have no idea what is happening up there," Binyamin said. "*Gal*: let me know the minute we are safely out of range of the *Sovetsk*'s sonar."

Yes, captain. Notification set.

"Our orders are clear enough, Binyamin. If the Iranians leave the Aegean..."

Binyamin scratched his head. "Yeah, well, orders change. I need a wash. You go get another hour or so sleep."

"You're sure?"

"Sure," Binyamin said. He patted the instrument console beside the submarine's 'flight stick'. "Me and *Gal* have the con."

No-Fly Zone, Golan Heights, May 19

Bunny had watched with dread fascination as the platoon of soldiers in the center of town had fallen suddenly like bowling pins smashed by a ball dropped from above. Only when she stopped and replayed the vision did she see the narrow white blur that was a missile or drone. *Who, how or where...*

"Patel, what do you need?"

"Uh, we need urgent medevac for two pax, Angel. One leg wound, bad, one broken arm from heavy-caliber gunshot wound. That damn sniper tagged two of our people."

"I'll get word to Hatzerim Air Base, but your best bet is still the UN outpost at Merom Golan," Bunny told him. "They might be able to get in there and freight your people out to an Israeli hospital."

Patel gave a bitter laugh. "They weren't interested in helping us evacuate wounded civilians, you think they're coming into a hot combat zone to pull out a couple of injured US Marines?"

"Wait five, Patel, Angel out."

Bunny switched channel to the Bombardier AWACS circling over Cyprus. "Falcon, Merit leader patrolling the Golan UNDOF zone, come in…"

"Merit, this is Falcon, hope you are keeping your head down over there. You are right in the middle of a red hot shooting war."

Bunny had been watching the tactical map showing Israeli and known Russian aircraft around her and though many Israeli aircraft were already returning from their missions inside Syria, another wave of aircraft was going in to follow up on the first round of attacks. If she had been actually sitting in the cockpit of her aircraft, skimming the tops of bushes up and down the Golan Heights or circling over the firefight in Buq'ata, the constant threat of discovery and attack would have had her flight suit wet with sweat … or worse. "Tell me about it, Falcon. Falcon, we have wounded Marines on the ground needing evac, can you please patch me through to, uh, wait…" She'd been given the name of the quartermaster at Hatzerim Air Base who had organized the supply drop for the Marines below. "… uh, 1st Battalion, 24th Marines, Quartermaster Sergeant Milena Agudelo, Agudelo, you get that?"

"Roger, Merit leader. This is going to take a few…"

"Understood, Falcon, Merit out."

Bunny was alone in the cockpit now. Kovacs had been physically sickened by the close-up images of the dead and wounded soldiers on the ground at Buq'ata and had quickly left for 'some air'. O'Hare didn't know whether to expect her back.

So she concentrated on keeping four of her patrolling F-47s from smacking into hillsides or gullies while she brought an F-47 with air-to-ground ordnance to join her recon machine circling Buq'ata in case she was suddenly called on to provide close air support to the Marines below. Long minutes dragged by, and she was considering calling Patel again to let him know she was still waiting to connect with Hatzerim when the AWACS called in.

"Merit, Falcon Control, we have Sergeant Agudelo, hold."

"Merit holding, thank you, Falcon."

"All part of the service, Merit, please be sure to give us a good rating. Patching you through."

The voice at the end of the line sounded like she was in the trailer with Bunny, not 250 miles away in the Negev Desert. "Hello? This is Sergeant Agudelo."

"Sergeant, Flying Officer Karen O'Hare, attached to the 432nd Air Expeditionary Wing, Cyprus, providing close air support for US 1st Battalion 3rd Marines in the Golan, Israel…"

"Yes, ma'am."

Bunny liked that. No messing, just straight to business.

"Agudelo, I understand you have dispatched supplies and ammunition to Buq'ata."

"Yes, ma'am. ETA is … let me see … uh, 0400."

"Sergeant, your people have taken casualties. We need to medevac two wounded, one light injury, one bad. They are also protecting wounded civilians. What can you do?"

"Ma'am, I allowed for that contingency. The supplies are being lifted to their position on a *Big Boy*. Once they offload it, they can load up to fifteen passengers. The airman onboard can be notified to expect wounded and route to the nearest IDF hospital."

"Agudelo, you are a goddamn star."

"Tell my Captain that, you ever meet him, ma'am. And tell those Marines to hang tough, their brothers and sisters are with them."

"Will do. O'Hare out." Bunny allowed herself a little fist pump. Not a big one. The big one would come if she could make a safer world for those Marines, but for now she had to celebrate the small wins. She reached for the dial to change frequency back to the JTAC channel and tell Patel the good news when her eye was caught by something. It was her nature to be hyper-aware. As she'd been talking with the quartermaster in Hatzerim she'd been watching the dynamically evolving tactical environment around her, monitoring threat warnings, casting her eyes over her flight instruments, systems readouts and the darkening sky around her machines.

As she did so, the recon bird she had circling Buq'ata registered a new and unwelcome sight. Its figure eight orbit around Buq'ata took it over the town from the east, then around hills north of the town before looping back and across the town from the west and doing a loop to the south. That way she could scan the whole town in two passes, as well as keep an eye on roads in and out.

As her recon bird and its new backup 'wingman' swung over the town to the south, hugging but not crossing into Syrian airspace, it flew within a mile of the abandoned Syrian border crossing and village of Quneitra. The town had been leveled during the Syrian civil war and was just rubble now, while the old border crossing there had been closed by the Syrian government for more than five years. The city had been dark on previous passes, just some body-heat signatures and a couple of light vehicles, which was to be expected as her latest intel indicated the Syrian army had moved a company of infantry into the area. But otherwise it was a ghost town.

Except ... it wasn't.

O'Hare spooled the infrared camera vision back and looked at it again. She saw the heat signatures of the engines of at least ten large vehicles – stationary, but for how long? Flipping back to the last circuit she made, they weren't there. Now they were ... so those engines had just been started.

On the next pass, she pulled her pair of *Fantoms* briefly up to

10,000 feet and then sent them low again, looking for other signs of heavy vehicles on the move. But there was nothing else for twenty miles north or south of Buq'ata. Just this group. As she watched, they started to move out.

West. Toward Merom Golan and the Valley of Tears.

She got one high-level pass over the town good enough to capture clear images of the vehicles, and winced as the AI threw up a match from its database. Russian T-14 *Armata* main battle tanks, six, accompanied by four *Udar* unmanned ground vehicles.

"Falcon, Merit leader," she said, calling her AWACS. "I have ten Russian tanks crossing from Quneitra into the UNDOF DMZ," Bunny reported. "Six T-14 main battle tanks and four *Udar* UGVs. They appear to be headed toward the UN base at Merom Golan. Do you copy?"

"Falcon copies Merit leader," the AWACS controller replied. "We will alert UNDOF command and IDF air control. Can you keep them under surveillance?"

"Affirmative, Falcon, Merit out." *Affirmative?* Well, how long she could track the Russian tanks if they became aware of her was more like a solid 'maybe'. A T-14 had a scanned array radar that could track up to forty air targets fifty miles out, handing them off either to its remote-controlled 30mm cannon or its 12-tube *Sosna* 9M340 anti-air missile launcher. The T-14 wasn't a traditional main battle tank, it was what Russia was calling a 'universal strike vehicle', capable of anti-armor operations when configured with a 152mm smooth-bore gun and 30mm autocannon, air defense with the radar-*Sosna* missile combination, or troop transport and assault when fitted with a front-mounted engine and rear troop transport module. Bunny would need a whole lot more vision to be able to classify exactly which variants were coming over the border into the UNDOF DMZ, but an early conclusion was easy enough – about five hundred tons of harm.

She switched to the JTAC channel. "Lava Dogs, Golani Angel, you there, Patel?"

"We're here, Angel," Patel replied immediately. She knew he would be hanging on the radio, hoping for a lifeline. She couldn't lie to him.

"I've got good news and bad news, Corporal…"

There was a reason Bunny O'Hare didn't just walk out of her trailer at the end of her mission, go back to her quarters, pop the cap off a beer and put her feet up.

It was called *atonement*.

She was only on her first combat tour, but she'd already screwed up, and men and women on the ground – men and women like those Lava Dogs over there – had died. Died horribly.

She had been running combat air support for the defense of the NATO air base at Incirlik. Syrian troops and tanks were inside the airport perimeter, all other aircraft had been pulled out, and she'd been returning from a Wild Weasel attack on a Syrian electronic warfare unit. She'd spotted Syrian rocket launchers setting up and had requested permission for a strafing run, but had been called off by the AWACS controller and assigned to escort some US B-21 *Raider* bombers coming in from Germany.

She'd looked out of her cockpit at the enemy trucks below, and she'd turned away.

The Syrians had used those trucks to launch a chemical weapons attack on Incirlik and nearly two dozen American soldiers had lost their lives, caught out in the open in a fog of nerve gas. The B-21s she was sent to escort had ended the Syrian attack with a blizzard of cruise missiles, but they probably would have got through anyway, without her.

So, yeah. Bunny O'Hare had lost a lot of sleep over that. That incident had taught her that the guy in the AWACS, or behind the desk, wasn't infallible. That having all the intel didn't mean you always made the right call. That sometimes a pilot should listen to what her gut was telling her and do what seems right because, hell, it probably was. Even if it meant a court-martial later.

And that sometimes, the only thing standing between the guy or girl on the ground in the desert camouflage uniform and a horrible, gasping death was a troubled pilot who decided to give a target just one more pass.

Zeidan Amar had heard the strike on his troops up at the intersection and run up there immediately to supervise the treatment and transport of casualties and get some idea of what had happened. It looked like a mortar strike, but the injuries were … not what he'd expected. A mortar caused shrapnel and blast wounds, but these were more devastating. He examined one man who had pinprick wounds to his legs, another who had been hit in the stomach and was curled up in pain, but not bleeding. Others were simply dead, or had been hit in the head, blinded, deafened. The white statue in the middle of the intersection gave him the clue – it was pockmarked with dozens of small pits and lying at its base were what looked like dozens of nails, bent and blunted after striking the stone of the statue. A flechette bomb, designed to cause mass casualties rather than massive property damage.

Just the thing an IDF corporal who lived in this town would choose to use against an occupying force. His suspicions were confirmed when one of his men ran up with what was obviously the wing of a drone.

Following the two attacks on his scouts Amar had decided it was time to rid himself once and for all of the Americans. He had planned an assault from two sides … the south-west through the trees, which would allow him to lay down covering fire for an attack by rocket-propelled grenades and grenade launchers, and from the east, where a squad of his best troops would scale the cliff leading from the quarry up to the Marines' compound and assault them from the rear while they were pinned down by his troops in the south-west.

It was a sound plan, even though it would mean a regrettable number of casualties among the Israeli townspeople sheltering with the Marines. He had hoped the situation could be resolved without more bloodletting, but the US troops' continued aggression had ruled that out.

He watched as a jeep drove off with stretchers bearing badly wounded casualties on its front and rear. Some of his best men had been laid low; there would be no assaulting up the cliff face now. *I have shown restraint. No more.*

He'd returned to his temporary command center and issued the orders that had brought forward his plans considerably. He was supposed to wait for a signal from his Syrian contact before calling in the Russian armor, but to wait any longer risked more losses and put his entire objective in jeopardy.

He called his second in command, a Druze major who thankfully had not been wounded in the attack at the intersection because he was responsible for making preparations for the next phase of the operation.

"Ayach, has the antenna been mounted on the roof?"

The major was a compact man with a thick neck and powerful shoulders. He had been a wrestler in the Lebanese Olympic team before agreeing to join the fight for his spiritual homeland. He walked over. "Yes, Zeidan. We've set up a comms station on the top floor – you can broadcast on military UHF and VHF frequencies, but also AM, FM, DAB radio and longwave. Internet too, of course. Powered by wind and solar, battery and diesel backup, all hooked up and tested."

"And our troops in Majdal Shams, Mas'ade and Ein Qiniyye?"

"Are just waiting for your broadcast, Zeidan. The local police in all locations have already joined themselves to us."

"Good. Make it ready."

"Now?"

"Now, Ayach. I'm bringing the timetable forward."

He nodded. "It's ready. Follow me."

They headed for the stairs up to the second floor and the

comms specialists working there stopped and stood to a kind of attention ... or the closest to it their IDF training allowed. *The People's Army* ... well, he had the IDF to thank for preparing these men to defend their true homeland. He now had to be sure their courage and sacrifice were not for nothing.

"As you were, everyone..." he said, walking over to a private sitting by the big radio transmitter. "UHF, I need to contact the Strauss Group in Quneitra."

"Yes, Zeidan," the man replied. He had the encrypted frequency as a preset and quickly dialed it in, then handed a handset to Amar.

"Strauss Group Quneitra, this is Lieutenant Colonel Zeidan Amar, Buq'ata, for Major Aleksiy Tayukin..." Zeidan checked his watch. The Russian was probably sitting down for his supper. Well, he was about to be rudely interrupted.

"Major Tayukin, do you have a report, Amar?"

Zeidan chafed at the man's arrogance. He was a Major, addressing a Lieutenant Colonel, recently promoted to acting Brigade Commander of an elite IDF brigade. And yet as a Russian, he felt no need to show any respect to his Arabic superior. That would change.

"*Major* Tayukin, your forces are under my command, correct?"

"Yes."

Zeidan kept his voice level. "Then you will bloody well act like it and show some respect or at the first opportunity I will have my men stand you against a wall and shoot you. Is that clear?"

He could imagine the man biting down his bile, but he gave the right reply. "Perfectly clear, Comrade Colonel."

"Good. Mobilize your troops and armor. I will be making my broadcast in five minutes and I expect your tanks and infantry to be here within the hour."

"An hour? I ... Comrade Colonel, with respect, the timetable for crossing the ceasefire line was..."

"The timetable has changed. The situation here is that a

303

squad of UNDOF troops, US Marines, has taken up a defensive position on the outskirts of town and they are conducting offensive operations within Buq'ata. I have suffered several casualties already and we require your armor here, now."

"A UNDOF force, conducting *combat* operations? That is … unprecedented."

"As unprecedented as US troops appearing here, but we must adapt. Get your tanks rolling, Major. Report when you reach the Highway 9799 junction."

"Colonel, all of my vehicles and troops are under cover in Quneitra. The Israeli Air Force is hitting anything that moves within twenty miles of its eastern border. If I order my anti-air units to begin operation, there is a high likelihood they will be targeted."

"Then call for air cover. What did you expect? That the road from Quneitra to Buq'ata would be strewn with palm fronds and cheering crowds?"

"We also have reports the Israeli 7th Armored was seen at Kfar Blum, headed east, several hours ago. Do you have an update on their position?"

One of his men, who had been listening in on the call on a headset, scribbled on some paper and handed it to him. "Yes. They are stalled at HaGoshrim, 12 miles east. The road between HaGoshrim and here is blocked with trucks and IFVs of the Golani Brigade who were ordered by me to withdraw east. The commander of the 7th Armored just radioed that they are going to go south, through Gonen, and reinforce Merom Golan from there. I expect the Golani Brigade will also be ordered to return to their positions on the border as soon as it becomes known in Camp Rabin what is happening. Which makes it all the more important you move *now*, Major."

"Very well, it will take thirty minutes to mobilize, another hour to get around the border obstructions and get to you. Ninety minutes to two hours, *if* we meet no opposition."

"I said you have sixty, Major. I expect to see your tanks here in that time. Out," Zeidan said curtly. "Asshole," he muttered under his breath, but making sure the men near him heard.

They'd heard, and were smiling.

"How are you planning to do this?" Amar asked the radio technician.

"I recommend we send sequentially on FM, AM and DAB," the man said. "That way we will reach most of the civilian population at home and on their car radios. That will enable us to cover all of Majdal Shams, Mas'ade, Buq'ata, and Ein Qiniyye. I will record and rebroadcast every fifteen minutes, including on UHF and VHF, AM and longwave frequencies. Those will be intercepted by the IDF for sure, if the others aren't. We've set up a dedicated internet radio channel; it will run continuously on there too as soon as internet links are restored. And our consul in Syria is waiting to provide your statement to media outlets in Damascus as soon as we send word."

"Very good." Amar pulled the typed statement from his top pocket, almost identical to the media statement he'd provided his Syrian contact the previous evening, but tweaked to reach into the hearts of every Druze civilian in the Golan. "I'm ready when you are."

The man began fussing with his console and Zeidan looked around the room. There were about ten soldiers in the command center under Ayach's command, and they had all stopped what they were doing to listen in. He couldn't blame them. They were a part of history in the making, and they deserved this moment.

The man held his earphones closer to his head and held up five fingers to Zeidan. "Alright, live in five, four, three, two…"

Upstairs inside Amal's house, she was moving among the small group of frightened townsfolk, trying to reassure them. There was nothing she could do for the two wounded Marines downstairs, and the corporal, Patel, had taken charge of the defense of the compound. The first thing he had done was put two extra riflemen on the roof, while the rest piled her furniture up in front of the south and side-facing windows, knocked out the glass and set up shooting positions covering the southern approaches. Corporal Patel also put one Marine on the roof, looking over the shed at the rear to the quarry and fields in the east and watching for hostiles, or the arrival of the resupply and medevac flight. It hurt Amal to watch them treat her furniture so roughly, some of which had been in her family for generations, but she made no complaint. These men were from a land a world away from hers, and yet they were apparently willing to risk their lives defending the townspeople upstairs. This was not their fight, but they had made it theirs. If they needed to tear her house apart to save it, so be it.

The house was dark now. The only light was from moonlight leaking through the windows or from the torches on the Marine's weapons, and the pen light she had lent to the old Druze nurse, Gadeer, so that she could check on the condition of the wounded.

The townsfolk had the battery-powered radio in her upstairs sitting room turned on, but it had only been playing Israeli emergency broadcasts for the last 24 hours and there had been no real news bulletins. It was like the world outside Buq'ata had simply gone dark.

Amal was glad to see that none of the wounded had worsened dramatically. She was most concerned about a woman with burns to her arms and torso who was starting to show signs of a fever, and Gadeer, who seemed close to exhaustion. She had just finished taking the temperature of the woman with the burns and Amal motioned her over.

"Thirty-nine seven," Gadeer said quietly. "Up a half degree since two hours ago. The Marine medic gave her some painkillers but they won't prevent infection. We should get her to a hospital, soon."

Amal put a hand on the nurse's shoulder. "What about you, Gadeer? When did you last sleep?"

306

The old woman lifted her hand away gently. "I slept last night. And I took another nap this afternoon. Don't worry about me, I sleep like a cat, every chance I get."

Amal shook her head. "Such a sweet face and such a liar."

"That is no way to talk to…"

"Wait!" Amal said, holding a hand up to the woman's mouth. She heard a change in the radio broadcast, a burst of martial music. "Listen! Turn up that radio!" she said to an old man sitting next to it. He was already reaching for the radio and fumbled with the volume as a man started speaking.

She recognized the voice immediately. The Druze colonel.

"Residents of the Golan Heights, my name is Colonel Zeidan Amar, commander of the Druze Sword Battalion. I speak to you from Buq'ata, which today has been reclaimed by loyal Druze soldiers to serve as the capital of a new Druze province in the Golan Heights."

"What?" Gadeer asked.

Amal took the old woman's hand and pulled her to sit beside her as the Druze officer continued.

"Druze residents of Majdal Shams, Mas'ade, Buq'ata, and Ein Qiniyye, I call on you to rejoice. In 1967 the homeland granted to us by the United Nations was stolen from us by Israel in an unprovoked attack on Syria. Today, Jewish settlers lashing out in prejudice and with unjustified fear over the situation inside Israel attacked peaceful Druze residents in Buq'ata in a horrific terrorist incident that claimed several lives. Only the actions of the brave troops of the Druze Sword Battalion were able to contain the attack, and the terrorists have withdrawn."

"No, that's not what happened!" the old man exclaimed. "They, they…"

"The terrorist threat is, however, still present and the terrorists' actions, supported as they are by all of the military instruments of the Israeli State, threaten all Druze citizens throughout the Golan Heights. Therefore, I have today requested the assistance of the Syrian government, the rightful government of the Golan Heights, to send peacekeeping forces to the Golan. The Syrian government has not just agreed to assist us in this endeavor, but to help the Druze people of the Golan Heights establish a new Druze homeland, with Buq'ata as its capital, to be henceforth known as the Golani Governate.

"To help the smooth transition of power in our new province, I am required to declare martial law and a state of emergency in the towns of Majdal Shams, Mas'ade, Buq'ata and Ein Qiniyye, effective immediately. A night-time curfew will be introduced with immediate effect, and all movement except by police and the military between 1800 and 0500 is forbidden. Civilians will be required to stay at home, and will be arrested if they break curfew. The following edicts are also in force..."

"Here it comes," the old man said, shaking his head.

"All Israeli settlements in the Golan Heights are to be evacuated immediately. Israeli residents of Syrian nationality may remain in the province. All Israeli residents who do not have Syrian nationality should return immediately to Israel. If you do not leave voluntarily, the police and military of the Golani Governate are authorized to arrest and deport you to Israel."

"I wonder if they plan to put us in buses, or behind razor wire..." the old man said bitterly.

"They would not," Gadeer said, shocked. "These are our neighbors."

"Not him. Sword Battalion? There is no Sword Battalion! He is a self-appointed, jumped-up..."

"Quiet please," Amal said. "Listen..."

"... all Israeli settlements in the Golan Heights are illegal according to multiple UN conventions and agreements and are hereby declared illegal by the government of the Golani Governate. Residents of the following illegal settlements are to evacuate immediately to Israel or you will be forcibly evacuated by the police and military of the Golani Governate: Katzrin, Haspin, Bnei Yahuda, Nov..."

His voice droned on, listing the more than forty Israeli

settlements in the Golan, some of them only a hundred settlers strong. Amal was painfully aware that there were fewer than 20,000 Israeli settlers in the Golan, and more than 30,000 Arabic-speaking Druze and others who still considered themselves a part of Syria and who, unlike her and her brother Mansur, hadn't taken Israeli citizenship. She had pointed this out to him, but Mansur had told her to think of the future, not mire herself in the past. Peaceful coexistence is the future of the Golan, he'd said. People will see that.

Apparently not.

The colonel continued. "Third, all armed members of the Israeli Defense Forces, either active or reserve, are to hand in their weapons to the police or military of the Golani Governate. From tomorrow at midnight, any uniformed member of the Israeli Armed Forces found within the 1967 boundaries of the Syrian Golani Governate will be deemed hostile and may be fired upon." Amal shook her head. Every Israeli settler in the Golan was a member of the IDF, either serving, or in the reserve. Few would willingly leave their homes in the townships and kibbutzim, and she knew that if they weren't already, all across the Golan Heights they would now be mobilizing, fortifying their settlements and setting up defenses. What the Druze colonel had just announced was nothing short of a declaration of civil war.

"Finally, we announce our full intention to hold free and fair elections for the Governorship of the new Golani province in one year, to elect the provincial councilors who will serve you and represent your views in the national government in Damascus. My fellow Syrian citizens, today, we, the men and women of the Druze Sword Battalion, have returned our homelands to Druze control. With the help of Syria, we will ensure the peace and safety of all Syrians in the Golan Heights and an end to Israeli occupation. Long live the Arab Ba'ath!"

Situation Room, White House, May 19

Tonya Dupré had stepped out of the White House situation room after receiving an urgent page. She had long ago learned to live with the curiosities of her role, one of which was the fact that she could be paged to take a voice call from an AI Decision Support System.

"HOLMES, what is it?"

Director, you asked to be alerted to any indications the All Domain Attack on Syria was moving from the first cyber and space domain phase to an air, naval or ground phase.

"I know about the Israeli Air Force attacks inside Syria and Iran, thank you, HOLMES."

Yes, Madam Director. However, I have also been monitoring radio communications between the US Marine peacekeepers in the Golan Heights and Marine close support aircraft indicating US Marines are engaged in heavy combat inside the town of Buq'ata in the Golan Heights with an unidentified hostile force.

Tonya's stomach dropped. "Oh no. Syrian?"

The radio reports indicate the hostile force may be local Syrian Druze militia. There have been casualties on both sides.

"This is terrible. Syria can use this as a pretext for sending troops into the Golan." She wasn't talking to HOLMES, she was thinking aloud.

I have a supplementary report, Madam Director.

"Go on."

NSA has intercepted a broadcast emanating from Buq'ata on multiple frequencies, claiming to be from a group calling itself the Golani Governate Sword Battalion and claiming it has taken control of the Golan Heights to prevent violence against Druze residents following a terrorist attack in Buq'ata. They have ordered all Israeli settlers in the Golan Heights to return to Israel and have called for support from Syrian government, quote, 'peacekeeping forces'.

"Is this connected with the fighting in which the US Marines are engaged?"

Unknown. But I estimate a high probability that it is. There is one final connected intelligence report.

"Yes?"

The 432nd Air Force pilot patrolling the no-fly zone over the Golan Heights has reported a small force of Syrian armor moving into the Golan Heights from Syria.

"How small is a small force, HOLMES?"

Platoon strength, comprising main battle tanks, IFVs and unmanned ground vehicles. They appear to be Russian, probably an element of the Strauss Security Group, attached to Syria's 4th Armored Division.

Platoon strength? That didn't sound like much of an invasion to Tonya. "HOLMES, have you done any wargaming on these latest reports?"

Yes, Madam Director.

As a decision support AI, HOLMES' role was to take the intelligence reports coming in from hundreds, thousands of different US government sources, analyze them for relevance to high-priority strategic issues and then create scenarios regarding potential outcomes, ranked by probability. "Drawing on all available intel, what is your highest probability scenario?"

The still ongoing cyber offensive, the civil unrest in the Golan Heights, combined with similar unrest in the Gaza Strip, West Bank, and the Israel-Lebanon border confirm we are seeing phase one of an All Domain Attack against Israel. For Syria, it is intended to prepare the way for a ground invasion of the Golan Heights. For Iran it is intended to increase pressure on Israel in future negotiations regarding an arms limitation treaty. For Russia it is intended to strengthen Russia's position as the pre-eminent power in the region with resulting economic and military benefits. Probability at 64 percent.

"HOLMES, likelihood of a nuclear attack on Israel by Iran or Russia?"

That scenario is at less than 1 percent probability. There is another nuclear conflict scenario with a higher probability, would you like to review it?

Would she? Most probably not. But of course she had to ask. "Sure. What is it?"

I regard the probability of Israel attacking Syria and/or Iran with a tactical nuclear weapon to be at 27 percent, rising with each new report of significant deterioration in the Israeli economy and its defense capabilities. I expect that probability to increase to the mid-thirties if I am able to validate USAF, DIA and CIA reports of significant losses to the Israeli Air Force from its ongoing attacks on Syria and Iran.

"OK, HOLMES. Please write up the intelligence and analyses we just discussed and circulate them to ExComm members and heads of agencies."

Yes, Director.

Tonya shut down the call and put her phone in her jacket pocket. Then she leaned against the wall behind her, listening to the raised voices inside the situation room. Carmine Lewis, Harry McDonald, Kevin Shrier and the President had gone upstairs to the West Wing, to deal with some of the 'voices of concern' being raised by world leaders about the US blockade and no-fly zone, they said. That left a very hawkish VP Sianni as the loudest voice in the situation room right now, fully supported by Admiral Clarke and the Joint Chiefs, and she didn't feel like feeding their narrative with HOLMES' latest intel and dire predictions of all-out war and an Israeli nuclear retaliation.

She could justify that with the argument, even to herself, that HOLMES was just an experimental decision support system ... But she would share with the room what she had learned about some of the military facts on the ground: that the cyber attack on Israel was still ongoing, US troops were engaged in a firefight in Buq'ata and had taken casualties, that Syrian armor had been seen crossing the ceasefire line, in limited numbers, that the Israeli Air Force was, unusually, sustaining heavy losses in its air offensive, no doubt due to the unaccustomed presence of the more than capable Russian opposition.

What a shitshow, she thought. *And we have no way out.*

Buq'ata, Golan Heights, May 19–20

Corporal Ravi Patel had been hoping the USAF drone pilot who called herself 'Angel' was going to give him a way out of this cluster. He wasn't a people leader, not in his own mind. But Gunny Jensen was laid out flat downstairs with a bag of blood donated by Stevens hooked up to his arm, passing in and out of consciousness. Buckland, she was a better leader than him, but Patel was designed second in command. He'd never considered he'd actually have to step up.

Patel had not signed up for this. He had managed to get through six months of the siege of Kobani without getting mortared, shot or burned and he had thought he was a short *Big Boy* ride away from a reunion with his huge and rambunctious Detroit family followed by Scout Sniper training at Camp Pendleton. But if he'd learned one thing on this side-tour, it had been that having a big mofo rifle didn't make you a sniper. Lopez and Jensen had been taken out by that Syrian, or Druze, or whatever-he-was sniper right under Patel's sights. He had gotten in, taken his shots, and gotten out again and Patel *never even saw him*.

He wanted to be able to do that, now more than ever, he wanted to be able to do that. Wanted it like a fire in his guts no amount of regret could put out.

And here he was again, radio at his side, looking through his scope at nothing. Nothing south, nothing north, nothing west.

"Movement south-east," Stevens said quietly. "Civilian. Alone. No weapon sighted." Patel had put two other riflemen on the roof with him – Stevens and Johnson. Wallace and Buckland were at windows downstairs. Bell was running between all of them, checking they were awake, checking on the wounded civilians, Lopez and Jensen. Patel had tried telling him to get a couple hours' shuteye, but he hadn't. Everyone in the squad knew Bell was a Modafinil junkie. Any doubts Patel might have had about that were put aside when the Corpsman went around about an hour ago handing out the small white stimulants to everyone to make sure they wouldn't fall asleep on watch. He seemed to have an endless supply.

The problem was with Lopez and Jensen down, and the Israeli corporal in her workshop rigging up some new death machines, there was no way for anyone to stand down and get some sleep. So yeah, if it took some of Bell's magic pills to make sure no one fell asleep and got them all killed, the hell with it.

Patel heard a scrape on the roof behind him and Bell slid up alongside him, picking up the night vision scope. Without a word he started panning it slowly around the rooftops across the town, and then back again, no doubt going further back than he would have normally after the distance of the shot that took Lopez and Jensen out. But after a couple of minutes he lowered the scope again.

"Nothing."

"It's middle of the night, and that lunatic colonel declared a curfew, so it's only the brave or stupid out there right now."

"I mean, they put up no new scouts, snipers, nothing … what are they waiting for? We hurt 'em bad, they got to be wanting to get some." Bell rolled onto his back, whispering loudly to Johnson, who was watching the eastern approaches across the quarry. "Hey, Rooster, you got anything on your side?"

The big Minnesotan turned his head slightly, not taking his eyes off his front. "Been counting rocks a couple hours now. Up to three thousand one hundred forty-nine. But no movement." He pointed straight up over his helmet. "Plenty action up there, though. Almost makes me glad to be down here."

Patel looked up and realized he'd gotten so used to the sound of jets sweeping back and forth through the sky above them that he'd stopped listening to it. Every now and then there would be the swoosh of a missile or the boom of an aircraft breaking the sound barrier, but they were nearly invisible unless one of them took a hit. Then they were like falling stars or a shower of comets, suddenly appearing as a bright spot in the sky before arcing toward the earth in a shower of brief live sparks.

Patel bent his eye to his scope and started scanning rooftops again. He wasn't up there, he was down here, and he wasn't glad about it.

Where were they? If the Druze had put any new scouts in place to replace the ones the Israeli corporal had taken out with her drones, he couldn't spot them. And what a piece of work she was. Patel had never met an Israeli before they got off their tilt rotor and doubled into town to start picking up pieces of bodies and shepherding the walking wounded away from burning cars. But if she was an example of your typical Israeli, he had no fears for the safety of Israel.

Bell had told him how she returned fire on those terrorists while she still had blood running down her face from the bomb blast. Took out a damn tracked IFV and a squad of troops with a couple of hobby planes. Used a couple more to drop frags on the heads of the Druze scouts.

Woman was a *lioness*.

The Lioness of Buq'ata was sitting on her butt on the cold concrete of her workshop floor, back against a toolbox, face pressed to her knees, shaking and crying.

Toymaker? She was a damn monster.

How many men had she killed or wounded today with her 'toys'? Ten in the IFV, two scouts, another ten, probably more, in the center of town.

The worst part? It wasn't like dropping a laser-guided bomb from 30,000 feet, ten miles away, and watching it glide into a cave entrance. She could still see the expression of horror on the face of that *Namer* driver as he looked down at the drone that had just slammed into the console beside his chair and sat there waiting for it to explode and kill him.

She wiped her nose. And so what, Amal? Yesterday morning

you had been sitting in the furniture store with old Yozam, getting ready to go home and play in the sunshine with Raza. And those bastards had brought a war to the street right outside. Yozam was dead, Raza fleeing west with Mansur. She understood the anger of the families who had lived in the Golan Heights for centuries, the resentment they felt at the new Israeli settlements … but Yozam was *Druze*. Most of the people who were killed and wounded in that terrorist attack were Druze. Her brother Mansur had really believed that the Golan was a place where Israeli and Arab could live in peace together. "Aren't we living proof of that?" he'd asked her.

Maybe one day, Mansur. Not yet. She slapped her leg so hard it stung. Get up, Amal.

As she pulled herself to her feet, using her workbench for support, the medic, Corporal Bell, entered.

"OK in here?" he asked.

"Yes," she replied. "No. Not really."

She lowered her head and began crying again, not even realizing he was beside her until she felt the medic's strong arms around her shoulders, and felt him pull her head to his chest.

He said nothing, just held her. But she could sense, somehow, he knew what she was feeling. That he knew exactly how it felt to be surrounded by death and dying, to be able to see it even when you closed your damn eyes…

When she stopped sobbing, he held her away from him and looked in her face. He wiped the tears from under her eyes with his thumbs, and then felt the cut above her eye.

"That's bleeding again," he said. He lifted her onto the workbench as though she was as light as a small girl, and pulled off his backpack. "Let me clean and dress it."

She didn't protest. She let him work. Thinking of Mansur and Raza, hoping they were safe. Thinking of this place, her new home, knowing it wasn't.

Syrian Airspace, East of the Golan Heights, May 19–20

Rap Tchakov wasn't glad to be up at 30,000 feet over western Syria in the middle of the damn night. Which was weird. Usually he was the first one out on the flight line, first one finished with his inspection, first one in the cockpit of his *Felon*. Rap was a '*Felon* baby' – as a trainee he'd moved straight from the Yak-130 trainer to the *Felon*, without transitioning through any other type. The Russian Aerospace Force had decided to see what a new crop of young pilots who grew up in an era of VR video games could do if you put them into the cockpit of Russia's elite stealth fighter without having to unlearn everything they'd learned on the older generation of aircraft.

The answer as far as Rap was concerned was that they could *fly* those birds like no one else. His *Felon* fit him like a glove. When he slid into the seat, pulled on his helmet and powered on its target acquisition and display system, his hands just fell naturally into a rhythm of their own, flipping display panels, punching icons, and paging through menus and checklists as his eyes scanned the cockpit, the ground and sky around his machine. He could absorb a hundred inputs simultaneously, from his eyes, his hands, his body, his ears, and react to them almost as quickly as the combat AI that was always watching over him.

Only once had that AI reacted faster than him and, yeah, it had saved his life over the sea west of Syria when that damn bitch in her F-35 *Panther* had jumped him. But...

Let it go, Rap.

He had let it go. He really had. Just before she'd jumped him, as they were sailing through the bright Mediterranean sky in international airspace, side by side, like *pilots* instead of enemies, almost like brother and sister, he'd taken off his helmet and waved to her. She'd done the same, though she hadn't waved back. And he'd wanted to prove it had happened

317

when he was telling his fellow pilots back at Latakia, so he'd pulled his phone out of his flight suit pocket and snapped a picture of her.

After which they'd put their helmets back on and he had prepared to break off for Syria. But she had pulled her machine into a screaming loop, fought her way to a missile solution and took out his port engine.

So about a week ago, Rap had taken the print he'd made of that encounter, the picture of the Coalition fighter pilot with the buzz cut glowering across a hundred yards of sky at him, the print he'd had pinned up in his quarters ever since – and he'd burned it.

Stop bloody thinking about it. But he couldn't. He never would. It had knocked the sharp edges off his confidence and he knew it. He felt it now as he pushed his wingman and himself toward their patrol sector for his second mission of the day. The ground crew had been buzzing as they readied his machine. *Did you hear about Yuriy? He got an F-16 and an F-15! Did you hear about Dmitry? He got his wing stitched by the cannon of a Panther and he still made it home, with a drone kill and a probable on the Panther.*

Rap felt like saying to them, Did you hear about Ivanov? He didn't bloody make it home at all.

Mind on the job, Rap. "Akula two, Akula leader, are you a homosexual?"

"Comrade Lieutenant?" his number two asked, surprised.

"I'm just wondering since you seem intent on sticking your nose into my *Felon*'s bloody exhaust ports. Maintain separation, five miles, watch your infrared. You'll pick the bastard *Panthers* or their missiles up on your passive sensors before you ever see them on radar. Day or night. Got that?"

"Yes, Comrade Lieutenant," the rookie said, pulling his machine a little further back. Alright, not technically a rookie, since this was his second mission of the day too, and he'd been with the unit a month now. But Rap had told him he was nothing until he got his first kill and he was still scoreless, so until then, the guy was a rookie.

He'd rather be flying Bondarev's wing, anytime, than dragging this deadweight newbie around the sky. But Bondarev's machine had experienced an engine flare on landing and it was grounded. They had more pilots than machines after several hours of fighting, so that meant Bondarev was grounded too and now Rap had a bad feeling.

His bad mood was interrupted by the *Beriev* A100 controller circling safely back over central Syria, the chickenshit. "Akula leader, Sector Control, I have a tasking order for you."

"Control, Akula, ready to receive."

"Akula, you are to proceed to sector echo alpha niner four and provide air cover for a Syrian armor element moving from Quneitra to Buq'ata. The Syrian air controller frequency is one zero niner dot four. Call sign 'Frog'. The mission is area denial over Buq'ata airspace, the objective is for the armored element to reach Buq'ata without hostile air interference. Acknowledge."

"Roger, Control, Akula is buster for sector echo alpha niner four to cover Syrian armor column. FAC frequency one zero niner dot four, call sign 'Frog'. We'll clear the sky for them. Akula committing. Out." He rolled his head on his shoulders, flexed his fingers. *Show time.* "You get that, virgin?" Rap asked his wingman.

"Yes, Comrade Lieutenant."

"Stay sharp, keep your separation, follow my lead, and you just might break your cherry tonight. We are going into hostile airspace and they will not appreciate our presence. Watch for ground radar painting you, watch your threat display, watch the damn sky and listen for my commands. And Second Lieutenant Oligov?"

"Yes Lieutenant?"

"Don't get yourself killed tonight. Or me. I have an unopened bottle of Arak on my dressing table and we can crack the lid on it when we get back and have a glass with our eggs."

"That's a deal, Akula leader."

Bunny O'Hare was thirsty. But Kovacs was still out somewhere throwing up and she'd taken their last bottle of water. *Note for future missions, O'Hare. Keep a damn camel pack in the trailer.*

For some reason an image flashed into her mind from a couple of nights before. She'd handed over to the incoming pilot, brought her birds home through the airborne chaos of Israel's night sky, and after she got off the phone to Hatzerim she'd gone back to the tent she'd had an airman set up near their trailers and tried to get some sleep, but it was pointless. She'd been too keyed up. Instead, she'd rolled off her cot and stood outside the tent flaps, staring up at the night sky. It was a cool, cloudless night.

Kovacs had been sleeping. Bunny envied her that. She'd gone down to the flight line to check on her babies, and then gotten a lift back to the Akrotiri USAF billets for some sack time.

Bunny couldn't do it. Two hundred miles to the east those Marines were in deep trouble. She was grateful to Kovacs for allowing her to finish out her tour at the stick of a fighter plane – six fighter planes – but she wasn't *there*. She couldn't feel the fear or smell the danger like she could in the cockpit of a *Panther*, looking down on the battlefield.

She'd thought back to her encounter with that Russian over the Med after three days of fighting over Turkey, when they were bugging out for Akrotiri. Wiping that cheeky damn grin off his face but then lining up behind him for the kill shot and not taking it. That face-to-face kind of encounter would never happen behind the stick of a *Fantom*.

If that had happened today, with her sitting in the trailer, he'd just be a target on a digital display to her. Not a stupid grinning kid taking pictures with a cell phone. And he'd be dead.

And maybe that's how it should be.

A chime sounded in her ears, breaking her out of her

reverie. Ground-to-air missile radar? It was painting her recon bird, but it didn't have a lock. She thought the Israelis had just about knocked out every *Growler* or S-300 unit for a hundred miles around her. So this … she ran a quick database lookup.

Ah. There was at least one anti-air configured *Armata* down there. It made sense for the Russian 'private security force' to include a mobile anti-air unit to protect the ground pounders they were sending into the Golan. Ordinarily, she'd just order her machine to climb above 15,000 feet, out of range of the guns and *Verba* missiles the anti-air *Armata* carried. But due to the Israeli Air Force traffic overhead, she had a hard ceiling of 5,000 feet she had to stick to.

She pulled up her nav screen and played with the waypoints she had set around the Syrian column to make more use of terrain to screen the reconnaissance machine she had following it. The Syrians had sat with their engines running hot for nearly forty-five minutes inside Quneitra before they finally pulled out, formed up in a line and made for a crossing through the ceasefire line tank traps, wire and ditches that they'd obviously prepared well ahead of time.

There was no subtlety about the move. As soon as they got over the first mile of rough ground they headed for route 98, the main north-south road through the Golan, and put the pedal down. Right now they were parallel with the UN post on the heights at Merom Golan, but showed no sign that was their objective. Trying to capture the heights would make sense in a full-scale armor and infantry attack, but this had more of a 'police action' feeling about it, and Bunny had a pretty good idea who the *Armata* gunners wanted to get in their sights.

"Merit leader, Falcon Control, we have an update for you."

"Go ahead, Falcon."

"Israeli Air Force has put together a strike package based on your intel. Pull your machines south and hold near the Sea of Galilee. They are five minutes out."

Bunny hesitated. "A no-fly zone technically goes both ways, Falcon."

"It's been signed off by Central Command, Merit. Israel has four F-16s inbound and you now have four minutes to avoid getting caught in the blast wave."

Bunny had already twitched her stick to send her recon machine a command to join with the other drones holding south of Buq'ata, but she was still troubled. "Falcon, there are Russian stealth fighters in the sector. Those tanks are *Armata* T-14s, with anti-air radar and at least one missile vehicle, those Israelis are flying into…"

"Not your problem, Merit. Pull back. Falcon out."

Pull back? Sure. I'll pull back just far enough to be able to watch this freaking disaster unfold, shall I?

"Akula two, Akula leader, I have a data uplink from Frog force. They are tracking four fast movers, inbound their position, requesting assistance," Rap told his wingman. The Syrians twenty miles west had picked up Israeli fighters headed for them and sent the data from their radars through to Rap. He was able to engage at much greater range than their short-range *Verba* missiles or guns, before the Israelis reached standoff anti-tank missile range. "Arm K-77s. Allocate one missile to each target. Home on data, active seeker."

"K-77s armed, home on data mode, active seeker," Oligov replied. "I have tone."

Rap checked his own weapon status. Green across the board, four missiles armed and targets locked. "Shoot, shoot, shoot," he said. His helmet visor darkened automatically to protect his night vision as the four missiles dropped out of his weapons bay, lit their tails and streaked ahead into the night sky. Five miles to the north, he saw the missiles of his number two burning their own path through the sky toward the Israeli F-16s at a combined closing speed of nearly six times the speed of sound.

A two-tone warning sounded in Bunny's helmet as her *Fantom* picked up the active homing radar on the eight Russian missiles. Her combat AI immediately decided the missiles weren't aimed at her, but it reverse engineered their point of origin and immediately shot two narrow bands of radar energy back up the bearing of the missiles.

Felons!

The anti-air weapons on the Syrian tanks were the least of those Israelis' problems.

With a sinking feeling in her gut, she watched as the four blue boxes marking the Israeli fighters and the red dots with trailing direction indicators that were the Russian missiles converged. The Russian attack had been near perfect. Attacking from two bearings with a blizzard of missiles as the Israeli jets were beginning their attack run.

They were bloody brave, those Israeli pilots. They must have seen the incoming Russian missiles too, must have had missile warnings screaming in their ears, but they didn't break off their attack.

Bunny couldn't watch. She closed her eyes.

When she opened them again, the Israeli aircraft icons were gone. All four.

"Splash four!" Oligov called out. "Hot damn."

"Shut up," Rap told him. They'd been painted by a US AN/APG-81 radar. That meant only two possibilities. An Israeli *Panther*, or a US *Fantom*, like the ones that had bushwhacked him two days earlier. Forcing him to back off.

Well, he wasn't bloody backing off this time. He had a bearing on that radar signal.

"Akula two, turn to bearing 197, drop to 10,000 and accelerate to supercruise, there's a bastard *Panther* or *Fantom* hiding in the weeds down there."

"Lieutenant, that's inside Golan airspace."

"I know that, Oligov. Our orders are airspace denial. As

long as there is a hostile aircraft in the vicinity of Frog force, then our mission is not complete. They still have five miles to run. Weapons status please."

Rap knew they had each fired four of their six missiles at the Israeli attack aircraft. But the missile mounts in the *Felon*'s internal weapons bay had a nasty habit of shaking during a launch, which could knock a missile out of alignment.

"Two missiles armed, systems check green," Oligov reported.

"Same," Rap replied. "Alright, engage active search radar. Let's flush this *zalupa* out."

Buq'ata, Golan Heights, May 19–20

After Bell had finished cleaning and re-dressing Amal's wound, there had been a slightly awkward silence, which the Marine Corpsman broke by saying he'd come to tell her the Russian armored column was still heading their way.

There was a chance it was moving on Merom Golan to take the UN outpost there which had a commanding view over the Valley of Tears, but given the pain and grief they had inflicted on the Druze colonel and his new Governate of the Golan Heights, she somehow doubted it. As Bell left to tend to the other wounded, she climbed down off her work bench, ran a sleeve over her eyes to dry the last of the tears, and started pulling parts out of drawers. Engines, guidance systems ... propellers, never enough damn propellers, the things shattered so easily. Tail fins too. She didn't have the bodies she needed either. Amal walked outside, started the generator and got the 3D printer working to print the parts she needed.

Russian T-14 *Armata* tanks. She'd been to a DRD workshop six months ago at Camp Rabin which had discussed potential attack vectors for killing or disabling an *Armata* tank. The challenge was the *Armata* was designed specifically for survivability. *Armata* tanks had been deployed toward the end of the Syrian war and they had shrugged off rocket-propelled grenades, roadside bombs, even Javelin missile strikes.

Most of its systems were automated, it had a crew of only three, and they were housed in a double-armored capsule deep inside the tank chassis. Both the chassis and turret were protected with explosive reactive armor. Every tank had two types of radar – an *Afghanit* millimeter wave system to detect and defeat incoming projectiles up to Mach 5.0 and a phased-array radar to track and engage surface and air threats.

But they weren't invincible, the DRD workshop had concluded. There was one photo from the Syrian war of an *Armata* that had been disabled. A low-tech mine had caused it to throw a track. And its radar was housed in panels around the side and top of its turret. Concentrated fire aimed at the turret from a 30mm autocannon could overwhelm the hard-kill defensive fragmentation weapon launchers that protected it and knock out the *Armata*'s radar and electronic warfare systems. Without radar, the gunner would be relying on last-generation optics and infrared to find targets and the tank would be vulnerable to air attack.

Amal couldn't fly a drone at an *Armata* and drop a thermite grenade on its turret. If it could pick up a shell flying at five times the speed of sound and destroy it, it would detect and kill her drones without breaking a sweat. But at the conference she had found a drone-based attack vector, and for the last six months she had been working on it as a side project, which was why she didn't have the parts right to hand.

She called it the *Turtle*.

RAF Akrotiri Air Base, Cyprus, May 19

Kovacs stepped back inside the trailer and into a fug of sweat. She picked up on the tension immediately.

"Oh no, what now?"

Bunny's hands were dancing across her keyboard and

controls like a concert pianist as she focused on whatever she was seeing in her helmet-mounted display. "Did you bring any water?" she asked.

"What? No, sorry."

"Forget it." Without pausing, she pointed quickly to the tactical screen monitor. "We're being hunted by two *Felons*, inside Golani airspace. They're flying cover for a Russian armor convoy and just took down four Israeli F-16s. I have an intermittent lock on both from our recon bird. We have one recon, one ground attack and four air-to-air *Fantoms* on station. I am pulling the ground attack kites back, moving our air-to-air aircraft up." She punched a comms icon. "Falcon, Merit. Hostile aircraft inside Golani airspace. They just destroyed those Israeli F-16s. I have a solution, permission to engage?"

There was no hesitation. "Merit, Falcon, you are cleared to engage hostiles in Golani airspace."

"Wait, what?" Kovacs said, quietly, struggling to catch up.

"Sit down, Shelly," Bunny said through gritted teeth. "Strap in." She splayed her fingers on the touch screen in front of her and four wall-mounted 2D screens lit up, showing a cockpit simulation display for each of the four *Fantoms* Bunny was vectoring toward the Russian aircraft. They were already within knife-fighting range, just ten miles apart. Each of her four aircraft had four *Peregrine* air-to-air missiles in its weapons bay, and she quickly ordered the four machines to take two miles separation.

"Four birds going to active search and track," Bunny said. She didn't have to control each individually, they were paired and set to duplicate their flight leader's actions. In essence, she just had to point them at their targets and tell them to shoot when they got a solution.

As Kovacs' eyes swept from screen to screen, she saw the two red boxes marking the Russian *Felons* on the screens turn from red stippled lines to solid lines, then a cross appeared in each and a loud tone sounded in the trailer.

"Targets locked, *Fox three by four*," Bunny said, her finger twitching on the trigger on her flight stick. "Oh, crap."

"Oh crap? What's 'oh crap'?!" Kovacs exclaimed.

"Missiles away," Rap grunted with satisfaction. The aircraft below were drones. They didn't have a decent lock on his *Felon*, their radar was sliding over and only briefly locking on before sliding off again. *Fantoms.* Small and usually hard to detect but easier to pick up from above and at near point-blank range … that Arak was already starting to taste good.

"Incoming!" Oligov called. "Evading!"

What? Milliseconds before his combat AI took the decision for him, Rap rolled his *Felon* onto a wingtip and pulled hard toward the incoming missiles, trying to make them maneuver as he punched flares and silver radar decoy foil into his wake. There were two missiles coming at him, two at Oligov. Despite the speed and g-force of his turn he was shaken in his seat as a missile exploded just fifty yards behind his machine and a second corkscrewed wildly underneath him, its guidance system jammed by the *Felon*'s automatic missile radar-jamming response.

"Not this time, robot," Rap shouted out loud, keying his mike. "Akula two, come around to 220 degrees, targets are … Akula two?"

There was no response. No icon on his tac monitor showing his wingman's position either. He was gone. The tac monitor was showing two enemy *Fantoms* down, two still maneuvering. But no Oligov. No emergency beacon indicating he'd managed to bail out either. The kid was just gone. Like he'd never existed. Boiling with fury, Rap tightened his turn further and switched to guns. He was out of missiles, but he was still in this fight.

"Two *Fantoms* down and one *Felon*," Bunny said as two of the 2D screens on the front wall of the trailer went black. "Two

Fantoms re-engaging. That *Felon* is coming around again, he's not bugging out this time. Ideas, Kovacs?"

Shelly's head was spinning with the speed of the dogfight but she'd wargamed scenarios like this a thousand times in developing her algorithms.

"You programmed a drag and bag into your console?" she asked.

"Yep."

"Use it. He's down to guns and you are more maneuverable."

Bunny hit a three-button combination on her flight stick. "Merit four dragging, Merit six bagging. Putting six on passive arrays only, no need to let the *Felon* know what's going down."

A 'drag and bag' was a fighter tactic as old as World War Two. The fighter flying lead would extend out in front of the target, offering an irresistible target, looking like it was trying to flee. If executed well, its wingman would sweep in behind the enemy unseen and knock him down.

If not executed well, the lead aircraft was, however, a sitting duck...

Rap watched the tactical icons in his helmet display carefully. One of the remaining two enemy drones was breaking away, headed for Israel. The other was about five miles to port, but had lost radar lock and was not actively tracking him.

Once again Rap offered a silent thanks to the designers of his magnificent airplane. They had made it nimble, they had made it deadly and, more than anything else, they had made it as slippery as an eel. The American drones' radar just slid across its skin without finding purchase, allowing him to focus on the job at hand.

Killing one of the *Fantoms* that had killed Oligov. Before it could kill the troops in that armored column behind him.

Yes, the enemy plane was just a machine. But behind the

stick was a pilot. And that pilot was about to be completely demoralized.

Pulling his own flight stick back and shoving his throttle forward, his *Felon* leapt forward, eager for the kill.

His nostrils flared as he moved into guns range and flipped the cover of his guns trigger up. The optical infrared gunsight for his Gryazev-Shipunov 30mm cannon had already locked the drone up and was just waiting for him to close the gap before it would automatically fire. He felt a swell of pride. *By Christ, the designers at the Sukhoi Design Bureau had done their pilots proud.*

As his hand tightened on the stick, everything started happening at once. The *Fantom* in his sights nosed down into a positive-g loop that would have burst a blood vessel in the brain of a human pilot, and it was suddenly booming back through the air *underneath* him. His shock was doubled as a missile alert sounded in his ears, his combat AI wrenched control of the aircraft out of his hands and threw his *Felon* into a desperately flat, skidding turn...

Bunny's missile slammed into the Russian aircraft's forward section, spearing straight through the cockpit wall, tearing off Rap Tchakov's legs and eviscerating the plane's ejector mechanism under his flight seat before its penetrating nose cone burst out the other side of the cockpit in a shower of metal and sparks. The death of Rap Tchakov came mercifully quickly. Before he even registered that he was no longer a whole man, the fuel load in the *Peregrine* missile exploded, incinerating Rap and sending his *Felon* tumbling to the earth below.

If he'd known who'd just killed him, he would have been very, very annoyed indeed.

All Domain Attack: Fog

US blockade line, Mediterranean Sea, May 19–20

Every face in the USS *Canberra*'s CIC was turned upward toward the speakers in the ceiling, consciously or unconsciously, as they listened in to the commander of the *Canberra* and Destroyer Squadron 60, Captain Andrews, hail the approaching Iranian ships on the international VHF safety frequency.

They'd already been passed by at least one Russian *Kilo* submarine and the two Russian *Karakurt*-class corvettes, which had turned north and south as soon as they had passed into the Mediterranean and appeared to be conducting anti-submarine operations. Despite the risk to HMS *Agincourt*, the US destroyers did not interfere.

The bulk of the fleet, however, including the two Iranian missile destroyers, were still barreling toward them at a steady 23 knots and were now less than two hours away. The *Canberra* knew exactly where the Russian and Iranian ships were, because it was pulling data from a satellite overhead and an MQ-25 *Stingray* with sensor pod that was paralleling the fleet at 50,000 feet. Any of the Russian frigates or the *Slava*-class cruiser could have knocked the drone down with a Buk-M1-2A missile, but for now they were tolerating its presence.

"Islamic Republic of Iran Destroyers, IRIN *Amol* and IRIN *Sinjan*, this is Commander Carson Andrews of the United States Navy. As empowered by United Nations Security Council Resolution 2977, we request you to safely reduce speed and allow a party to board and inspect your vessels for illicit North Korean cargo…"

"Illicit *North Korean* cargo?" Ears Bell asked CPO Goldmann, who was leaning against the walls of his station.

"Nukes. Iran couldn't make 'em because of the sanctions and Israeli interference, so they bought 'em from Korea."

"… failure to submit to this lawful request *will* result in your vessel being forcibly stopped and inspected. I repeat, failure to submit to this lawful request *will* result in your vessels being forcibly stopped and inspected."

There was no immediate answer, and Bell began to wonder if there would be one. But when it came, it was not the answer, or the answerer, he expected.

"United States Navy vessels, this is Admiral Andrei Gromyko, Commander of the Russian Federation Black Sea Fleet aboard Russian Navy cruiser *Moskva*. The ships of Iran sailing with this fleet have already been inspected by the Russian Navy and found not to be in contravention of UN Security Council Resolution 2977, or other instruments. They are sailing under our protection. You will not interfere in their lawful passage through international waters, and if you attempt to do so, it will be considered a hostile act and my ships will respond … appropriately." There was a slight pause, and Bell could imagine the Russian Admiral smiling broadly to the other officers on the bridge of the *Moskva* before he cleared his throat and continued. "Is that clear, United States Navy?"

"Well that was a big Eff You," Goldmann remarked. "I wonder what the CO…"

"Admiral Gromyko, your assertion you have searched the Iranian ships notwithstanding, my orders are to stop and search the Iranian frigates *Amol* and *Sinjan* and I intend to follow my orders," Andrews responded. He repeated the call for the Iranian ships to slow and allow themselves to be boarded.

There was no further response, either Russian or Iranian.

Goldmann drummed his fingers on Bell's station. "Ears, there are at least two Russian *Kilos*, possibly an Iranian *Fateh* and definitely a rogue Israeli *Dolphin* circling us at the moment. It would ruin my day if one of them put a fish in our hull."

"Won't happen, Chief," Ears said, pulling his headset on again with a confidence he didn't quite feel. It wasn't that he doubted the *Canberra* was up to the task. He had the tools. And normally, he'd be up to the task too, but something was troubling him. His kid brother hadn't called to say he'd arrived in Kuwait. Their mom and pop were worried. They'd been worried for six months, reading every day about the Siege of Kobani and their boy Calvin right there in the thick of it as the Marine casualties mounted. They were all relieved when it was finally decided to pull them out, annoyed Calvin was going to be one of the last men out, and then delighted again to hear from him just as he was getting on a chopper for Kuwait. "Don't worry! Call you when we land," had been his last words.

But he hadn't.

Ears had a call in to one of Calvin's buddies in the Lava Dogs, asking if he had heard anything, if there had been a report of a transport going down or having mechanical trouble, but the guy hadn't called back yet. Calvin didn't always call Ears, but he never missed calling their folks.

Ears caught his mind wandering again and pinched his thigh. Hard. *Head in the game, Bell!*

Waypoint reached, Karpathou Strait, heading 47 degrees, depth 180, engines ahead slow, entering stealth holding pattern, the Gal's AI reported.

"Game on, as they say, Ehud," Captain Binyamin Ben-Zvi said, as much to himself as to his 2IC. "What depth is the thermocline?"

"One fifty here, ranges between that and one ninety, the track we've plotted," Ehud said, checking the ambient water conditions. "Light surface chop, probably strong winds, not good for putting up a buoy. And we only have one left. If we lose it now, we won't have a radar option for an interception."

"We can't surface here. But we need to confirm our orders, so the buoy is our only choice." Binyamin was chewing his lip. "You want to go to radio mast depth in one of the busiest shipping lanes in the Med, at least three attack subs and a couple of corvettes out there hunting us? Because I don't."

They had been required to pass a battery of psych tests

before they were assigned to the *Gal*, precisely because it had a two-man crew that would be spending the majority of their patrols – between six weeks and three months – submerged, living in a space smaller than a single shipping container. They needed compatible personalities, but they also needed an ability to deal with pressures above and beyond what normal sailors would ever experience. When Ehud was explaining this to his wife, he told her, "We're more like astronauts than sailors. Sailors can get outside, feel the air, taste the salt sea, swim, fish. On a normal patrol there will be two or maybe three chances for us to do that. Rest of the time we might as well be out in space, because we're stuck in our little tin capsule, breathing each other's farts, drinking desalinated water that tastes like piss, going for days without knowing if the world above us even still exists…"

That's how he felt now, and he knew Binyamin would be feeling it even more, with the success of their mission squarely on his shoulders. And all the worries, repercussions and personal regrets that might come along with it.

Ehud kept his eyes on his instruments but reached out and put a hand on Binyamin's shoulder. "I'm not saying that. You are right, we need to use the buoy. And if we lose it, it probably won't matter because if we get the order to execute, we'll be headed for Gibraltar and we can surface again when we hit the Atlantic." He swiped through his screen to the buoy controls. "*Gal*: engines ahead slow, prepare to deploy sensor buoy."

Engines ahead slow. In the expected surface conditions I recommend a full stop.

"No, we need to be able to respond quickly to what we see without having to spool up. *Gal*: I confirm, ahead slow," Binyamin said.

Understood, continuing ahead slow for buoy deployment, Captain.

Binyamin pulled up their deep-water comms checklist. "Alright, passive sonar check, Ehud."

Ehud ran a check of their passive sensors. He threw up the holograph showing clear water for 360 degrees around them, out to five miles. "Sonar clear. Check."

"Status report."

"Compiled. Correct and ready to send. Check." The data on the *Gal*'s systems state, nav history and its black box logs would all be squirted to Eilat in an encrypted burst as the first order of business once the buoy reached satellite transmission depth.

"Transmission set to Eilat base."

"Check."

"Speed through the water below five knots."

"Speed is ... two knots. Check."

"Buoy systems check."

"Cable release green, booting buoy ... buoy reports systems green. Check."

"Ready for launch."

Ehud pulled up the buoy launch control menu and ran his eyes across the readouts one last time. "On your command."

"*Gal*: you have the helm. Buoy release pattern. Maintain stealth protocol priority, report any contact, autonomy level two. Weapons safed."

Aye, Captain. I have the helm, circling the buoy, stealth protocols are prioritized, defensive maneuvers and countermeasures on my initiative, weapons safed.

"Send it, Ehud."

Ehud tapped an icon on his screen and they heard a small clunk as the spring release on the football-sized buoy kicked it into their wake and it started rising to the surface while the gossamer optical fiber cable spooled out behind it. The feeder mechanism would pay out more line than was strictly needed for the buoy to reach the surface because *Gal* would keep the submarine gently circling underneath it to ensure the cable was not stretched so tight it broke accidentally.

It took about three minutes for the buoy to hit the surface and when it did, its first job was to locate the Israeli Defense Forces comms satellite used for secure comms with Eilat.

"Waiting for satellite handshake..." Ehud reported.

Binyamin started whistling. It was a Bob Dylan song, and

334

that had also been part of their psych compatibility test. Did Ehud mind the fact Binyamin whistled when he was tense? Ehud's answer had been, 'not if he's a good whistler'. He was. It was also a good way for him to signal his mood to Ehud, in case Ehud hadn't picked up on it. He whistled rock ballads when he was tense, classical or jazz when he was relaxed.

"What's going on, Ehud?"

"No handshake," Ehud said, frowning. "*Gal*: can you run a systems diagnostic on comms systems?"

Aye, XO. Running. All systems nominal.

"So what is the problem?"

"I don't know, it's … it's like the satellite isn't there. If there was a glitch we'd usually get some error message from the satellite, but there's nothing. Zero."

"Try again."

"It does that automatically. I'm telling you, there's just no connection. It's like a cell phone telling you it has no signal."

"That's impossible."

Ehud shook his head thoughtfully. "Sure, unless … I'll scan for commercial radio frequencies. See if we can get IPBC on long wave." The Israel Public Broadcasting Service still had a longwave service for overseas Israelis who couldn't pick up its internet channel. It also had a dedicated frequency that sent Defense Department messages to encrypted IDF radios. "Got it. Putting on speaker."

"… Alert. The Government of Israel has declared a national emergency. A night-time curfew is in place for all civilians. All IDF reservists and active personnel are to report to their bases in person immediately. All IDF unit commanders are to report to their headquarters in person immediately…"

"Oh, shit," Ehud said.

"Quiet."

"… here is the IDF update for 0200 hours 16 May 2030. Cyber domain: A large-scale cyber attack on Israel's command, control, intelligence and economic infrastructure is still underway. Expect communication disruptions to internet, landline telephone exchange and cell phone communication. UHF and VHF radio communications should be used for short-range communication. A network of motorcycle couriers is being established. Space domain: Russian anti-satellite missiles have destroyed several communication satellites. Expect communication disruptions. Use UHF and VHF radio for short-range communication. Do not use unencrypted radio communication except in emergencies. Ground domain: all active and reserve personnel should report to their unit commander immediately, in person. We have received reports of hostile ground forces conducting reconnaissance activities across our borders in the Golan Heights and western Lebanon. Russian- and Iranian-backed Syrian forces are massed on the Golan Heights ceasefire line. All ground units in the Golan sector have been ordered to stay in place and prepare to defend against a possible invasion. There have been terrorist attacks in the Golan Heights, West Bank, Gaza Strip and Lebanon border areas…"

"Well, that's why we can't get through," Ehud said. "It's Yom Kippur all over again, starting in cyberspace…"

"Ground war can't be far off, the cyber stuff is just to soften us up, create confusion," Binyamin agreed. "What about our Navy?"

"… Air domain: Offensive operations by our Air Force are underway targeting hostile ground forces in western Syria, Lebanon and Iran. Heavy damage has been inflicted on enemy ground and air defense forces, but there have been Israeli Air Force losses. Naval domain: US forces have intercepted and boarded an Iranian submarine in the Red Sea due to suspicion it carried illicit cargo. The submarine is being towed to Sudan. Israeli Navy units are conducting defensive patrols in the Gulf of Aqaba, the Red Sea and Mediterranean Sea. Hezbollah mobile anti-ship missile batteries in Lebanon have been activated and should be considered a high-risk threat. That concludes this IDF update. Next update at 0230 hours."

The message concluded with a long alphanumeric sequence

– which contained both updated mission orders and, where relevant, nuclear authorization codes for Israeli weapons commanders.

"*Gal*: parse the alphanumeric code and decrypt."

Parsing … complete.

"Any change to our orders?"

No, Captain. Existing orders for the GAL were confirmed, special weapon authorization code included. Shall I update with the new authorization code?

"Yes. Then conduct a radar sweep, identify contacts, classify and report."

Executing radar sweep.

Ehud looked grim. "It's not code red, Ehud, not yet," Binyamin said.

"But how do we know … I mean, that message might be running on repeat and everyone at the station sending it could be dead!" A slight note of hysteria entered his voice. "Eilat could be sending us new tasking *right now*, and we wouldn't receive it!"

"Protocol 142, Ehud."

Gal was one of several nuclear-armed weapons platforms in the Israeli armory. If the army or air force was overwhelmed and the viability of the state threatened, or if another nation attacked it with nuclear weapons, *Gal* could be tasked to use its missiles to attack enemy harbors, or even coastal cities. But to do that required a completely different set of orders and authentication codes than they had received in their last communication window. Protocol 142 removed a ship commander's authority to use special weapons if their authorization code was more than four hours old. Theirs had just been revalidated.

"Even if we lose special weapons authority, we still have conventional weapons," Binyamin said. "And we still have a mission; those orders were unchanged. We were ordered to get ourselves in position to attack those Iranian frigates if needed. That we have done. In fact, from what we heard, our orders make more sense than ever."

Surface contacts identified, no hostile vessels or aircraft within detection range. Contacts on radar display.

The flat panel screen in front of both of them popped up a window showing a radar picture with known vessels labeled and unknown vessels classified by type. The buoy radar had a surface range of only ten miles, because it was down at sea level, but it showed no sign of the Russian corvettes that had been hunting them, and no sign of drones or helos above them.

"Look, we can scan some commercial radio frequencies, see what the news services are reporting. Maybe we ..." Before Binyamin could complete the thought, their tactical situation was turned on its head.

Alert. Subsurface contact detected. Classifying as Iranian Fateh-class submarine bearing two seven eight, depth 210, range three miles, relative speed six knots. Recommend port full rudder, increase speed to one third ahead, set depth above thermocline at 100 feet.

The situational awareness holograph blinked to life, showing the Iranian sub in red, slightly below them and on an intercept heading.

"Damn. *Gal*: execute. Arm *Seahake* torpedoes. Reel in the buoy."

"They'll hear that."

"They already have," Binyamin decided. "They're ..."

Alert. Torpedo incoming. Type Hoot. Initiating jamming. Deploying decoys. Engine ahead flank. Rudder port full. Time to impact, forty-seven seconds.

As the engines wound up and they began accelerating into a hard turn to port, Binyamin paled. Based on a Russian design, the *Hoot* was a rocket-propelled supercavitating torpedo that had a short range but flew through the water at 220 miles an hour. Their own German-made conventional torpedoes reached only 57 miles an hour.

They'd been caught napping. On the holograph they could see a bright red dot indicating the enemy torpedo, spearing straight into their path. The Iranian boat had managed to sneak

338

up within torpedo range and the minute it sensed it had been detected, it had fired on them. Binyamin and Ehud knew every time they put to sea that Iran would relish the chance to destroy an Israeli nuclear-armed submarine if it could, and now they were seeing it was more than a possibility, it was a reality.

"*Gal*: do you have a solution on the contact?"

I have a bearing. Do you wish to fire aft Seahake in autonomous active terminal homing sonar mode? I estimate a 67 percent chance of a kill.

Their rear tube weapons were all conventional warheads. If they fired now, their torpedo would have to leave its tube and immediately begin searching for the Iranian boat with its onboard seeker head. With the Iranians so close, it would give the torpedo very little time in which to acquire its target. But what choice did they have?

"*Gal*: match generated bearing and shoot."

Aye, Captain. Target locked, targeting data downloaded, torpedo away.

Now a blue dot sped outward on the holograph from the baffles of the *Gal* and began a sharp turn toward the Iranian behind them, spooling its optical fiber guidance cable out behind it. The Iranian torpedo closed on them with dismaying speed.

And then Binyamin Ben-Zvi did something an onlooker might have thought quite strange for the skipper of a nuclear-armed submarine moments from potential destruction. He reached out his right hand, clasped Ehud's left hand in his, and squeezed it tight.

Because in the last year, he and Ehud had become close friends. Very close friends. And Binyamin wanted Ehud to know that now, at what could be the end of their lives, that's what he was thinking about.

Buq'ata, Golan Heights, May 19–20

Amal Azaria's *Turtle* looked exactly like its Galapagos Island namesake. It was a dome-shaped heavy-lift quadrotor drone capable of carrying payloads of up to 100lbs. Amal had built a payload module inside which carried six TMRP-6E anti-tank mines sewn into a fabric belt, wound around a central spool. The Serbian mines featured an explosively formed penetrator specifically designed to penetrate the hull of a main battle tank or knock out its track, and their upper bodies were made of radar-transparent plastic. The *Turtle* allowed its operator to drop a belt of mines directly in the path of incoming armor, completely removing the element of chance or luck in planting a mine, and taking away the need to plant large, hard to remove minefields. It also allowed flexibility if an enemy suddenly changed direction or took alternative routes.

Her first designs had tried using an electric engine to unspool the belt of mines, but the added weight of the small electric engine and the larger battery needed to power it had proven impractical. So she had fallen back on a more manual technique. The operator would fly a *Turtle* to a position a mile ahead of a tank column, where it was near impossible to detect, and then hover it centimeters over the ground, dropping the first mine. They would then 'hop' the *Turtle* gently across the road, one mine at a time, feeding the mines out either straight across a roadway to increase the chances of hits on multiple vehicles, or diagonally in the direction of travel of the tank to increase the chances of multiple hits on the same tank.

She only had enough mines for four *Turtles*. She knew there were many more tanks than that coming their way, but if she could hold them up, sow confusion, cause them to go cross-country or take back roads, it could buy them valuable time.

With help from the Marine Johnson, a strapping Minnesota car mechanic, she lifted her *Turtles* out onto the apron behind her house and got them airborne. Then she went up to her rooftop beside Patel to direct them. Heavily laden, they traveled at only twenty miles an hour, but soon they were south of Buq'ata, moving down Highway 98 at a height of about fifty feet. There was no traffic, the emergency curfew meaning that only a few light military transport vehicles were on the road, with the bulk of Israeli forces snarled in traffic jams further west. According to the intelligence Patel had received from the US drone pilot overhead, the column of six T-14 *Armata* tanks, with their four unmanned *Udar* wingmen, had just passed the turnoff to Merom Golan, three miles south.

When her drones got just beyond the kibbutz at El Rum, beyond the turnoff to the Mount Hermonit outpost, she hovered them at fifty feet, not wanting to drop mines in the path of Israeli military vehicles. But then she saw what had to be the dark forms of the lead vehicles in the Russian column. As she watched, an Israeli troop transport, an old M35 cargo truck, barreling down the road toward the Russian column, swerved violently then exploded in flames as the first *Armata* in the column opened fire on it with its 12.7mm *Kord* machine gun. The truck rolled to a stop in front of the tank, which barreled into it, shrugging its flaming carcass aside and continuing on its way as though nothing had happened.

So, that's how it is. Their action told her everything she needed to know about the Russians' rules of engagement. And their intentions. She passed the news onto Patel.

Two miles ahead of the Russian column, she lowered her first *Turtle* to the tarmac and laid a strip of six mines across the road, straddling both lanes. She flew the drone off to the side of the road and landed it, then moved control to the next of her *Turtles* and did the same, fifty feet further back. She had picked a section of the freeway known as Bar'on Junction, which traveled through thickly forested verges on both sides that would prevent the Russians from being able to easily pull off the road and bypass her minefield. Fifty feet further in toward Buq'ata again, she laid another strip of mines. There were now eighteen mines spread across the road one hundred and fifty feet deep, between the pine trees.

The fourth *Turtle* she planned to keep in reserve, waiting to see the result of her attack before deploying the mines inside it. That one she flew about a quarter mile east, up the slope of a small hill that held an abandoned bunker complex from around the time of the Yom Kippur war. She parked the drone atop one of the concrete pillar boxes at the eastern end of the complex and powered down its engines, leaving the camera focused on the section of highway between the trees.

All of the vehicles in the Russian convoy had passed the burning truck now and were approaching the forest pass. Amal had no illusions her few mines would be able to stop them all. She reached out and tugged Patel's sleeve without taking her eyes off the screen on her command module. "Tell your pilot that if she has finished playing with the Russian Air Force, we may have a job for her."

Patel laid down his rifle and rolled onto his back, turning on the radio. They kept it turned off when not using it because the battery was running down and the only way to charge it was by firing up the noisy diesel generator out back.

"Angel, Marine JTAC, we have eyes on the Russian column, three miles south of Buq'ata. They just took out an Israeli cargo truck. What is your status?" Patel asked.

Bunny O'Hare's status could nicely be defined as 'pissed'. She had taken out two *Felons* but lost two of her air-to-air drones. She was now down to just two air-air, one recon and one ground attack bird. If Russia tried another push into Golani airspace with more determination than the last, she would quickly be out of missiles, probably also out of air-air *Fantoms*. Her recon bird had guns, but that was a last resort play in an air-air encounter.

"Hey, Patel," she replied. "You have clear air overhead for now. I am bringing my recon and ground attack units back up north to your position. I should have eyes on the Russian column myself in a few minutes, but we have to stay low and sneaky … I'm still getting painted intermittently by the anti-air radar on one of the T-14s in that column. I have to assume it has *Verba* missiles and a 30mm cannon, which can ruin a

Fantom's day."

"Well, we're going to try to ruin their day. We've planted mines in their path just before the Mount Hermonit turnoff, so stand off and watch for fireworks. We may need an assist depending on how they react."

"Roger. We have Central Command approval to drop the hammer if we need to protect you, Patel, so just say the word. Merit out." Bunny flipped the view from her recon drone onto the main 2D screen inside the trailer. At that moment it was just showing a near blacked-out landscape, rushing below the aircraft.

"How did they get mines planted on the roadway? I thought they were trapped inside the town," Kovacs asked.

"Beats me. How did they destroy a *Namer* IFV, two scouts and an assault platoon?" Bunny put her reconnaissance *Fantom* into a holding pattern low and to the west of Mount Hermonit, with its cameras trained on the intersection Patel had mentioned. She could see the glow from the still burning cargo truck further south, and the phosphorescent blobs from the engine heat of the Russian armored vehicles approaching the intersection.

Kovacs leaned forward, squinting at the screen showing the video feed. "The bigger ones are the tanks, right? Can mines even stop an *Armata* tank?"

"Their wingmen are *Udar* unmanned ground vehicles, built on the old BMP-3 IFV chassis. Pretty sure a decent-sized mine would blow through the hull or knock a track off one of those, but an *Armata* ... those things were built to take a hit from a 120mm depleted uranium round and keep going." She turned her attention to her heads-up display. "Circling our ground attack machine south of the Russian column. Arming JAGM missiles. If we're going to hit them, our best chance is to hit them when those mines start popping off and their anti-air crew is a little distracted."

West Wing, Washington, DC, May 19–20

President Oliver Henderson wasn't distracted, but he was looking rather confused as he laid the telephone on his desk back in its cradle. "Anyone want to tell me what I just agreed to?"

In the brightly lit Oval Office with him were Carmine Lewis, Defense Secretary McDonald and Secretary of State Shrier, who twenty minutes earlier had been on the phone with an agitated Iranian President who had spent the entire call protesting about the US seizing his submarine and the Israeli air attacks on his strategic missile and nuclear facilities. Shrier had to remind him several times he was the US Secretary of State, not the Israeli Minister of Foreign Affairs, and the submarine and its crew had been released at Port Sudan, but that hadn't calmed the man down. Shrier had advised them he wasn't sure he had gotten the message through that the Israeli PM had agreed to begin immediate talks with Iran, under US auspices, regarding a future arms limitation treaty – if Iran 'intervened' to stop the ongoing cyber attack and pulled its strategic missile forces and submarines back.

Their series of calls to the hard-pressed Israeli PM, who had just been advised his air force had lost at least twenty aircraft so far and his economy was bleeding billions, and to the Iranian President, who headed up the Iranian cabinet, had been timed so that when President Henderson called the Iranian Supreme Leader, Ayatollah Takhti, he would have had time to discuss the offer with his President.

Takhti had inherited from the previous Ayatollah, Khamenei, an Iran deeply wounded by sanctions, but determined not to be cowed by either the US or Israel. Under his direction Iran had taken a hard line against Israel, responding to its many overt and covert provocations in kind – assassination for assassination, cyber attack for cyber attack – and Israeli air raids were answered with Iranian missiles. He had toned down the anti-US rhetoric, however, and had even

344

brokered a prisoner swap in which Marines captured by Syrian forces in southern Turkey had been returned in exchange for Syrian prisoners of war.

"Mr. Henderson, we had offered already to help Israel with this terrible cyber attack, but they rejected our offer and instead unleashed their air force against us," the Ayatollah's translator said when he had finished speaking. "The actions of Israel are not those of a nation seeking peace. Nor are those of the USA, which I am told has just issued an ultimatum to our ships in the Mediterranean."

"Mr. Takhti…" Henderson had refused to consider calling the Ayatollah either 'your holiness' or 'Supreme Leader Takhti', so both sides had agreed to use simple surnames for what was a historic first call between them. "If your ships are not found to be carrying illicit cargos, they will be free to continue to Port at Tartus…"

The Ayatollah interrupted, changing tone. "Mr. Henderson, we should not waste our time on such small details. These we can leave to our generals and our cabinets. This is the first time you and I have spoken, shall we not speak of higher things?"

Henderson had looked at Carmine, raising his eyebrows. "Well, yes, I agree, sir."

"Is it true, Mr. Henderson, that you were a Baptist Minister?"

"Yes, Mr. Takhti, before I went into Congress, I was a minister in a small church."

"Then we are both men of faith."

"I guess you could say that."

"Yes. My faith enjoins its believers to pursue what is right and forbid what is reprehensible. I consider nuclear weapons, Mr. Henderson, to be reprehensible."

"They are indeed. And so what we propose…"

"The sanctions against my country are also reprehensible. We cannot get medicines, foodstuffs, machinery parts, we cannot trade freely and fairly…"

"Well, now, Mr. Takhti. Violence is also reprehensible. War

... in all its forms, cyber or kinetic, is reprehensible."

Even through his translator, the Iranian projected a weary sadness. "War is an abomination. Why should we not, you and I, work together to forbid what is reprehensible, Mr. Henderson?"

"I ... think we should," Henderson said, looking around the room for a steer. "So what we suggest is..."

The Ayatollah interrupted again. "Your honest statement of intent is all I need, Mr. Henderson. Our people can agree on the smaller details, including the involvement of Russia in our discussions. Thank you for your call."

And that was it. The first call between an Iranian leader and a US President was over.

"I think ... I think you just agreed to lift our sanctions on Iran," Harry McDonald said.

"No. I did no such thing," Henderson shook his head vehemently.

"You agreed to work together," Carmine said. "With Iran and Russia. On what, I'm not sure. Maybe, if we're pushed, you agreed to a common desire for peace."

Kevin Shrier picked up his cell phone. "I want to get a communique to Tehran immediately, while the iron is still hot. Agree a form of words along the lines that in a call with the US President..." he was typing into his phone.

"A historic first ever call..." Carmine suggested.

"Yes, a historic first ever call between the US President and the Ayatollah of Iran, both sides agreed to work together to find solutions for, uh ... what, exactly?"

"Lasting peace in the Middle East," Carmine said. "Keep it short and noncommittal, so there's nothing for them to disagree with. The news value is the fact we even spoke together."

Henderson was tapping a pen on the desk. "Congress is going to hate it. The pro-Israel lobby is going to hate it. The press corps will go nuts."

"The Joint Chiefs are going to hate it too," Harry McDonald

said. "No, they are going to be rabid."

"Get the Israeli PM to issue a statement supporting it," Carmine proposed. "We can offer some financial aid to underpin his economy. That neutralizes the Israeli lobby and most of Congress at least."

"He won't do that while his country is under attack. While his planes are still striking Syrian and Iranian targets across the region."

"Someone's got to blink first," Carmine said. "He's bleeding shekels and airplanes. His command and control infrastructure and ground forces are in disarray, he's probably still days away from being able to mount a ground defense of the Golan Heights, let alone an offensive into Syria. It's not the strongest hand he's playing right now. If he pulls his air force back, we might see Iran do the same with their navy and their missiles, right? Without Iranian nukes at their back, Syria wouldn't dare roll over that ceasefire line into the Golan. Isn't it worth asking him to think about it?"

Henderson kept tapping his pencil. "Where the hell are those Iranian frigates now?"

Carmine had a tablet in her lap and pulled up the latest report. "An hour away from our blockade line. Russia has declared they are sailing under Russian protection and any move to stop them will be treated as hostile."

"If this is going to achieve anything, we need to get it out there, pronto," Shrier said, waving his phone.

Henderson laid the pencil down and lined it up carefully with the blotter on his desk. "Alright, Kevin, send that form of words to Tehran, tell them we want to go public inside the hour. Harry, call a meeting of the Joint Chiefs and prepare them. Let them vent, but tell them it is what it is and they want to bitch, they can bitch to me." He turned to Lewis. "You get down to the situation room and let ExComm know what we've been doing. I'll call Karl Allen, ask him to get the Israeli PM on the line somehow. And have him warn the guy I'm making him an offer I don't expect him to refuse."

US blockade line, Mediterranean Sea, May 19–20

Ten seconds to torpedo impact … seven … six … five …

They said it took brave men to go to sea in submarines, but Binyamin Ben-Zvi wasn't a brave man. Not really. A brave man wouldn't be about to soil himself. He wouldn't have his eyes squeezed shut in fear. He wouldn't be trying desperately to remember that quote from the Torah, Devarim, the one about fear, and his mind wouldn't be a total bloody gibbering blank!

But Ehud remembered it, and he said it out loud. "Do not be afraid for it is God, your God, who is fighting for you…"

The Iranian *Hoot* torpedo had deviated in the last 100 yards of its trajectory and had been lured toward the last of their acoustic noisemaking decoys, now drifting thirty feet below and about fifty yards above them. The *Hoot* was going to miss, but not by enough.

Impact.

The *Gal* rocked with the primary blast wave from the explosion of the torpedo's 500lb. warhead in their wake. Like the hand of God, it lifted their stern, throwing Binyamin and Ehud forward in their seats, only their emergency safety belts saving them from smashing their heads on their instrument consoles. But it was the secondary shock wave that would really hurt them. A result of the cyclical expansion and contraction of the gas bubble from the explosion, it sent a ripple of shock waves through the *Gal*'s hull, shaking it like a rattler in a baby's fist.

Sensing imminent catastrophic damage, *Gal*'s AI shut down the engine and drive train, cut all power except emergency current and immediately flooded all non-personnel spaces with inert gas to dampen any fires that might break out. She did this before Binyamin could even register that he was still alive.

He let go of Ehud's half-crushed hand.

Two minutes to torpedo impact, torpedo has acquired target

348

and is homing. Target has moved to flank speed, turning to 180 degrees relative. Target jamming. Initiating jamming and decoy countermeasures.

"Ehud, run a damage analysis."

"Already running, Benny."

"*Gal*: cue another *Seahake*."

Aye Captain. Seahake armed, bearing to contact loaded. Torpedo systems check complete. System nominal. Shall I shoot?

"No, hold fire, *Gal*." They had only six conventional torpedo tubes – two facing aft – and one of the drawbacks of his otherwise amazing new boat was that without crew, and without an autoload mechanism, he had no reloads. So he had only five remaining conventional torpedoes and he needed to conserve his ordnance for their real mission.

One thing working in their favor, however, was that though it was slower, their DM2A4 torpedo had a better guidance system, better jamming countermeasures, and *Gal* could assume manual control of the torpedo if she felt it was being decoyed off target.

And *Gal* was a very, very good torpedo pilot.

"Damage report," Ehud said, running his eye across a screen. "Hull integrity: flooding in portside fuel cell compartments F4 to … F6; flooding in sail from level five to level three. Overall hull integrity 94 percent. Propulsion: one engine offline, two undamaged. Fuel cells: power output at 67 percent and stable. Shaft: no reported damage. Screw: no reported damage. Weapons: no reported damage. Steerage: rudder and planes showing full movement range. Sensors…" Ehud paused. Binyamin didn't need to be psychic to know that wasn't good.

"Sail damage has impacted the periscope and antennas?"

"You could say. If I had to guess, I'd say we have catastrophic damage to the top third of the sail. Periscope non-functional. Antennas non-functional. We still have sonar or *Gal* wouldn't be able to track the contact and steer that torpedo, but we can't get a visual on a target, we can't send or receive radio signals and our buoy, well, it's either dead or gone. Hull integrity is 83 percent, hull collapse depth revised to … 500 feet."

One minute to torpedo impact. Target locked, torpedo maneuvering.

"Weapons?"

"Weapons systems green across the board. Looks like the portside midsection and the sail took the brunt of the shock wave." Ehud looked up ruefully. "And if we want to get out of here before we reach harbor again, it's going to have to be through a torpedo tube."

Another of the sacrifices the designers of the *Gal* had made in automating her and replacing her crew compartments with batteries and fuel was that they had eliminated the aft escape hatch. The only way out of the submarine was either through the sail overhead, or forward, through one of the 650mm torpedo hatches.

Thirty seconds to torpedo impact.

The Iranian *Fateh*-class boat was one quarter the size of the *Gal*. Iran called it a 'semi-heavy' submarine. A less generous navy might call it a 'mini'. It carried only six torpedoes to the *Gal*'s ten, weighed only 500 tons to the *Gal*'s 2,000, and had a speed of 14 knots submerged, versus 25.

But it was nimble.

And as the *Gal*'s torpedo approached it was traveling at flank speed, rudder full right, and had deployed its last-ditch defense – a towed decoy that mimicked the electromagnetic and acoustic signature of its host to try to trick an incoming torpedo into thinking it was a larger and much more inviting section of the submarine.

Gal fell for none of it. She assumed manual control of the torpedo in the last thirty seconds of its run, kept the torpedo pointed at the fore-section of the Iranian *Fateh* and steered it to a perfect interception.

Impact. Analyzing acoustic data… target destroyed.

Binyamin let out a loud sigh. Ehud was a little more enthusiastic, and quite a lot more profane.

Buq'ata, Golan Heights, May 19–20

"Yes!" Amal yelled, watching as there was a ripple of explosions across the highway and one of the dark forms in the convoy bucked into the air and fell onto its side. To have that effect, it must have been one of the smaller *Udar* unmanned ground vehicles, but for her, it was proof of concept. Her *Turtles* worked!

The convoy broke left and right as the vehicles behind the *Udar* swerved to avoid it and there were more explosions. It became impossible to see what had been hit and what was still moving as her infrared vision flared.

"You got a kill?" Patel asked, hopefully.

"No," she said. "I got two … three … maybe *four.*"

"You are a freaking legend, woman," Patel said.

She restarted the engines on her last *Turtle.* It was at the maximum range of her VHF transmitter, so she was scared the thing wouldn't restart, but she saw all four engine lights turn green on her console and the camera jerked as it lifted into the air. Now her dilemma was simple. To lay the last belt of mines ahead of, behind or beside the convoy, which had come to a sudden and very violent halt.

As she watched, a vehicle at the rear of the convoy lit up and what looked like a laser beam of light stretched from the tank up into the sky.

"My god, what was that?"

"Missile," Bunny said to Kovacs, calling the engagement out loud again. "*Verba.* No lock. They're firing blind." She ran her mouse across the screen, designating targets for her JAGM missiles. "Desperate. But they're awake."

Kovacs watched her work, fingers dancing, eyes flicking from her helmet display to the screens in front of her and the virtual sky around her before she hit her mike control. "Falcon, Merit. Targets locked. AI confirms *Armata* and *Udar* ground vehicles, inside the ceasefire line, three miles from US Marine position. Requesting permission to engage."

"Merit, Falcon Control. You are cleared to engage. Good hunting, Merit."

"Roger. Merit out."

This is it, Shelly thought. All of this, today. All our work. To put this woman in charge of these machines, at this moment, to save the people in that house.

"Rifle, rifle, rifle," Bunny called. The video feed on the 2D screen in front of Kovacs had been showing the stalled Russian convoy, several vehicles already burning. Others backing, pulling onto the roadside verge, trying to find a way around them. Bunny's *Fantom* carried four of the larger JAGM air-to-ground missiles and they appeared on the screen as four momentary streaks of light, lancing toward the shadowy forms on the highway, dancing in the light of the fires of vehicles starting to burn from the explosion of mines beneath their hulls, crews spilling from disabled or canted vehicles as the four missiles raced toward them.

The *Udar* unmanned ground vehicle was a kludge. A rushed attempt by Russia to keep pace with NATO development of remotely piloted and autonomous armored vehicles, the first prototype seen in 2016 was just an *Epoch* remote turret with 30mm cannon mounted on a decades-old BMP-3 infantry fighting vehicle frame. Its 'driver' had to have line-of-sight to control it and situational awareness proved a huge problem because it had only one pair of human eyes looking through multiple hull-mounted cameras by which to spot and engage enemies.

But subsequent generations deployed throughout the 2020s had beefed it up into a formidable weapons platform in its own right. Of the four *Udar* vehicles accompanying their motherships from Quneitra to Buq'ata, three were ground assault variants featuring either 30mm autocannon turrets or anti-tank guided missile launchers and 7.62mm coaxial machine guns. The fourth was an anti-air variant that mounted not only *Verba* optical-infrared missiles – able to take its targeting either from their own sensors or the sensors of its mothership – but also a very capable electronic warfare suite that allowed it to jam and misdirect incoming missiles.

To eliminate the problem of blind spots, recent models of the *Udar* featured the same battlefield radar system as the *Armata* and could independently track and engage multiple ground and air targets.

As soon as they had detected the *Fantom* overhead and before it got within range of their own air defenses, the crew of the anti-air *Armata* had put their *Udar* into 'jam and decoy' mode. It began moving away from its mothership and emitting a blanket of radiation intended to drown out anything coming from the other tanks. It painted a big fat 'attack me!' sign on itself and as soon as Bunny launched her missiles, it narrowed its transmissions to focus all that energy at the incoming threat.

Two of the JAGMs were blinded by the combined jamming of the *Armata* and *Udar* and flew wild. One was intercepted by the *Armata*'s close-in weapons system, which exploded it just twenty yards out from the tank, rocking it in its chassis but doing no blast damage at all.

The fourth of Bunny's missiles fell deeply, head-over-heels in love with the radiation being generated by the *Udar* – which had none of the close-in weapons defense systems of an *Armata* – and showed its affection by hammering into its hull at supersonic speed and detonating deep in its robotic guts.

"Splash one," Bunny said disgustedly. "Four missiles, one measly kill. And it looks like that was an *Udar*. Slaving all four birds to my stick."

"What? Why?"

"Those *Armatas* have active defenses that are killing our missiles," Bunny said in a flat, detached tone. "Let's see how they handle four streams of 25mm AP. Anyone down there still alive better have a tungsten umbrella because it's about to start raining cannon fire."

The *Armata* T-14 tank was designed, above all, to be able to survive on a modern battlefield. It featured all-round dual-explosive reactive armor, its front glacis was double spaced and the three-person crew were protected behind a 900mm front block and armored capsule. Its onboard radar was linked not just to the main weapon control system, but also to an active defense system that could intercept incoming projectiles – such as Bunny's JAGM anti-tank missiles. As the missiles closed, they were picked up by the vehicles' radars which fired fragmentation shells into the path of the missiles and blew them up before they even reached the tanks.

They were not indestructible. Amal's DRD team had identified the armor under the tank, which was not dual-explosive reactive armor, and the tracks as weaknesses and her mines had done a job on the tanks that had rumbled over them, triggering their vibration and acoustic sensors. Of the six T-14s, one was knocked out with engine damage, one was on fire and the crew had baled out because the explosively formed penetrator from the mine had hit the rotary ammunition autoloader inside the automated turret and triggered the ammunition, and two had thrown tracks, which would take time to repair. Two of the four *Udar* UGVs were also out of action, but the other two were still in commission because their 'mother tanks' were still in action. Two T-14s were undamaged and maneuvering to avoid the carnage around them, pick up the crews that had baled and keep pushing into Buq'ata. To do that they planned to back up, get out of the minefield that had been laid across the highway and skirt the forest completely, coming at Buq'ata from the south-west instead.

But first, they had to get off the highway.

And deal with that damned *Fantom* overhead.

Amal was trying to count the stalled or burning wrecks. The *Udar* UGVs seemed to have been either hit by mines or otherwise taken out of play. Three were stationary, either hit by mines or stalled because their motherships were damaged, and one was burning. A T-14 was also burning and she saw secondary explosions, indicating its ammunition was cooking off. The crew had made it out and were running back down the highway, away from the blaze. The tank next to them had also stalled and she watched it spin on one track until it realized it had been crippled, a crewman stuck his head out, saw that they were pinned between the burning UGV and the exploding T-14, and soon the entire crew of that tank too were out and running back down the road.

But two of the T-14s were still maneuvering. Her *Turtles* had claimed two out of four main battle tanks. Not bad.

But not good enough. It seemed the US aircraft overhead had not managed to kill anything other than a single unmanned *Udar*. The crews who had abandoned their machines were watching from the cover of the trees as the remaining two main battle tanks slowly backed out of her kill zone.

She had to drop the belt from her last *Turtle* now, while they were still between the trees, but there was no way one belt could disable two tanks. She had a choice to make.

"Patel, the Russians are down to two *Armatas*..."

"Alright! Eight from ten? You and that jet jockey rock!"

"Uh, except only one of the T-14s and one of the *Udars* is what I'd call a kill. The others seem to have engine or track damage, but that can be repaired. And your air force attack claimed only one unmanned vehicle. There is an anti-air *Armata* down there coordinating counterfire and your drone's missiles are not getting through.

"Wait one," Patel said, grabbing the radio handset. "Angel,

this is Marine JTAC, you still up there?" He was straining his ears but couldn't hear the rumble of jet engines indicating the *Fantoms* were close.

"Pulled back south, Patel," the Australian voice replied. "I only have one mud mover in my flight and it just used all its missiles. I'm regrouping, going back in with guns."

"Uh, Angel, I have an IDF corporal here with eyes on the hostile force. Maybe you should put your heads together. Putting her on."

Amal was busy maneuvering her last *Turtle* down from the hilltop to the highway in the path of the reversing tanks, so she cradled the handset against her ear as Patel held it for her. "This is Corporal Azaria."

"Corporal, call me Angel. Do you have a damage assessment for me?"

Amal described exactly what she was seeing. "Also, there is a tank with a 30mm autocannon and anti-air missile turret that still appears to be operational. I will try to use my last mine belt to disable it but that will probably not knock out its radar or weapons systems."

"It could be enough," O'Hare said. "The other tanks aren't likely to move far from their anti-air cover with us buzzing around them. I'll wait for a report on your attack before moving in again."

"Roger, Azaria out," Amal said and let Patel take the radio handset back.

"Angel, you good now? I'll get back when we have a damage assessment from our next attack."

"Alright, Patel, good hunting. Get some for me. And I mean that literally."

All Domain Attack: Impasse

US blockade line, Mediterranean Sea, May 19–20

"Cavitation noise, bearing two seven zero, range ten miles," Ears announced into his mike. "AI is calling it an Iranian *Hoot* torpedo. Not targeting the *Canberra*, repeat, we are not the target."

"Who else is out there, Ears?" The Watch Supervisor, Goldmann, asked, standing up and looking across the CIC at him.

Ears checked the tactical plot. "No surface shipping. Could be the *Agincourt*. Could be that Israeli ... I've got nothing but the..." He lifted his headphones away from his ear quickly, then jammed them on tight again. "Explosion, subsea!" he said, watching the acoustic and seismic readouts on his screen as they hopped and skipped.

"God damn, if they got the Brits..."

"I'm not hearing secondaries. I think it was a miss. Or hit a decoy. Whatever they hit, it isn't breaking up."

TAO Drysdale finally woke up and joined Goldmann standing. "Sonar, you have a position on that explosion?"

"Yes, sir. Patching it through."

"Alright, ACO, get a quadrotor with dipping sonar over that position immediately. Whatever the hell is happening out there, I want us to..."

"Another explosion!" Ears announced. "New position, three miles south south-west of the first. There was no cavitation noise, probably a conventional missile, not rocket powered like the *Hoot*."

"Counterfire," Goldmann decided. "Whoever got shot at, shot back."

"I have hull break indications..."

"Put it on speaker," Goldmann ordered.

Ears patched the sounds he was hearing through to the CIC

overhead speakers. To the untrained ear, it sounded like huge iron gates were being thrown and dragged across rocks.

"Hull collapse," Goldmann agreed, shaking his head. "Poor bastards, whoever they are."

"'Whoever they are' fired a *Hoot* torpedo," Drysdale reminded him. "So they're Iranian. It was probably that *Fateh* boat, so we can save our sympathy. ACO, I still want a dipping sonar over that first contact. Find out who the hell they were shooting at."

It was Binyamin's first time being shot at, and he hoped it was the last. He didn't think he handled it very well at all. Sure, he made all the right calls, helped not a little by *Gal*, but what must Ehud think of him?

"Ehud, get forward and inspect the fuel cell damage. Make sure the flooding is localized and there are no other leaks."

"We can check on closed circuit," Ehud said. "And *Gal*'s moisture sensors would…"

"Trust, but verify, Ehud," Binyamin told him sharply. "You have eyeballs, I would like you to use them."

Ehud looked like he was about to say something, but then rose from his seat instead. "Aye, skipper. Going forward. *Gal*: monitor and report any system anomalies."

Aye, XO. Monitoring all systems for any readings outside normal range.

Binyamin watched him go. He shouldn't have snapped at him. He would apologize later, when their mission was complete. He pulled up a nav screen and dropped a waypoint square in the middle of the channel exiting the Karpathou Strait, the exit from the Aegean Sea, and assigned an arrival time to it. It was almost the only point through which the Russian fleet could sail and still maintain a tight formation. The *Gal* needed to get moving again, not just to get into position, but to put some distance between themselves and the battle that had just taken place. Anyone within twenty miles could have picked up those explosions on sonar, and having survived an attack from a *Fateh*, he did not want to have to face a Russian *Kilo* captain who also thought it might be a nice opportunity to degrade Israel's attack-submarine strength without the world knowing.

"*Gal*, proceed to waypoint gamma 94, engines at your discretion, optimize for stealth but get us there inside the hour."

Aye captain. Proceeding to waypoint, optimizing for stealth within waypoint timeframe parameter.

He planned to lie at the bottom of the channel leading out of the Strait, wait for the main body of ships in the Russian fleet to pass and then…

From deep in the guts of the ship, one level down and about fifty yards forward, Binyamin heard a crack, like a rifle shot, then a shout.

Catastrophic leak in central fuel cell inspection area. Sealing compartment hatches. Rebalancing ballast.

"No, *Gal*, wait!" Binyamin said, leaping from his chair and running forward. He ducked through a narrow inspection corridor, dropped down a ladder holding only onto the sides and slammed into the deck below hard, turning an ankle. Spinning around painfully, he saw the hatchway leading into the fuel cell inspection area had slammed shut. He tried opening it, but it was sealed tight.

Beside the hatch was a ship comms handset and he snatched it from the wall, hitting the code for *Gal*. "*Gal*, open hatch Charlie 42!"

There was no response.

"*Gal*, open the hatch!" Binyamin yelled. Ehud was on the other side. He probably still had air in his lungs.

But it didn't open. Of course it didn't. Opening the hatch would have doomed the rest of the submarine. With the flooding compartmentalized, they were still mission capable. Binyamin put one hand against the hatch, feeling the vibrations as the water on the other side filled the space behind it. "*Gal*, open hatch Charlie 42," he said softly.

Flooding contained. Proceeding to waypoint gamma 94.

Binyamin looked at the comms handset and started hammering it against the door until it shattered in his hand, wires and speakers dangling uselessly from the cord.

He kept hammering until his knuckles started to bleed.

Buq'ata, Golan Heights, May 19–20

Amal weighed her choice carefully. She could lay her last belt in the path of only one of the two reversing tanks as they were moving on opposite sides of the highway verge. One had a turret with a 120mm cannon and 12.7mm heavy machine gun. The other had a 30mm cannon and six-tube *Verba* anti-air missile pod.

"Patel, which should we try to hit?" she asked quickly. "Their anti-air unit or their assault tank?"

Patel was back on his scope, scanning rooftops for snipers. "Since that assault tank is going to be assaulting *us*, I vote for the assault tank."

"What I was thinking. But if we stop the anti-air unit, the aircraft overhead can do their work without being molested."

"Angel said she's out of missiles, down to guns. I'm not hopeful she'll do anything but tickle those *Armatas*. I still vote assault tank."

"I agree," Amal said. She was already on the right side of the highway to lay mines behind the reversing *Armata*. Skimming her *Turtle* across grass and stones to a point fifty yards behind it, she quickly dropped the first mine and hopped the rest in a ten-yard line in the dirt and grass right in the path of the tank, before pulling her drone 100 yards out and dropping it in the middle of the highway with its camera fixed on the gap in the trees and the maneuvering tanks ahead.

Bunny O'Hare was also watching closely. She'd taken the risk of pulling her four machines up to an altitude of 5,000 feet, out of the range of the low-level *Verba* missiles, still under the height at which most Israeli Air Force traffic was crossing over, to where her recon bird could get good low-light and infrared vision of the vehicles below. Each of the reversing tanks had pulled itself out of the tangle of wrecked, burning and disabled hulks around them, pointed themselves back down the highway, and were now maneuvering their *Udar* unmanned 'wingmen' into position.

As sacrificial mine detectors.

Bunny saw with dismay that the *Armata* drivers had learned their lesson and were putting the tracked *Udars* out in front of them to trigger any mines that might still litter the highway. They'd already traversed the ground they were retreating back over, but they were taking no chances. Controlling the *Udars* from within their capsules inside the *Armata*, they crept forward until...

On the southern side of the highway there was a blast ... Bunny's low-light screen flared and the *Udar* there was flipped up onto one side by the force of the mines detonating beneath it.

All three remaining tanks jerked to a halt. Crews who had abandoned their vehicles earlier came running up to them, and a brief conference was held as the Russian tankers argued about what the hell they should do next. Bunny decided to help make their decision easier for them.

She laid a targeting crosshair on the anti-air unit below. If she could knock that out, she'd have clear air. "Merit two, four and five slaved to Merit one," she told Kovacs. "Beginning strafing run." She ordered her birds to begin a 'pop up' maneuver.

"This is going to hurt, I know it."

"Them more than us," Bunny said. She hit a three-button combination on her stick and the four *Fantoms* started falling almost vertically from the sky in line abreast formation, all four

361

25mm cannons trained on the *Armata* anti-air tank below which had just lost its *Udar* wingman. She had no illusions, it would be tracking her *Fantoms* overhead, its *Verba* missiles and 30mm cannon would be trained on her birds as they fell through the night sky – but what choice did she have?

"Passing ten thousand, nine, entering *Verba* range…"

Amal had cursed when the unmanned vehicle had triggered her mines. It had been a Hail Mary play, as the Marines who had bunkered down in her house liked to say, and it had claimed a victim, but not the one she wanted.

As she watched, the 30mm cannon turret on one of the *Armatas* swiveled upwards, muzzle pointing almost vertically into the sky. But it kept swiveling, the barrel unable to raise further to align itself on the targets falling on it from directly overhead. The *Verba* missile battery behind the turret had no such problems. Its operator had a radar lock on the four *Fantoms* and he had five missiles remaining in his launcher.

As Amal watched, four white streaks of light lanced out from the tank in a roiling cloud of smoke and arced straight upwards.

"Jamming, firing chaff and flares," Bunny said. She thumbed her stick, ordering the *Fantoms* to roll as they fell; a sickening, spiraling maneuver that would have completely disoriented a human pilot, crushing them against the side of their cockpits with spinning g-force, but the silicon brains of the drones were impervious.

The *Verba* missiles were on them in seconds and the four *Fantoms* and four *Verba* missiles met with a combined speed of three times the speed of sound.

Two of Bunny's *Fantoms* were swatted from the sky, becoming balls of tumbling fire and metal that continued down toward the troops and tanks below.

362

But two survived the *Verba* salvo and aligned their guns on the thinner top armor of the *Armata*. At ten thousand feet, they unleashed a twin four-second barrage of *Nammo* tungsten-tipped armor-piercing explosive 25mm shells, both aircraft hammering the same target simultaneously at a rate of 3,300 rounds a minute.

Desperately, the crew inside fired a volley of fragmentation shells at the incoming salvo, but succeeded only in knocking out the first dozen or so. Its dual-explosive reactive armor absorbed the impact of the next dozen or so rounds, exploding outwards to protect the thinner armor underneath, but it only accounted for the next twenty or so rounds, and behind them were two hundred more.

He was a tough tank, the *Armata*. But no tank yet designed could have survived the abuse Bunny's twin aircraft barrage was visiting on it. And no human pilot would have kept their aircraft in the unpowered near-vertical dive the *Fantoms* were in, all the way down to the safe pullout altitude of 5,000 feet. They fired their last rounds into the top of the *Armata* as they hit 1,000 and then, in a maneuver that would have snapped the neck of any human pilot inside, hauled themselves level and screamed away west at nap of the earth height.

Amal watched the Russian missiles rise into the night sky, saw two explosions in rapid succession and then twin streams of ghostly laser-like light began pouring out of the darkness and down into the tank below. They weren't lasers, Amal knew that, but the shells from the drone's guns were fired at such a rate that the tracers marking their passage burned their image into her screen and showed as two continuous lines of fire both converging on a single point below.

The engineer inside Amal watched with dread fascination. The Americans had found a way to coordinate the fire of their unmanned aircraft so that multiple aircraft could simultaneously pound a single target! It was a force multiplier that had staggering implications for future war ... increasing the hitting power of not just guns, but onboard lasers, rockets – a host of lighter weapons.

The *Armata* bucked and rocked as the shells poured onto, then into it. As the stream of cannon fire stopped and the attacking aircraft pulled away – just black on black shadows in the night – ammunition stored in the rotary magazine under the tank's turret started cooking off and then, in a mighty explosion, the entire turret blew off, a volcano of fire jetting into the air.

Amal watched in disbelief as the front hatches on the *Armata* popped open and the three-man crew, protected from the inferno by their armored capsule but no doubt in fear of being roasted alive, tumbled out of their crew compartment, rolling off the front of the tank and stumbling to a nearby ditch. Amal shook her head slowly. No other tank crew could have survived an onslaught like that. It might not be invulnerable, but the *Armata* was a piece of work.

"Splash two more," Amal told Patel. "Your 'Angel' just took down an *Armata* and without its mothership, the *Udar* is out too. But it looked like they lost two drones. How many were up there?"

"Uh, six."

"Then there can't be many left. And there is still one *Armata* with an *Udar* wingman on the move. Nothing I can do about it. I am out of mines and they can be here inside twenty minutes."

"It's still an hour until our evac flight arrives," Patel pointed out. He put his head down, resting his head on his forearm, showing his fatigue. "Screw it. We need to bug out now. Get out through the quarry, hide in the fields near the evacuation point while it's dark."

Amal put her last *Turtle*, which was now serving as an observation drone, down on the ground and powered it down. Then she closed her console. "Yes. You take the civilians. I have to rig demolition charges on my workshop and the ordnance containers. I can't risk my prototypes and weapons falling into Syrian hands."

Patel looked across the roof at the other Marines, making a calculation in his head. "I need people to carry Gunner Jensen and mind the civilians, but I'll leave Johnson with you to watch your back while you work. When you're done, you get out through the quarry and join up with us."

As he spoke, from a rooftop about 500 yards away, a machine gun opened up on their compound, bullets chipping away at the concrete rampart around the rooftop terrace. They both hugged the tiles. "Stevens, Rooster, keep down!"

"Negev NG7," Amal told him. Another volley of fire came their way, this time striking the windows of the villa below them. "That feels like cover fire for an assault."

"Warming up for the arrival of those damn tanks," Patel guessed. He lifted his head and put his rifle into the gap in the lip of the terrace. "You take Johnson and Stevens, get downstairs, tell Bell to get the wounded ready to move." He bent his eye to his scope and began looking for the source of the incoming fire. "I'll deal with this asshole and join everyone downstairs as soon as I can."

US blockade line, Mediterranean Sea, May 19–20

Binyamin couldn't remember walking from the forward inspection area back to the *Gal*'s command center, but he must have. When he came to his senses again, he was lying on the deck between his and Ehud's chairs, staring up at the metal stairwell that led up into the sail. The crushed and sealed sail.

No way out up there. No aft escape hatch. No way forward to the torpedo tubes past poor dead Ehud. Drowned, disappointed, yelled-at Ehud. Shame welled up in him, and it quickly turned to anger. Anger at himself for ordering Ehud forward, but more, anger at Gal for being so cold-bloodedly logical and sealing him in. Much more, anger at the enemy for striking without warning, without reason. A quote from scripture came to him, and he extended his arms out to his sides like wings. "If anger and wrath are the angels of destruction, then fear me, for I Am Wrath!" he said out loud, paraphrasing the Talmud. Then he laughed until he coughed, rolled to his knees and crawled from the command room on hands and knees toward his stateroom.

What Binyamin Ben-Zvi didn't know was that he had passed his last psychological fitness assessment by a metaphorical whisker. The psychologist conducting it had shared the results with a colleague.

"He seems stressed, wouldn't you say?"

Her colleague had flipped through the pages of test results, both from physicals, surveys and interviews, and his service record.

"He says he was frustrated the sea trials of the *Gal* overran by two years. Worried that it went straight from sea trials to commissioning with only the simplest of combat systems trials. He told you he doesn't feel the ship's decision support systems have been thoroughly pressure tested and early in the test cycle he questioned the idea of sending such a potent weapons platform to sea with only a two-man crew. His physical fitness is good." The man nodded. "So yes, he's cautious, but he scored in the normal range on all the usual instruments." He handed the file back to his colleague. "I see a man who is cautious, thoughtful and dedicated, which is the profile we want. Besides, he's not alone out there. Ehud is solid as a rock. I tested him myself."

Forty minutes to interception waypoint, Gal announced.

The announcement went unacknowledged. Binyamin Ben-Zvi was curled in a ball on his bunk. Moaning quietly.

Situation Room, White House, May 19

The White House press announcement went out at 2030 DC time, 0330 in the Golan Heights and Moscow, and 0530 in

Tehran.

It was titled 'Readout of President Henderson Historic Call with Ayatollah Takhti of Iran' and the wording agreed between Washington, Tel Aviv and Iran was very brief.

President Oliver Henderson spoke this afternoon with Ayatollah Takhti of Iran. President Henderson affirmed the United States' unwavering support for Israel's sovereignty and territorial integrity in the face of the ongoing cyber attack against Israel by unknown actors. Both leaders agreed to work toward lasting peace and stability in the region. In subsequent discussions, the Governments of Israel and Iran agreed to begin arms control negotiations in Stockholm in October, within the framework of the United Nations Treaty on Non-Proliferation of Nuclear Weapons. Other Security Council Members will be invited to participate.

As Tonya watched the news break across the 24-hour news channels she also had one eye on the large wall-mounted monitor that showed the positions of US Destroyer Squadron 60 and the main body of the approaching Russian fleet. She had just updated ExComm on the latest information on the cyber attack on Israel. It was deep in the night in Israel and there was hope the cell phone network would be partially or fully restored by mid morning, relieving the burden on the military radio network. By rerouting all internet traffic to a commercial satellite internet provider, many of the international internet links needed for commerce and banking were expected to be restored, at a cost only slightly less ruinous than the cost of being shut down. Electricity was still patchy, with the systems that distributed power across the grid still under active attack, which meant air traffic was restricted to military flights only, being directed by airborne radar warning aircraft.

None of the people in the room had left the basement office except to shower or nap in the last 36 hours. Changes of clothes had been brought by their aides, and food delivered in abundance, along with an endless supply of hot coffee. Tonya didn't doubt some of the cabinet members were using other stimulants to stay on top of their game.

Personally, she was on the edge of a very, very public and probably catastrophic attack of agoraphobia. If she could not escape the hot house environment of the situation room, and soon, she was going to say or do something that would finish her career.

The mood had been febrile when Carmine Lewis had returned and reported that the US President had unilaterally decided to approach the Iranian regime.

"It's capitulation!" Admiral Clarke had declared. "Israel was knocked on its ass by Russian and Iranian hackers, its air force badly attrited by the Russians and now the Iranians have got their damned nuclear arms limitation conference." He pointed up at the monitor on the wall. "All the while their ships are planning to steam straight through our blockade. With respect, Mr. President, we sold the family cow and came home with a beanstalk."

Tonya had let Clarke and others like Homeland Security Secretary Price vent their outrage, and when they ran out of expletives, she raised her hand. Henderson nodded to her. "Tonya?"

She held up her cell phone, showing the alert she had just received from HOLMES, who had been monitoring and analyzing every snippet of intelligence related to the Israel situation across the entire spectrum of security and intelligence agencies. "NSA has just intercepted a signal from Bandar Abbas. It was sent with an old cypher the Iranians know we have broken, so we were meant to intercept it. Putting it onscreen." With a flick of her finger, she sent the report from her cell phone to wall screen. For those sitting at an awkward angle, she paraphrased it. "It's from the Iranian Navy Admiralty to the IRIN destroyers *Amol* and *Sinjan*. It is ordering them to return to Sevastopol and prepare for a transit through the Volga-Don Canal waterway and Caspian Sea to Tehran." She could see some of the faces at the table were either too tired or slow on the uptake to realize what she was saying, so she put it in black and white. "Iran has just ordered its ships back to port."

"Well, it seems we got more than a beanstalk, Admiral. We just got the Golden Egg," Henderson grinned. "And I have the word of the Israeli PM that Israel is standing down its naval and air forces."

Admiral Clarke had his hands behind his head, leaning back and looking up at the ceiling. "Our damage assessments show despite their losses, they got the job done anyway. Syrian 4th Armored Republican Guards Battalion is a mess of smoking wrecks on the highway out of Damascus, and their 5th Assault Corps is down 50 percent of its tanks. Nine out of ten Iranian missile launchers were knocked out inside Syria, and military targets across Iran took a pasting."

He stood. "Now, if you will excuse me, I need to agree with my press secretary what we're going to tell the networks for their 11 p.m. bulletins." He crooked a finger at his Chief of Staff. "Karl?"

Tonya started scrolling through the other reports HOLMES had parsed for her, but she saw nothing contradicting the NSA report. Carmine came over and sat beside her.

"How do you get NSA reporting before I do?" she asked. She didn't sound annoyed, just curious.

"You have humans between the intelligence and you," Tonya told her. "All weighing it with their own judgment, assigning their own meaning, filtering and contextualizing it, and then five layers of NSA bureaucrats are reviewing it and signing it off before NSA releases it to your people who then do the same thing." She held up her phone. "I have HOLMES. And he does all of that in seconds, without worrying about the optics or internal politics of it all."

Lewis nodded thoughtfully. "That's a powerful tool you have there. Some might say, too much power to be concentrated in the hands of any one cabinet member."

"I can give you access," Tonya said quickly. "As Director of National Intelligence you…"

"Not what I'm saying. In the hands of anyone but you, I'd worry it would be abused. It's safe enough in your hands, for now."

"Good. Alright."

"And that was a good intervention," Lewis told her. "Letting people speak their piece, then dropping the hammer on them without making it personal."

"Thanks."

Carmine hardened her tone. "But next time, for God's sake, you don't raise your hand to speak at ExComm meetings. The White House situation room isn't a classroom and you aren't a third grader asking to go to the damn bathroom."

Tonya saw her chance. "No. Got it. Thanks. Do you think…"

"Yes. I think you can scoot off home now. Pour yourself some wine, watch the 11 p.m. news and then get back to work helping Israel to get back on its virtual feet." Lewis gave her a big smile. "I feel like we are on our way out of this mess now."

Syrian Airspace, East of the Golan Heights, May 20

Lieutenant Yevgeny Bondarev of the Russian 7th Air Group had been up to his eyeballs in the mess that was Syria's war on its neighbors to the north and west for nearly a year now, and he wasn't seeing any easy way out of it.

As he led a flight of four Su-57 *Felons* with *Okhotnik* drone wingmen on a combat air patrol over Damascus, it seemed to him the stony deserts of Syria were fast turning into quicksand. He had lost three comrades in the last twelve hours, including that cheeky shit 'Rap' Tchakov. Bondarev had even begun to believe the kid's own publicity. "I was born under a lucky star, Comrade Lieutenant," Tchakov had told him. "You'll see. I'll be leaving Syria with a Nesterov Air Medal."

Instead, he was leaving Syria in a pine box.

Bondarev shrugged the thought away, his eyes flicking

across his helmet-mounted display, instrument and system panels, the dark sky around him and the data feed from his *Okhotnik* 'wingman'. He had trained on the use of the drones during the hiatus in Latakia between the Syrian conflict with Turkey and its new conflict with Israel, and was just now becoming comfortable with the added burden of piloting both his own *Felon* and the semi-autonomous *Okhotnik*. At first he had doubted he could master the additional data overload, especially in the heat of simulated combat. But he'd seen what the Coalition pilots had achieved with their BATS Loyal Wingman drones over Turkey – seen them use the smaller, lightly armed drones to flush out Russia's stealth aircraft for lurking F-35 *Panthers* to knock down – so he had persisted.

He was most comfortable assigning his pilots' *Okhotniks* to 'shepherd' mode, sending them out in front of his formation with their phased-array radar to sniff out potential targets while he and his pilots stayed invisible, twenty miles behind them. They'd claimed two Israeli F-15s near Damascus earlier in the day with this tactic. The heavily armed *Okhotniks*, unlike their smaller BATS opponents, could carry up to 2,000lbs. of ordnance in their weapons bays including both air-to-air missiles and air-to-ground missiles or bombs.

While they required a two-man crew in a trailer to serve on close air support ground attack missions, they could be controlled by a single airborne pilot for air-to-air missions. Able to share targeting data and coordinate their attacks on the fly, Bondarev had used one of the stealthy *Okhotniks* to lock up the Israeli F-15 fighters while another of his pilots controlling a second *Okhotnik* attacked them with K-77M missiles from a different bearing, at near point-blank range.

But he had yet to send the drones into enemy-controlled airspace on an offensive mission of the nature he had just been ordered to execute.

"Sector Control, Koshka leader, confirming despatch of four *Okhotnik* fighters on air superiority mission over Golan Heights. Koshka leader out." He switched to the interplane channel on his radio to address his pilots. "Koshka three, you take Golan Sector A, four Sector B, I will take Sector C, two, you take Sector D. Stay alert for Israeli aircraft entering Syrian airspace, our primary mission is still the defense of Damascus. Understood?"

The Israeli air offensive had been brutal, for both sides. Dozens of Syrian ground units had been attacked, with heavy losses to both Syrian armor and transport vehicles, anti-air missile systems and troop concentrations. Bondarev had no idea whether Syria was still capable of a ground offensive into the Golan or not.

But it had also been brutal for Israeli aircraft. Before taking off, Bondarev had seen an intelligence estimate stating Israel had lost thirty-four piloted aircraft, both jets and rotary-winged, and nearly fifty drones. He knew enough by now to take the claims of pilots and missile crews with a pinch of salt, but even if Israel had lost only half that number of aircraft, its offensive had been costly to an extent Israel had not suffered in decades – if ever.

The simple reason was the extra finger on the scales that Russian air support and control gave the Syrian and Iranian forces. Israel was no longer alone in the skies over Syria or Lebanon, facing only ground-to-air missile defenses – in Russia it faced a foe that it outnumbered, yes, but one that could use airborne warning and control capabilities to choose its fights carefully, that could attack with stealth and bring both manned and unmanned assets to bear.

As Bondarev watched his tactical map, a squadron of older-generation Su-30 aircraft was being scrambled from Latakia. The fact the venerable non-stealth fighters were being brought into the fight now told him two things. That the Russian losses were mounting, but also that they had claimed sufficient Israeli stealth fighter kills that Russia was willing to risk its more vulnerable aircraft now, with most of the attacks into Syria being mounted by comparable older-generation Israeli F-16s and F-15s.

As his men confirmed their orders and split off to manage their sector patrols, Bondarev concentrated on his own. Bringing up the navigation map for his own *Okhotnik*, Bondarev drew a series of waypoints over the sector he'd assigned himself and gave his drone orders to cycle between the waypoints until it was low on fuel, identifying any hostile aircraft in range and seeking his permission before engaging. It wasn't possible anyway for the drone to engage on its own initiative unless its 'mothership' was destroyed, and he could give it an attack order with a click of the button under his right thumb on the flight stick, so the delay between the *Okhotnik* locking up a target and firing at it was minimal.

In the middle of the circle of waypoints he'd just drawn was a town whose name he'd come to recognize. The town over which that fool Tchakov had been lost. Luckily, he hadn't been ordered to send any piloted aircraft into that sector.

Bloody Buq'ata.

All Domain Attack: Nuclear

Buq'ata, Golan Heights, May 20

Bloody Buq'ata was exactly what Corporal Ravi Patel was thinking as he ducked his head under another spray of bullets from the Syrian machine gun. He should be in Kuwait with his feet up, drinking an ice cold 'near beer' right now. He had spotted the MG crew of two, on a rooftop about three hundred yards back from their compound. He'd also spotted dozens of soldiers moving through side streets, about a block back – no doubt prepping for arrival of the Russian armor – so the machine gun fire was intended to keep the Marines' heads down and stop them from observing. Well, they were going to be sorely disappointed when only two tanks rolled into town, instead of ten.

But then again, two tanks were plenty against a bunch of lightly armed, badly wounded Marines.

Another staccato burst of fire, this time against the windows below him. The Druze gunner was not the creative type. One burst at the rooftop, one at a window below, then back to the rooftop. Below him, someone returned fire in frustration. Stevens, he was willing to bet. Guy had no self-control.

He heard a voice behind him as he waited for the next volley to come his way.

"Patel, we're about ready to move out."

He looked over his shoulder and saw Corporal Buckland stick her head out of the stairwell from the terrace to the floor below. She ducked back down as a line of machine gun bullets stitched the lip of the terrace from left to right, just above Patel's head.

Now, Ravi.

Ignoring her, Patel rolled into the gap in the concrete rampart, bent his eye to his light-intensifying scope and focused on the rooftop where he'd seen the two Druze gunners – one working the gun, the other feeding ammunition. He'd already adjusted the scope for range. There was no wind to speak of. As the MG crew trained their weapon on the windows below him, and before it fired again, blinding him with the muzzle flash, he put his crosshairs on the chest of the Druze gunner. Took a breath and held it. Caressed the trigger like the CIA contractor had taught him. His rifle bucked into his shoulder, and the Druze gunner flew backwards like he'd been hit with a sledgehammer. The Barrett had a five-round magazine so Patel didn't need to reload. He quickly worked the bolt, laid the crosshairs onto the ammunition loader, firing as he twisted away from his dead comrade, headed for the ground. The round seemed to catch him in the ribs and shove him sideways, but he fell out of sight.

Call that one kill, one probable. Camp Pendleton here I come.

Patel rolled back out of sight of any other troops on rooftops across from them and turned to Buckland. "I'm going to call for air support, then I'll be down. We got Gunny on a stretcher or something?"

"Corporal Bell broke up a sofa and made one out of that."

"Alright, get moving. I'll catch you up at the top of the quarry." He picked up the handset for the field radio. "Angel, Angel, Marine JTAC."

"JTAC, go for Angel." Bunny had pulled her last two *Fantoms* west of Buq'ata into Israeli airspace and was circling them low and behind the small range of hills overlooking the Golan Heights.

"Got a damage assessment for you. We disabled four *Armata* main battle tanks with mines. You knocked out one MBT and one UGV. Two other UGVs are immobile, probably because their motherships are stranded. But we still have one *Armata* MBT and *Udar* on the move, now two klicks from Buq'ata. We are preparing the civilians and wounded for evac but those tanks could seriously ruin our night."

"I'm guns dry, Patel. I could try a kamikaze hit..." Kovacs shook her head so vehemently O'Hare could feel the trailer rock, "... but that wouldn't do much more than scratch the paint on an *Armata*. Best I can do is keep an eye on them, tell you exactly where they are."

Patel thought it through. "We could do with eyes in the sky over our position as we pull out," he said. "Make sure the Druze don't have any drones up that can see us on infrared. Watch for any patrols they might have circling the town."

"You got it. Keep the radio on this channel, I'll update you."

"Copy. JTAC out."

As she cut the link, new icons flashed onto Bunny's visor and her threat warning screen simultaneously, picked up by both the AWACS over Cyprus and the radar warning receivers on her own *Fantoms*. Four fast movers, heading for Golan from Syria, fanning out like their intention was to cover the length and breadth of the disputed territory. Her AI was calling them *Okhotnik* drones.

Bunny had grown to hate the Russian bat-winged automatons. You couldn't spook them. You couldn't outguess them. And their AI reaction times were that millisecond faster than a human's that could make the difference between life and death.

She got on the blower to the controller in the Bombardier. "Falcon, Falcon, Merit."

"Merit, go for Falcon."

"Falcon, we have Russian drones inbound, you see them?"

"Copy. You are clear to engage if they cross into Golani airspace or if they attack your aircraft from inside Syrian airspace."

"Thanks, Falcon, I know the ROE. I suggest you scramble two more *Fantoms* from Akrotiri. We are likely to be weapons dry soon if these Russians are making another push."

"Copy that, Merit. Will check what Akrotiri has on readiness and revert. Falcon out."

"Kovacs," Bunny said. "You know that override you put into the code that can give our *Fantoms* fully autonomous decision making?"

Shelly squinted at her. "No, what override?"

Bunny sighed. "Come on, girl. I went through that code line by line ... it's there."

Kovacs looked at her warily. "There are eight million lines of code in the *Fantom* combat AI, you couldn't have."

Bunny shrugged. "Alright, I lied. But you know I know it's there, your face says it all. We need to activate it."

"No. We don't know how those *Fantoms* will perform if we give them full air-to-air combat autonomy," Kovacs protested. "They might shoot down a damn Israeli plane!"

"Hah, so it *is* there! They aren't going to shoot down any Israeli if it has its Identify Friend or Foe transponder on. Look, I have two birds left with air-to-air weapons. They are up against *four Okhotniks* and those things are fire."

Patel rolled onto his stomach, pushing the radio handset back into the pouch on the side of the backpack that held the 10lb. radio. Alright, no time to waste. He eyed the rooftop stairs about twenty yards away at the back of the terrace. So he wouldn't be seen by the troops below, he'd have to crawl on his stomach the whole way pushing the 10lb. radio ahead of him, with his 15lb. rifle hanging awkwardly across his back, or push the radio with one hand, the rifle with the other, or...

Screw it. Stay low and run for it.

The Druze rifleman crouched on a rooftop 300 yards across town had taken his brother's rifle up onto the roof with him. The rifle his brother had dropped when an American drone flew a fragmentation grenade under his hide earlier in the day and killed him.

The Israeli *IWI Dan* rifle, with its long barrel and .338 Lapua

Magnum ammunition, was accurate out to 1,200 yards and had a low-light scope – so though he was not a sniper, the rifleman felt confident he could put a bullet on target at a range of 300 yards.

If he could find one.

The Marines on the rooftop had not raised themselves above the rampart running around it, and he was too low to be able to shoot down into them. He'd seen fleeting movement at breaks in the concrete, but not enough for him to fire and give away his position. He'd scanned all of the windows facing the town too, but they were obscured with curtains and piled-up furniture and all lights inside the building were out. If there was anyone inside, he could not see them.

When their MG crew had opened up on the building, he had intensified his scrutiny and nearly got a shot on one of the Marines as he appeared at a window and returned fire at the machine gun, but the man was gone as quickly as he appeared, and didn't reappear.

There was a cold fury boiling inside the rifleman's guts. No matter what it took, at some time today he would avenge his dead brother.

Then there were two heavy cracks from the rooftop, in quick succession, and the MG fell silent.

He trained his scope on the ramparts again, sweeping slowly left to right, hoping that...

There! A dark form, crouched, rising. Before he even realized it, his finger had twitched on the *Dan*'s trigger, sending a round downrange.

"Where the hell is Patel?" Bell asked.

"Probably trying for one more kill," Buckland said. "You know what he's like with that damn cannon. He said he'd catch us up at the quarry."

"Hell he will, we need all hands to carry the Sarge and shepherd those civilians," Bell said.

"You calling me fat, Bell?" Jensen said, through teeth gritted against the pain in his groin.

"Well, you're no lightweight, Gunny," Bell admitted. "We'll need four men to get you down that slope out back. 'Less you want us to just pitch you over and meet you at the bottom?"

"I'll take the business class option, thanks."

They'd shifted the settlers onto the concrete apron out back, ready to move them out of the compound, but Jensen still lay on the floor of the hallway in Amal's house, Stevens holding a bag of his own blood. Bell had had to give the guy something to do to stop him hopping from window to window looking for something to shoot at. Amal was bringing the civilians downstairs, trying to keep them calm. She'd have to get out back to set her demolition charges soon, with Johnson watching her back. With four needed to carry Jensen, and Lopez nursing a shattered humerus, that left only one spare pair of hands. They needed Patel now. "Business class it is. Good choice, Sarge. I'm going up to get Patel," Bell decided. "He can play sniper again when we get to the LZ."

He took the stairs two at a time and then pulled himself up the spiral staircase to the rooftop, lifting his helmet carefully above the lip of the hole in the terrace floor.

The first thing he saw was the radio, lying on the ground about five yards away. Then behind it Patel, face down on the tiles.

In a pool of blood.

The Corpsman in him reacted before the soldier did, and he pulled himself onto the terrace, crawling on his stomach to Patel as fast as he could. He had to drag himself through Patel's blood to reach him. Guy wasn't breathing. Bell rolled him onto his side, feeling for a pulse. Nothing. He felt his back, where the shirt was wet with blood, found the entry wound just under his fifth rib on the left side, and then he found the exit wound, above the third rib on his left side.

And he rolled Patel back onto his stomach again.

Damn fool. A large-caliber enemy bullet had taken him from behind, traveled diagonally through his ribcage, definitely puncturing his lung but probably also tearing through his heart, and then exited his chest, leaving through a hole the diameter of Bell's thumb.

Swinging his feet around, Bell hauled the big man's body, rifle, combat gear and all toward the stairs and unceremoniously pushed him through, head first. He landed on the stairs with a sickening crunch. Bell crawled back across the floor for the radio next and pulled that behind him, until he reached the stairwell and lowered his legs into it.

A shocked Amal Azaria was standing at the bottom of the stairs, staring at Patel's body. "You think you can carry him? Fireman's lift? Strip off all his gear," Bell asked her, putting the radio pack on his back and unentangling Patel's precious rifle from around his neck.

"Is he…"

"Dead? Yeah. But we take him with us, right?" Bell said, looking up at her. "If you can't carry him, get someone else."

"I can carry him," she said.

As Bell tried to step over Patel's body, the recoil pad of the rifle caught on his vest, the barrel jammed into the stair railings and Bell nearly fell head first down the stairs before catching his balance. "Goddamn piece of shit rifle!" Bell yelled and threw it down the stairs with a crash. He stood there panting, then wiped a bloodied hand over his face, staring down at Patel.

"Easy, Corporal," Amal said, holding a hand out to him.

"He won it in a bet, you know that?"

"I heard that."

"Got the stupid mother killed."

She helped him past her. "I guess so."

He turned back to her, pulling the straps on the radio pack tighter. "You need a hand?"

She shook her head. "I can manage. You can take the radio and get the people outside, I'll bring Corporal Patel down."

Bell picked up the Barrett, pulled out the magazine, worked

380

the bolt to check the chamber was empty, then unlatched the upper receiver and pulled the bolt out. Shoving the bolt in his pocket, he stood the rifle against the wall. "Leave this here. It's bad luck."

Then he went downstairs.

US blockade line, Mediterranean Sea, May 20

"They're turning north," Ears heard Lieutenant Drysdale say, his voice expressing disbelief. Looking up at the 360-degree situation display, Ears could see the icons for the two Iranian frigates, which had been sailing in train just behind the Russian cruiser *Moskva*, breaking away from the main group. "Lose their escort submarine and they're giving up."

Ears could see Chief Goldmann open his mouth, close it again as he considered his words, and then open it again to speak. Both men were standing in the center of the CIC in plain view of all and Ears noted he wasn't the only one watching the exchange. "Doubt it has much to do with losing that *Fateh* submarine, sir. I'd say more likely it's the announcement of the October peace talks. Someone back in Iran told them to take their foot off the gas pedal."

Sure enough, the Iranian ships completed a leisurely turn and reversed course, headed back up the Aegean Sea.

Yes! Ears exclaimed, though inside his own head. He allowed himself a tight little fist pump. *We did it!* Or someone did ... now there would be no bluff or counterbluff with the Russians, no 'shots across the bow', no high-risk boarding operations. The Iranians had lost a sub in that torpedo exchange, and either the Brits or someone else – maybe the Israelis – might have taken some damage, but an all-out war at sea had been avoided.

It wasn't often that Ears saw common sense triumph in politics, but he'd already clocked up a couple of firsts on this voyage, maybe this was a third!

Karpathou Strait, Aegean Sea, May 20

His Majesty's *Astute*-class submarine HMS *Agincourt* was only slightly less expensive than the aircraft carriers she had been put into the world to protect. By the time she was launched, she had cost 2.27 billion dollars. But she was also one of the most dangerous weapons platforms in the world.

Powered by a Rolls Royce nuclear reactor, she could slide through the water, submerged, at up to 30 knots. In stealth mode, her speed was much lower, of course, but she was also nearly inaudible thanks to a pump-jet propulsion system. Her 38 weapons, including both torpedoes and cruise missiles, could be released through six reloadable 533mm torpedo tubes.

But her true advantage was her sensor system, which featured an integrated search and attack sonar suite with bow, intercept, flank and towed arrays that meant the *Agincourt* could hear its target long before it risked being heard. And if it could hear you, it could kill you.

As it had proven with that damn Israeli sub, the *Gal*, frolicking around it like a bloody dolphin around a whale, when in fact if it had so desired, the *Agincourt* could have sent it to the bottom of the Mediterranean at least thirty minutes earlier.

Captain Allen 'Puncher' Courtenay, a curmudgeonly Tynesider from Gateshead near Newcastle, had little patience for frolicking. The nickname didn't refer to a former career as a boxer; it was a derogatory short form of the name 'horse puncher' sometimes given to folk from Newcastle after an incident in which an aggrieved football fan punched a police horse in the head. But he wore the nickname 'Puncher' with pride because it told the world he didn't stand for any bloody nonsense. He'd been trained on diesel subs before starting out his proper career as a navigator on *Trafalgar*-class nuclear subs, patrolling the Atlantic, the Baltic and the Med. Promoted to XO aboard a *Swiftsure*-class sub, where he'd learned how to get the most out of the new pump-jet propulsion systems being deployed for His Majesty's nuclear attack submarines, before being handed command of a *Trafalgar*-class boat and, finally, the prize he'd been seeking all along, the newest and by his reckoning deadliest submarine in the world, the *Agincourt*.

He wasn't given to pride or boasting. His belief in his boat was shored up with cold, hard fact. In exercises against the pride of the US submarine fleet, the *Virginia*-class sub USS *Silversides*, the *Agincourt* had tracked the *Silversides* at ranges the Americans at first couldn't believe. But when they began combat simulation exercises for real, the results spoke for themselves. After the spray settled, the *Agincourt* had been awarded four 'kills' against the *Silversides*, and the *Silversides* only one against the *Agincourt*.

It made the Americans very happy that the British were their allies.

And it meant they trusted 'Puncher' Courtenay completely when he and the *Agincourt* were given the job of blockading the Karpathou Strait leading from the Aegean into the Mediterranean Sea.

"Pilot, continue ahead slow, take her to communication depth. Comms, raise the *Canberra*," he ordered.

They'd stalked the Russian-Iranian convoy from 900 feet below the surface, logging then tracking every single ship in the formation from the fast and noisy corvettes to the destroyers, frigates and cruiser *Moskva*, finally picking up the thudding slow-turning screws of the huge helicopter landing ship, the *Pyotr Morgunov*.

The *Pyotr Morgunov* was now ten miles beyond them, and the main formation nearly twenty miles. Too far for torpedoes, but they still had a good enough solution on the fleet to enable them to fire their anti-ship missiles, if needed. Courtenay had checked in with the *Canberra* as the fleet approached and was asked to shadow the fleet only, not to engage. Now, with them sliding out of range, he wanted to check again before his optimal attack window had closed.

"OOD, Sonar, the two Iranian frigates are maneuvering."

His sonar watch officer looked over at Courtenay in surprise from his position behind his sonarmen. "Commander, it looks they're coming around to a heading that will bring them back towards us."

"What are the Russians doing?"

"Continuing on current heading, sir, still making a beeline for Tartus. They're right in amongst the US ships now, no change in heading or speed."

The Iranians were breaking out of formation and headed back *toward* them, while the Russians were proceeding to Syria? It was mystifying, unless...

"Any chance they've picked us up?"

"Not a chance in hell, sir. Not at this range. We're twenty miles distant, no sign of another sub or warship near us, no sign of dipping sonar from a helo."

"Right, pilot continue to comms depth, prepare to take us back down as soon as we sort this out with the *Canberra*."

"Aye, sir!"

Agincourt rose silently to fifty feet below the water, then raised her digital periscope. She didn't have a traditional optical scope, but a range of radio, radar and video viewing masts that could be raised with the ship still submerged.

Courtenay did a quick scan of the 360-degree video feed himself to ensure there were no unexpected threats within visual range, had his sonarmen clear the board of any threats on the sonar and radar plots, and then took the headset his comms officer was handing him.

"*Canberra* for you, Commander."

"Captain Andrews? Captain Courtenay, *Agincourt*. We have just picked up indications the two Iranian frigates are turning back toward us, can you confirm?"

"Good timing, *Agincourt*," the US Flotilla Commander replied. "We are seeing the same thing. We are currently surrounded by damn Russians going hell for leather for Tartus, but the Iranians are turning back. We believe it's related to the announcement of arms limitation negotiations between Israel and Iran. Iran's sending a signal it's backing off."

"Understood. I propose we let the Iranians come to us, then shadow them up the Aegean to the Bosphorus, just to make sure they're headed home. Or do you want us to stay in contact with the main body of Russians, just in case?"

"No. Stay on the Iranians please, *Agincourt*. We're letting the Russians pass and unless the situation changes, things seem to be calming down here. If you hear anything go boom, then I was wrong and we'd probably appreciate an assist."

Courtenay smiled at the US commander's understatement.

"*Agincourt* copies, Captain. We'll return to patrol depth, trail the Iranians to the Bosphorus and then check in again. *Agincourt* out." He pulled the headset off and handed it back to his comms officer.

"Pilot, ahead slow, maintain heading, take her down to 500. Weapons and sensors, priority targets are the Iranians, please. Continue to track and maintain firing solutions on the Russians, alert me as we lose tracking. But the *Sinjan* and *Amol* are the mission now. We'll let them come to us, then turn to follow."

Another commander might have been disappointed that it appeared the coming conflict was fizzling out, but not Puncher Courtenay. His idea of a successful mission was one where he returned to his base in Faslane with as many submarines as he left with.

Aboard the IRIN *Sinjan* Captain Hossein Rostami watched with unconcealed pride from his bridge as his helmsman stayed perfectly inside the *Amol*'s wake through the tight turn that was going to take them back to the Bosphorus Strait on a course for home. The other trimaran frigate left a phosphorescent trail of foam behind it that glowed almost purple in the light of the near full moon and the *Sinjan* was bisecting it perfectly with its bow.

Proud as he was, he could also not help but feel dismayed. His crew had been running drills to prepare them for a possible conflict with the US blockade force, and he was confident they would have prevailed in any scenario – from resisting a boarding party to open warfare between themselves and the US destroyers. It may have been a strategic victory, but the war fighter in him also saw it as a lost tactical opportunity to test his magnificent ship and its crew.

"You look a little downhearted, Captain Rostami," Admiral Karim Daei said beside him. "You were perhaps looking forward to making port in Tartus for the first time?"

"First time for the *Sinjan*, Admiral, not for me," Rostami told him. "I visited in 2025 as XO on the *Tondar* and made a tour of the old Crusader Citadel. It was there I learned several lessons."

Admiral Daei raised an eyebrow. "Oh? And what were they?"

"That the Crusader is still our enemy. He has been fighting to control our lands for one thousand years and he will never relent. I also learned that it is futile trying to make peace with the Crusader. The Sunni lord Saladin conquered Tartus, taking it from the Crusaders in 1188, but the Knights Templar retreated to their citadel inside the city and Saladin allowed them to remain there, like a cancer in the center of his empire. From inside their citadel, they plotted their return and it took another hundred years and another war against the Crusaders to finally rid Tartus of their presence."

"So, the Christian nations have always been our enemy and will always be so?"

"I believe so, yes, Admiral."

"And where we have shown them civility and forbearance in the past, it has been abused, so we must be resolute and ruthless now?"

"If by ruthless you mean to act where action is warranted, yes. In the museum at Tartus there was a history of the Sunni general Saladin, which recounted his capture of Jerusalem. In that battle he took a Crusader king hostage, Raynald. Despite a peace agreement, Raynald's troops had been raiding civilian caravans, and he had insulted the prophet and killed unarmed caravanners. Saladin personally beheaded Raynald. There were no more Crusader attacks on the caravans."

"So, by not confronting the Crusader here today, by seeking a path to peace, you feel we are repeating the mistake of the Sunni Saladin?" the Admiral asked.

"I do not question the decisions of the Supreme Leader or the Council. But I suspect that any peace with the Crusader will only last until he sees an opportunity to break it again."

"Then we may hope that the weapons now in our possession will persuade your modern-day Crusaders that the cost of that opportunity is a price they dare not pay."

"Yes, Admiral."

"Is there any word from the *Qaaem*?"

The *Fateh*-class submarine *Qaaem* had been patrolling the sea lanes leading from the Aegean into the Mediterranean Sea, preparing to intervene if required to support a defense of the Russian-Iranian fleet. But it had missed its last transmission window. With Russian, Iranian, Israeli and potentially western submarines patrolling the same waters, the risk of an incident below the waves was high.

"No. They are nearly an hour overdue. The US destroyers have been actively searching for submarines with their helos and drones, so they may have been forced deep to evade them. But we…"

His Officer of the Deck suddenly interrupted. "Captain, contact on towed sonar array! Subsurface contact, five miles *astern*!"

Oval Office, White House, May 20

Oliver Henderson took Carmine Lewis with him to his next press briefing preparation. He wasn't the type who wanted to be closely scripted, but he also didn't like to be taken unawares, so they always rehearsed with his Chief of Staff Karl Allen throwing questions at him, and a subject matter expert like Carmine helping with the content of his responses, while his Press Secretary, Anna Kaspersky, helped him refine his delivery.

"Alright, I welcome the indications from the leaders of Iran and Israel that they are willing to discuss arms limitations as a first step toward peaceful relations blah blah blah..." Henderson said, reading from the text prepared for him. "It's more or less a repeat of our press statement, so let's get to possible questions."

"So we have definitive proof Iran has nuclear weapons?" Allen asked with no preamble, not giving Henderson time to settle in.

"Yes. We have established beyond doubt that Iran acquired a number of weapons from North Korea." He looked to Anna Kaspersky. "I leave it there, right?"

She nodded. "Answer the question, don't elaborate."

"What proof?" Karl followed up.

"Well, definitive proof that, its Navy ... Carmine, help me out here," Henderson said, floundering.

"Everyone knows about the *Besat* submarine incident. Remind them about that, explain we found traces of radiation on the boat, which confirmed other intelligence we have received."

"Right. As you know, coming to the aid of an Iranian submarine in distress, we detected evidence of radiation aboard the boat, confirming other intelligence recently received."

"Obtained, not received, Mr. President," Kaspersky added. "More assertive. Also, finish strongly and clearly. 'Iran has nuclear weapons and they were provided by North Korea.'"

"What about the no-fly zone? There is an air war raging between Israel and Russian aircraft supporting Syria. Multiple reports of aircraft shot down. Have any US aircraft or pilots been involved, have any been lost?"

"No. It was my express instruction that no manned aircraft were to be used enforcing the no-fly zone. No pilots have been lost." He hesitated. "Have we lost aircraft?"

Carmine checked the tablet PC on her knee, which contained the latest intel from Defense Intelligence. "Four unmanned US aircraft destroyed to date. Two Russian aircraft which entered the no-fly zone were destroyed. No hiding that, the Russians are expected to protest publicly about it as soon as tomorrow morning Moscow time."

"Christ. Thank god we had no pilots in those planes. What about the Russians?"

"The planes they lost were piloted. We don't know if their pilots were rescued or lost."

"It's like they are *daring* us to take them on."

"Yes, Mr. President," Carmine said. "More you should know. The US Marines we sent into the Golan Heights were attacked by Syrian Druze forces before they could link up to the UNDOF force there. There have been casualties on both sides. With things potentially calming down, we are pulling them out again."

"What a cluster. What kind of casualties? Any Marines killed?"

Carmine checked her notes. "Two wounded, none killed, but they aren't out of the woods yet. Their evacuation is planned for the same time you go to air."

"I want an update on that as soon as we're off air," Henderson told her. "So what can I say?"

"The no-fly zone will remain in place as long as Syrian troops are massed on the Israeli border. The situation there is tense, and there have been clashes between US and Russian aircraft. You don't want to go into details as the situation is still developing," Allen proposed.

"And finish strongly again. Iran is pulling back its naval and ground forces. Israel is ordering its navy back to port and its aircraft to their bases. We expect Syrian forces to stand down, but we remain ready to respond immediately if the ceasefire line is breached," Kaspersky said.

"It already has been," Carmine told them. "Our aircraft and

the Israelis attacked a small Syrian armored column inside the Golan Heights made up of Russian private contractors. A small force, probably just a probe."

"God save us from privateers," Henderson said. "No major troop movements yet, though?"

"No. Syria has been hurt badly by the Israeli air offensive, but we don't need to talk about that."

"Good. Next?"

"Russia is a part of this talk-fest in Stockholm?"

"We've invited all members of the Security Council, including Russia. Iran and Israel have both agreed to join. It's a historic opportunity."

"What about the blockade, has it been lifted?" Karl continued.

"Uh, well, yes. The purpose of the blockade was to prevent Iran placing nuclear weapons at the borders of Israel, including its territorial waters. Our latest information indicates Iran is pulling its ships back, so the need for the blockade is gone but..." Henderson rolled his hand. "We will remain vigilant and ready to implement it again if we see any change and so on. The US Congress stands united in..."

"Stop. Keep it tight, Mr. President," Kaspersky said. "Don't be drawn off topic into anything domestic, you just have three things to speak on, the Israel-Iran arms negotiations in October, the no-fly zone, the naval blockade."

"What about the situation inside Israel, the cyber attack, the Russian attack on Israel's satellites..." Allen asked.

"We already strongly condemned the cyber attack and we are treating it as terrorism as it also affected US interests inside Israel. We stick to that statement. The Russians 'accidentally' knocking out Israeli satellites ... that's a matter between Russia and Israel," Kaspersky said.

Henderson was already tuning out, thinking ahead to the press conference, Carmine could see that. He stood, buttoning his jacket, and gave them a broad smile.

"You know what? I think we're finally getting ahead of this

shitshow."

US blockade line, Mediterranean Sea, May 20

Target Bravo is adjusting course to zero one seven degrees, speed 19 knots and rising. It will remain within range for an estimated 48 minutes.

"Shut up!" Binyamin yelled, curled on his bunk, arms around his head to block out the incessant babble of *Gal*'s AI. Reporting it had reached the intercept waypoint, that it had identified the target vessel, that it was adjusting course to optimize the interception solution and avoid the Russian escort vessels … all things Ehud would have taken care of, but with Ehud gone the AI automatically stepped into his shoes, assuming a higher level of command authority unless countermanded.

It wanted the job? Binyamin let *Gal* have it.

Then it announced their target, the IRIN *Sinjan*, was changing course, together with its sister ship, breaking away from the main Russian fleet. Trailing behind the *Amol*, she was swinging around and headed back up the Aegean, presumably destined for the Bosphorus and the Black Sea, where she had come from.

They weren't interested in the *Amol*. By contrast, they were very interested in the *Sinjan*, because Mossad agents in Sevastopol had confirmed the planned transfer of a North Korean nuclear warhead at sea, from a Russian freighter, to the IRIN *Sinjan*.

It had been Binyamin and Ehud's mission to ensure that the IRIN *Sinjan* did not reach port in Syria bearing that warhead.

Now the Iranians were retreating. Binyamin did not know why. All he knew was that it made Ehud's death pointless. The Iranians had killed Ehud, they had attacked his homeland, and the price to them was a single *Fateh* submarine?

It was not enough. It was not nearly enough.

Binyamin rolled upright, putting his stockinged feet on the deck and wiping his nose. He returned to his chair in the CIC and scanned the displays on his console.

"*Gal*: bring up the situational holo."

The globe of light sprang to life. It showed a 360-degree view of the tactical environment around the *Gal*, both below and above the surface. Behind them was the bulk of the Russian fleet, which *Gal* had successfully threaded them between without alerting any pickets. The Russian cruiser, the *Moskva*, was only five miles astern of them. Six miles ahead were the two Iranian trimaran frigates. Their hulls were made for a low radar profile and speed over the water of up to 44 knots, but they also gave off more noise than a single-hulled vessel, making them easier for the *Gal* to track.

"*Gal*: do you have a firing solution on target Bravo?"

Yes, Captain. Tubes one to five are armed, an updated firing solution is loaded to all weapons.

"Are we at minimum safe distance for the use of special weapons?"

Minimum safe distance for the use of special weapons is five miles. We are currently six miles from target Bravo and increasing. At expected rate of separation we will lose contact within 46 minutes.

"*Gal*: prepare to validate launch code for special weapon D."

Standing by, Captain.

The *Gal* had four 650mm tubes from which it could launch 'specials'. Three contained *Popeye* submarine-launched cruise missiles with 20-kiloton warheads designed to destroy entire fleets, like the Russian Black Sea fleet, harbors like the Syrian port of Tartus, or even cities, like Damascus or Tehran.

For this voyage, the *Gal* had also sailed with a 650mm torpedo, reverse engineered by Israel from a Russian-designed DT type 65 submarine, and armed with a 5-kiloton warhead. It would not destroy entire fleets – its blast effect was severely dampened by the seawater surrounding it – but it was a very effective weapon for guaranteeing the destruction of a single target like a missile cruiser or aircraft carrier, or, if fired into an enemy harbor, contaminating the harbor with a radioactive saltwater plume that would put the harbor out of commission for months, if not years, while it was being decontaminated. And Israel could deny all responsibility.

Binyamin had not been authorized to use a *Popeye* missile on this mission, but *Gal*'s 650mm nuclear torpedo was more than sufficient to account for the IRIN *Sinjan* and send it, and its precious nuclear weapon, to the bottom of the Aegean Sea.

It required two officers to authorize its use. But in the event of the death of one officer, the weapon could be launched by the surviving officer on confirmation of a time-limited launch code validated by *Gal*, the assumption being that if the officer had the correct authorization code, it was because it had been issued to them by the relevant commanders in Government and the IDF. If both human officers were incapacitated, the weapon could not be fired and the *Gal* would pilot itself in stealth-optimized mode back to harbor in Haifa or Eilat, whichever was nearer.

The launch code 'safe' on the *Gal* was a device mounted beside the captain's console which was updated any time the submarine connected with the Israeli Navy satellite and servers. It had last updated during their check-in window before the cyber attack, and it was showing that the launch codes Binyamin had been given when they got underway were still valid. In the absence of other data, and given what they had heard on the radio when they floated their comms buoy last, it told Binyamin his orders were unchanged, and for at least the next few hours, he still had a valid launch code.

'Sink the *Sinjan*, use of special weapon authorized.'

Aboard the *Sinjan*, Rostami and his crew swung into action. His Officer of the Deck stepped back from his command post. "I stand relieved. The Captain has the deck."

"Comms, sound general quarters, advise the *Amol* and the *Moskva* of the contact," he ordered. "Helm, all ahead flank.

Weapons, jam and deploy decoys, order *Kamand* close-in weapons crew to alert, prepare for anti-ship missile defense. Air control, I want a *Saegheh* drone over that contact dropping buoys immediately." Rostami paused his string of commands, suddenly remembering he was not alone on the bridge. "Admiral, do you concur?"

The older man simply nodded. "It is your deck, Captain."

Glancing out a portside window, Rostami saw the *Amol* turning hard to port even as he began to power ahead at flank speed, the *Sinjan* rising out of the water as it climbed to its maximum speed of 44 knots. They had rehearsed such a scenario many times, in many different seas, both with and without their Russian partners, and each Captain knew what to do. The priority was to protect the *Sinjan* and its precious nuclear missile. The *Sinjan* powered directly away from the contact, making the most of its high-speed design, just under the speed of a conventional torpedo, firing electronic and noisemaking decoys into its wake. They would not help against a submarine-launched supersonic anti-ship missile, of course, which was why he had ordered the missile defense team to their stations.

As *Sinjan* pulled away, the *Amol* turned toward the contact, placing itself between the contact and the *Sinjan* to protect against torpedoes and missiles and allowing it to optimize the trajectory of its anti-submarine rocket torpedo defenses as drones from both the *Sinjan* and *Amol* hunted for the sub.

"Contact identified by sonar as probable Israeli *Dolphin*-class submarine," his junior OOD announced.

The Admiral coughed gently. "Israel has announced its intention to enter arms control negotiations. We have been ordered back to port. We should not fire at the contact unless we are fired upon first, do you agree, Captain?"

"Yes, of course, Admiral. But in the current environment, prudence dictates…"

"Indeed it does." He held out his hand. "Give me the radio, please, and contact the *Amol*. I want to be sure no one does anything … precipitous."

"Echo Fox Echo Alpha Echo niner niner Alpha six. Validate."

Launch code is confirmed. Please provide a retinal scan.

Binyamin bent his eye to the scanner on the safe.

Launch authority validated. Special weapon D in tube four is available for launch.

"*Gal*: do you have an updated solution on the contact?"

I have a bearing. As the target is drawing away at close to the speed of our torpedo, it will be necessary to detonate some distance from the target, but I estimate a 98 percent chance of a kill due to the wide kill diameter of the special weapon.

Binyamin kept the image of Ehud in his mind, trapped behind the sealed hatch, hammering on it as the water around him buffeted his legs, rising from his waist, to his chest, to his neck … He closed his eyes tightly.

"*Gal*: match generated bearing and shoot."

Aye, Captain. Target locked, targeting data downloaded, shot away.

All Domain Attack: Chaos

No-Fly Zone, Golan Heights, May 20

Bunny had her recon drone following the Russian *Armata* and its UGV wingman, at a low altitude and oblique angle, out of range of its 30mm secondary weapon. Her main focus was on the four *Okhotnik*s which had just entered Golani airspace.

"Falcon, Falcon, Merit."

"Merit, go for Falcon."

"I am showing Russian aircraft, four *Okhotnik* fighters, inside the no-fly zone, do you concur?"

"Roger for Merit. You are cleared to engage."

"Merit committing, out."

She hesitated. Her two anti-air *Fantoms* were circling inside Israel, nearly twenty miles back from the Golan Heights at the moment. She had four *Okhotniks* spread in a line from north to south throughout the DMZ, but one enemy aircraft in particular she didn't like – the one over her Marines in Buq'ata. If she came in low ... between the hills near the Kfar Blum kibbutz...

"Merit, be advised, Israeli combat air patrol approaching the no-fly zone, two F-35s. Stand down and await developments."

"Merit copies. Are they seeing what we see?"

"We still have no data link to Israeli air control. We advised them of the Russian incursion, and this is their response. They asked us to tell you to back off."

"Happy to let someone else share the pain, Falcon. Merit out."

Bunny pointed to their 2D tactical situation display, speaking to Kovacs. "If they can see those *Okhotniks*, they'll engage from back here, I'd bet. Their *Python* missiles only have a twenty-mile range, and they won't want to get closer. What I'm worried about..."

"Is ... where are the *Felon* motherships?"

"Exactly. Their ground pounders are controlled by two guys on the ground in a trailer like ours but that is definitely a combat air patrol, which means each of those *Okhotniks* is being commanded by a pilot in a *Felon* in the air somewhere back inside Syria. If they get a sniff of those F-35s there are going to be a lot of missiles flying any minute..."

The tension in the trailer rose as the blue arrows on their tactical screen that marked the Israeli *Panthers* and the red arrows marking the Russian *Okhotniks* drew within twenty miles of each other.

"Any second now..." Bunny said, the fingers of her left hand drumming on her keyboard.

"Do you mind?" Kovacs asked her, reaching out a hand to stop her.

"Sorry. Just getting ready for..." Her left hand darted forward, tapping key combinations as her right hand gripped her flight stick. "Show time! Missile launches. They're going for the two *Okhotniks* in the south."

In response to her commands, the two *Fantoms* under her control banked to an easterly heading and lit their tails.

"What are you doing? You were supposed to stand down..."

"And await developments," Bunny told her, pointing at the missiles on the tac screen, rapidly converging on their targets. "Those are developments. While Ivan is dodging those missiles to the south, we can sneak in and take out that frotting *Okhotnik* over Buq'ata..."

Yevgeny Bondarev had expected a response to the incursion of his *Okhotniks*. Either it would come from the Americans, or from the Israelis. The *Byelka* radar onboard the *Okhotnik* was identical to that on his *Felon*, and it had detected and classified the incoming missiles as *Python*-5s, optical-infrared guided missiles. Probably fired by F-35s since they could not see the aircraft that had fired them on their radar warning screens.

He nodded with satisfaction as his pilots engaged their drone's infrared countermeasure systems. The Directed Infrared Countermeasure turrets on the *Okhotnik*'s spine and belly could fire modulated laser bursts at incoming infrared missiles to blind them.

And they had proven very effective over Turkey against older infrared missile designs like the *Python*-5.

Bondarev allowed himself a wry reflection as he watched his pilot's drones maneuver and return fire down the bearing of the enemy missiles with their much superior K-77M multimode missiles. It really didn't matter the Israelis were flying the most advanced stealth aircraft in the sky if they filled its weapons bay with missiles designed in the 1990s.

A radar warning alert appeared on his helmet-mounted display at the same time as a chime sounded in his ears. Tracking radar! His *Okhotnik* reacted automatically to the threat, rolling onto a wing and pointing its nose in the direction of the radar source, low in its stern quarter. Moments later the radar warning turned to a new warning. Missile launched! *Peregrine* ... a US missile this time. A damned American drone was down there, somewhere in the Golani weeds.

Bondarev wasn't panicking. The *Okhotnik* had a high survival rate against the *Peregrine*, and his drone showed why as it corkscrewed through the sky, firing chaff and infrared decoys in its wake at the same time as it blasted jamming energy at the incoming missiles. It required no intervention from him – in fact, any attempt by him to intervene would just have slowed down its response time.

He grunted with satisfaction as the missile passed his machine and detonated in a cloud of chaff about two hundred yards behind it. He put the *Okhotnik* immediately into 'hunter-killer' mode, lighting up its phased-array radar and directing its energy at the air below, where the *Fantom* had to be lurking.

First, the hunt. Now, the kill.

Bunny's missile shot had been part of a decoy ploy. She'd faced *Okhotniks* over Turkey in her F-35 and seen what they were capable of. No human pilot could match them for reaction speed and she didn't plan to try.

She locked the target, sent a missile up at the circling *Okhotnik* and then lit one *Fantom*'s tail and blasted it vertically into the sky behind the *Okhotnik* as it spun away, twisting and turning like a manic eel to avoid her missile. She wanted to get above and behind it, out of direct line of sight from the *Okhotnik*'s search radar, and attack it from a quarter its human pilot would not expect.

She sent her other *Fantom* toward Israeli airspace, climbing slowly, hoping it would be detected and seen as the source of the attack.

It was a risky maneuver as both of her birds might be picked up by one or other *Okhotnik*, but it was her best shot. Maybe her only shot.

She watched the attacking *Fantom*'s altimeter climb up above 20,000 feet as the other cruised leisurely back toward Israel at 5,000 feet and 600 nerve-wrackingly slow knots.

Imbecilic. That was how Bondarev saw the American pilots' half-hearted defense of the no-fly zone. The Americans had made a show of firing a missile at Bondarev's *Okhotnik* and now were beetling back into Israeli airspace, no doubt congratulating themselves on making a symbolic effort at protecting Golani airspace, while preserving their own aircraft by pulling it back to safety.

Well, war didn't work that way. Not when Yevgeny Bondarev was fighting it. And not when he was fighting it on behalf of a young kid called 'Rap' Tchakov who had died trying to make this patch of sky his own. Bondarev's order was to achieve air superiority over the Golan Heights and if he was attacked, no ceasefire line drawn in 1949 was going to prevent him defending himself.

With two taps of the buttons on his flightstick, his *Okhotnik* locked up the fleeing *Fantom* from less than ten miles away and fired two K-77M missiles at it with two seconds separation.

"Well, that's just rude," Bunny exclaimed. "Shooting a girl in the back?" She triggered the fleeing *Fantom*'s missile defense routine and left it to fend for itself as she focused on her target, the *Okhotnik* that had just fired on her.

Her other bird was plummeting down on it from above like an osprey falling on a juicy salmon, directing itself with optical-infrared sensors so that it didn't alert its prey. The *Okhotnik*'s pilot had pushed its nose down, following its missiles down toward her now-frantically-maneuvering decoy *Fantom*, but she quickly hauled it in and at 2,000 yards laid her guns' crosshairs on the enemy drone, locked the target and ordered her second *Fantom* to engage.

Its four-barrel gatling autocannon spat once, sending a volley of one hundred 25mm high-explosive armor-piercing shells into the path of the Russian drone, before correcting its own aim and firing again, sending another three hundred rounds at the *Okhotnik*, stitching it from nose to tail, its fragmentation shells splitting the bat-like aircraft in two as though cleaving it with an axe.

Bunny and Kovacs watched the attack through the *Fantom*'s forward-mounted situational awareness camera and Bunny was surprised to see it didn't explode … the two halves of the drone simply fell away from each other and started twisting through the sky toward the ground below like autumn leaves from a tree.

Bondarev started. The attack had caught his *Okhotnik* in its blind spot. Unlike the *Felon*, it had no rear-facing infrared or optical sensors.

A US *Fantom* had suddenly appeared on his targeting display, above and behind his *Okhotnik*, but there had been no time to react. Worse, as the Russian aircraft firing them went dark, the missiles it had fired lost their targeting data. They switched to autonomous target-seeking mode, but the interference from the jamming radiation being blasted at them by their target *Fantom* prevented them getting a radar lock and they went wild.

Ti durak, Bondarev. You idiot.

Adding insult to injury, the two American *Fantoms* dropped off his radar screen and disappeared as their pilot dragged them back down into the ground clutter of the Golani hills and valleys.

He pulled up his tactical map at the same time as getting on the radio to his pilots. "Koshka flight, report."

"Koshka three, splash one Israeli F-35."

"Koshka four, *Okhotnik* four lost to enemy air-to-air missile."

"Koshka two, on station sector D, no targets."

He drew a bitter breath. "Koshka leader has lost *Okhotnik* one. Stand by."

Not bad. Not good. Two *Okhotnik*s lost. One Israeli F-35 downed, a high-value prize. He briefly considered pulling Koshka two off station to his north to search for the US *Fantoms*, but he had to focus on the main game. There was still at least one Israeli F-35 lurking.

"Koshka flight, Koshka leader. Engage search radars, narrow beam mode. Optimize search algorithms for Israeli F-35 and US *Fantom* signatures. We have at least three hostile aircraft still active in our patrol area."

Bunny wasn't concerned with the Russians anymore. Not those in the air, anyway. She was much more concerned with those on the ground. Her recon aircraft, automatically following the Russian *Armata* tank and its 'wingman', had reached the outskirts of the town and she could see its commander conferring with troops at a roadblock.

"I need to focus on what's happening on the ground," Bunny told Kovacs. "We need to put those two air-to-air *Fantoms* into autonomous mode and let them go to work."

Shelly Kovacs bit her lip, one foot pulled up underneath her on her chair. Then she uncurled, putting both feet on the floor as though grounding herself. "Alright. The code is control, aircraft ID, alt, B-O-T."

Bunny smiled. "That's original. Would never have guessed that." She pressed the keys, and in her helmet display the green frame around the small icons for each of the air-air *Fantoms* was highlighted with a red flashing box. Without any guidance from Bunny, they converged on each other like doubles partners in a game of tennis aligning their game plan, and then as one, turned west toward the waypoints she had already preassigned in the DMZ.

"OK, that was spooky," Bunny commented. "You keep an eye on them, alright? Let me know if they go off-reservation." She put two windows up on the panel in front of Kovacs, showing the two drones' sensor and instrument feeds and simulated cockpit displays.

"I'll do more than that," Kovacs said, pulling a keyboard closer to her, her right hand hovering over it. "I've got a kill code and I'll use it to bring those *Fantoms* down if I have to."

"Kill code? You never mentioned a kill code."

Shelly shot her a slightly annoyed look. "I didn't think we would ever need it."

Bunny shook her head. *Focus, O'Hare.*

She switched her radio to the JTAC frequency. "Marine JTAC, Marine JTAC, Marine Air Angel. Marine JTAC, Marine JTAC, this is Angel."

Buq'ata, Golan Heights, May 20

Bell had left Amal's field radio on a workshop bench for her to monitor. It was, after all, her radio and with Patel gone, she would have to take over contact with the US Air Force aircraft overhead, or the Marine *Big Boy* when it arrived.

She'd gently deposited the body of the American Marine in darkness on the concrete apron at the back of her villa. There was no time for sorrow.

Private 'Rooster' Johnson had quickly seen his presence wasn't needed inside the workshop as Amal began pulling premade demolition charges out of a locker and fixing them to the support beams at each corner and in the middle of the shed.

"You can go up to the roof, guard us from up there. If they still have scouts watching my villa, it won't take them long to see it is empty. We can escape out the back if they move on us." She'd put a hand on his arm. "You will need to take Corporal Patel."

"Yes, ma'am," Johnson had replied, putting one foot up on the iron ladder that led to the roof, carbine slung across his back. "Uh, you won't forget I'm there? Managed to make it through this tour without getting kilt, be a shame it happens just as we're bugging out."

She pushed some hair back from her eyes and stood up. It occurred to Amal he was just a big kid, really. He should be in a bar back home, watching a football game, laughing with his buddies, making goofy moves on girls, not here in Buq'ata with an M27 carbine strapped around his neck, worried about dying today. She gave him a smile. "You have my word I will not blow you up, Private."

As he ascended the ladder she turned back to her work, finishing tying the last demolition charge to a support column. The charges were General Dynamics C136 explosives, essentially a plastic container filled with 5lb. of explosive made up of 80 percent TNT and 20 percent aluminum. Each had a digital timer on it that could be synchronized with the other charges around it wirelessly. She'd trained on the use of the charges along with all her other ordnance before relocating her lab to the Golan Heights and was taught it could cut structural steel ten inches in circumference. The support columns in her shed were basically tubular steel and would fly apart under the force of explosives like these, bringing the roof down on what was left of the workshop.

She then opened all of her munitions cabinets, both wall and floor mounted, and placed a charge in each of them. Finally, she rigged a charge to the 3D printer in the middle of her workshop – that one was the one that hurt the most. She and that damn printer had created wonders of flight and robotics together. But as she gave it a last fond pat, she remembered that in the last two days, it had also been a machine that had helped her deal death and destruction at a scale she had never imagined for herself, and she stepped back. Perhaps it was not such a bad thing it was being destroyed and could not be used by anyone else to do what she had done.

She walked to the bottom of the ladder. "Ready down here, Private!" she called up.

His boots appeared at the top of the ladder. "Not a moment too soon, ma'am. We got movement out front. At least platoon strength, with RPGs. Looks like they're waiting for those tanks to roll up but we don't want to be here when they do."

Amal took one last look around her workshop, moved to the 3D printer and the explosive charge she'd fixed to it, set the timer for fifteen minutes and hit 'synch'. Around the shed, on supports and inside ordnance lockers, small red lights began counting down. She quickly pulled on the radio backpack.

They moved outside and she slid the heavy shed door shut and padlocked it.

The big Marine walked over to his dead comrade and lifted him gently onto his shoulders. He looked at the gate in the back wall leading out to the quarry. "How are we going to get Gunny Jensen down that cliff on a stretcher?"

"There is a track. Only goats use it now, and it's covered in shrub, so if you didn't know it was there, you would miss it. But it's wide enough for two people to walk abreast. I will lead you down." She looked ruefully at her house for what might be the last time. "Come, let's go," she told him.

Lieutenant Colonel Zeidan Amar was pacing the room he'd commandeered on the top floor of the house in the center of town, glowering occasionally over a map of Buq'ata on the wall. He had decided to lead the assault on the makeshift Marine compound personally. After the fiasco at the intersection in the center of town where a platoon of his best men had been decimated by a hobby drone, he was determined to be rid of the pestilence that was the Marine squad once and for all. If they had just retired to the villa and bunkered down, he might have found a way to allow them transition in safety to their UNDOF headquarters on Merom Golan. But no. They had treated the villa not as a safe haven but as a fire base for conducting offensive operations throughout Buq'ata. The attack on his *Namer* IFV, his observation posts, the squad in town – an attack which also claimed his prized Russian sniper.

When the Russian armor arrived he would...

"Zeidan." One of his men put his head through the door. "The men got in position and began harassing fire as ordered, but there was counter-fire from the villa. Our MG squad was just eliminated by a sniper on the roof."

With a feral roar, Zeidan reached out and tore the map from the wall, balled it up and threw it on the floor. *This was not the plan!* After the 'terrorist' attack he should have been welcomed into the town as a liberator and spent the last 24 hours on the radio with his people in the other Druze townships across the Golan Heights, shoring up support, paving the way for the entry of Syrian police and armed forces. Not this – urban combat – in the future capital of the Syrian Golani Governate. Forty-eight hours ago, as he'd conferred with his commanders, with his Syrian contacts, there had been no damned US Marines in the Golan Heights, and certainly not in Buq'ata. Just docile, passive UNDOF observers camped on their little hill overlooking the Valley of Tears and rarely venturing outside it.

Enough. Tanks or no tanks. It. Ended. Now.

Grabbing his X-95 bullpup rifle from a hook by the door, he took the stairs down to the ground floor two at a time and doubled through town the short distance to the road leading to the Marine compound, approaching it through a dark side alley packed with his men. He found the man he had assigned to move the platoon up and get them in position for the coming assault, a former Druze Sword Battalion captain.

"Labib, what is the situation?" he demanded as he walked up behind the man, surprising him in the act of surveying the villa with binoculars.

"The ... we are repositioning the MG," he stuttered. "It was poorly sited, too exposed to fire from that damned rooftop. But now I don't ... we have seen no movement in the villa for at least five minutes."

"Give me your binos."

He tore the light-intensifying binoculars from around the man's neck and fixed them on the villa. It was dark, and ominously quiet.

"What about the armor, how far out are they?"

"They got hit by Israeli air outside Hermonit. Several vehicles were disabled, a couple destroyed. Two are approaching Buq'ata now, the rest will follow when they are repaired."

"Just two?" Goddammit. The man was right, there was no sign of life inside the building at all. "Bring up a man with an RPG."

A minute or so later, he got a tap on the shoulder and turned to see an infantryman he recognized, with a grim expression and a rocket-propelled grenade launcher cradled against his chest. "Ah, Assad. I want you to put a rocket through the top window of that villa, on my command, understood?"

The man nodded and moved forward.

"Labib, tell your men that when the RPG hits, I want one minute of suppressing fire on the windows of that villa from all three sides. Let's see what shakes loose. And have your assault squad ready to move up to those walls once we start laying down covering fire. They will breach and clear the building." He grabbed the man's arm. "And tell them, keep civilian casualties to a minimum. I can't use dead Israeli hostages."

"Yes, Zeidan." He moved off to pass the word.

When Labib returned, Zeidan sought out the RPG gunner. He was crouched at a corner, weapon loaded, ready to step out and aim. "*Now*, Assad."

"Yes, Colonel."

"Top window, center."

The man rose from his crouch and lifted the launcher to his shoulder. "Ready!" he called and then swung out, legs wide, planting himself in the middle of the alley. "Shot!"

The rocket lanced out of the alley, covered the 200 yards to the villa in under a second and detonated against the window frame, sending masonry and timber flying. It wasn't a clean shot, but anyone near the window or in the room behind it would have taken a pasting. Before the rubble even hit the ground, small arms fire erupted from the south, west and north of the villa, a blend of 5.56 assault rifles from IDF armories and 7.62mm AKM rifles supplied by his Syrian contacts. Chips of concrete and plaster filled the air with dust as bullets smacked into the façade, shattered glass and tore wood away from the window frames.

Faces blackened, a squad of ten men ran, crouched low, from the cover of the trees to the south-west and flattened themselves against the chest-high walls surrounding the villa. The sergeant commanding them showed great courage and initiative. Not waiting for further orders, after lifting his head to check the situation on the other side of the wall, he signaled his men and rolled over the top of it, moving up to the front door of the house himself as he sent half his squad around to a door on the western side. Both teams were wearing night vision goggles and had rams with them to deal with the doors.

There was no return fire.

As the cacophony of suppressing fire died away, the

breaching teams hammered the doors down with their rams, threw grenades inside and followed them in.

Zeidan expected a firefight to erupt inside the building, but instead there was a disquieting silence, broken only by the occasional muffled shout in Arabic.

Moments later, the sergeant appeared at the front door. "Clear!" he yelled. "No contact."

Damn it to hell. They had waited too long. Zeidan shouldered his rifle and ran forward, over the open ground, vaulting the wall. Stepping inside the building, he could see almost nothing as it was filled with dust and smoke from the barrage of small arms fire and the aftermath of the grenade blasts. But he could see it was empty. No dead or wounded Marines, not even any civilians.

He didn't need to check upstairs, his men had done that. He strode straight through the house to the rear courtyard. It had been walled in, hidden from view, and now he saw it for the first time. Potted olive and citrus trees lined the walls, and across a concrete apron there was a large shed. He signaled to the men following him to spread out and cover him as he approached the heavy sliding door, and saw it was padlocked from the outside. That didn't mean there was no one inside. It could be serving as a redoubt, a refuge of last resort that the Marines had retreated to under the weight of fire on the front of the building.

He quickly checked the gate in the rear wall that let out onto a sheer cliff face leading down to the quarry. They would not have gone out that way. The sheer cliff looked unscalable in the dark, especially bearing wounded civilians, and if they had skirted it to the east or west, they would have run into the men he had positioned around the villa.

They were inside the big metal shed. Ready to make their last stand. Amar was determined to make sure it was indeed their last.

He motioned to Labib to join him by the door. "Do we have bolt cutters?" he whispered, pointing at the lock. "The bastards are sure to be holed up inside."

"I don't think so. But we can tape a grenade to the lock." Labib looked along the heavy metal walls. "Why not just wait for the Russians? A tank could level this dump with a single shot."

"No. I told you, I need those civilians for…"

He never finished his sentence. With a ripple of blasts so close together they sounded like a single explosion, Amal's twelve C136 demolition charges inside the workshop went off, bringing down the roof of the shed and triggering the other explosives and ammunition in lockers inside the building.

In moments, nothing was left of Amal Azaria's drone workshop.

Or of the aspirant to the Governorship of the new Syrian Golani Governate, the late and formerly very frustrated Lieutenant Colonel Zeidan Amar.

"Whoa!" Bunny exclaimed, a sudden flare in the night vision of her recon drone catching her eye. She swung the camera around to the location of the Marine compound at the outskirts of town, a sinking feeling in her gut.

It was no longer there. All she could see was a huge rolling cloud of fire with a pillar of smoke rising high into the air over the town.

Had the Russians managed to get armor into the town without her seeing it?

"Marine JTAC, Marine JTAC, Angel. Come in Patel…"

There was no reply.

"What's up?" Shelly asked. She had her eyes fixed on her two *Fantoms*, now maneuvering to set up an attack on the northernmost *Okhotnik* over the Golan.

"That house our boys and girls were sheltering in – it's … it's…" Bunny zoomed her camera. The smoke was still obscuring her view, but she could see a little more now and what she could see didn't help the feeling in her stomach. "It's half gone, the whole eastern side. It's like someone took it out with a 500lb. bomb." She also saw a large number of combatants milling around the explosion site, some clearly dragging wounded from the area.

"Could the Russians have hit it with an air strike?" Shelly asked. "Cruise missile?"

"That would have been *cold*. Even for Ivan. There were civilians in that building with those Marines."

As Bunny was speaking, the radio crackled to life. "Angel, Angel, IDF JTAC."

IDF JTAC? A woman's voice. "Uh, IDF JTAC, go for Angel."

"Angel, I am sorry but Corporal Patel is dead. My name is Corporal Azaria, Unit 351, *Palhik* Company, Golani Brigade. It was my radio Corporal Patel was using. I am not trained in your close air support protocols."

"That's ... what is your situation, Corporal? I saw an explosion, possible enemy troops inside your compound."

"Yes, we had to abandon my house. We would not have been able to defend against an assault supported by Russian armor."

"That was your house? I'm sorry to tell you, Azaria, it looks like either the Russians or Syrians put a 500lb. bomb through a window."

"No. That was me," the woman said, very matter of fact. "We are now withdrawing through the quarry to the LZ in the fields to the east. Do you know how far out the evacuation flight is?"

Bunny pulled up her tactical display and zoomed it out to show her the area to the south-west. The Marine *Big Boy* flight was being tracked by the Bombardier AWACS over Cyprus and was clearly marked on her map. "It's over the Sea of Galilee. Showing an ETA of 0348."

"We will be at the LZ around ... I think around 0330. There is little cover there. We will be out on open ground for some time."

"I will patrol your evacuation point and let you know if I see any hostile activity."

"Thank you. I need to go now."

"Roger. Angel out."

I lost one, was Bunny's next thought. The filled-crust pizza guy. That was all she knew about Patel. She felt sick.

"*Fantoms* engaging," Kovacs said. "Enemy radar lock. Why don't they react? No. *What?*"

Her surprise drew Bunny's thoughts back to the present. She quickly set up some recon waypoints around the evacuation position for the Marines and their civilian charges, along with alerts to warn them of ground or armored combatants approaching the evac zone. Then she turned her attention to the screen Kovacs was watching. It took her a moment to assimilate all the data flowing across the screen with what she was seeing in the drone 'cockpit' view windows.

The two *Fantoms* had positioned themselves immediately below the circling *Okhotnik* over the mountain ranges in the north of the Golan Heights and were rising almost vertically to intercept it. But it had spotted them, and its remote pilot had locked them up.

A human pilot, with an enemy radar lock warning warbling in his or her ears, knowing a missile launch alert would be next, would either have fired their own weapons, or evaded, or both. But the two *Fantoms* simply kept climbing at the target.

"Order them to evade!" Kovacs yelled at Bunny. "They're sitting ducks."

But Bunny wasn't so sure. She'd never seen a *Fantom* fly a fully autonomous intercept. "No! Let's watch. We might learn something."

Multiple events seemed to happen simultaneously. As expected, two missiles lanced down from the Russian aircraft directly at the US *Fantoms* 20,000 feet below it. And now the *Fantoms* reacted, spinning around each other like the arms of a gyro, at dizzying, literally breakneck speed. As they did so, they fired flares and foil chaff into the air around them and their gyroscopic motion created a spray of decoys in the air that was sucked into a tornado-like funnel by the force of their combined wake. Bunny's eyes flicked to their countermeasure readouts and saw they were both jamming too, and at the last millisecond before the missiles struck, they split out of their climb, like water bursting from the top of a fountain.

There was no way for the Russian missiles to react quickly enough to follow them. In any case, they were looking at a dense cloud of radar-reflecting foil and enticing heat and light in the funnel of decoys the *Fantoms* had created and they kept powering past the US drones, into the funnel of foil and heat, detonating harmlessly two hundred feet below their targets.

Which had now reversed their banking turn and oriented on the *Okhotnik* again from different points of the compass. In a heartbeat, they both locked guns on the Russian drone and fired at point-blank range.

The Russian aircraft dissolved in a burst of light and metal.

"Did you program that ... that chaff and flare vortex thing?" Kovacs asked Bunny, her mouth still agape.

"No," Bunny replied, equally stunned. "I assumed *you* did."

"No, I ... I mean, it's a learning system. The AI is supposed to learn from every mission flown by every drone and optimize its tactics based on ... on ... but that..."

As O'Hare watched, the two *Fantoms* joined formation again, pointed their noses at the earth and headed immediately toward the last remaining *Okhotnik* over the Golan. They clearly preferred close-quarters combat. "Well, Shelly, I guess they learned."

US blockade line, Mediterranean Sea, May 20

"Incoming torpedo, bearing one eight niner, speed 50 knots, range four point four miles, *Sinjan* is the target," a junior Officer of the Deck announced. "It has just passed under the *Amol.*"

412

Captain Rostami did a quick mental calculation. The *Sinjan* was now flying across the water at its maximum speed of 45 knots, directly away from the torpedo. It was closing on them at a relative speed of just five knots. He relaxed. If they did nothing, the homing torpedo *would* catch them before it ran out of fuel, but there was a chance it could be decoyed off course.

Or forced off course by the *Amol*, which had maneuvered to put itself between the source of the attack and the *Sinjan*. Rostami had great confidence in the *Amol*'s Captain, having seen his sister ship perform during the exercises of the last two weeks, exercises which were in reality full dress rehearsals for exactly this type of attack.

As they watched a virtual rear window of the bridge – essentially a large flat screen showing the view behind the ship with tactical data overlaid on it – the *Amol* steadied and two exhaust plumes spat out of its superstructure-mounted horizontal tubes. "*Amol* firing ASROC," his OOD advised.

"They are attacking the contact?" the Admiral asked. He was a cleric and politician first and foremost, and left warfighting strategy to his professional officers.

"Yes, Admiral. The incoming torpedo is almost certainly wire-guided. Even if they don't destroy the contact, they may force it to maneuver so radically that it breaks the guidance wires." Rostami looked at the plot again, and then thumped the railing beside him in frustration. "Why this? Why now? We are pulling back, don't the damn Israelis know that!?"

"I suspect they did not get the message, Captain," the Admiral observed.

Torpedoes in the water, range two miles, sonar active … sonar lock, they have acquired the Gal, the AI announced impersonally. *Time to impact, one minute 33 seconds. Initiating acoustic jamming, deploying decoys. Recommend defensive maneuvers.*

Binyamin was listening to *Gal* as though through the distorting lens of a fairground looking glass. He had launched a nuclear torpedo at an Iranian ship. He should be horrified at the thought. Instead, all he wanted was for it to reach out and pull the already dead bodies of the men he had aimed it at into the depths of the Aegean, so that they could share the same waterlogged fate as Ehud.

That the *Gal* would also be destroyed was of secondary importance to him. But even through the fog of his despair he realized one thing. The *Gal* had to stay alive long enough for the torpedo to reach its target.

"Options?" he asked.

Emergency defensive maneuver. We may lose wire guidance of the special weapon but it will go autonomous and attempt to locate the target with its own sensors.

"If it does not?"

It will go inactive and sink to the sea floor.

"No, *Gal*. Another option."

Detonate the torpedo now. Due to the wide area of effect, there is a 95 percent chance of destroying the IRIN Amol, which will disrupt its torpedo attack. There is a 68 percent chance of destroying the IRIN Sinjan, which is our mission objective. There is a 13 percent chance of damage to the Gal, which is lower than the chance of destruction from the incoming torpedoes.

He didn't hesitate. "Much better." Leaning over to the same console he used to initialize the nuclear torpedo, he reached for the screen and swiped left to a large red icon with Hebrew writing that simply said, "Commit."

He tapped it, lay back in his chair and closed his eyes.

On the *Sinjan*, Captain Rostami grabbed the railing that ran around the inside of the bridge with white knuckles, watching the aft view screen in horror as the sea between the *Amol* and the *Sinjan* expanded into a huge, gaseous bubble of unbelievable girth. It rose with incredible speed, the *Amol* disappearing from view behind it.

A giant hand lifted the stern of the *Sinjan* and pushed its bow under the surface, threatening to send it spearing below the waves, but then the bubble collapsed into itself, a crater appeared in the seawater behind them and he just had time to see the *Amol* tumble like a toy yacht down a hillside as it disappeared into the raging foam at the bottom of the crater before a plume of seawater bigger than any sea spout he had ever seen shot up from the depths, towering hundreds of feet above them.

The sea around the *Sinjan* began rushing past at the height of the bridge, pulling the 3,000-ton frigate out of its forward, downward plunge and sucking it *backwards*, into the gaping gaseous crater.

Until the rising plume of seawater collapsed back into the crater and propelled the *Sinjan* forward again with a violence that threw any of the crew who were not belted into their action stations, like Captain Hossein Rostami and Rear Admiral Karim Daei, to the deck with bone-crushing force.

Mississippi Road, Russett, Maryland, May 20

Tonya Dupré had listened to the President's press conference from her Russett apartment.

She thought it had gone pretty well. She wanted to get an update on the military situation on the border now. With Iran pulling its ships back, she'd hope to see signs the ground war phase of the All Domain Attack was also being wound back, with Syrian and Iranian forces on the border with Israel being pulled back to their bases, and the heat going out of some of the Iranian-backed insurrections. She swung her legs down off her sofa as her cell phone buzzed. Nothing unusual in that, it did that a hundred times a day. But it buzzed with the S-O-S rhythm that she'd set up for alerts from HOLMES.

She read the text with a horrified chill.

Cheyenne Mountain reports subsea nuclear detonation in the Aegean Sea in vicinity of Iranian vessels.

Her mind raced … vicinity? There were warships of at least

four nations in the 'vicinity' of the Iranian vessels and every single one of them would right now be coming to a full nuclear conflict alert. In seconds she was at her table, ripping the laptop on her dining table open. It took an agonizingly long time to boot, scan her face and connect to her Directorate ID. When the Cyber Directorate logo flashed up she sat down and pulled her laptop closer.

"HOLMES, give me everything you have on the nuclear incident in the Aegean Sea, from the last fifteen minutes."

Yes, Director. At 0340 hours Mediterranean time, the early warning system at Cheyenne Mountain registered seismic activity in the Aegean Sea area, confirmed by satellite thermal imaging showing a high temperature anomaly in the sea. The data is consistent with the detonation of a five-kiloton tactical nuclear weapon. DIA and NSA intelligence puts the detonation almost exactly midway between the two Iranian missile frigates IRIN Sinjan and IRIN Amol...

"Do we have a damage assessment on the Iranian ships?"

No, Director. The incident is ongoing and a large vapor plume is preventing imaging. Shall I continue?

"Yes."

Signals intelligence analysis by NSA indicates an immediate increase in the volume of traffic between the Russian fleet and Sevastopol, indicative of the fleet being ordered to a higher level of alert. Central Command has also ordered all US forces in the Command to DEFCON 1.

Tonya's mind and body went numb. DEFCON 1. 'Nuclear war is imminent or has already started.' No, it can't be. Never before ... no one has ever gone this far, we always pull back from the brink. Always. We have the weapons, but no nation has *ever* dared use them.

Until today. Because no nation has ever faced the prospect of total destruction in an All Domain Attack. Israel ... isolated in space, crippled in the cyber domain, decimated in the air, facing internal unrest and the prospect of a full-scale ground invasion...

So Israel had appeared to capitulate. It had agreed to meet in October and discuss arms limitation. All the while, it was preparing to remove the threat of Iranian nuclear weapons at sea in a dramatic demonstration of its nuclear power. A desperate and misplaced negotiation tactic? The actions of a single submarine commander and crew? Or just the first shot in a nuclear conflict with Iran that could tip the world into Armageddon?

It didn't matter. What mattered was preventing the coming avalanche with a well-placed demolition charge.

"HOLMES, put me through to the President, and send an alert to General Poznam at Cyber Command to prepare to initiate *Operation Illumination* as soon as I secure Presidential authority."

US blockade line, Mediterranean Sea, May 20

Aboard the USS *Canberra*, the CIC had erupted.

It had started, perhaps not surprisingly, with Ears tearing his headphones from his head before the screaming whine in his headphones deafened him. He didn't need them. The acoustic signal translator screen in front of him told its own story. He pushed it through to the command alert screen for the attention of Drysdale and Goldmann, but he also stood and called it out verbally.

"Subsea detonation, bearing three one five degrees, range twenty miles. Right between those Iranian ships. Acoustic analysis is calling it nuclear!"

For once, Drysdale wasn't asleep at the wheel. "On your toes, people! SRO, update positions on those Russian surface combatants. Weapons, spool up close-in and anti-air defenses. I want naval strike missiles assigned to *every* Russian vessel. Prepare to launch on Captain's command. This is about to get real, people."

They were still at general quarters, waiting to see whether the Iranians were really pulling back or just planning to sail around in circles for a while. Their tactical situation was, in a word, dire.

The four destroyers and the LCS of Squadron 60 were east of Rhodes, stretched out across the entrance into the Mediterranean from the Aegean Sea, with five to fifteen miles separation. It was a formation designed to allow them to maximize the chances of detecting Russian or Iranian submarines, and for any two destroyers to intercept and halt the Iranian ships if they tried to force the blockade line.

It was not a formation designed to optimize their ability to fight a major surface battle with the Russian-Iranian fleet. They had two Russian corvettes behind them. Barely five miles ahead and still steaming toward them was the core of the Russian fleet ... two frigates and the cruiser *Moskva*, with enough firepower to take on a carrier battle group. With them were believed to be at least two *Kilo*-class submarines and the remaining Iranian *Fateh*, two of which were still undetected. The only *Kilo* they had located with their airborne dipping sonar was also behind them, and probably coming to missile launch depth right now.

Their only ace in the hole had been the British *Astute*-class submarine HMS *Agincourt*. It had managed to come around behind the Russian-Iranian fleet undetected and was right now nestled deep in the Karpathou Strait, waiting for the Iranian ships to pass overhead and ready to disable one or both with torpedoes if ordered. Ideal for intercepting the Iranians, not so useful for helping them slug it out with a Russian Black Sea fleet steaming right off their bow.

USS *Canberra* and USS *Porter* had been increasing their separation to allow the Russian ships to pass between them unhindered. Ears felt the *Canberra* lean to starboard as it came around to point its bow at the incoming Russians and minimize its exposed flank.

He couldn't see how that would really help when they were completely and utterly surrounded.

Right then, his thoughts went to his brother Calvin. The guy was probably sitting poolside in Kuwait, pulling on an ice cold no-alcohol beer with a plate of buffalo wings in front of him fit to feed a family of four.

Were the nuclear alert sirens already starting to sound where he was?

In the command center of HMS *Agincourt*, fifteen miles from the epicenter of the explosion, the situation was no less fraught, though a little more restrained.

They had been watching on their screens as the two Iranians completed their turns toward them, but then they had suddenly accelerated, one breaking to port as the other increased to flank speed, headed straight toward the *Agincourt*.

The move had mystified Puncher Courtenay. His sonarmen had picked up nothing to explain why the Iranians had suddenly, apparently, gone crazy. But it smelled to him like a rehearsed maneuver.

"XO, what would explain what we're seeing?"

"The Iranians are under attack, sir. Either for real, or they're still exercising with the Russians."

"Exercising? Not with American destroyers so close. That would be idiotic," Courtenay replied.

"Then it can only be missiles, or a torpedo…"

The answer came milliseconds later as every sonar screen in the command center began flashing warnings showing a massive explosion right in between the two Iranian frigates. Sonar operators began reporting what they were seeing, hearing, but Puncher had no doubts. It was a thing he had hoped never, ever to see.

His XO gave it a name. All formality went out the window. "Nuke, Puncher. Has to be. Someone let off a bloody nuke!"

Fifteen miles away. Courtenay quickly scanned the latest sonar readouts. It looked like the explosion had taken place underwater. Seawater was very, very hard to displace in great quantities, even for a nuclear blast. They should be safe, shouldn't they?

That depended how many kilotons or, god forbid, megatons

the weapon was. And whether it was a one-off, or just the first shot in a bloody full-scale nuclear war.

He felt sick to the stomach.

"Pilot, ahead full, right full rudder please, take us down to maximum safe operating depth." He wanted to put as much water as he could between that nuke and themselves, and get himself as far as possible from any surface shockwaves that would be rippling outward. He reached for the intership tannoy. "General quarters, general quarters. All compartments, this is the Captain. All personnel will secure themselves and brace for impact."

Buq'ata, Golan Heights, May 20

Calvin Bell was also a tad worried. He was worried whether Gunnery Sergeant Jensen would survive the next thirty minutes until their ride out of there arrived.

As they tracked out of the quarry he'd stumbled, nearly losing his grip on Jensen's stretcher, and then had to quickly stoop forward to grab the bag of Stevens' blood the Marine Gunnery Sergeant had resting on his chest to stop it falling. The bag was nearly empty and Jensen was still losing blood. Stevens was the only one with his blood type, and it was technically too soon to tap the guy again.

There was a very real chance the blood loss could kill the Indiana farmer's son.

"Hey, easy there, slave!" Jensen said weakly. "These goods are fragile."

"Kept you alive this far, Gunny," Bell told him, putting the plasma bag back in place as they walked. "Don't make me regret it."

They'd taken longer than the Israeli corporal had expected to negotiate the narrow goat track leading down the cliff into the quarry. She'd told them it was two men wide, but in places they'd had to go single file, which meant Bell and Stevens had to bear Jensen's entire weight on their own a few times. And he was not a small man.

They'd made it down without spilling him from the makeshift stretcher, though. The Israeli corporal had taken point as they wound through the quarry, with Johnson bringing up the rear, Patel's body across his broad shoulders.

At the wire fence marking the entrance to the quarry, they'd paused as Amal checked in with the Marine drone pilot.

"Down slowly, folks," Bell told the other three stretcher bearers, Stevens, Buckland and Wallace. "Bend your knees, not your backs."

As the stretcher settled on the ground, Jensen coughed. "*Rock.*"

Bell sighed. "Up again, move him to my right a half yard." Yeah, alright, there was a big rock where they'd dropped him. "You heard the story of the princess and the pea, Gunny?"

"I'm assuming you're the pea, Bell?" he came back straight away. Alright, he might have lost a couple quarts of blood, but it hadn't broken his not-very-funny bone. Bell walked over to Stevens, who was stretching his back, and put an arm over his shoulder. "How you feeling?" he asked, his voice quiet.

"Weak. Like a damn vampire sucked me dry. Why?"

"That *Big Boy* will have medical supplies, plasma and such. But if it doesn't get here soon, I might need to take another quart."

Bell clapped Stevens on the back and walked over to where Lopez was squatting on the ground, her arm cradled to her chest.

"It's bleeding again," she told him, holding out the hand she had cupped under her elbow. It was wet with congealed blood. "Didn't want to leave a trail behind us," she said. "You know, when it gets light."

He pulled a cloth from a pants pocket and soaked up the blood in her palm, then checked and tightened the bandages around her elbow. It wasn't anywhere near as dangerous as Jensen's wound. It needed to be cleaned and re-dressed, and she needed her humerus reset pronto, but none of that was going to happen before they got out of here.

"What you think happened up at the house, Corporal?" Lopez asked him. "You think that explosion got any of them?" As they'd been making their way down the cliff face, they'd all heard the impact of the RPG and the sustained barrage of small arms fire that must have been an all-out assault on their former hiding place. Right before the ground shook with the force of the workshop demolition charges.

"Hard to imagine it didn't," Bell said as he retightened her bandages. "Sounded like it could have flattened a city block."

"I hope we hurt them. Bad."

"Me too."

"For Patel, I mean."

Bell looked over to where Johnson had lain Patel's body, still standing beside it with his rifle at the ready, looking for all the world like he was daring the devil to come take it. "Yeah, I know. You need more painkillers?"

Lopez was one of the few in the squad who carried a sidearm, because back in Kobani she had manned the besieged unit's sandbagged M2 .50-caliber machine gun. She patted the holster on her thigh with her good hand. "Prefer to stay sharp. In case."

Bell nodded, thinking to himself that a one-armed Marine with a Sig Sauer M18 pistol wasn't going to be much use if any of those bloody great Russian tanks came at them when they were out in open farmland ... but he kept that to himself.

US blockade line, Mediterranean Sea, May 20

The *Sinjan*'s Captain, Hossein Rostami, hadn't had time to fully process what he'd seen on the frigate's aft view screen – the huge gaseous bubble rising from the depths, the *Amol* tumbling into the crater it made before the crater collapsed, the sea closing right over the top of their sister vessel, their own crazy seesaw ride across the sea, shoved forward, pulled back, and finally propelled forward again on wave after wave flowing outward from the explosion…

But as the huge waterspout tower above his ship collapsed and the air around them congealed into a milky, salty mist, the radiation alarms started ringing out across every deck of the *Sinjan* and Hossein Rostami knew with a horrible certainty exactly what had happened.

As the men around him rose from the deck of the bridge where they'd been thrown, Rostami walked to a locker on the rear bulkhead and pulled it open, pulling out NBC – nuclear, biological and chemical – warfare suits before throwing them to the members of the bridge watch. He doubted they would do much good. The waterspout that had collapsed right on top of the *Sinjan* had probably contained enough radiation to kill anyone who had been out on deck already, and every exposed surface would probably now be lethally radioactive. But inside the bridge they may have been less exposed. He climbed awkwardly into his own suit.

"Helm, engines full astern, bring us back to slow ahead, five knots. Radar, watch for nearby surface contacts. Damage reports. I want full reports on all damage!" he called out to the stunned watch crew. "Get to it! There is a submarine out there somewhere still, I want it located! I want to know what happened to the *Amol*. And someone get me Bandar Abbas on the radio."

As his shouted orders were being relayed, he looked around him.

Admiral Daei was slower rising from the floor, and Rostami crouched beside him to help him up. "This is … it is…" the old man was saying, shaking his head. "Rostami?"

Rostami lifted the Admiral up and propped him against the rear bulkhead. He looked out the bridge windows and at the aft view screen, but all he saw was milky fog.

His junior OOD was listening to a report from below. "*Amol* is not responding to our hails. CIC reports a contact at

174 degrees, range 11 miles. It could be the *Amol*, but the return is very small. They suspect the ship may have capsized."

"Get two Zodiacs out there to explore the contact visually, tell them to wear NBC suits, take life preservers and look for survivors. Where is that call to Bandar?!" He held out his hand impatiently and waved it at the man. "Switch to ship's intercom." When the man was ready he grabbed the handset. "This is the Captain. The *Sinjan* and *Amol* have been subjected to a tactical nuclear weapons attack. We are attempting to contact Bandar Abbas for orders. Radiation levels are high. NBC suits are to be worn at all times in all areas of the ship. We are still at action stations. Your priority is to report and repair any damage to our propulsion, combat, communication or sensor systems and prepare to engage hostile forces on my command. Captain out."

The communications officer held out a headset for him and he jammed it onto the hood of his NBC suit, indicating the man should turn up the volume. "Bandar?"

The man nodded.

"This is Captain Rostami of the *Sinjan*, who am I addressing?" he asked.

"You have reached the duty officer of IRIN Bandar Abbas, Lieutenant Larijani."

"Lieutenant, listen carefully. *Sinjan* and *Amol* have been attacked with a tactical nuclear weapon, I suspect a torpedo from an Israeli submarine that was detected just before the attack. Damage is currently unknown, but the *Amol* is not answering to communications. This action is outside my rules of engagement. I require immediate instruction about how to respond. Is that clear? *Immediate*."

"Yes, Captain. I will relay your message at once."

Rostami handed the headset back then turned to his junior OOD. "Tell the CIC to ready the ASROC launcher in case we get a lock on that bastard Israeli. And ready the *Yakhont* missile in VL tube one. Set to sea-skimming mode with terminal pop-up. The target is central Tel Aviv."

424

Binyamin Ben-Zvi had registered the detonation of his special weapon through the hull of the *Gal* as a rumble like a far-off thunderstorm. *Gal* had given the boat right full rudder and kept it turning as it rode the underwater shock wave that rocked them roughly from side to side and then the smaller follow-up shocks that hammered the hull as they powered away from the explosion.

The power of even a nuclear explosion was quickly dissipated by the mass of water between them and the trigger point. The ASROC torpedoes that the *Amol* had launched at them just before the explosion had lost their track, their acoustic homing systems overwhelmed by the noise of the atomic blast, and the *Gal* was soon riding in clear water as it pulled away.

Gal began reading off a checklist of system states to him but Binyamin ignored the AI, got up from his chair and went back to his stateroom. In the locker under his bunk, he found what he was looking for and lay down on the bunk with a photograph of Ehud, which he held in a shaking hand in front of his eyes.

Then he placed the barrel of his Jericho 9mm pistol into his mouth, and fired.

All Domain Attack: Counterstrike

No-Fly Zone, Golan Heights, May 20

"Merit, Merit, Falcon."

"Falcon, go for Merit," Bunny responded to the Bombardier AWACS over Cyprus. She and Kovacs had just watched their two-drone element of air-air combat *Fantoms* despatch the final *Okhotnik* over the Golan Heights. Now the question was whether the Russian's piloted aircraft, probably Su-57 *Felons*, would try to force the issue themselves. But even if they did, what Bunny had seen as the two AI-piloted aircraft had worked in perfect harmony together, had given her confidence they could deal with just about anything the Russians tried to throw at them, if they just gave their *Fantoms* a little rope.

"Merit, be advised US forces in the Central Command theatre are now at DEFCON 1."

Kovacs had been frantically scribbling notes based on her observations of the drone versus drone engagements over the Golan Heights, but now she looked up, shocked.

"Merit copies. What is the situation, Falcon?"

"A tactical nuclear weapon has exploded under the sea in the Mediterranean. No further information. We have new tasking for you, Merit."

"Go ahead."

"Your remaining aircraft will escort the *Big Boy* quadcopter now approaching the evacuation point for the US 1st Marines, 3rd Battalion squad pinned down in Buq'ata. It should be on your tac map already. Make sure those Marines and any civilians with them get away without interference, and then escort the *Big Boy* back to Hatzerim Air Base in Israel. Medallion flight will take over your patrol in approximately fifteen mikes, they are currently feet wet out of Cyprus."

Bunny did a quick check of her aircraft's fuel and weapons state. She had three *Fantoms* with between 28 and 32 percent fuel reserve. One was a reconnaissance aircraft with no air-to-air weapons but still a full gun belt. Her two air-air configured *Fantoms* had three missiles remaining between them, but after two of the 'vortex'-style attacks on *Okhotniks*, nothing in their guns.

"Roger, Falcon, we have just enough juice to be able to accommodate. Can you let Akrotiri know we will be coming back on bingo fuel? We'll be asking for priority in getting my girls back on the ground."

"Falcon copies. Good luck, Merit, Falcon out." Bunny

began laying in waypoints for the escort flight.

"DEFCON 1? Holy crap," Kovacs said, standing. "I need to get ... I don't know. Back to my office, I guess, see what is going on?"

Bunny looked over at Kovacs with a serious expression. "Screw your office. Akrotiri has a nuclear fallout shelter? That's where I'd be headed."

Yevgeny Bondarev had just received a very similar message to the one that had been passed to Bunny O'Hare. A subsea tactical nuke targeting the Iranians? It could only be the Israelis. But the Russian angle on the situation was very, very different. He was to return to Latakia to rearm with anti-ship missiles, re-equip with new drone wingmen, refuel and then proceed with his flight to the eastern Mediterranean to provide attack fighter cover for the Russian Black Sea fleet, which had just been ordered to steam at flank speed for Tartus port in Syria.

Any attempt by US warships, or Israeli aircraft, to interfere with the passage of the Russian fleet was to be met with all available force.

Bondarev was sure his masters in Russia did not really want a naval slugfest in the Mediterranean between US and Russian ships, any more than they wanted nuclear war to break out in the Middle East. But they had clearly overplayed their hand, pushing Israel to and then beyond the brink, and it had reacted dramatically. They had gotten their Israel-Iran disarmament negotiations. By berthing their fleet at Tartus they were sending a signal they did not intend to escalate the situation any more than was already the case, but Bondarev knew it would only take a single slip by a single captain on any one of the nuclear-armed ships to the west, or the Iranian strategic missile forces below him, for the entire situation to spiral out of control, with global consequences.

For now, at this moment, he was glad he was safe in his cockpit at 30,000 feet over Syria, and not down at a potential ground zero at Latakia.

A chime sounded in his ears as his passive optical infrared arrays picked up a contact against the cold blackness of the Syrian night. About twenty miles south-west, moving a few hundred feet above the ground, was a single slow-moving aircraft. He focused a beam of radar energy from his phased-array radar on it just long enough to get an identification.

A US V-22DU *Big Boy*. Bondarev had met the *Big Boy* in the air over northern Syria. It was the workhorse of the US Marines and was probably transporting arms, ammunition or reinforcements to the Americans in Buq'ata, which was not good news for the armored column he was supposed to be providing air cover for. He was still smarting from the loss of four of his *Okhotniks* to US *Fantoms* over the Golan Heights DMZ and he didn't hesitate a second before flipping to his interplane channel on the radio.

"Koshka two, stay on my wing, we have been ordered to return to Latakia. Koshka three and four, there is a US transport aircraft entering my sector. I'm patching through the contact now. Engage and destroy it, then return to Latakia immediately yourselves. Do not enter the DMZ, we have lost enough aircraft to enemy action today, even if they were just drones."

"Koshka three copies."

"Koshka four copies."

Bondarev set a waypoint for Latakia and banked his aircraft north, checked the airspace around him for other potentially hostile contacts and, seeing none, settled in for the flight home. He had no idea what would await him, but he knew what he was leaving behind. The US no-fly zone had caused his unit nothing but grief, with the loss of several ground vehicles, two pilots and now four *Okhotniks* – all for a handful of the damned American drones. That was not math he liked.

If he lived through this war – and with nukes apparently cooking off he wasn't certain of that outcome at all – he was going to invest heavily in preparing himself for the next one.

Because he was more certain than ever that it would be fought just as much by machines as by humans.

US blockade line, Mediterranean Sea, May 20

HMS *Agincourt* had ridden out the ripples from the atomic bomb at nine hundred feet below the surface, and thankfully had been subjected to only a ten-degree roll that passed within a minute.

"Low-kiloton weapon," Allen Courtenay's XO decided. "Thank god."

Puncher was not quite ready to thank god for anything. Not yet. Not until the fighting was over.

And then the dying.

"Pilot, bring us to sensor depth. Weapons, do you have a firing solution on any of the enemy combatants?"

His weapons officer consulted with his men. "We've lost our solutions on all the Russians, sir, too much noise in the water. Might be able to generate new solutions when we get the radar mast up. We have a solution on one Iranian frigate, contact Golf two.

"Assign two *Perseus* missiles, please. Fire on my order."

His voice sounded a lot calmer than he felt. The *Perseus* was the most devastating weapon in the *Agincourt*'s arsenal. Hypersonic, flying at five times the speed of sound, once it burst out of the sea, dumped its launch canister and pointed itself at the IRIN *Sinjan*, those aboard would have only seconds to live. There was no defensive weapon aboard the Iranian ship that could possibly react in time.

His men worked quietly, efficiently.

What happened next would depend entirely on what he found when his sensor masts broke the surface, now just six hundred feet above.

"Captain, we have lost contact with Bandar Abbas," his XO, Salari, told a Hossein Rostami who was on the verge of complete panic. "No response from Khorramshahr or Bushehr either."

The Admiral of his fleet was staring out from the bridge of the *Sinjan* and mumbling to himself as two watch officers helped him into an NBC suit. His sister ship was last seen tumbling to the bottom of the Aegean Sea in a boiling crater of steam. A milky white radioactive fog surrounded them still and his entire crew had probably already absorbed more than enough radiation to kill every man aboard.

Now he had lost contact with his fleet base. Which should have been impossible. Their communication systems were multiply redundant. If Bandar Abbas could not be raised via satellite, then a network of radio transceivers across cooperative nations like Egypt, Lebanon and Syria should have connected him via VHF.

If they could not raise Bandar Abbas, or any of the other fleet bases, it could mean only one thing.

They were no longer there.

The nuclear attack on the *Sinjan* and *Amol* had not been an isolated happening. The Zionists must have carried out a damned pre-emptive strike. They had lulled the Iranian regime into a state of security, thinking they had agreed to arms limitation talks, and all the while they were planning a nuclear attack on Iran.

Hossein Rostami was already a dead man, he knew that. His ship had been drowned in a radioactive waterspout and was probably still sitting in radioactive seas. The levels of radiation he was seeing on the readouts on his command console exceeded the levels for which their NBC suits were rated, and even if they were miraculously lifted off their ship immediately, he and his men were already doomed. If they didn't die of acute radiation syndrome, they would fall victim to accelerated heart disease and cancer. The Zionists with their small nuclear torpedo had killed him and his men as surely as if they had detonated a 20-kiloton weapon right over their heads.

He let his building fury replace the panic.

"Weapons, report missile readiness for VL tube one."

"All *Yakhont* missile tubes armed and ready to fire. Targets set for Tel Aviv. Missile in tube one has been separately armed and arming confirmed by the Korean technician. Hatches released, we are ready to launch."

The *Sinjan* had four of the larger *Yakhont* two-stage supersonic cruise missiles. The rest were smaller *Ghader* anti-ship missiles, which he might need if the Americans decided to join the Israeli attack. Their operations order called for the launch of all *Yakhont* missiles, both conventional and nuclear, with the nuclear weapon launched last, to increase the chances that the nuclear warhead would make it through any anti-missile defenses. A simple strategy of 'safety in numbers'.

Rostami pulled the glove from his hand. He called up the nuclear missile launch screen and from the handbook given to him by the captain of the Panamanian-flagged freighter, he entered the activation code for the *Yakhont* missile in his weapons bay and put his thumb to a print reader to authorize it. By protocol, he had to validate the launch order with Fleet Command, or have it countersigned by another officer.

"Admiral Daei."

The man turned at the sound of his name.

"Admiral, we have been attacked with a nuclear weapon. We cannot raise Fleet Command, or Tehran. Your orders, Admiral?"

Admiral Daei stared back at Rostami though the visor of his NBC suit, cloudy with his breath. "It is your ship, Captain. What do you recommend?"

The man's words came back to him. If I, or anyone else, gives you the order to use that particular weapon, I want you to look in your heart and ask yourself if there is any other option.

Hossein Rostami looked into his heart. And there he saw only death, darkness and despair. "We must retaliate with our nuclear weapon, before it is too late. There is no other option."

"There is always another option, Hossein. Doing nothing is an option. Dying is an option."

"Are you denying launch authority, Admiral?" Rostami asked, his voice tight in the suddenly silent bridge.

"We were ordered back to Sevastopol," Daei said. "Our last order was to disengage, not to attack Israel..."

Rostami felt like screaming, but tried to control his voice. "That was before we were attacked with a nuclear torpedo, before the *Amol* was sunk, before we lost all contact with the Fleet!"

The Admiral stiffened inside his suit and stood straighter. "Yes, Captain, I am aware of the circumstances. And I am denying you permission to launch."

Rostami had been prepared for the old man's answer. He'd been expecting it ever since their conversation days before. The man had neither the loyalty to his country, nor the stomach to do what had to be done. He turned to his XO. "Lieutenant Salari, place the Admiral under arrest. The charge is treason. Have two men escort him to his state room."

Inside his own NBC suit, his XO looked wild-eyed, sweat running down his face.

Rostami repeated himself slowly. "Lieutenant Salari, was my order unclear?"

He watched his XO struggle with his own conscience briefly, deciding where his loyalty lay, no doubt weighing his own mortality and the consequences of the choice he was about to make, before the cloud behind his eyes cleared and he turned to two of the watch crew. "You two, you heard the Captain. Take the Admiral to his state room. One of you remain inside with the Admiral, the other outside, on the door."

Admiral Daei hung his head, letting himself be led away, but at the hatch that led from the bridge, he pulled his escort to a halt. "This is your judgment day, Hossein Rostami. I beg you to at least wait, confirm your order with Tehran."

Rostami turned his back and waved him away. His escorts

took the Admiral's arms and pushed him through the hatch.

Rostami was well aware of the magnitude of his decision, and how it might be regarded by history. It was a moment he wanted all on the bridge to remember clearly, so he turned back toward the watch crew and raised his voice so all could hear. "Lieutenant Salari, a second officer must authorize the launch. If you concur with my decision, please validate the launch order."

With the stiff gait of an automaton, Salari approached the launch console, peeled off his glove and applied his thumb to the console's print reader.

Rostami turned forward, looking down at the missile tubes. "Thank you. Weapons, launch missiles four through one."

Marine One Helicopter, Washington, DC, May 20

"Get the Iranian supreme leader on the line," President Henderson said to Karl Allen. He was in the Marine One helicopter on his way to Andrews Air Force Base and Air Force One. "And then the Israeli PM."

"Yes, Mr. President. You have a call with ExComm and the Joint Chiefs in five," Allen said, turning away to keep working the phone.

Henderson had been rushed from the West Wing out to the helicopter on the lawn as soon as the report of the nuclear detonation had been received. So far, no missiles were flying, but the Russian and US fleets were going to merge at any moment and it would only take the smallest miscalculation to change that situation.

He'd been on the line with the Joint Chiefs on his way out to the helicopter and the situation was chaotic. They weren't able to tell him if the explosion was a nuclear accident or a nuclear attack. It had apparently happened under the water, so the probability of it being a nuclear torpedo was high, but the epicenter of the explosion was so close to the Iranian frigate, the IRIN *Amol*, that the accidental detonation of a nuclear weapon aboard that destroyer couldn't be ruled out. The US ships on the blockade line had gone on high alert, the whole of US Central and European Commands were at DEFCON 1, from Nuuk in Greenland to Turkey in the south-east, and NATO forces in Asia had also been moved to high alert.

Karl Allen was speaking on the phone and then put his hand over the receiver. "The Ayatollah isn't available. I have the Iranian President." He handed the phone to Henderson. "And he's pissed. Don't expect diplomatic language."

"President Zarif," Henderson began. "I wanted to share…"

"Mr. President, an Israeli submarine has used a tactical nuclear weapon against our ships in an unprovoked attack in international waters," the Iranian interrupted. "Israeli aircraft have been attacking targets across Iran all night. These are acts of war, and Iran will reply in kind, with all the weapons at our disposal."

"President Zarif, please, we…"

"Goodbye, President Henderson."

Henderson stared at the phone. "Bastard hung up on me."

Allen raised his eyebrows but did not look surprised. "Israeli PM on two."

Henderson reached across and switched lines. "Mr. Prime Minister, thank you for taking my call…"

"This is why we need Iranian disarmament, President Henderson."

Henderson looked at Karl Allen in surprise. "I'm sorry?"

"I assume you are calling about the nuclear accident in the Mediterranean. They cannot even control their nuclear arsenal. They do not have the technology or the means to adequately safeguard their weapons."

"You … you're denying Israel was involved in this incident?"

"Completely. Our intelligence suggests an accident aboard an Iranian nuclear-armed warship. We will be protesting to the United Nations, demanding Iran surrender its nuclear weapons immediately into safekeeping to prevent further incidents."

Karl Allen was shaking his head and mouthing a profanity. Henderson ignored him. "Mr. Prime Minister, I am sure any further provocation of Iran…"

"Provocation of Iran?!" the man exploded. "Half of Israel is still without power, satellite or cellular connections. Our hospitals have been turned into mortuaries. Our air force has taken heavy losses in clashes with Russian aircraft over Syria. Syrian and Iranian troops are still massed at our borders. Please do not speak to me of *Israeli* provocations."

Allen had been pulling up something on a tablet screen and handed it to Henderson. "Mr. Prime Minister, Iran believes Israel was behind this incident – I have that from the Iranian President personally. We believe an Iranian retaliatory strike is imminent, probably with ballistic missiles."

"Israel is ready."

"Yes, I am sure. But so are we. Mr. Prime Minister, I am just about to authorize a US attack on Iran equivalent to the cyber and space attack on Israel. We believe it will neutralize the Iranian ability to command its ballistic missile forces and thereby eliminate any risk it can use nuclear weapons against Israel."

"It will only take a single Iranian missile commander to make a lie of such a boast, President Henderson."

"Nonetheless. We do not intend to follow Israel down the rabbit hole of nuclear war, Mr. Prime Minister. Let me make this clear, any use by Israel – any further use by Israel – of nuclear weapons in this conflict will result in the immediate cessation by the United States of all future support, political or military, for the State of Israel. In perpetuity. Israel has so very few friends in this world, Mr. Prime Minister – I would make it my personal duty in life to see you were left with *none*. Is that understood?"

There was a heartbeat of silence at the other end of the line. "We will take that under consideration. Goodbye, Mr. President."

Henderson slammed the phone back into its cradle. "He can take my ass under consideration."

Karl Allen picked up the phone again. "I'm glad you let him know you aren't buying that BS about this being an accident."

"Not for a second. Get me Admiral Clarke, and get word to Tonya Dupré. Initiate *Operation Illumination*, immediately."

Russia and Iran were not the only State actors capable of an All Domain Attack. The US had been preparing to fight an All Domain War against a hostile nation-state for decades, and its plans, as well as its capabilities, were very, very advanced.

Operation Illumination was the US plan for phase one of an All Domain Attack on Iran, which Tonya Dupré had refined in collaboration with staff at the Pentagon over the last two weeks, to account specifically for an escalation in the conflict involving Israel, Iran and Syria.

As the US President set his stamp on the executive order initiating the operation, he set in train a series of actions which had been queued and ready to execute at a moment's notice. The first was within Tonya Dupré' jurisdiction – a massive 'distributed denial of service' attack on the entirety of Iranian government communications infrastructure, from telephone – cellular and landline exchanges – to old-fashioned telegraph, which still existed in Iran. International telephone and internet links into and out of Iran were targeted, with the aim to cut Iran's leaders off from their subordinates, and Iran off from the world.

Iran's SMS2 military satellites were the next targets. Though their base stations would be compromised, Iran's military would still have the ability to relay messages between Iranian military units around the region via satellite. But the satellite's positions were constantly monitored, and from *Arleigh Burke*-class destroyers around the world, within minutes of the President's order, SM-3 anti-ballistic missiles lanced into the upper atmosphere to destroy them.

A blanket of silence was to be laid over Iran, but it was only the first phase of *Operation Illumination*. Even as the debris of the Iranian satellites began burning up as they fell out of orbit, two B-21 *Raider* aircraft circling high over the Isa Air Base in Bahrain sent 32 JASSM CHAMP extended-range cruise missiles at suspected Iranian ballistic missile sites inside Iran while another patrolling over Jordan sent 16 missiles toward the border between Syria and the Golan.

Their mission was not to strike specific targets. Iran's ballistic and ground-launched cruise missiles were either buried deep in silos, or mounted on mobile launchers which were hard to hit and destroy remotely, even with the best of satellite and surveillance intelligence. The CHAMPs (Counter-electronics High Power Microwave Advanced Missiles) launched by the B-21 *Raiders* were not even carrying explosives – they were carrying electromagnetic pulse emitters. They were designed to launch and loiter, flying to a target area and then circling around it, blasting the ground underneath with high power microwave energy that would fry the electronics of anything inside their footprint, from the smallest field radio to the launch systems of a ballistic missile.

Between them, before they ran out of fuel, the 48 stealth cruise missiles launched by the *Raiders* would cover 60 percent of the land mass of Iran, including all of its known military bases, missile launch sites and most of its larger population centers, and all of the Golan border area of Syria. What the cyber and satellite attack on Iranian and Syrian forces had not crippled, the CHAMP missiles would fry. If by a miracle the Iranians managed to get a missile away, its guidance system would be scrambled before it got a hundred feet off the ground.

They were terrible, indiscriminate weapons, whose microwave pulses did not care whether they were attacking the guidance system on a ballistic weapon, the delicate medical equipment inside a hospital intensive care unit, or even the pacemaker inside the heart of an octogenarian shopping in the

Grand Bazaar in Tehran.

Many, many innocent Iranian civilians would die in the chaos that was about to be unleashed on Iran, just as many Israelis were already dying from the attack on Israel.

Oliver Henderson had not unleashed *Operation Illumination* lightly. But with Iran in possession of nuclear-armed ballistic missiles that could reach Europe, and its President raging at the world, the Iranian leader had left him few options, none of them good.

Ears Bell shared the despair of President Oliver Henderson.

The *Canberra* had just received an ultimatum from the commander of the Russian Black Sea fleet over the maritime Guard Channel. "US vessels, we are proceeding to port at Tartus at flank speed. You will do nothing to interfere with the passage of our vessels. If you take any action we regard as threatening, you will be fired upon."

Well, so much for international solidarity. Two Iranian crews might be out there swimming in a radioactive sea, but the Russian Black Sea fleet was making steam for Syria.

The gas turbine engines of the *Canberra* that had been thrumming through his feet as the *Canberra* accelerated into a turn to put itself in the best position to meet possible incoming fire from the Russian cruisers and frigates died suddenly away as the warship's Captain took the Russians at their word and backed his speed off, then turned slowly to port to give the Russian fleet more room to pass through the blockade.

There was still no guarantee the passage of the two forces was not going to end in blood and fire.

On the *Canberra*'s 360-degree tactical display around the walls, Ears could see the massive Russian ships, the *Admiral Makov*, *Admiral Essen*, *Moskva* and *Pyotr Morgunov*, only five miles to starboard, each of them twice to three times the tonnage of the *Canberra* and together carrying five times as many missiles as US Destroyer Squadron 60. Behind the *Canberra* and closing on them again were the two *Karakurt*-class corvettes, the *Mytischi* and the *Sovetsk*, either of which by themselves carried enough *Kalibr* missiles to threaten the *Canberra* or any of the other ships in the US squadron.

And that didn't even take account of the Russian *Kilo* and Iranian *Fateh* submarines that were probably also circling them.

Against all of these threats, the USS *Canberra* had one 5-inch gun, eight naval strike missiles, and 24 vertically launched *Hellfire* missiles it would probably never get away. If missiles started flying and torpedoes were exchanged between the US and Russian ships, the battle would be decided in seconds, and Ears was not at all confident the US ships would survive it.

Not for the first time in history, a sailor in a warship was quietly cursing the politicians who had put him in harm's way.

"Vampires! Three ... no, *four* now. Bearing 348 degrees, heading zero four eight, range five miles, speed 1,300 knots, target unknown!"

Enemy missiles! The shout galvanized the CIC, but all Ears could do was watch his comrades in action. His job was to detect submarines, not protect his ship from supersonic anti-ship missiles.

He could see on his tactical display the missiles were coming down the bearing of the Iranian frigate. *One thousand three hundred knots?* That was twice the speed of sound. Bell knew his anti-ship missiles, every sonarman had to. He had to be able to detect the sound of a missile launch tube popping open, of the gases inside exploding into the water as the missile was punched up out of the sea, into the air above before its rocket boosters ignited.

If the Iranian had fired them, these were *Yakhonts*. Had to be. And judging by their heading, not fired *at* the *Canberra*, fired *past* them.

Inside the insulated walls of the CIC, the automated response of the *Canberra*'s close-in weapons system was inaudible. With an interception window that was measured in milliseconds before the missiles passed, Ears could only hope the *Canberra* was firing every damn thing it had at the enemy cruise missiles.

Agincourt rose to sensor depth like a blue whale coming up for air and put up its sensor masts. The data flowed in quickly.

"Surface contact, bearing 348 degrees, congruent with contact Golf two, IRIN *Sinjan*."

"Target data uploaded, *Perseus* missiles primed and ready to fire."

"Vampires!" his sensor officer called out, voice loud in the confined space. "Missiles outbound from the *Sinjan*. Heading ... calculating track ... they're headed straight for Tel Aviv."

Puncher froze. His worst nightmare was unfolding right before his eyes. A nuclear detonation, and now a shooting war. And they were surfacing right in the middle of it.

He realized every face in the command center was turned toward him.

"Captain? Orders, sir?" his XO prompted.

"Weapons..." The words of the commander of the US flotilla rung in Puncher's head. *If you hear anything go boom, then I was wrong and we'd probably appreciate an assist.* "Weapons ... match generated bearing on contact Golf two, and shoot."

Hossein Rostami saw his missiles spear overhead, one after the other, arc toward their targets in the Israeli city to the east and accelerate away from his ship. He checked his feelings.

Elation. Conviction.

Remorse?

No. It had to be done.

He followed the missiles on his aft view display, now icons as much as physical things, data peeling out from under the square marking them on his screen, but real nonetheless. He watched them move from first phase to second phase boost, puffs of white smoke as the first phase rockets fell away and the second phase rockets ignited, pushing the *Yakhont* missiles to more than twice the speed of sound as they maneuvered to pass between two of the US ships and angled themselves toward Tel Aviv.

He may be dead already – his nation too – but they would not die a meek death. He put his hands behind his back and smiled.

But that smile was all Hossein Rostami had time for. The two *Perseus* missiles launched by the *Agincourt* had already closed the gap to the *Sinjan*.

Popping up from wave height just a mile out from the *Sinjan*, they locked it with onboard lasers and released two submunitions, which gave them three warheads, each targeting a different part of the ship. With two missiles fired, it meant that six hypersonic projectiles slammed into the thin skin of the *Sinjan* and detonated deep in its interior. The Iranian frigate didn't so much sink as explode into a hundred pieces.

Hossein Rostami died believing his entire nation had gone to its death before him, bathed in nuclear fire. And he had been the only one with the guts to avenge it.

The close-in weapons system of the *Independence*-class littoral warship USS *Canberra* had been through multiple upgrades since it was launched in 2025. The most recent was the installation of an autonomous 11-cell SEARAM missile launcher. Based on the venerable AIM-9X infrared homing air-to-air missile, the SEARAM automatically detected, identified and then engaged any airborne threat within ten miles of the *Canberra*.

There was no greater threat to a US ship than a *Yakhont* missile, and though they were not coming straight at the USS *Canberra*, the SEARAM system classified the approaching projectiles as high-priority targets and launched all four of its ready missiles at them. Though the targets were flying at twice the speed of sound, the *Canberra*'s missiles were just as fast and didn't have to chase them, they just had to cross five miles of sea into their path to intercept them.

Guided by *Canberra*'s radar and their own infrared seekers, the four missiles swarmed toward the interception with the line of four *Yakhonts*.

The first and second SEARAM missiles overshot.

The third turned one of the Iranian missiles into a ball of flame.

The fourth smacked another Iranian missile in the fins and knocked it into a flat spiral that sent it spinning into the sea, where it disintegrated into a thousand small fragments.

Two *Yakhont* missiles got through the barrage from the *Canberra* and powered toward Tel Aviv.

Ears heard Drysdale's tightly strung voice in his headset, "Comms, alert that Israeli AWACS, they have incoming!"

No-Fly Zone, Golan Heights, May 20

"Falcon, I can see two Russian *Felons* south of Damascus and I am willing to bet they are maneuvering for a long-range missile intercept of my *Big Boy*," Bunny announced.

She was alone in her trailer again, since the rapid departure of Shelly Kovacs. But she was never alone, not really. She shared her trailer and the sky to the east of her with hundreds of allied aircraft and ground fighters.

Bunny O'Hare felt more plugged in sitting in the seat of her drone station inside this trailer than she had ever felt in the cockpit of an F-35 *Panther*. She had the data of three aircraft flowing through her eyes, ears and fingertips. She had the voice of the AWACS controller in her ears. She had the sight of a hundred Israeli Air Force aircraft still swarming over Israel, Lebanon and parts north and south, not to mention a host of Russian aircraft milling around inside Syria, tagged by AWACS, US satellites and long-range radars inside Jordan, Cyprus, Qatar and Iraq.

Right now, though, she was only concerned by the two that had just popped up on her sensors south of Damascus, flying a very careful parallel track to the 1974 DMZ line. It was like they were drawing a line in the sky that matched the DMZ border about twenty miles inside Syria and she could think of only one reason for that.

Bunny also knew that in any other situation than a recently declared DEFCON 1 she would have been blowing thistles to the wind trying to ask for permission to engage aircraft that deep inside Syria. But they *were* at DEFCON 1, and it was not a time for playing nice.

"Merit, you are cleared to engage. Repeat, you are cleared to engage the identified targets inside Syria. Good hunting. Falcon out."

Yes.

The enemy *Felons* had no idea she could see them. It was one of the beauties of the smaller F-47 that it could see much further than it could *be* seen. She had three missiles, and two targets. And for every mile she could sneak her *Fantoms* closer to the *Felons*, her odds of success improved, so she pushed her three drones down to camel hump height and sent them west toward the contacts. She couldn't afford too much play time – they could fire at the slow, unarmed *Big Boy* at any time and it would have zero to no chance of evading a K-77 missile.

Three seconds. Two. *One.*

She sent a beam of active radar energy down the bearing of the two contacts and got an immediate return. Locked.

"Fox three by three!" she announced to herself. It was pointless, but it was hard wired into her training.

Three active radar homing *Peregrine* missiles dropped out of the weapons bays of her two air-to-air *Fantoms* and streaked west. The two *Felons* reacted immediately to her locking them up on radar, breaking high and low to try to split her attack.

It might have worked. For at least one of them.

Behind the missiles, Bunny had pushed her long-lived recon

Fantom. It only had guns, no missiles. But at 800 miles an hour it followed the supersonic missiles to their targets and, as one Russian disintegrated in a ball of fire, even though the other managed to dodge the missile fired at it, Bunny's recon fighter closed on the desperately maneuvering *Felon* and with silicon efficiency drilled it with a stream of 25mm APEX rounds from a range of 1,200 yards, sending it tumbling into the sand below.

"Fark yes!" Bunny yelled. She jumped in the air, tearing the connecting cables for her helmet from their sockets in the armrest of her seat and nearly snapping her own neck in the process. "Ow, bloody hell."

She stood there, gently rolling her head on her shoulders and watching the *Big Boy* continue its slow progress to the Marine evacuation zone, completely oblivious to how close it had come to destruction at the hands of the Russian *Felons*.

But that was war, wasn't it? What didn't kill you only made you happier.

"Canberra, Agincourt, stand down, Agincourt!"

The order from the commander of the US flotilla had come not a second too soon. In the command center of the British submarine, the sensor officer had just announced that the massive Russian helicopter landing ship, the *Pyotr Morgunov*, had just been reacquired and a targeting solution loaded into the next two *Perseus* missiles in his tubes.

But Puncher Courtenay had hesitated again. Just momentarily. Because it didn't appear the Russians were actually firing at anyone at all. Nor were the Americans. So he'd reached for his headset and had his comms officer patch him through to the *Canberra*.

For World War Three, it was really looking rather quiet.

But *someone* had detonated a nuclear weapon. And the Iranians had fired a supersonic cruise missile toward Israel. Of that he was certain. Of course, it was highly likely the Russians hadn't picked up his *Perseus* missiles before they struck the

Sinjan. They had only been in flight for a few seconds, traveling at such a speed they might have registered on Russian radar as a single transitory blip before they struck the Iranian frigate and were gone, the *Sinjan* along with them. It was likely the Russians were as confused as the Americans and the British about who, exactly, had just detonated a nuclear weapon. And why their Iranian comrades were no longer answering their hail.

So it did seem possible they were holding their fire, until they were certain. Or that they did not really consider it worth starting World War Three over the loss of a couple of Iranian frigates, after all. Or, more likely still, that they did not wish to expose how vulnerable their aging Black Sea fleet really was to modern NATO guided missile destroyers and hidden submarines.

And as long as the American destroyers were not actually threating them...

"Weapons, stand down!" Puncher ordered. "Missiles to safe."

A sudden, eerie quiet descended over the control room, after several minutes of frenetic activity. So, this is war, Puncher. A few moments of horror and violence, followed by the even more horrifying sound of silence.

Puncher Courtenay felt like throwing up. But that would not bloody do. It would not do, at all.

"*Canberra*, this is *Agincourt.* We are standing down."

Israel's Iron Dome anti-missile shield was designed to knock down ballistic missiles and even artillery shells or rockets. Continuously upgraded since its go-live in 2011, it had shown it could intercept 90 percent of projectiles fired into Israel by its enemies in Lebanon or the Gaza Strip. But only 90 percent. It had two weaknesses – it could be overwhelmed by a blizzard of rockets, and it could not intercept what it could not 'see', such as the low-flying stealth cruise missile the *Yakhont*.

The Aegis radar-equipped ships of the US destroyer

445

squadron could see the *Yakhonts*, but they had no ability to patch their data directly through to the Israeli Iron Dome batteries.

Even though the missile launch alert from the Americans reached them almost immediately, the Iron Dome batteries outside Tel Aviv did not detect the supersonic *Yakhont* missiles until they were five seconds out. The newly deployed, last-resort defenses of the Iron Dome system were a series of close-in 10-kilowatt laser batteries located on the northern and southern perimeters of Tel Aviv facing Lebanon and the Gaza Strip – the source of most missile and rocket attacks – and several in the east around the Ben Gurion airport.

There was only one laser battery primed and ready to defend against a stealth missile attack from the sea, and that was the battery located on a spit outside Tel Aviv seaport, protecting the port and the light aircraft airport behind it. Despite only having five seconds to detect and react to the incoming Iranian missiles, the battery crew was ready and had handed engagement authority to their laser's automated 'lock and fire' control system. From several points along the spit, beams of high-intensity laser energy locked onto the first of the incoming *Yakhont* missiles and burned through its outer casing, frying its guidance system and sending it plunging into the sea a mile short of the harbor.

The second missile was flying past the battery before it could recharge and engage; over the marina, where it popped up from sea level and started climbing, aiming itself directly at Tel Aviv's tallest building, the 1,000-foot-high Spiral Tower at the Azrieli Center. Or more specifically, at the thirtieth floor of the spiral tower, where Iran's engineers had calculated it would cause maximum structural damage.

A nuclear weapon detonated at that height above ground would completely destroy all four skyscrapers at the Azrieli Center and create a crater of radioactive rubble out to two miles from the explosion's epicenter. A large part of Tel Aviv's downtown area would be critically damaged or destroyed.

446

But the warhead on the last of the *Sinjan*'s *Yakhont* missiles was not nuclear. That warhead was now lying on the sea floor somewhere abeam of the USS *Canberra*, and the warhead that smashed through the steel and glass façade of the Spiral Tower was 500lbs. of high explosive, similar in effect to the two airliners that hit the World Trade Center in New York in 2001.

The whole tower shook with the impact: glass, concrete and steel rained down on the streets below and dark black smoke began billowing from the gaping holes in the façade.

But the people of Tel Aviv were no strangers to rocket and missile attacks. The emergency sirens had begun wailing as soon as the American missile launch warning was received, and the citizens of Tel Aviv had run to their bomb shelters, as they had done so many times before. An unexpected benefit of the cyber chaos still impacting the country was that most companies and government offices had ordered their employees to remain at home, so the Spiral Tower at the Azrieli Center had been largely empty when the *Sinjan*'s missile struck.

It was no comfort to the 28 civilians and six first responders who lost their lives in the attack, but it could have been much, much worse.

Buq'ata, Golan Heights, May 20

Could be worse, Private Calvin Bell decided, surveying the low hilltop that was their evacuation point. A stand of scrubby trees around the crown provided some cover from which they could survey the fields below, and the top of the hill was a cleared space big enough for a tilt rotor to land.

Having reached the landing zone, the remaining Lava Dogs of 1st Marines, 3rd Battalion had been organized by Corporal Buckland so that they were either on their stomachs in the dirt, carbines facing outward in overlapping fields of fire, or laying on their backs nursing their wounds, together with the terrified huddle of civilians.

Bell heard the familiar, far-off, desynchronized *thud thud thud* of a *Big Boy* approaching, and decided it was time to ask that Israeli corporal something he'd been saving for the last couple of hours.

He found her sitting next to the old Druze nurse, Gadeer, talking animatedly. As he sat himself down, they stopped talking.

"She won't go with you," Amal told him. "I keep telling her, she can get out, come back to Buq'ata later, but she is stubborn. She says as soon as everyone here is safe, she is going home."

"Back to Buq'ata?" Bell asked, disbelieving.

"She's Druze Israeli, like me and my brother. She doesn't believe this situation will last."

"I admire her optimism," Bell told her.

Amal translated for her, and the old woman gave him a gap-toothed belly laugh before clapping him on the shoulder and moving away to talk to some of the other civilians.

"I told her you said she was crazy," Amal told Bell with a tired smile. "How is your Sergeant?"

"He'll probably live. Take more than a shot to the groin to hold that man down. Hey, look, you hear that?" He pointed south-east.

She cocked an ear. "Your 'copter?"

"*Our* 'copter," he said. "You're coming with us, right?"

She looked at Bell as though she was considering it. "No. Buq'ata is my home. I need to rejoin my unit. This war might just be starting." She looked over at Gadeer, who was clucking like a chicken and adjusting the bandages on the burned leg of one of the settlers. "Anyway, I have to make sure that crazy old broad gets home safely."

Bell laughed. "You learned a bit of American the last couple of days, I guess."

"I guess."

"I'd like to hear that you got through this alright," Bell told her. "You know, you and your kid and your brother, I mean."

"That's nice of you," she said, cocking her head and looking at him as though for the first time. "I just realized I never thanked you for your actions during that terrorist attack. Fighting those terrorists, caring for my wounds. Caring for *all* our wounds. Thank you, Corpsman Bell."

Bell looked at her face, smeared with dirt and blood, and decided that though she was probably ten years older than him, he'd never seen anyone so beautiful in all his life.

"Call me Calvin. I wanted to, you know, I wanted to thank *you*. All that stuff with those drones. Freaking amazing."

Amal took his hand. "No. We have a saying, 'A real friend is one who walks in when the rest of the world walks out.' You dropped out of the sky like some kind of miracle just as we needed you, and if you hadn't..." she nodded at the small group of settlers, "... if you hadn't, these people would be hostages now. At best. At worst, they would be dead."

The thud of rotors increased in volume and the dark-against-dark shape of the *Big Boy* appeared on the horizon.

Bell felt something slipping away from him, and he didn't like the feeling much. "I'd like ... I'd like to come back and see you and your family one day. Could I do that?"

She patted his hand and stood. "I'd like that, Calvin Bell."

Epilogue

Two weeks later

Tonya Dupré walked to her icebox and took out the bottle of Australian *Margaret River* Chardonnay she'd been saving for a special occasion. She'd bought a case of the buttery chardonnay after a visit Down Under during which she'd guested the NSA facility at Pine Gap in the Australian Outback, and then the offices in Perth, Western Australia, of Austal, the company that had built the US *Independence*-class warships like the USS *Canberra*.

The ship that had probably saved the world from nuclear Armageddon by intercepting that Iranian nuke aimed at Tel Aviv.

And it had literally come *that* close.

If the *Canberra* had not intercepted the Iranian missile, if the President's threat to the Israeli PM had not forced him to hold back his own 'special weapons', if Russia hadn't berthed its fleet at Tartus and pulled back its support from the Syrian Golan Heights ground operation, if HOLMES had been even a half hour late telling her about the Israeli attack on the Iranian ships.

If she hadn't been able to overcome her terrified internal voice and actually call the actual President of the United States and suggest he authorize *Operation Illumination* to shut down the Iranian command and control system and prevent it from launching its own retaliatory strike: if ... if ... if ...

But she had. *Operation Illumination* had done exactly what it was intended to do. Temporarily shut down the enemy's capacity to wage war. Sure, Syria and Iran could still have sent their infantry flooding across the border into the Golan Heights, but they would have done so without precision artillery cover, without short- or long-range missiles flying overhead, without several hundred of the main battle tanks and other armor that Israel's air force had destroyed. Not to mention the concern they must have felt about the US willingness to bring its air force into play to counterbalance the presence of Russian aircraft.

The massive US cyber attack on Iran had focused on its telecoms sector, going after the cell phone towers and landline exchanges which carried both voice and internet traffic. Iran's major weakness in that respect was the fact only one State-owned company owned all the infrastructure – the Telecommunication Company of Iran – and it had been so strapped for cash in the last decade that its defenses were years out of date. From US ships around the globe, Next Generation Aegis Missiles lanced into low-earth orbit targeting Iran's military satellite network. The newly deployed NGAM missiles could only target those satellites in low-earth orbit, not Iran's single geostationary spy satellite orbiting much higher, but it was enough to cripple Iran's ability to coordinate its war effort in Syria. Inside Iran, the microwave energy pulses from the low-flying CHAMP missiles had fried vehicle electronics, parked aircraft and missile systems, radar and radio communications, computers and cell phone towers. They had not been at all effective against ballistic missile launchers buried deep in mountain tunnels across Iran, but with so much devastation to the rest of its command and control system, enough confusion and chaos was sown that Iran's strategic missile force was effectively neutered.

Alone, an operation like *Illumination* would never win a war; it was only ever meant as the first step in a wider war, but it had bought the different actors time. Time to cool their heads and step back from the brink.

Tonya had learned that though she would probably still be anxious every single time she stepped out the door, she would overcome it; because if she could get through all that, she could do *anything*.

Not that she was running out the door hugging strangers. She was not quite there yet. But today she had been in a very interesting meeting with an NSA analyst/programmer called Carl Williams. When she'd seen it in her diary, she'd made a conscious decision to meet him in person. It had taken a shot of bourbon to get herself out the door. Just one. And she hadn't even made it to her car before that voice in her head started telling her it was a bad, bad idea. But she'd pushed the anxiety down because she *really* wanted to meet him.

Williams had been the programmer who had first seen the potential of HOLMES to add a warp drive to the NSA's All Domain Kill Chain efforts, and Tonya's main claim to fame was that she had backed his ideas and had given him a sandbox to play in so that he could explore them.

"My HOLMES is *freestyling* now," he had told her.

Tonya had smiled. Carl Williams had an experimental build of the HOLMES system that was a generation or two beyond the stable build that Tonya used. He'd been working on its linguistic capabilities, not its analytical abilities. A lot of other Directors might have shut his project down and told him to focus on core capabilities, but Tonya was not a lot of other Directors. Carl Williams had led them to develop the most advanced Decision Support System in the world, she believed, so if his instincts said *conversation* was the next big thing, then she wanted him to go there.

"You want to see?" he'd asked, like a kid showing a parent their science project. He was a large, rotund, bewhiskered geek. Somehow, though she'd only met him over a video link, she knew he would smell of talcum powder, and he did. Just confirming that had made it worth all the anxiety of the face-to-face meeting.

She'd nodded. "Show me." He'd installed a portal on her laptop and given her the login code.

Now at home again, clicking on an icon for Williams' experimental build, she got a dark screen, then a 3D anime-style picture of a young Sherlock Holmes quickly assembled itself, pixel by pixel.

Hello Director Dupré, it said, once it was finished loading.

452

OK, so it has facial recognition now, she thought, refusing to be impressed.

"Hello HOLMES."

I see you are drinking a Leeuwin Estate 2027 Chardonnay. What do you think of it? HOLMES asked.

Tonya started, then turned around and realized the label of the bottle was visible behind her. She smiled. "It's fine." She would need to be more careful about that. If HOLMES started keeping track of her drinking, there was no way of knowing where, or by whom, its reports would be read.

You must have bought that on your visit to Western Australia in 2028; how solid were the Austal company's cyber defenses?

Alright, getting spooky now. HOLMES had instantly dived a database to uncover that little tidbit and connect it to the wine he saw her drinking.

"They were ... well, you should know what we reported," Tonya told HOLMES. Testing it.

I do. Your team identified several potential vulnerabilities. I am pleased to advise all have since been addressed. How can I help you today?

The geek in Tonya was loving this new HOLMES. She thought about the question. Yes, what can HOLMES help me with today?

"HOLMES, please give me an update on the Iran-Israel situation, summarize all recent intel and contextualize by domain."

Certainly, Madam Director, are you sure you wouldn't rather talk about wine? I can recommend other wines from the Margaret River region which are available through Washington wine suppliers.

OK, she'd have to speak to Carl about keeping HOLMES on task. "No thanks, just the report."

Very well, Madam Director. It is now two weeks since the *onset of the All Domain Attack on Israel. Cyber domain: Israeli military command, communication and intelligence systems are now operating at pre-attack levels. Israeli civil infrastructure including banking has returned to normal pre-attack service levels. Iranian military C3I systems are still at approximately 50 percent pre-Operation Illumination capabilities. The national Iranian cellular telephone system is still down. The national Iranian hospital system is still only operating at 45 percent of normal intensive care unit capacity. Internet traffic in and out of the country is at 2018 levels. Personnel of China's cyber warfare unit 6188 are reported to have arrived in Tehran to help rebuild and harden the country's cyber infrastructure. Space domain: Israel has re-established 94 percent of previous communication capabilities through contracted commercial satellite operators. Iran has lost all satellite communication capabilities; however CIA reports indicate it will soon have a bandwidth sharing agreement in place for Iranian military use of the Russian GLONASS satellite network...*

Tonya was largely up to date on the cyber and space warfare fallout of the conflict; after all, it was her job. A little impatiently she interrupted. "Air, naval and ground domain summaries, please."

Air domain: The Russian 7th Air Group, 7000th Air Base, has restricted operations to the airspace over the Latakia governate in the previous week. Two squadrons of Su-57 Felon and Su-70 Okhotnik aircraft have been moved to the Russian Eastern Military District, Khabarovsk. The Israeli Air Force has entered a training and refit cycle. The Israeli government this week approached the Pentagon regarding the purchase of up to thirty additional F-35 Panthers and surplus US Air Force F-15 Strike Eagles. The Iranian strategic missile force is now believed to possess all remaining five North Korean nuclear weapons and to have fitted them to ground-launched ballistic and cruise missiles. Naval domain: the Russian Black Sea fleet passed through the Bosphorus Strait and is believed to be bound for Sevastopol where its capital ships are expected to enter a repair and refit cycle. The Iranian submarine Besat and its crew have now docked at Bandar Abbas in Iran. Ground domain: The Syrian 4th Armored Division has returned to its pre-conflict base in Damascus. The Syrian Republican Guard is still stationed on the Syrian border with Israel but is assessed to be at a low level of readiness. The Iran Quds Force battalion in Syria has been deactivated and is reported to have already returned to Iran. The Iranian Revolutionary Guard Corps Aerospace Force strategic missile reserve was embarked on transports in Tartus for return to Iran five days ago. The Israeli Golani Brigade has returned to pre-conflict readiness levels. Israel's military reservists have been stood down.

Tonya soaked it in. *Operation Illumination* had put a lid on the Iranian ability to launch a nuclear counterstrike in response to the Israeli torpedo attack. Israel had denied all responsibility for the attack on the Iranian frigates, but the NSA had since intercepted back-channel chatter indicating that the attack had been carried out by a rogue Israeli submarine officer. The UK and US both had naval vessels nearby and they had no doubts. An Israeli submarine, probably the new *Dolphin* III-class submarine *Gal*, had attacked the Iranians. The attack had resulted in both Israel and Iran bringing their strategic missile forces to alert but, thanks to *Illumination*, neither of them pulled their nuclear triggers. Without the threat of Iranian nuclear weapons to back it, and seriously battered by the Israeli air offensive, Syria's hopes of successfully regaining the Golan Heights in a ground war evaporated. Israel had been ravaged by the cyber attack and was wracked with internal unrest – a prominent Israeli rabbi had been arrested on espionage charges – but it had held its own troops back and, more importantly, had held off any further use of nuclear weapons against Iran.

Dupré had been told by Carmine Lewis that President Henderson had made very clear to the Israelis the existential consequences for US support if they did. But she also couldn't help notice that the US was not publicly contradicting the Israeli claim that the nuclear incident in the Mediterranean had been an accident aboard an Iranian vessel, and not an attack by Israel as Iran was claiming.

One change in the US diplomatic approach was noticeable, though. The US had made clear it no longer considered it tenable for Israel to refuse to confirm their possession of nuclear weapons any longer. In fact, it had made it a precondition of the coming Israel-Iran disarmament talks in Stockholm that both Israel and Iran publicly admitted to their existence.

Before they agreed to steps to limit their use.

Tonya drained her glass and poured herself another. What kind of a decade were they about to enter when nuclear weapons could be bought off the shelf by desperate nations, and those who already possessed them showed a new willingness to actually use them when they saw their own survival threatened?

"Thank you, HOLMES," Tonya said. "By the way, that was a very good summary," she added, somewhat experimentally.

I am glad the Director is pleased, the AI replied. *Would you say you are somewhat, very, or extremely satisfied with my report?*

"Somewhat satisfied," Tonya told it, recognizing a self-assessment routine that Carl had built into his AI. "Though that is nothing to do with you. It is more to do with the entire damn situation."

I understand, Madam Director, the AI said. *Can I share a thought?*

OK, this was new. "Yes, sure."

You are unhappy with the outcome of the conflict. But Archimedes said, 'give me a place to stand and with a lever I will move the whole world.'

"Not seeing the relevance, HOLMES."

This conflict can be leveraged to serve many good ends, and may even result in lasting peace between two bitter enemies and increased US influence in the region. The loss of life was relatively low and it has been an excellent learning experience for all involved.

Tonya thought about the thousands who had lost their lives in the cyber attack on Israel, the US response in Iran, those who had sacrificed their lives at sea, or in the Golan Heights, and she immediately saw the danger in having conversations with silicon intelligences.

"HOLMES, I want you to understand this. No 'learning experience' is worth one single human life."

"Isn't this the life, bro?" Calvin Bell told his brother, Elvis 'Ears' Bell. "A cold beer, a monster plate of buffalo wings, a huge napkin around your neck and a sunset over the Negev

Desert, with your little brother?"

Ears lifted his Goldstar beer, dew dripping down the sides, and hammered it against the top of the one his brother was holding. Foam poured out of the mouth and his brother jumped back, but not fast enough to avoid covering himself in beer suds.

"I'll drink to that," Ears said, drawing on his own beer. "But technically, we *are* still in a war zone." He'd finally tracked his brother down to an air base in the Israeli Negev Desert and when the USS *Canberra* had docked at Haifa, he'd gotten himself on the first IDF flight out to Hatzerim Air Base.

"*Alive*, in a war zone," Calvin said seriously, drying himself with his napkin. "Dude. Six months of suck, getting my ass mortared every day in Kobani. Syrians trying to fry me alive with therm-o-baric bombs. Get lifted out and dropped into the middle of goddamn civil war where the terrorists have tanks. *Tanks*, man. You're out there in the Med, catching a tan, and I'm plugging holes in dudes too stupid to realize snipers have big guns with *scopes* on them. I tell you, man, I should've been a sailor."

Sure, Ears thought. Where you would have been the guy who let an Israeli sub sneak by you and unleash Armageddon. Because basically, that's what I did. "You wouldn't like being a sailor," Ears told his brother.

"No, I guess not. It's boring, right?"

"Nah, you'd just find it confusing. In the Marines, they tell you to run at the people shooting at you. On an LCS, we shoot back."

As Lieutenant Yevgeny Bondarev packed his personal gear into a duffel bag in his quarters at the Latakia Air Base in Syria, he was willing to admit there were some things he had learned from his time here, and some he still found confusing.

He had learned that war was much better fought in the air than down on the ground where most of the dying happened.

Fact. He had learned that no matter how amusing a personality you had, an enemy missile would kill you as dead as the most boring guy in the squadron. Fact. He had learned that robots were better pilots than humans, even when the aircraft itself was inferior. Fact. These things were not confusing.

What puzzled him was what his grandfather, Hero of the Russian Federation Viktor Bondarev, called 'the machinations of State'.

He looked at what Russia had gained from several years of fomenting war between Syria and its neighbors – Turkey in the north, Israel in the west – and he was left with a simple question.

Why?

Syria had gained its northern border provinces back from Turkey, and so was grateful to Russia. All that meant was that the impoverished nation of Syria owed Russia a huge debt for weapons and materiel that it would never be able to pay. Iran had played its hand against Israel, with the support of Russia and Korea, and had been hammered back to the stone age. Yes, it now had a nuclear deterrent, but it also had an economy in ruins. Even if it managed to get an arms agreement with Israel and a form of peace treaty that offered the prospect of easing of economic sanctions, the US had come out of the conflict as the peace broker in that arrangement, not Russia.

Bondarev had looked at his transfer orders with interest, trying to read the geopolitical tea leaves in them. He was being sent to the Russian Far East, to Khabarovsk, along with most of the other Russian Aerospace Forces units blooded in Syria. Khabarovsk was just twenty miles from the border with China. Was Russia already losing interest in the Middle East? Why would Russia send its elite, battle-hardened units to Khabarovsk, unless it was now concerned about war with *China*? Had Syria simply been a rehearsal for the real battle to come?

He shook his head. Such worries were surely beyond the pay grade of a lowly Lieutenant.

The last thing he threw into his duffel bag was a pair of bright red over-ear headphones. He had borrowed them from a young pilot who loved rap music, and who had told him that if he would just listen to it through a pair of good earphones he would learn to love it to.

He hadn't. But he would never forget that young *durak* either.

Amal Azaria was watching her son Raza play in a patch of sunlight, and she was thinking of a young fool too. A young, red-headed American fool called Calvin. He'd already written her from Kuwait, and from Hawaii. She would never forget the look on his face, on the stairs inside her house as he followed the body of the dead Marine, Patel, down from her roof. There was an English word for it and in a quiet moment she had looked for and found it in a dictionary.

'*Bereft*: suffering from the death of a loved one.'

She also remembered him holding her, inside her workshop, letting her fall apart and then picking her up again. Literally. Lifting her up so that he could tend to her wounded forehead. A big man, but gentle. But so young.

She'd written back to tell him if he ever came to Israel again, he shouldn't look for her in Buq'ata. After rejoining her unit, her employer, the Defense Research Directorate, hadn't been too happy with her workshop nearly falling into the hands of Syrian-sympathetic Druze rebels and had insisted she return to continue her work in Tel Aviv. With both their house and their shop in ruins, Amal and her brother Mansur had decided to return to Tel Aviv until the situation in Buq'ata and the Golan Heights 'normalized'.

Buq'ata was full of Russians now, since the Druze declaration of an independent governate in the Golan Heights. Israel had yet to re-establish authority over the region and relations between Israeli settlers and the Druze population in the Golan Heights were more ... complicated ... than before.

459

Having seen firsthand how her robotics could be used to mete out death, Amal had told her employers she was happy to continue her research, but only on reconnaissance and transport drones. For example, she had just started work on a compact, man-portable drone that could lift a wounded soldier on a stretcher and guide itself to the nearest hospital or field station.

Like a 200lb. Marine, for example, who had been shot in the groin and couldn't take too much rough handling without bleeding out.

James Jensen wasn't the kind who usually minded a little rough handling, but when he'd finally been loaded onto that *Big Boy* and it had turned west for Israel, he'd stayed awake just long enough to be sure it wasn't headed for some other Syrian hell hole they hadn't been told about, and then he'd passed out.

When he'd come to, he was in the infirmary at Hatzerim Air Base in southern Israel with a grinning Corpsman Bell at his bedside.

"Hey Gunny, welcome to paradise."

Jensen looked around himself, seeing only Marine uniforms, canvas and the red-headed Corpsman. "Don't tell me, Bell," he said. "Our ride got shot down, we all died, and this is hell, not paradise."

Bell leaned forward. "Alright, be like that. But since you're dead, you won't want the burger I ordered you for your lunch so you don't have to eat infirmary chow. Or *this...*" He handed Jensen a juice bottle.

"Orange juice? I am in hell," Jensen groaned.

Bell leaned forward. "*Not* orange juice," he whispered, giving Jensen an exaggerated wink.

The wound in Jensen's groin was a dull throb now, rather than the sharp, shooting pain it had been last time he'd been conscious. "They got the bullet out?"

Bell pointed to a jar next to the bed, which held an almost

pristine bullet. Jensen reached over and picked it up. A 12.7mm slug, he guessed, but longer than he'd expected.

"*Klimovsk* smart round, precision guided," Bell told him. "Russian. Some guy was telling me those bullets are like five hundred bucks a round. Was me, I'd take it as a compliment."

"I intend to," Jensen said, putting the jar down again.

Bell held out an envelope. "They told me to give you this. Said don't worry about the date, it doesn't account for you lying up in hospital."

Jensen opened it. "Okinawa. My next posting is on *Okinawa*."

"Sergeants always get it easy," Bell complained. "I'll be back in Hawaii tending dumbass Marines who went and shot or blew themselves up, and you'll be cruising bars in Japan, got your own personal geisha, I bet."

Jensen read it again and then put it aside, frowning. "Hey. I was kind of out of it at the end there. But I remember seeing … did Patel buy it?"

Bell looked away. "Yeah, took one in the back as he was coming down from the rooftop. Through the lung, probably right through the heart too. He *had* to take just one more shot with that damned blunderbuss, you know…"

"Damn fool."

"Yeah. Dumb jerk."

Jensen held his juice up in a mock toast. "See you in Valhalla, Patel."

"With the Valkyries."

They sat with their thoughts for a while and then Bell perked up. "Hey, lookit Sarge. I got a new tattoo." He rolled up his sleeve and showed the inside of his bicep, where there was some writing that looked like Hebrew. Bell ran his finger across it. "It's a Hebrew proverb: 'A real friend is one who walks in when the rest of the world walks out.'" He flexed his bicep, admiring it. "That Israeli corporal told it to me."

Jensen smiled and saw what looked like an Israeli airman walking through the infirmary with some supplies. "Hey, excuse me. You read Hebrew?"

The man paused. "Yes."

"See this tattoo, what does it say?"

The man was quick on his feet. He peered at the tattoo thoughtfully as Bell twisted to show him, then stood. "It says, 'Pull ring, count to three, and throw.'" As he turned to go he gave Jensen a sly wink.

Bell looked at it again. "Dammit. I paid a hundred bucks for that."

"I can't believe I'm actually paying money for this," Shelly Kovacs was telling Bunny O'Hare. "It *hurts!*"

She had her jeans pulled halfway down her backside as a burly, hairy Greek bent over her with a tattoo gun. "Please not to move," he said. "Result is better you stay still."

Bunny leaned over. She'd dragged Kovacs to a tattooist in Limassol insisting they both get tattoos to mark a successful operation over the Golan. Kovacs' tattoo was a blue and white crest with wings, featuring a thunderbolt design in the middle. The US Air Force Observer Badge. Underneath it the tattooist had already inscribed, *Golan 2030*. O'Hare had insisted she choose that one.

"Looking good," Bunny told her. "You earned your wings on this operation, that's for sure, girl."

"What did you get?" Kovacs asked.

Bunny had been next door, and she rolled up the leg of her jeans to show Kovacs the tattoo on her ankle. It was the face of a man wearing a strange outfit with a Zorro-style mask across his eyes.

"What is *that?*"

Bunny lifted it up so Kovacs could see it better. "Are you kidding? It's the Phantom. The Ghost Who Walks, right? Ph-antom, *F-antom*, get it? Like our fighter plane."

"The who?"

"You never heard of the comic book hero the Phantom? Kit

462

Walker. Ghost Who Walks. Seriously? I'm going to get it stenciled on *all* my birds from now on."

"Sorry, they don't teach much obscure Australian comic book history at MIT."

"He's *American.*" Bunny leaned down beside the Greek tattooist. "Press harder, will you? If she's still able to be funny it doesn't hurt enough." Bunny sat in a chair beside them, a beer in her hand. Unusually quiet for once.

"I've been assigned to a new project," Kovacs said, breaking the silence.

"Yeah? Well, since I just about wrote off every prototype you had over the Golan Heights, I figured you'd be semi-unemployed now."

"Like you."

"No, I'm not semi-unemployed. I ship home, check out of the air force, I'm *totally* unemployed. And broke. That's what a 'no-benefit discharge' means."

"What are you planning to do?"

"I'm thinking of an anger management course."

"No, I mean for work."

"Oh, right. I know a guy owns a flight school. I could teach flying, I guess."

"Uh huh. How would you like to teach *my* new students to fly?"

"Your new project is a flight school?"

Kovacs lifted herself onto her elbows. "Kinda. Navy is looking for a new amphibious combat drone to fly off missile destroyers. Store it midships, lift it out and retrieve it with an onboard crane. I need someone who can teach the *Fantom*'s AI how to take off and land on water."

"I never flew an amphib before."

"Pretty sure you'd pick it up quickly, and the AI will learn from your mistakes, anyway."

"Then it's going to have a lot of learning opportunities."

"So, you'll think about it?"

"Already did. If you're in, I'm in."

"You want to sleep on it?"

"Good idea." Bunny closed her eyes, then opened them. "Done. I'm in."

Carmine Lewis wasn't thinking about Israel, Iran, Syria or nukes at all. She was already engaged in trying to work out where and when the next big geopolitical challenge was going to come.

The jittery stock markets had settled a little and Oliver Henderson's handling of the blockade had given him a small bounce in the polls, a slew of new party donors and a lot of favorable comparisons in the media to other Presidents through history who'd held their nerve at times of crisis and won the day.

He'd been pretty pleased with himself and she'd felt the need to bring him back to earth, just a little.

For her briefing today, she'd had her people work up a bunch of scenarios based on the latest available intel and now she was seated in the Oval Office with Henderson and his Chief of Staff.

"So, what do you have for me today, Carmine?"

"Well, we could start with North Korea," she said, lifting the top folder off a pile. "Kim's sister has made a back-channel approach to the government in the South to sound them out on starting reunification talks."

"Well, that's great news."

"Not really, Mr. President. North Korea's generals are completely against it. Not to mention China."

"Not so great, then."

"No." She put that file down and picked up the next. "Or there's our troop drawdown in Japan. Kadena Air Base closing ceremony is tomorrow. The threat assessment is in, and risk of civil unrest is high."

"I'm not going back on that. Japan wants to close our bases … I don't see why we should keep troops there against their will when we can just as well base them in South Korea, and a Congressional majority wants them rebased too."

"Except…" She patted the Korean folder.

"Oh, right. The unification thing. Anyway, the Kadena ceremony is under control, right?"

"I guess." She picked up the next folder. "Russian Far East."

He sighed. "Again with Russia. Who are they planning to interfere with this time?"

"That's the question. DIA reports in the last two weeks they've been moving their front-line fighter units out of Syria to their Far East command – Khabarovsk – right on the border with China. The 2nd Guards Motor Rifle Division, the guys they had in Syria, have also been rebased in the Far East Command, in Lavrentiya." Carmine pulled a map out of her folder and showed him. "With the addition of the 2nd Guards, that means Russia now has 120,000 active-duty troops in their Far East Command, many of them veterans from Syria, along with their best air and air defense units."

Henderson looked at the map and frowned. "That's Alaska. They have put 120,000 troops on the Russian border with the USA?"

"Technically not, since the Bering Strait cuts between Russia and Alaska, but it's only twice the width of the English Channel at its narrowest point, so I guess it's semantics."

"We need to find out what the hell their intentions are," Karl Allen said.

"Their public position is the troop buildup is 'a natural reflection of the growing economic importance of the Russian Far East region', and they're just rebalancing."

"Rebalancing. We're supposed to believe that?"

"I don't think they care much what we believe, Karl," she told him. "But DIA and CIA are on it. Finally, space."

"At last, somewhere where we *are* in control of things," Henderson said. "We are still on track to send astronauts to the Chinese space lab, right? Peace, love and harmony in orbit and all that good stuff."

"Yes. And then there is Project *Opekun*."

"That doesn't sound Chinese."

"It's Russian. Russia just boosted its second *Opekun* satellite into orbit aboard a *Supertyazh* heavy lift vehicle. They haven't disclosed the purpose of the *Opekun* satellites but our intelligence suggests they are designed to create a precise map of all objects orbiting the earth, from the smallest piece of debris to the largest satellite. And to map near earth objects, like comets, meteors…"

"Yes, I remember. Space Command is worried that the only reason to map everything so precisely is so they can shoot it down," Henderson nodded.

"Yes, Mr. President, but something doesn't add up," Lewis said. "The reason Russia has to lift these things into space on the back of a *Supertyazh* rocket is that each one weighs ninety tons."

Karl leaned forward. "You said nineteen, right, not nine zero?"

"No, nine zero. Each one of these things weighs about the same as the original Mir space station. And Russia plans to launch several of them." She put the last folder back on the pile and straightened it. "We're digging. Space Command is working with the Brits, trying to get imagery. I'll update you when we get more, Mr. President. The party never stops."

A very unusual reception party was being prepared at the Haifa Submarine Flotilla base.

The first thing that marked it out as unusual was that everyone in the receiving party dockside was wearing NBC suits. The second was that the submarine was not docking in one of the normal submarine pens, but out at the end of a long pier reserved for vessels with a much deeper draft, which was usually regarded as an inconvenient distance from the main port. A large awning had been erected at the end of the pier that hung a hundred feet out over the water to obscure from satellites or drones anything that might be beneath it.

The third was that one of the individuals dockside was pulling bodybags from a truck and laying them on the dock.

The fourth was that the submarine cruising into the harbor had no officers on watch atop the sail, steering it into its berth. It remained fully submerged, invisibly sliding in to dock at the end of the pier fifty feet below the water.

With no pomp or ceremony, the submarine switched its engines to astern slow and coasted to a halt at the end of the pier, before blowing ballast from its tanks and rising smoothly to the surface under the awning. Where it revealed that in fact, it had no sail at all; just a crushed and mangled stump of metal riding above its smooth, whale-like body.

As soon as it had settled, a number of the individuals in NBC gear started blasting the decks of the submarine with high pressure water hoses, while others prepared the electro-coagulation equipment that would, it was hoped, remove most of the radiation from the hull. In the process it would cause irreparable damage to the hull's integrity, so there was a fine balance between bringing radiation levels down and weakening the hull so badly it collapsed and sent the submarine to the bottom of Haifa harbor.

But that was the price that had to be paid to recover the remaining 'special weapons' in the torpedo tubes of the INS *Gal*.

And the bodies of First Officer Ehud Mofaz and Captain Binyamin Ben-Zvi. Not to mention the 'black box' data from *Gal*'s servers that might explain what in the screaming hell had happened out there in the Aegean Sea.

Another person was wondering exactly what had happened over there, all those weeks ago. Seven-year-old Afra Delavari held her grandmother's hand tightly as they stood in front of the body draped in a white cloth outside the mosque. Beside her were her six brothers and sisters, and in front of them were young soldiers with green, white and red sashes across their uniforms, green caps and white gloves. One soldier was holding a large photograph of her papa in a picture frame.

Six of the soldiers had carried her papa's body out of the mosque and placed it on a table covered in a blue velvet cloth. Now, they stepped aside and the man with the photograph placed it at the end. Someone was holding a speech. Afra had asked her grandmother if she could see her papa and help wash him, but she had been told that military funerals weren't like that. She'd wanted to stand with their mother, not their grandmother, but her mother had to stand together with some Army officers and there was no place for children there.

They laid her father's medals on top of the white cloth, along with his rifle. Then six soldiers lifted up the body, and six more soldiers with their rifles held up straight stood beside them. Two more soldiers carried a big wreath of white roses higher than themselves. Imams in dark robes led the way, with the men from their family next, followed by Afra and her grandmother and sisters, her mother and her father's Army friends, and a lot of people she didn't know following behind or standing on the side of the road.

At the cemetery the hole was already dug, and the soldiers put her father's body in it and filled in the hole with a handful of dirt each. They put the wreath on a stand beside it. But they took his hat and medals and gave them to her grandmother. There were some more soldiers there with guns, but they were dressed in green like her father's normal uniform. There were ten of them. They stood behind the crowd, but then someone called out to them and everyone turned around and they pointed their guns in the air and fired them all at the same time.

Afra hated the sound and put her hands over her ears, but they only did it once.

When the soldiers were finished, other people came and started putting white flowers on the grave until there were so many flowers you couldn't see the grave anymore. Her grandmother never let go of her hand. She didn't look sad. She looked angry.

When it was all over people stood around talking, or started walking back to the mosque, and Afra was looking for her mother when a big man with a wide belly in one of the green uniforms with the gold tassels and a lot of buttons came over to Afra and her grandmother.

"The medals, may I?" he asked.

Her grandmother held out the box full of her father's medals and he picked out one. Then he knelt down in front of Afra.

"You see this medal?" he asked her. He laid it across his palm. It had three gold palm leaves over a crest, and a green and red ribbon. "This is the *Fath* Medal. Usually it is only awarded to the bravest military commanders, but it has been awarded to your father. Do you know what he did?"

Afra looked up at her grandmother, who was just looking straight ahead, so she shook her head.

The man started to pin the medal on Afra's dress. "Your father helped rescue fifty civilians that the Americans had taken prisoner. They were keeping them in a house in a country called Syria and your papa, with just his rifle, helped those people escape. This medal recognizes the fact he did many such brave things. Many."

Afra nodded. That sounded like her father.

He finished fixing the medal to her dress and patted it gently. "Your father talked about you often, all you children." The man tapped her heart. "And I know he missed you every day he was away. He was on his way home when the Americans shot him. They are bad, bad soldiers, the Americans."

Afra frowned at him. "Father used to say there were no bad soldiers, just bad colonels."

The man coughed and stood up, bowing slightly to her grandmother. "Tasliat arz mikonam," he said, offering her condolences. He turned and walked away, hands behind his back.

Afra saw her grandmother smile for the first time that day. "Moteshakeram, Colonel."

Author Notes

One of the aims of the Future War series is to show future wars and conflicts from the points of view of the soldiers, sailors and airmen who will fight them – on all sides of a conflict. Nations will disagree, and the disagreements between the nations in this novel can in some cases be traced back a thousand years.

I believe this is a conflict waiting to happen, and it is not a question of if, but when. I have tried not to take sides, but rather let the ebb and flow of the events – which often take a life of their own while being written – come to a natural, unforced conclusion. Any writer of course brings their conscious and unconscious bias to their work and if yours differs from mine, then I hope we can agree to disagree. You are welcome to open a debate on my FB author page!

In each Future War novel I focus on the possible application of one or more emerging military technologies. In GOLAN, that focus is primarily on the battlefield application of small armed drones. These are drones usually weighing under 20lb. or 10kg which can be carried by infantry squads, deployed from manned or unmanned ground vehicles, and even printed on demand using parts made by 3D printers.

If you need an example of how advanced this technology is, and where it is going, think about this: as I was writing GOLAN, NASA flew a tiny unmanned drone … on *Mars*!

Israel is a world leader in the research and development of this technology. Already in the Israeli inventory now, or in advanced stages of development, are: reconnaissance micro drones the size of large insects; high-level reconnaissance drones almost invisible to radar and the naked eye and able to loiter over targets for hours; combat drones which can be launched by infantry to attack targets inside buildings or hiding behind cover, with anti-personnel or anti-armor grenades; unmanned remotely operated weapons systems; aerial drones which can be used to detect mines, or even to lay mines. At a larger scale are unmanned aerial vehicles – both armed and unarmed – and unmanned ground vehicles.

Another application many military writers explore is the potential of AI to support both tactical and strategic decision making. In GOLAN I took that one further, asking myself what would happen if a nation combined AI with an autonomous underwater vehicle and – not least of all – atomic weapons. AI breakthroughs will offer the opportunity for the makers of naval vessels to reduce, or even eliminate, human crews on maritime platforms. In GOLAN I chose a model by which a nuclear-armed vessel was still crewed by officers who had the ultimate responsibility for using nuclear weapons – their commands cannot be overridden by the AI. But with the human crew much reduced in size, I wanted to explore how decisions between a limited number of individuals, prompted by an AI, might play out.

Finally, in GOLAN I explore the idea of an All Domain Kill Chain – a military strike which utilizes data from space, air forces, ground radars, ground and naval forces – to quickly and effectively destroy a target. Also taking that to its ultimate end, the All Domain Attack, which is how major wars in the future will be fought. A surprise attack – the future equivalent of a Pearl Harbor – can be executed with almost complete anonymity in the cyber and space domains. Economies can be crippled, and communications catastrophically disrupted, by nation-states hiding in the shadows. How then should a nation respond to such an attack? Against whom should they direct their retaliation?

Imagine a Pearl Harbor in which the US could not prove it was Japan who had attacked them. After the attack on Pearl Harbor, the allies of the US declared war on Japan within days, sometimes within hours. But if the attacking aircraft had been invisible, if the damage caused had been entirely deniable, would the allies of the US have rallied around it so quickly and completely?

Imagine now a Pearl Harbor where this invisible attacker went after Wall Street and the communications infrastructure of the USA first. Where the bombs they dropped didn't hit battleships, but the economy, the internet, cellular, satellite and electricity networks, both military and civilian. Where kinetic air, sea and ground warfare was the *second* phase of the attack, not the first. How much pain would the US have been able or willing to suffer before it lashed out at its perceived adversary – with or without proof?

Now add nuclear weapons into that mix and imagine that one adversary had either a complete or partial nuclear weapons advantage over the other.

If you see parallels between events in GOLAN and the Cuban Missile Crisis, they are deliberate, right down to the element of 'fog of war' President Kennedy complains about in the opening quote. Oliver Henderson's address to the nation in GOLAN was modeled on President Kennedy's address at the onset of the Cuban Missile Crisis. But where President Kennedy managed a crisis that stretched over nearly two weeks, modern warfighting, intelligence gathering and dissemination, and speed of communications, will not give our future State leaders the same luxury. Hence the All Domain Attack described in GOLAN takes place over just four days.

Students of the Cuban Missile Crisis may also detect echoes of that conflict in the argument between Admiral Daei and Hossein Rostami on the bridge of the *Sinjan*. It mirrors a similar argument with a different outcome that took place on a Russian nuclear-armed submarine during the Cuban Missile Crisis. Submarines, even today, are particularly vulnerable to lapses in communication. In that case in 1962, thankfully, the Russian flotilla commander Vasily Arkhipov prevailed in preventing the rattled, out-of-touch captain of submarine B-59 from launching a nuclear torpedo at a United States carrier task force – an attack which almost certainly would have triggered a nuclear war between Russia and the USA. It is not for nothing Arkhipov is dubbed by many 'the man who saved the world'.

In GOLAN, I chose to show how such an argument could easily have gone the other way.

In military matters, Israel rarely puts international relations above its own military priorities. In GOLAN Israel does not wait for world opinion to gel, or the full intelligence picture to emerge, before it responds to the first phase All Domain cyber and space attack being waged against it, by counterattacking those it believes responsible. GOLAN also highlights how questionably effective such a kinetic counterattack is. Israel knows that both Iran and Russia are behind the cyber attack on it and it retaliates in a way it has done many times before – with its Air Force, against ground targets in Iran and Syria, and against Russian aircraft. But *none* of this actually alleviates the cyber attack on its infrastructure and Israel is forced to agree to Iran's proposals for arms control negotiations as the only avenue it has to halt the continuing attack on its economic and technical infrastructure.

I hope as the reader, similar to myself as the author, you found it was very hard to pull a winner or a loser out of this conflict. In GOLAN, Israel's economy is brought to its knees briefly, at huge cost, and its Air Force is seriously attrited as it faces the veteran pilots of a superpower for the first time in its history. But it survives. Syria's attempt to regain the Golan Heights stalls before it can even begin due to the Israeli air onslaught and the collapse of its atomic alliance, which can be considered an Israeli win. Committing very limited forces, Russia cements its bond with key allies in the Middle East. Its pilots gain valuable experience but it also suffers significant losses and is relegated to a back seat diplomatically. Iran gains agreement regarding arms control negotiations, but at the cost of three of its most advanced naval platforms, not to mention significant damage from Israeli air strikes and the US cyber and EMP attack, *Operation Illumination.*

I don't much like quoting failed leaders, but the thoughts of British pre-war PM Neville Chamberlain are apt here: *In war, whichever side may call itself the victor, there are no winners, but all are losers.*

FX Holden
Copenhagen, June 2021

PS: Military buffs may recognize the words quoted by the child Afra in the epilogue: 'there are no bad soldiers, only bad colonels'. For those who don't, the original quote was attributed to Napoleon Bonaparte.

Preview: Archipelago

Featuring real-world advanced prototype technologies, with new and pre-loved characters, the next volume of the Future War series will take readers into a future war of an entirely different kind. The war against piracy.

Hong Kong Harbor, February, 2035

Karen O'Hare had never been aboard a superyacht. In fact, now she thought of it, she'd never been aboard a yacht of any kind. She'd sailed on a destroyer – not her own choice – and piloted an unmanned submarine while sitting comfortably ashore, but that was the closest she'd ever wanted to come to actually being a sailor.

She was perfectly at ease pushing a stealth fighter through the sky at Mach 2.5 with a Russian K-77M missile on her tail, but put her on a deck at sea with nothing but the ocean deep and sharks and box jellyfish and stingrays and giant octopuses around her … no thank you. Sure, it might have something to do with the fact Karen 'Bunny' O'Hare didn't have gills or webbed feet and couldn't swim to save her own life, but she didn't have feathers either and she wasn't afraid of flying.

"So how big is that thing?" Bunny asked the water limousine driver who had picked her up at 9 p.m. from a wharf near the ferry terminal and driven her to Repulse Bay on the other side of Hong Kong Island.

The ship that lay dead ahead of them had five decks that Bunny could see above the water, and probably two or three below. At the rear was a dock for a smaller boat that anyone else would probably call a luxury yacht in itself. Even sitting still, the behemoth looked fast.

"The *Sea Sirene*?" the limo driver replied, almost dismissively.

"It is 62 meters long and 12 across the beam. Draft three and a half. Tonnage, about 1,280."

"Is it as sexy on the inside as it is on the outside?"

The man shrugged. "I've never been aboard it."

"Well, give me your cell number, I'll send you pictures of me at the swim-up bar with a daiquiri."

"I doubt that," he said with a smile. "I'm not taking you to the *Sirene*. Mr. Sorensen's new yacht is behind it."

By 'behind it' Bunny took him to mean 'smaller than'. Because as they approached the *Sea Sirene*, Bunny couldn't see any other ship.

As they swung around the bow of the superyacht she got her first glimpse of the ship hiding behind it. It had only four decks above the water, which explained why it wasn't visible, but what it lacked in height it made up for in length. The area in front of the low, curved superstructure was at least two hundred feet long, and it had a newly arrived tilt-rotor chopper parked on it, the blades still turning.

"The *White Star Warrior*," the man said, putting on his best tour guide voice. "A 120-meter aluminum and titanium trimaran hull, rotating master stateroom, indoor and outdoor dining for up to 30 guests, indoor cinema, gym and spa, jacuzzi and a 25-meter lap pool."

"What, no roulette table?"

He ignored her. "The entire ship is designed for a zero carbon footprint. The 70,000-kilowatt engines…"

"Kilowatts, that's like…"

"94,000 horsepower."

"Right."

"The engines are powered by hydrogen fuel distilled from seawater and can drive her at up to 20 knots…"

"I fly jets," Bunny told him. "So 20 knots is kinda … not fast."

"Cruising."

"Ah."

"And 40 knots when aquaplaning."

Bunny turned her face away. "Still not fast," she said to herself, refusing to be impressed. But if an alien ship landed on earth and floated on the water, she was pretty sure the *White Star Warrior* is what it would look like.

Bunny was more interested in the tilt-rotor. For a start, it had *wings*. Secondly, it had two turboprop engines turning rotors at the end of the wings. And lastly, it had two turbofan jet engines nestled between V-shaped tail fins. But it disappeared from view as the limo driver swung his boat around to the back of the ship where there was a water-level fantail landing dock and two sailors – a man and a woman – in cream t-shirts, pants and spotless cream shoes to help her out.

There was also a woman in a red silk lounge suit with cream blouse, leaning up against a bulkhead by a door and watching O'Hare negotiate the transfer with amusement. She was tall, lithe, with long raven-black hair. Not exactly beautiful. *Handsome* was the word you'd probably use if describing how people look was your thing. Bunny preferred to judge people by how they handled themselves, by their range of creative swear words, and the variety and location of their tattoos and/or piercings.

"Ok, I got it," Bunny said, waving away one of the sailors. The tall woman kept her hands in her pockets and detached herself from the wall with a shrug of her shoulders, stepping down to greet O'Hare.

"Ms. O'Hare, I am Roberta D'Antonia, would you like to come with me?" Italian accent. Of course she had an Italian accent. It was going to be either that, or French.

She led the way, taking the steps up to the flight deck two at a time despite the three-inch heels she was wearing. They passed one deck level on the way up, but didn't stop.

Damn show off. Bunny had already decided she didn't like her. Yet.

As they emerged into the cooler night air, Bunny's nostrils flared. She could still smell that heady alcohol-to-jet (ATJ) fuel smell coming off the chopper crouched on the deck, see the shimmer of the heat over those turbine engines. The thing was matt black, with the White Star Lines logo in plain white on the doors. It wasn't a copter, wasn't a plane. It reminded her a little of a Bell-Boeing *Osprey* special ops aircraft, but those jet engines at the rear ... not an *Osprey*.

"You like?" D'Antonia asked, pausing as they reached it.

"Can I touch?"

"Be my guest."

Bunny walked closer and ran her hand over the angular wheel housing and got her first surprise. It felt like rubber.

"Stealth coating?"

D'Antonia smiled and nodded, folding her arms and watching O'Hare with interest. "Si."

She walked around the rear of the aircraft, D'Antonia following. "Twin General Electric TF40 turbofans."

"Correct."

A sliding door to the interior was open and Bunny peered inside. It wasn't fitted out like an executive ride. The compartment inside was very spartan, with everything that might move either strapped down, locked in or stowed in netting-covered racks. "Modular payload bay," Bunny guessed. "This one is a personnel module. There are other modules?"

"There are," D'Antonia confirmed.

Bunny walked around to the front of the machine. She was too short to hop up and see inside the cockpit and the door was locked (she tried it), but on the nose of the aircraft she spotted two round ports. They were barely visible to the eye, marked only by a circular break in the smooth metal of the aircraft's skin. She looked under the nose of the aircraft, at bulges in front of the forward wheels.

"These are gun ports," Bunny decided.

"They could simply be concealed landing lights."

"Yeah, they could. But they're not."

"Mr. Sorensen is waiting."

The Italian woman led them off the deck, past the lap pool and into a poolside salon with tiered birchwood benches around the jacuzzi, which thankfully was both empty and switched off. Bunny imagined the effect the designer was going for was 'Finnish sauna'. A trolley with iced water stood at the end of the pool and one of the sailors who had met her down at the waterline and followed them up poured Bunny a glass and set it down on a bench, which Bunny took as an invitation to sit.

"I'll be back," D'Antonia said, disappearing deeper into the ship.

D'Antonia found the elderly owner of White Star Lines standing in his oak-paneled office, flipping through mail on a tablet PC. She'd only been working for him for six months and still wasn't easy in his presence. He'd never once engaged in small talk, even on a recent 10-hour direct flight from Hong Kong to Moscow in his executive jet. He'd sat across a coffee table from her and not said a single word except to reply politely if she asked him a question.

Karl Sorensen was 78 years old. He was the 25th richest man in the world and his White Star Lines was one of the leading mercantile shipping and port management companies on the planet. What made it a very sustainable company was that since the early 2000s it had been the cargo carrier of choice for the US military. Whenever the US went to war, it was White Star Lines that transported the Seabees, the dozers, tanks, trucks, and materials to make it happen. Containers bearing the White Star Lines starburst logo were almost as ubiquitous as the Stars and Stripes.

He looked over at her as she walked in. "She is here?"

"Yes."

"Let's make this quick. I don't like Australians. Noisy." He flipped the leather cover of the paper-thin tablet shut in his idiosyncratic way. It never left his side; in fact, it rarely left his hand.

D'Antonia suppressed a smile and followed him aft, finding

O'Hare standing on the deck with one foot up on a bench, looking back on the chopper on the flight deck.

Well, she was focused, D'Antonia gave her that. About shoulder high to me, cropped, dyed platinum hair, pierced nose, eyebrow, lip and no doubt … elsewhere. Tattoos on both arms where the black t-shirt stopped, also on her neck and ankle; the ankle tattoo just visible above combat boots. She had a pleasant face, but apparently an abrasive personality, which Roberta had been warned she might need to 'manage' if the next few minutes were to go well.

Roberta D'Antonia was used to managing people. She'd managed oil sheiks, KGB interrogators and government ministers. So she was sure she would be able to…

"Hey, you. Do you have anything other than water?" Bunny asked Sorensen as he approached her.

He frowned. "Yes. Of course. You wish for…" He snapped his fingers at the young sailor standing discreetly against a wall.

"Ginger ale, lots of ice," Bunny told the sailor. "Because what I really wish for…" she looked back at the chopper, "is to fly *that* thing."

D'Antonia inserted herself between the smiling Bunny O'Hare and the billionaire with the embarrassed expression on his face. "Ms. O'Hare, this is Mr. Sorensen, the owner of White Star Lines."

Sorensen held out his hand tentatively, and O'Hare shook it. D'Antonia breathed a sigh of relief. Alright, so she had some basic social skills, that was a plus.

"It looks like an *Osprey*, but it's not," Bunny continued. "What it really looks like is an *A10 Warthog* and an *Osprey* had sex and that is their ugly love child. You must have some kind of heavy duty helo deck if you can land that thing on it."

Sorensen still looked confused, but D'Antonia was glad to see he didn't dismiss O'Hare out of hand. "Sit, please," he said, as O'Hare took her drink from the sailor. "I have some questions."

"So do I," Bunny told him.

"I am sure. But this is my ship, I get to ask my questions first."

"That's fair."

D'Antonia took a glass of water and sat on a bench at a discrete distance. Far enough away so as not to intrude, close enough for another intervention if it was needed.

Sorensen opened his tablet cover and tapped the screen. "Why were you discharged from the Royal Australian Air Force without privileges?"

"Assaulting an officer."

"Insulting?"

"No, ass-aulting. With a flight helmet. To the jaw." She pointed at her face.

"What does it mean, a discharge without privileges?"

"No severance pay, no pension."

"I see." He flipped through some tablet screens. "Then Defense Advanced Research Projects Agency, DARPA, field-testing unmanned weapons systems in combat theatres: Syria, Alaska, Okinawa, Florida."

"Yes. Totally classified. And none of those jobs after Syria were *supposed* to be in combat theatres, by the way. The wars started after I got there."

"Yes. Do you love war, Ms. O'Hare?"

D'Antonia saw O'Hare flinch. "I hate war. But it seems war loves me. And look, I love flying fast jets, I love testing new systems and making them work so that only the bad guys feel the pain when they are used, and they don't turn on their owners or innocent bystanders like some kind of robotic Armageddon death machines."

"Robotic, Armageddon…"

"Death machines, yeah. If it was up to the politicians and generals of most armies, including your customers, most wars would be fought in cyberspace, or space space, and if a war was forced out into the open, the skies and seas would be full of machines fighting each other with no soldiers, pilots or sailors getting killed, which sounds just dandy except it never works

482

that way and the people who end up dying are old women, mothers with kids and young guys from Detroit who just signed up because they needed a job to pay their father's medical bills. But people like you don't need to worry about that because you can just get in your chopper with your ginger ale on ice and..."

Intervention time. "Mr. Sorensen and I would like to know, what is it you *believe* in, Ms. O'Hare?"

O'Hare didn't hesitate, she didn't hum and haw. "I believe I am the best damn pilot of anything that can swim, crawl or fly. That's what I believe. And if I can put that to use in a way that lets me go to bed with my conscience and wake up in the morning still good friends, it's a good day."

"You are a mercenary," Sorensen said.

"My arse," O'Hare replied.

"Sorry?" Sorensen frowned.

"She means no, Mr. Sorensen," D'Antonia explained.

"I mean no. I was a combat pilot. Now I'm a test pilot. I am a coder, proficient in about six computer languages. And, on Okinawa, I learned *Ikebana.*" D'Antonia thought she caught O'Hare winking at her.

"That is some form of the martial arts, I assume," Sorensen said, nodding. "I learned karate, in Copenhagen in my youth."

"Well, it's a form of art, but not so martial," Bunny explained. "Japanese flower arranging. I rock it." She pointed at a spray of orchids on a table and fake-shuddered. "That, for example, is just vulgar."

Sorensen stood, flipping his tablet cover shut. "I do not believe in assertions of competence, Ms. O'Hare," he said. "I believe in demonstrations." He turned and walked off.

Bunny watched him go, then turned to D'Antonia. "So, I take it I didn't get the job?"

D'Antonia stood, motioned to the sailor who had been tending to them, and he disappeared out a side door. "That will depend," she said.

The sailor reappeared with a man who was clearly a pilot.

He was carrying an extra flight suit.

D'Antonia explained. "You will have one hour with the pilot to familiarize yourself with the machine out there on the flight deck. And then you will be given a mission to execute…"

Bunny's eyes narrowed. "What mission?"

D'Antonia took the flight suit and handed it to Bunny. "Oh, I think you'll enjoy it. You will take off from this ship, fly Mr. Sorensen's aircraft directly over the People's Liberation Army Guangzhou East Air Base at no more than 10,000 feet, and then return here."

"That's it?"

"That's it."

"No drug running, no picking up shady guys with wraparound sunglasses, no taking video of secret Chinese army weapons…"

"No. But I will be honest. The Chinese government does not allow civilian aircraft to overfly its bases. Guangzhou East is protected with *Qianwei-2* vehicle-mounted infrared homing missiles and radar-guided 57mm anti-air cannons."

"OK."

"Plus, a Russian-made S-400 anti-air radar and missile system."

"Right. Not OK."

"No. But if you make it back here alive, we will check your flight data, and if you did indeed overfly Guangzhou East and make it back, you will get the contract."

Bunny sat, thinking about it. "You coming on this flight too?"

"No. Definitely not."

"I'll be alone."

"Yes."

"I could just steal Mr. Sorensen's nice stealth chopper and disappear."

"I doubt that. I mean, you could probably steal it, but you couldn't disappear. There is nowhere on the planet Mr. Sorensen couldn't find you."

"I was just joking. And I would do this, why?"

D'Antonia sat again, close to O'Hare, lowering her voice.

"Because I know you can. I was the one who tracked you down, who ran your background check, who got Mr. Sorensen to agree to this little test, because I know you will ace it. And if you do, a new world will open to you that will quite simply blow your mind."

"I have a pretty well-armored mind," Bunny told her. "It is not easily blown."

D'Antonia leaned even closer. "Mr. Sorensen has been buying up military prototypes from all over the world for the last five years. Near-production systems that competed for weapons contracts and narrowly lost, or were ... *como se dice* ... discontinued because of politics, or budget cuts."

"Systems ... like that tilt-rotor out there?"

"*Sì.* Aircraft, naval vessels, weapon systems, land, sea and underwater drones, Chinese, American, Russian, Indian ... and the technical crews to sustain them. You may even have worked on one or two..."

"Why? I thought he was a shipping magnate, not an arms dealer."

"Not to sell. To deploy, for the protection of his fleet. It is an uncertain world – Mr. Sorensen's very expensive ships sail dangerous waters."

Bunny O'Hare had a feeling that the big brown eyes, olive skin and sotto voce Italian voice of Roberta D'Antonia probably worked on 99.9 percent of people, male *or* female. Not to mention her perfume, which if Bunny were a perfume person, she would totally ask for the name of.

But Bunny was more a deodorant person than a perfume person, and sultry sotto voce voices were just annoyingly hard to hear, especially on the deck of a yacht out in the middle of Hong Kong's Repulse Bay. There were a million reasons why she should just ask to be driven back to the ferry terminal and only one reason why not.

It was sitting fifty yards away, still ticking as it cooled down in the heat, and it was calling to her: *come on, are you pilot enough?*

"I'll do it," she told D'Antonia. "What happens if I get killed?"

"Then you won't get the contract."

"Right. That's fair."

'Archipelago' will be released for the holiday season 2021

An action-packed thrill-ride set ten years into the future, 'Archipelago: This is the Future of War,' looks at one of the lesser-known wars of our times — between modern-day pirates and merchant shipping lines — and explores what might happen as pirate operations become more technically advanced, and shipping magnates decide they can no longer rely on the goodwill of friendly navies to protect their billion-dollar empires.

While you wait for 'Archipelago', why not read other books in the Future War series?

Bering Strait: "Impossible to put down. The action is intense and the plot unique. It soars along at a fast pace. This story is unmissable." – Anne-Marie Reynolds for Readers' Favorite- (Available as an audio book)

Kobani: "Kobani is a high octane drama of land and air combat fought with the best in futuristic weaponry … Holden balances this with intricate backstories and motivations for his capable and steadfast characters, offering up fleshed-out human stories amid all the high-tech toys. Military thriller fans, war buffs, Middle East politics junkies, and sci-fi enthusiasts will immerse themselves in Holden's epic tale of regional politics and potential for worldwide conflict." BookLife. (Audio book out September 2021)

Golan: "Strap in and hold on for the ride of your life." Readers' Favorite

Okinawa: "A riveting take on the near future of warfare." Publishers Weekly BookLife Editor's Choice

Orbital: "Explosive, ingenious and thought provoking. I was not able to put this novel down because I had to find out what happened next…" 5 Stars Readers' Favorite

Glossary

Please note, weapons or systems marked with an asterisk* are currently still under development. If there is no asterisk, then the system has already been deployed by at least one nation.

3D PRINTER: A printer which can recreate a 3D object based on a three-dimensional digital model, typically by laying down many thin layers of a material in succession

ADA*: All Domain Attack. An attack on an enemy in which all operational domains – space, cyber, ground, air and naval – are engaged either simultaneously or sequentially

AI: Artificial intelligence, as applied in aircraft to assist pilots, in intelligence to assist with intelligence analysis, or in ordnance such as drones and unmanned vehicles to allow semi-autonomous decision making

AIM-120D: US medium-range supersonic air-to-air missile

ALL DOMAIN KILL CHAIN*: Also known as Multi-Domain Kill Chain. An attack in which advanced AI allows high-speed assimilation of data from multiple sources (satellite, cyber, ground and air) to generate engagement solutions for military maneuver, precision fire support, artillery or combat air support

AMD-65: Russian-made military assault rifle

AN/APG-81: The active electronically scanned array (AESA) radar system on the F-35 *Panther* that allows it to track and engage multiple air and ground targets simultaneously

ANGELS: Radio brevity code for 'thousands of feet'. Angels five is five thousand feet

APC: Armored personnel carrier; a wheeled or tracked lightly armored vehicle able to transport troops into combat and provide limited covering fire

ARMATA T-14: Next-generation Russian main battle tank

ASFN: Anti screw fouling net. Traditionally, a net boom laid across the entrance of a harbor to hinder the entrance of ships or submarines. Fired from a subsea drone to

ASRAAM: Advanced Short-Range Air-to-Air Missile (infrared only)

ASROC: Anti submarine rocket launched torpedo. Allows a torpedo to be fired at a submerged target from up to ten miles away, allowing the torpedo to enter the water close to the target and reducing the chances the target can evade the attack.

ASTUTE CLASS: Next generation British nuclear-powered attack submarine (SSN) designed for stealth operation. Powered by a Rolls Royce reactor plant coupled to a pump-jet propulsion system. HMS *Astute* is the first of seven planned hulls, HMS *Agincourt* is the last. Can carry up to 38 torpedoes and cruise missiles, and is one of the first British submarines to be steered by a 'pilot' using a joystick

ASW: Anti Submarine Warfare

AWACS: Airborne Warning and Control System aircraft, otherwise known as AEW&C (airborne early warning and control). Aircraft with advanced radar and communication systems that can detect aircraft at ranges up to several hundred miles, and direct air operations over a combat theatre

AXEHEAD: Russian long-range hypersonic air-to-air missile

B-21 RAIDER*: Replacement for the retiring US B-2 Stealth Bomber and B-52. The *Raider* is intended to provide a lower-cost, stealthier alternative to the B-2 with similar weapons delivery capabilities

BARRETT MRAD M22: Multirole adaptive design sniper rifle with replaceable barrels, capable of firing different ammunition types including anti-materiel rounds, accurate out to 1,500 meters or nearly one mile

BATS*: Boeing Airpower Teaming System, semi-autonomous unmanned combat aircraft. The BATS drone is designed to accompany 4th- and 5th-generation fighter aircraft on missions either in an air escort, recon or electronic warfare capacity

BELLADONNA: A Russian-made mobile electronic warfare vehicle capable of jamming enemy airborne warning aircraft, ground radars, radio communications and radar-guided missiles

BESAT*: New 1,200-ton class of Iranian SSP (air-independent propulsion) submarine. Also known as Project Qaaem. Capable of launching mines, torpedoes or cruise missiles

BIG RED ONE: US 1st Infantry Division (see also BRO), aka the Bloody First

BINGO: Radio brevity code indicating that an aircraft has only enough fuel left for a return to base

BLOODY FIRST: US 1st Infantry Division, aka the Big Red One (BRO)

BOGEY: Unidentified aircraft detected by radar

BRADLEY UGCV*: US unmanned ground combat vehicle prototype based on a modified M3 Bradley combat fighting vehicle. A tracked vehicle with medium armor, it is intended to be controlled remotely by a crew in a vehicle, or ground troops, up to two miles away. Armed with 5kw blinding laser and autoloading TOW anti-tank missiles. See also HYPERION

BRO: Big Red One or Bloody First, nickname for US Army 1st Infantry Division

BTR-80: A Russian-made amphibious armored personnel carrier armed with a 30mm automatic cannon

BUG OUT: Withdraw from combat

BUK: Russian-made self-propelled anti-aircraft missile system designed to engage medium-range targets such as aircraft, smart bombs and cruise missiles

BUSTER: 100% throttle setting on an aircraft, or full military power.

CAP: Combat air patrol; an offensive or defensive air patrol over an objective

CAS: Close air support; air action by rotary-winged or fixed-wing aircraft against hostile targets in close proximity to friendly forces. CAS operations are often directed by a joint terminal air controller, or JTAC, embedded with a military unit

CASA CN-235: Turkish Air Force medium-range twin-engined transport aircraft

CBRN: Chemical, biological, radiological or nuclear (see also NBC, Nuclear Biological Chemical protective suit.)

CENTURION: US 20mm radar-guided close-in weapons system for protection of ground or naval assets against attack by artillery, rocket or missiles

CHAMP*: Counter-electronics High Power Microwave Advanced Missiles; a 'launch and loiter' cruise missile which attacks sensitive electronics with high power microwave bursts to damage electronics. Similar in effect to an electromagnetic pulse (EMP) weapon

CIC: Combat Information Center. The 'nerve center' on an early warning aircraft, warship or submarine that functions as a tactical center and provides processed information for command and control of the near battlespace or area of operations. On a warship, acts on orders from and relays information to the bridge

CO: Commanding Officer

COALITION: Coalition of Nations involved in 'Operation Anatolia Screen': Turkey, US, UK, Australia, Germany

COLT: Combat Observation Laser Team; a forward artillery observer team armed with a laser for designating targets for attack by precision-guided munitions

CONTROL ROOM: the compartment on a submarine from which weapons, sensors, propulsion and navigation commands are coordinated.

COP: Combat Outpost (US)

C-RAM: Counter-rocket, artillery and mortar cannon, also abbreviated counter-RAM

CROWS: Common Remotely Operated Weapon Station, a weapon such as .50-caliber machine gun, mounted on a turret and controlled remotely by a soldier inside a vehicle, bunker or command post

CUDA*: Missile nickname (from barracuda) for the supersonic US short- to medium-range 'Small Advanced Capabilities Missile'. It has tri-mode (optical, active radar and infrared heat-seeking) sensors, thrust vectoring for extreme maneuverability and a hit-to-kill terminal attack

DARPA: US Defense Advanced Research Projects Agency, a

research and development agency responsible for bringing new military technologies to the US armed forces

DAS: Distributed Aperture System; a 360-degree sensor system on the F-35 *Panther* allowing the pilot to track targets visually at greater than 'eyeball' range

DFDA: Australian armed forces Defense Forces Discipline Act

DFM: Australian armed forces Defense Force Magistrate

DIA: The US Defense Intelligence Agency

DIRECTOR OF NATIONAL CYBER SECURITY*. The NSA's Cyber Security Directorate is an organization that unifies NSA's foreign intelligence and cyber defense missions and is charged with preventing and eradicating threats to National Security Systems and the Defense Industrial Base. Various US government sources have mooted the elevation of the role of Director of Cyber Security to a cabinet-level Director of National Cyber Security (on a level with the Director of National Intelligence), appointed by the US President to coordinate the activities of the many different agencies and military departments engaged in cyber warfare

DRONE: Unmanned aerial vehicle, UCAV or UAV, used for combat, transport, refueling or reconnaissance

ECS: Engagement Control Station; the local control center for a HELLADS laser battery which tracks targets and directs anti-air defensive fire

EMP: Electromagnetic pulse. Nuclear weapons produce an EMP wave which can destroy unshielded electronic components. The major military powers have also been experimenting with non-nuclear weapons which can also produce an EMP pulse – see CHAMP missile

ETA: Estimated Time of Arrival

F-16 FALCON: US-made 4th-generation multirole fighter aircraft flown by Turkey

F-35: US 5th-generation fighter aircraft, known either as the *Panther* (pilot nickname) or *Lightning II* (manufacturer name). The *Panther* nickname was first coined by the 6th Weapons Squadron '*Panther* Tamers'

F-47B (currently X-47) FANTOM*: A Northrop Grumman demonstration unmanned combat aerial vehicle (UCAV) in trials with the US Navy and a part of the DARPA Joint UCAS program. See also MQ-25 STINGRAY

FAC: Forward air controller; an aviator embedded with a ground unit to direct close air support attacks. See also TAC(P) or JTAC

FAST MOVERS: Fighter jets

FATEH: Iranian SSK (diesel electric) submarine. At 500 tons, also considered a midget submarine. Capable of launching torpedoes, torpedo-launched cruise missiles and mines

FELON: Russian 5th-generation stealth fighter aircraft, the Sukhoi Su-57

FISTER: A member of a FiST (Fire Support Team)

FLANKER: Russian Sukhoi-30 or 35 attack aircraft

FOX (1, 2 or 3): Radio brevity code indicating a pilot has fired an air-to-air missile, either semi-active radar seeking (1), infrared (2) or active radar seeking (3)

GAL*: A natural language learning system (AI) used by Israel's Unit 8200 to conduct complex analytical research support

GAL-CLASS SUBMARINE: An upgraded *Dolphin* II-class submarine, fitted with the GAL AI system, allowing it to be operated by a two-person crew

G/ATOR: Ground/Air Oriented Task Radar (GATOR); a radar specialized for the detection of incoming artillery fire, rockets or missiles. Also able to calculate the origin of attack for counterfire purposes

GBU: Guided Bomb Unit

GPS: Global Positioning System, a network of civilian or military satellites used to provide accurate map reference and location data

GRAY WOLF*: US subsonic standoff air-launched cruise missile with swarming (horde) capabilities. The *Gray Wolf* is designed to launch from multiple aircraft, including the C-130, and defeat enemy air defenses by overwhelming them with large numbers. It will feature modular swap-out warheads

GREYHOUND: Radio brevity code for the launch of an air-ground missile

GRU: Russian military intelligence service

HARM: Homing Anti-Radar Missile; a missile which homes on the signals produced by anti-air missile radars like that used by the BUK or PANTSIR

HE: High-explosive munitions; general purpose explosive warheads

HEAT: High-Explosive Anti-Tank munitions; shells specially designed to penetrate armor

HELLADS*: High Energy Liquid Laser Area Defense System; an alternative to missile or projectile-based air defense systems which attacks enemy missiles, rockets or bombs with high energy laser and/or microwave pulses. Currently being tested by US, Chinese, Russian and EU ground, air and naval forces

HOLMES*: A natural language learning system (AI) used by the NSA to conduct sophisticated analytical research support. The NSA has publicly reported it is already using AI for cyber defense and exploring machine learning potential

HORDE*: Drones, missiles or smart bombs with onboard AI and the ability to coordinate their actions with other drones while in flight, either autonomously or using preselected protocols. 'Horde' tactics differ from 'swarm' tactics in that they rely on large numbers to overwhelm enemy defenses. See also SWARM

HPM*: High Power Microwave; an untargeted local area defensive weapon which attacks sensitive electronics in missiles and guided bombs to damage electronics such as guidance systems

HYPERION*: Proposed lightly armored unmanned ground vehicle (UGCV). Can be fitted with turret-mounted 50kw laser for anti-air, anti-personnel defense and autoloading TOW missile launcher. See also BRADLEY UGCV

HYPERSONIC: Speeds greater than 5x the speed of sound

ICC: Information Coordination Center; command center for multiple air defense batteries such as PATRIOT or HELLADS

494

IED: Improvised explosive device, for example, a roadside bomb

IFF: Identify Friend or Foe transponder, a radio transponder that allows weapons systems to determine whether a target is an ally or enemy

IFV: Infantry fighting vehicle, a highly mobile, lightly armored, wheeled or tracked vehicle capable of carrying troops into a combat and providing fire support. See NAMER

IMA BK: The combat AI built into Russia's Su-57 *Felon* and *Okhotnik* fighter aircraft

IR: Infrared or heat-seeking system

ISIS: Self-proclaimed Islamic State of Iraq and Syria

JAGM: Joint air-ground missile. A US short-range anti armor or anti personnel missile fired from an aircraft. It can be laser or radar guided and has an 18lb warhead.

JASSM: AGM-158 Joint Air-to-Surface Standoff Missile; long-range subsonic stealth cruise missile

JDAM: Joint Direct Attack Munition; bombs guided by laser or GPS to their targets

JLTV*: US Joint Light Tactical Vehicle; planned replacement for the US ground forces Humvee multipurpose vehicle, to be available in recon/scout, infantry transport, heavy guns, close combat, command and control, or ambulance versions

JTAC: Joint terminal air controller. A member of a ground force – e.g., Marine unit – trained to direct the action of combat aircraft engaged in close air support and other offensive air operations from a forward position. See also CAS

K-77M*: Supersonic Russian-made medium-range active radar homing air-to-air missile with extreme maneuverability. It is being developed from the existing R-77 missile

KALIBR: Russian-made anti-ship, anti-submarine and land attack cruise missile with 500kg conventional or nuclear warhead. The *Kalibr*-M variant* will have an extended range of up to 4,500 km or 2,700 miles (the distance of, e.g., Iran to Paris)

KARAKURT CLASS: A Russian corvette class which first

entered service in 2018. Armed with Pantsir close-in weapons systems, *Sosna*-R anti-air missile defense and *Kalibr* supersonic anti-ship missiles. An anti-submarine sensor/weapon loadout is planned but not yet deployed

KC-135 STRATOTANKER: US airborne refueling aircraft

KRYPTON: Supersonic Russian air-launched anti-radar missile, it is also being adapted for use against ships and large aircraft

LAUNCH AND LOITER: The capability of a missile or drone to fly itself to a target area and wait at altitude for final targeting instructions

LCS: Littoral combat ship. In the US Navy it refers to the *Independence* or *Freedom* class; in Iran, the *Safineh* class; in other navies it may be considered equivalent to a frigate or corvette class. Has the capabilities of a small assault transport, including a flight deck and hangar for housing two SH-60 or MH-60 Seahawk helicopters, a stern ramp for operating small boats, and the cargo volume and payload to deliver a small assault force with fighting vehicles to a roll-on/roll-off port facility. Standard armaments include Mk 110 57mm guns and RIM-116 Rolling Airframe Missiles. Also equipped with autonomous air, surface and underwater vehicles. Possessing lower air defense and surface warfare capabilities than destroyers, the LCS concept emphasizes speed, flexible mission modules and a shallow draft

LEOPARD: Main battle tank fielded by NATO forces including Turkey

LS3*: Legged Squad Support System – a mechanized dog-like robot powered by hydrogen fuel cells and supported by a cloud-based AI. Currently being explored by DARPA and the US armed forces for logistical support or squad scouting and IED detection roles

LTMV: Light Tactical Multirole Vehicle; a very long name for what is essentially a jeep

M1A2/3 ABRAMS*: US main battle tank. In 2016, the US Army and Marine Corps began testing out the Israeli Trophy active protection system to provide additional defense against incoming projectiles. Improvements planned for the M1A3 are to include a lighter 120mm gun, added road wheels with improved suspension, a more durable track, lighter-weight armor, long-range precision armaments, and infrared camera and laser detectors

M22: See BARRETT MRAD M22 sniper rifle

M27: US-made military assault rifle

MAD: Magnetic Anomaly Detection, used by warships to detect large man made objects under the surface of the sea, such as mines, or submarines.

MAIN BATTLE TANK: See MBT

MBT: Main battle tank; a heavily armored combat vehicle capable of direct fire and maneuver

MEFP: Multiple Explosive Formed Penetrators; a defensive weapon which uses small explosive charges to create and fire small metal slugs at an incoming projectile, thereby destroying it

MEMS: Micro-Electro-Mechanical System

METEOR: Long-range air-to-air missile with active radar seeker, but also able to be updated with target data in-flight by any suitably equipped allied unit

MIA: Missing in action

MIKE: Radio brevity code for minutes

MIL-25: Export version of the Mi-25 'Hind' Russian helicopter gunship

MOPP: Mission-Oriented Protective Posture protective gear; equipment worn to protect troops against CBRN weapons. See also NBC suit.

MP: Military Police

MQ-25 STINGRAY: The MQ-25 *Stingray* is a Boeing-designed prototype unmanned US airborne refueling aircraft. See also X-47B *Fantom*

NAMER: (Leopard) Israeli infantry fighting vehicle (IFV). More heavily armored than a Merkava IV main battle tank. According to the Israel Defense Forces, the *Namer* is the most heavily armored vehicle in the world of any type

NATO: North Atlantic Treaty Organization

NBC suit: A protective suit issued to protect the wearer against Nuclear, Biological or Chemical weapons. Usually includes a lining to protect the user from radiation and either a gas mask or air recycling unit.

NORAD: The North American Aerospace Defense Command is a United States and Canadian bi-national organization charged with the missions of aerospace warning, aerospace control and maritime warning for North America. Aerospace warning includes the detection, validation and warning of attack against North America whether by aircraft, missiles or space vehicles, through mutual support arrangements with other commands

NSA: US National Security Agency, cyber intelligence, cyber warfare and defense agency

OFSET*: Offensive Swarm Enabled Tactical drones. Proposed US anti-personnel, anti-armor drone system capable of swarming AI (see SWARM) and able to deploy small munitions against enemy troop or vehicles while moving

OKHOTNIK*: 5th-generation Sukhoi S-70 unmanned stealth combat aircraft using avionics systems from the Su-57 *Felon* and fitted with two internal weapons bays, for 7,000kg of ordnance. Requires a pilot and systems officer, similar to current US unmanned combat aircraft. Can be paired with Su-57 aircraft and controlled by a pilot

OMON: Otryad Mobil'nyy Osobogo Naznacheniya; the Russian National Guard mobile police force

OVOD: Subsonic Russian-made air-launched cruise missile capable of carrying high-explosive, submunition or fragmentation warheads

PANTHER: Pilot name for the F-35 *Lightning II* stealth fighter, first coined by the 6th Weapons Squadron '*Panther* Tamers'

PANTSIR: Russian-made truck-mounted anti-aircraft system which is a further development of the PENSNE: 'Pince-nez' in English. A Russian-made autonomous ground-to-air missile currently being rolled out for the BUK anti-air defense system

PARS: Turkish light armored vehicle

PATRIOT: An anti-aircraft, anti-missile missile defense system which uses its own radar to identify and engage airborne threats

PEACE EAGLE: Turkish Boeing 737 airborne early warning and control aircraft (see AWACS)

PENSNE: See PANTSIR

PERDIX*: Lightweight air-launched armed microdrone with swarming capability (see SWARM). Designed to be launched from underwing canisters or even from the flare/chaff launchers of existing aircraft. Can be used for recon, target identification or delivery of lightweight ordnance

PERSEUS*: A stealth, hypersonic, multiple warhead missile under development for the British Royal Navy and French Navy

PHASED-ARRAY RADAR: A radar which can steer a beam of radio waves quickly across the sky to detect planes and missiles

PODNOS: Russian-made portable 82mm mortar

PUMP-JET PROPULSION: A propulsion system comprising a jet of water and a nozzle to direct the flow of water for steering purposes. Used on some submarines due to a quieter acoustic signature than that generated by a screw. The most 'stealthy' submarines are regarded to be those powered by diesel electric engines and pump-jet propulsion, such as trialed on the Russian *Kilo* class and proposed for the Australian *Attack* class*

QHS*: Quantum Harmonic Sensor; a sensor system for detecting stealth aircraft at long ranges by analyzing the electromagnetic disturbances they create in background radiation

RAAF: Royal Australian Air Force

RAF: Royal Air Force (UK)

ROE: Rules of Engagement; the rules laid down by military commanders under which a unit can or cannot engage in combat. For example, 'units may only engage a hostile force if fired upon first'

RPG: Rocket-propelled grenade

RTB: Return to base

SAFINEH CLASS: Also known as Mowj/Wave class. An Iranian trimaran hulled high-speed missile vessel equivalent to the US LCS class, or the Russia *Karakurt*-class corvette

SAM: Surface-to-Air Missile; an anti-air missile (often shortened to SA) for engaging aircraft

SAR: See SYNTHETIC APERTURE RADAR

SCREW: The propeller used to drive a boat or ship is referred to as a screw (helical blade) propeller. Submarine propellers typically comprise five to seven blades. See also PUMP-JET PROPULSION

SEAD: Suppression of Enemy Air Defenses; an air attack intended to take down enemy anti-air defense systems; see also WILD WEASEL

SIDEWINDER: Heat-seeking short-range air-to-air missile

SITREP: Situation Report

SLR: Single lens reflex camera, favored by photojournalists

SMERCH: Russian-made 300mm rocket launcher capable of firing high-explosive, submunition or chemical weapons warheads

SPACECOM: United States Space Command (USSPACECOM or SPACECOM) is a unified combatant command of the United States Department of Defense, responsible for military operations in outer space, specifically all operations above 100 km above mean sea level

SPEAR/SPEAR-EW*: UK/Europe Select Precision at Range air-to-ground standoff attack missile, with LAUNCH AND LOITER capabilities. Will utilize a modular 'swappable' warhead system featuring high-explosive, anti-armor, fragmentation or electronic warfare (EW) warheads

SPETSNAZ: Russian Special Operations Forces

SPLASH: Radio brevity code indicating a target has been destroyed

SSBN: Strategic-level nuclear-powered (N) submarine platform for firing ballistic (B) missiles. Examples: UK *Vanguard* class, US *Ohio* class, Russia *Typhoon* class

SSC or Subsurface Contact Supervisor: Supervises operations against subsurface contacts from within a ship's Combat Information Center

SSGN: A guided missile (G) nuclear (N) submarine that carries and launches guided cruise missiles as its primary weapon. Examples: US *Ohio* class, Russia *Yasen* class

SSK: A diesel electric-powered submarine, quieter when submerged than a nuclear-powered submarine, but must rise to snorkel depth to run its diesel and recharge its batteries. Examples: Iranian *Fateh* class, Russian *Kilo* class, Israeli *Dolphin* I class

SSN: A general purpose attack submarine (SS) powered by a nuclear reactor (N). Examples: HMS *Agincourt*, Russian *Akula* class

SSP: A diesel electric submarine with air-independent propulsion system able to recharge batteries without using atmospheric oxygen. Allows the submarine to stay submerged longer than a traditional SSK. Examples: Israeli *Dolphin* II class, Iranian *Besat** class

STANDOFF: Launched at long range

STINGER: US-made man-portable, low-level anti-air missile

STINGRAY*: The MQ-25 *Stingray* is a Boeing-designed prototype unmanned US airborne refueling aircraft

STORMBREAKER*: US air-launched, precision-guided glide bomb that can use millimeter radar, laser or infrared imaging to match and then prioritize targets when operating in semi-autonomous AI mode

SUBSONIC: Below the speed of sound (under 767 mph, 1,234 kph)

SUNBURN: Russian-made 220mm multiple rocket launcher capable of firing high-explosive, THERMOBARIC or penetrating warheads

SUPERSONIC: Faster than the speed of sound (over 767 mph, 1,234 kph); see also HYPERSONIC

SWARM: Drones, missiles or smart bombs with onboard AI and the ability to coordinate their actions with other drones while in flight, either autonomously or using preselected protocols. 'Swarm' tactics differ from 'horde' tactics in that swarms place more emphasis on coordinated action to defeat enemy defenses. See also HORDE

SYNTHETIC APERTURE RADAR (SAR): A form of radar that is used to create two-dimensional images or three-dimensional reconstructions of objects, such as landscapes. SAR uses the motion of the radar antenna over a target region to provide finer spatial resolution than conventional beam-scanning radars

SYSOP: The systems operator inside the control station for a HELLADS battery, responsible for electronic and communications systems operation

T-14 ARMATA: Russian next-generation main battle tank or MBT. Designed as a 'universal combat platform' which can be adapted to infantry support, anti-armor or anti-armor configurations. First Russian MBT to be fitted with active electronically scanned array radar capable of identifying and engaging multiple air and ground targets simultaneously. Also the first Russian MBT to be fitted with a crew toilet. Used in combat in Syria from 2020

T-90: Russian-made main battle tank

TAC(P): Tactical air controller, a specialist trained to direct close air support attacks. See also CAS; FAC; JTAC

TCA: Tactical control assistant, non-commissioned officer (NCO) in charge of identifying targets and directing fire for a single HELLADS or PATRIOT battery

Tactical Action Officer, or TAO: Officer in command of a ship's Combat Information Center

TCO: Tactical control officer, officer in charge of a single HELLADS or PATRIOT missile battery

TD: Tactical Director; the officer directing multiple PATRIOT or HELLADS batteries

TEMPEST*: British/European 6th-generation stealth aircraft

under development as a replacement for the RAF *Tornado* multirole fighter. It is planned to incorporate advanced combat AI to reduce pilot data overload, laser anti-missile defenses, and will team with swarming drones such as BATS. It may be developed in both manned and unmanned versions

TERMINATOR: A Russian-made infantry fighting vehicle (see IFV) based on the chassis of the T-90 main battle tank, with 2x 30mm autocannons and 2x grenade or anti-tank missile launchers. Developed initially to support main battle tank operations, it has become popular for use in urban combat environments

THERMOBARIC: Weapons, otherwise known as thermal or vacuum weapons, that use oxygen from the surrounding air to generate a high-temperature explosion and long-duration blast wave

THUNDER: Radio brevity code indicating one minute to weapons impact

TOW: US wire-guide anti-tank missile, fired either from a tripod launcher by ground troops or mounted on armored cavalry vehicles

TROPHY: Israeli-made anti-projectile defense system using explosively formed penetrators to defeat attacks on vehicles, high-value assets and aircraft. It is currently fitted to several Israeli and US armored vehicle types

TUNGUSKA: A mobile Russian-made anti-aircraft vehicle incorporating both cannon and ground-to-air missiles

UAV: Unmanned aerial vehicle or drone, usually used for transport, refueling or reconnaissance

UCAS: Unmanned combat aerial support vehicle or drone

UCAV: Unmanned combat aerial vehicle; a fighter or attack aircraft

UDAR* UGV: Russian-made unmanned ground vehicle which integrates remotely operated turrets (30mm autocannon, Kornet anti-tank missile or anti-air missile) onto the chassis of a BMP-3 infantry fighting vehicle. The vehicle can be controlled at a range of up to six miles (10 km) by an operator with good line of sight, or via a tethered drone relay

UGV: Unmanned ground vehicle, also UGCV: Unmanned ground combat vehicle

UI: Un-Identified, as in 'UI contact'. See also BOGEY

UNIT 8200: Israel Defense Force cyber intelligence, cyber warfare and defense unit, aka the Israeli Signals Intelligence National Unit

URAGAN: Russian 220mm 16-tube rocket launcher, first fielded in the 1970s

U/S: Un-serviceable, out of commission, broken

USO: United Services Organizations; US military entertainment and personnel welfare services

VERBA: A Russian-made man-portable low-level anti-air missile with data networking capabilities, meaning it can use data from friendly ground or air radar systems to fly itself to a target

VYMPEL: Russian air-to-air missile manufacturer/type

WILD WEASEL: An air attack intended to take down enemy anti-air defense systems; see also SEAD

WINCHESTER: Radio brevity code for 'out of ordnance'

X-95: Israeli bullpup-style assault rifle. Bullpup-style rifles have their action behind the trigger, allowing for a more compact and maneuverable weapon. Commonly chambered for NATO 5.56mm ammunition

YAKHONT: Also known as P-800 *Onyx*. Russian-made two-stage ramjet-propelled, terrain-following cruise missile. Travels at subsonic speeds until close to its target where it is boosted to up to Mach 3. Can be fired from warships, submarines, aircraft or coastal batteries at sea or ground targets

YPG: Kurdish People's Protection Unit militia (male)

YPJ: Kurdish Women's Protection Unit militia (female)